He knew there was something unusual about his ship, but he wasn't expecting this...

Jabal settled back in his chair and stroked his whiskers. "Doesn't make much sense," he said. "The thing, or whatever it is, is a royal-pain-in-the-ass, but it hasn't harmed me or damaged any of my equipment. In fact, it reminds me of when my older brothers used to pick on me when I was a kid."

"Don't take it for granted, Jabal. We don't know what its game is, and it has killed before."

"Father, would you send me the files you have on the deaths, starting with the waste management officer?"

"Every scrap of information I have is already on board," Teller said. "Agoa."

"Yes, Admiral Shann?"

"I authorize Commander Shann to have full access to the entire ship's database about the um...*problem*. Nothing about this particular incident is to be withheld from him. Do you understand?"

"Yes, sir," she said.

"Thank you, Dad."

"Good hunting. By the way, your mother sends her love. Teller out."

Jabal rose from his chair, stretched and took a sip of tepid tea. "Bring up the file, Agoa. Let's see what we are up against."

"Commander Shann," Agoa said. "As embarrassing as this is..."

"What?"

"We have an intruder alert on deck seventeen, section three."

"What?" Jabal cried.

"Vital signs indicate a single adult Azurean."

"Give me a picture of that section, now."

"Impossible, Commander," she said. "I have indications that the section has been tampered with. I will send secur—"

"Belay that."

Jabal grabbed a machine pistol from a nearby weapon locker. "Show me a schematic of that section."

Instantly, the display showed a highlighted blueprint.

"Close off these sections," he said, indicating the screen with his finger. "I don't want him to get away."

"Commander, you can't risk yourself," Agoa said.

"I have to find this, because whoever it is keeps slipping through your security."

"That is hurtful, Commander," she said in an unmistakable pout.

Jabal rolled his eyes and rushed from the room. Running toward the ship's tram system, he asked, "Agoa, what is in that section?"

"Coma Unit Two."

The Great War with the Erest won, Commander Jabal Shann of the Azurean Sky Navy is ready to test a revolutionary new technology that would make it possible for a spacecraft to leap thousands of lightyears instantaneously. Unbeknownst to Jabal, he is dying of cancer and only has a few months to live. SD—an ancient, mythic being of immense power, called a Deverow—declares Jabal a "Dead End," or a being without a future and, therefore, free to be used by the capricious Deverow for their own convoluted purposes. Although no one on his home planet believes his radical idea is possible, Jabal is given a decommissioned ship, *The Blossoming Flower*, and told to test his theory far out in space, safely away from the Azurean planet. But as Jabel works to build his new drive, he uncovers deep, dark secrets, regarding not only *The Flower*, herself, but her mysterious cargo. Before Jabal can confront the leaders on his home world, Azurea is destroyed by an enemy with advanced technology. Jabal, along with several other Dead Ends, is tasked by the Deverow to use his new drive to annihilate the alien civilization before they can do more damage to the universe. But how can handful of misfits take on an entire armada and even survive, let along defeat them?

With no other choice, Jabal turns to the one ace he has up his sleeve, *The Flower* and her unnatural cargo, risking everything to save the remnant of his people, but at what cost?

KUDOS for *Dead Ends*

In *Dead Ends* by Ken Newman, Jabal Shaun is dying, making him a perfect pawn for a race of super beings called the Deverow. Since Jabal would die without intervention, the Deverow classify him as a Dead End, someone who can be used by the Deverow for the "greater good," at least as the Deverow define it. Jabal has invented a new technology that the Deverow want to use to defeat a race of beings who will do great damage to the universe. What Jabal and the other Dead Ends the Deverow have recruited want makes no difference to the Deverow. But they are in for a surprise as the group of misfit Dead Ends recruited have a few demands of their own. The story is intriguing and complex, told from several points of view, but I found it easy to follow and hard to put down—a thoroughly entertaining read. ~ *Taylor Jones, Reviewer*

Dead Ends by Ken Newman is the story of a group of young people with no future. All of them are going to die young, thus ending their influence on their home world. So the Deverow, a race of people with technology so advanced they seem almost like gods, arrange for the Dead Ends to continue living—at a price, the price being that the Dead Ends do the Deverows' bidding, whether they want to or not. But even the Deverow make mistakes, and some Dead Ends don't cooperate the way they should, so things don't go exactly as planned. I really enjoyed *Dead Ends*. While it reminded me at times of *The Hitchhiker's Guide to the Galaxy*, it's a lot more logical, easy to follow, and suspenseful, the characters more rational and realistic. If you are a science fiction fan at all, this one is a must read. ~ *Regan Murphy, Reviewer*

DEAD ENDS

KEN NEWMAN

A Black Opal Books Publication

GENRE: SCINECE FICTION/PARANORMAL THRILLER

This is a work of fiction. Names, places, characters and incidents are either the product of the author's imagination or are used fictitiously, and any resemblance to any actual persons, living or dead, businesses, organizations, events or locales is entirely coincidental. All trademarks, service marks, registered trademarks, and registered service marks are the property of their respective owners and are used herein for identification purposes only. The publisher does not have any control over or assume any responsibility for author or third-party websites or their contents.

To my wife Christian

CHAPTER 1

I am cold, wet, and feel like an utter fool," Jabal Shann mumbled to himself as he sloshed with single-minded purpose down the sidewalk. The wide street, normally bustling with activity, was empty, save for the miserable Jabal. It would be hours before the first shop owner opened their doors for business.

"How could I have let Darris talk me into betting on the *Thunder*? I would love to wipe that perpetual, cocky smirk off his face once and for all. To make matters worse, the virus I snagged seems to be getting worse. I feel so incredibly tired and the rattle in my chest is getting painful. The meds I got from the base pharmacy were a waste of pay credits."

He let out a ragged breath.

"As much as it pains me, after my meeting this morning, I will make a point to swing by the medic center and get a proper medi-spray from the base doc."

సౌసౌ

For two weeks, Jabal had endured a hacking cough and a nasty rattle in his chest that had grown steadily worse. Even though his wife was a topflight surgeon, he did not mention his ailment, just playing it off as an allergic flare up from the latest rounds of mandatory vaccinations.

One, he did not want her to worry, as she already had a full plate with her duties, and, second, Jabal had things to do, *historic* things. He knew his wife would force him to undergo a bevy of tests, and he did not have time or patience to be poked, prodded, and scanned.

Jabal, however, was wrong about the virus being a minor inconvenience. Deep inside the young officer's lungs, a rare, aggressive cancer grew at an alarming rate. The malignant tumor had made its way into the blood stream and his lymphatic system.

Jabal did not know it, but he was already beyond hope. The young Sky Naval Commander had exactly four months, twenty-two days, seventeen hours, five minutes, and sixteen seconds of life left to him.

All of which made him the perfect candidate.

෴

Jabal erupted into another hacking, coughing fit.

"This *foking* cough is driving me insane."

He took a few shallow breaths, as the persistent cough seemed to subside. "On the bright side, things could not possibly get any worse."

At that precise moment, a law enforcer's sleek, yellow-and-black trike pulled to a silent stop a few meters ahead of him. As if on cue, the icy rain he had been sloshing through suddenly turned into a torrential downpour.

"I just had to open my big mouth."

At the approach of the faceless law enforcer, Jabal stopped dead, removed his hands from his pockets, took a wide stance, and made no sudden movements while she scanned him for contraband and/or weapons. Sudden, suspicious movements could result in an unwanted interrogation by several very unfriendly officers, a week in a six-by-six-by-six foot, ice-cold steel can to teach proper respect for the law, or instant death. With zero witnesses, death was the most likely scenario.

While he silently swore he would never make another sport bet, Jabal noticed the enforcer's biomechanical armor was a vastly toned down version of the military's current M-390 Battleskin with which he was very familiar. His own was like a second skin in which he had spent weeks and even months at a time encased. *God, I hope those days are behind me for good.* Although a mere shade of the military version, the physically enhancing suit made the enforcer more than a match for a dozen armed thugs. With the built in Artificial Intelligent Companion, heightened senses, and a ten-fold increase in strength, the officer had little need for the fearsome S-3 magpistol strapped low on her right thigh.

Jabal's main goal in life, at the moment, was to keep the pistol resting comfortably in its holster.

ღოღ

"Good morning, Citizen. May I please see your vitals?" the law enforcer asked, as her armored hand came to rest lightly on her grim sidearm.

The well-modulated, artificial baritone postulated a polite, almost friendly request. It was, in reality, a demand.

"Why, of course, Officer," Jabal said. "It is my pleasure to comply."

While he didn't feel it, he tried his best to add a friendly tinge to his words. Managing a weak smile as he squinted against the stinging rain, Jabal pulled off his right glove and extended his hand, palm-up, toward the enforcer, exposing his thumb chip and his entire legal history.

He stood impassive as his exposed hand burned in the numbing cold rain, which flowed wickedly down his arm and into his uniform.

"Wonderful day for a stroll," law enforcer, Sakuna Izusa said, as her Artificial Intelligence Unit, scanned Jabal for any hidden weapons as well as the surrounding three blocks for company. Ambushes were rare, but not unheard of, and Sakuna was anything if not prudent.

To find a lone kenan, trudging along in the pouring rain when he should be sleeping, raised a few warning bells.

Jabal Shann was obviously not drunk or physically impaired, but since the war had ended, she had seen more than her fair share of mentally damaged veterans who had somehow slipped through the military's psych screens. All the returning soldiers were highly skilled at killing. Throw in a few mental quirks and a harmless encounter could explode out of control, and you were suddenly knee deep in trouble, fighting for your life.

Sakuna was newly assigned to Cobol City, having been here less than six months, yet her chest plate still bore the scar where a month ago a routine traffic stop ended in a wild shoot out.

It never got dull enforcing the law near a military base.

၉၁၅

"Yes...wonderful morning," Jabal said as he wiped a sheet of water from his face. "It's definitely a twofor."

"A twofor?"

"Two for one. Taking care of my exercise and getting a shower all at the same time."

While Sakuna kept a wary eye on Jabal, her AIU accessed the biochip embedded beneath the skin of his right thumb. Not only did the chip provide personal identification and legal records, but also gave the enforcer a complete toxicology of Jabal's blood.

"He's clean," the AIU whispered into the enforcer's ear. "Zero legal criminal record. I am picking up trace amounts of over the counter Antynol and Zetom...the commander must have a slight virus. However, not a hint of stems, numbs, or even herbs. As hard as it is to believe, the commander here is without flaw."

You can say that again, the enforcer mused as she observed the handsome, albeit waterlogged, military officer.

"Commander Jabal Shann of the Sky Navy, Fifth Fleet," the enforcer said. "No legal record and not even a trace of illegal, let alone legal, recreation drugs. You are too good to be true."

"I don't know about the too good to be true part," he said with an easy smile. "However, legal or not, a drug is a drug. Not my thing."

As he pulled on the glove, Jabal wondered what the enforcer looked like under her helmet. He knew she was a *fenan*, or female.

ↄↄↄ

For the last two hundred years, the Azurean people had fought a war of survival with a savage race called the Erest. The Erest had cut a path of destruction across the quadrant, as world after world had fallen to their insatiable appetite for conquest. Billions of slaves toiled endlessly, supplying the Erest war machine as they carved out a bloody empire.

Finding that war was inevitable, the Azurean nation had only two choices: death or total victory. Fortunately, for the Azureans, they had an aptitude for the art of killing that the Erest could scarcely imagine.

While every able body *kenan*, or male, was enlisted in some part of the war effort, the day-to-day running of society on the Home World fell on the shoulders of the fenans. All patrolling law enforcers were fenans, as were doctors, lawyers, firestormers, mech workers, and so on. Even pro sport teams were exclusively fenan.

An unsettling image came to his mind of a thick-necked combat foot soldier in lipstick and eye color. Jabal shuddered at the nauseous thought.

From the serial number printed on her chest plate, this particular officer was *785600*.

"As I am cruising by," the enforcer said, "I ask myself. Myself, I ask, what possible *legal* activity could bring a high and mighty Sky Navy Commander out on such a miserable day, well before sunup? We aren't up to anything naughty, now are we, Commander?"

Her tone was as icy and cold as the rain dripping off her distinctive black and yellow armor.

"Okay, you caught me," he said, throwing his hands up in the air. "I was trying to drown myself."

"Oh, do you think that was *funny*?" she said, cocking her head to the side. "I got news for you, Commander, that wasn't a bit funny. It sure won't be any funnier when we interrogate you down at the enforcer lockup after a night or two in the *can*."

"I see your point, Officer," Jabal said with a sheepish grin. "As ridiculous as this sounds, I lost a bet and am paying dearly for it."

"You *do* know that gambling is illegal, Commander?"

"It wasn't a monetary bet, Officer...*785600*...but one of humiliation. We call it *the walk of shame*."

"Who is *we*?"

"My *former* friend, Lieutenant Darris Oso."

"From the officer's compound to the Citadel, is a good ten kilometers," she said.

"That's what makes it so shameful. The rain was an unexpected bonus—"

Jabal turned away as he was racked hard with a ragged, painful cough.

"You obviously aren't physically well, Commander," Sakuna said as her hand finally left the butt of her automatic pistol. "You should not be exposed to this terrible weather."

"I'll be all right. Just a little tickle in my throat."

"It is against regulations, but...let me give you a ride to the base, Commander. That little tickle in your throat sounds bad enough to kill you."

"Thank you, Officer, but no, thank you."

"You are ill and in no condition to continue any farther. I insist. Don't make me put you in binders and arrest you for your own good."

Jabal laughed. "As tempting as that ride sounds, a bet is a bet. My word is my word. I have to do this."

"But no one would know I gave you a ride. It would be our little secret."

"I would know."

Sakuna looked long at Jabal. "Is there a *Mrs.* Commander?" she asked as her deep voice softened ever so slightly.

"Yeah," Jabal said. "At home, in a warm, dry bed, thinking I am a complete idiot."

"If—she is stupid and doesn't appreciate what she has— look me up. Have a good day, Commander."

Jabal smiled. "I'll do that, Officer. You be careful."

"By the way, Commander, if I run into this Darris Oso, I'll ruin his day."

"I would very much appreciate that, Officer."

Sakuna mounted her three-wheeled bike and, with a small, parting salute, roared off down the empty street.

Jabal pulled himself deeper into his thick, gray and blue greatcoat as the icy downpour turned to sleet.

"Barea is right," he said as he once again took up his march. "I am an idiot, but at least the enforcers like me."

Jabal could not help but laugh at his self-inflicted humiliating situation. However, his guffaw turned into another chest crushing, coughing jag. Leaning against the base of a lamppost, Jabal took a moment to recover his breath and gasped. His wet glove was covered with bright flecks of blood.

CHAPTER 2

Covered in a fine sheen of sweat, Darris Oso rolled off the softly panting Barea Shann.

"That was wonderful," he said, softly snuggling with his best friend's wife.

"It will do," she said as she pulled away from him.

Barea draped a sheet around her nude form. Reaching to the bed table, she snatched a small drug vaporizer and inhaled greedily.

"Be careful with that," Darris snapped. "That's the last one I have."

Smiling, she lay back as the drug entered her bloodstream. "Oh that feels so...delicious," she whispered. "Even makes *you* tolerable."

"Oh, I hate it when you gush," he said with a chuckle. "It's so embarrassing." Darris rolled over on his back. "So, Barea, when are you going to tell Jabal about us?"

"There is no *us*," she said as she closed her eyes. "You know that I hate everything about you."

"Everything?"

"Well, there is one thing I like," she said with a giggle.

"We are two of a kind."

"I am nothing like you," she said.

"Oh, yes you are. We both want to hurt Jabal Shann in the worst possible way. I wish I could tell him that while he marched like a moron to the base, I enjoyed having sex with his wife. God, the look on his face would be glorious."

"Jabal would beat you to death. With his family's connections, it would be ruled self-defense."

"He is quite a fighter. I could hire a few ex-military troublemakers, looking for a few extra credits to kidnap him. While I watch him being beat to a pulp, I would tell him in graphic detail how I have enjoyed your favors for over a year. That would be exquisite."

She giggled. "You are evil."

"And you aren't?"

"I don't want to kill Jabal," she said. "I love him."

"You have a funny way of showing your love for your beloved husband. It wasn't his name you were crying out earlier."

"You pretend to be his friend, but you are jealous of his family name. You are trying to use him to better your lot in life. You are a parasite."

"Guilty as charged. Berea, I have never lied to you. Yes, with all my being, I loathe Jabal Shann. It isn't fair that he should have the powerful family name and the most luscious wife in the city while I must scrape by with less. However, I have found that getting close to that fool has been very beneficial. After all, I already enjoy the favors of his beautiful wife. I am sure that, down the road, having ties to his important family will reap huge rewards."

"What if I tell him how you really feel?" she asked with a small smile. "What if I come clean and tell him everything and beg his forgiveness?"

"Go ahead," he said with a smirk. "That should be an interesting conversation. Sure, I would be good as dead, but his father would drop a hammer on you as well."

"I love Jabal, I really do. He is a good—a noble kenan. Much better than you can even imagine."

"Then why are you here, with me, in *noble* Jabal's bed?"

"I—I don't know."

"Well, I do know. Even if you will not admit it. Deep down, you want to destroy him. Probably even more than I do."

"N—no. You are wrong."

"It is true. You resent the times he leaves you alone. You feel less like his wife than one of his possessions. For the kind of fenan you are, that is too much to take."

"I hate you."

"Go ahead," he said. "Whether you want to admit it or not, I am here when you need me. I will always be here for you. Jabal will not."

Barea opened her mouth to reply, but her argument died in her throat.

Darris chuckled.

"I have to meet Jabal at the Iron Gate and rub in last night's victory. We have time for one more go around—if we hurry."

Barea gave Darris a thoughtful look then pulled back her sheet and embraced her lover.

CHAPTER 3

Marching through the stinging sleet, Jabal spied an unexpected oasis half a block away. One of the brightly painted food kiosks was open, its neon bright, carnival-like lights drawing Jabal like a moth to a flame. Jabal could see the vendor smile and motion for him to join him. It struck Jabal as odd for a vendor to be open at such an ungodly hour, but now wasn't the time to question good fortune. Jabal ducked under a wide, metal overhang of the street vender's booth and took a seat on the first of three, hard plastic, yellow stools. Heated air rising through hidden vents kept the customer area warm and dry. To Jabal, it was heaven sent. Taking off his dripping hat, he knocked off the excess water and ice before plopping it upon the stool beside him.

The vendor's fleshy face was a road map of wrinkles, clefts, and valleys that stood in sharp contrast to his neatly trimmed, snowy white beard and hair.

Despite the foul weather, the smiling old man was dressed in little more than a light jacket and immaculate green apron. A white nametag attached to his apron had the letters, *SD,* etched in simple black script.

Jabal had another uncontrolled coughing fit that left his rattling chest aching and his lips bright red with blood.

"Son, with a cough like that, you should be home in bed, not roaming through the streets in this terrible weather," the vender said. "This weather is only fit for ducks."

"What's a duck?"Jabal asked.

"A duck is an odd creature I ran across in my travels," SD

said with a chuckle. "Always fighting with rascally wabbits over which hunting season it is."

"Excuse me? What's a wabbit?"

"Never mind. Just a bad joke. Now, what will it be? I have fresh, warm sweet cakes that would melt in your mouth, and I just brewed a big batch of my world-renowned, spiced tea."

"Not much of an appetite," Jabal said, wiping his mouth with a damp pocket square. "But that spiced tea sure smells good. I'll take the biggest cup you have."

"Well now, just so happens that spiced tea is my specialty, Commander," the vender said as he stirred a white, ceramic crock.

As he filled a large plastic cup, Jabal noticed that the old man's left arm was artificial. Because of the conflict, such sights were sadly all too common.

Fortunately, six months before, the mighty Azurean armada destroyed the last stronghold of the Erest armed forces. The victorious fleet returned to their home system and a war-weary population, eager to close this terrible chapter in their history.

The old kenan handed Jabal a large steaming cup with his natural hand. "I guarantee that it will kill what ails you."

"I'll hold you to that," Jabal said with a warm grin.

SD laughed as Jabal pulled a glove off his right hand. The vender extended a thin plastic display the size of a paperback book and Jabal pressed his thumb against the smooth surface.

"Thank you, Commander Jabal Shann," the tiny voice of the credit machine said. "Have a nice day and come back often."

"I take it you were in the infantry?" Jabal asked, glancing at the artificial arm.

"And proud of it," the vendor said as he looked down at the information gathered from Jabal's thumb scan. His eyes widened slightly. "Jabal—*Shann?* You wouldn't be any relation to Major Gannon Shann would you?"

"He is—was—my grandfather," Jabal said, taking a sip of the tea.

"For the grandson of Major Shann, it's no charge," the older Azurean said as he voided the bill.

"I can't let you do that," Jabal protested.

"Already done, Commander Shann."

By the look in the old soldier's eyes, Jabal knew further protests were futile. "Thank you," he said, taking a sip. "I must say—this is wonderful tea, never tasted anything quite like it. What's in it?"

"Little bit of this—little bit of that—a lot of dreams."

Jabal smiled. "So, where did you serve under my grandfather?"

"I was with Major Shann at the invasion of Quester III. It was a damn hard fight, but we kicked the Erest off that rock."

"Quester III?" Jabal asked. "That was where he died. I wished I'd had more time to get to know him. I was only eight when he shipped out."

"He was quality, no doubt about it. You should be proud of him, son."

"I am. If you don't mind me asking, where did you lose your arm?"

"In the same offensive that killed the major. Blown off by a seeker round."

The old man held up his arm. The skeleton like prosthetic gleamed in the cold light. When SD wiggled his fingers, Jabal could see all the brass colored rods and pulleys moving in concert.

"I'm sorry."

"Don't be. I did my part—did what was needed. I am a better person for it. The government set me up with a dandy replacement. In many ways, the freaky thing is better than my natural born one, even got lifetime warranty on parts and labor. Besides, my grandchildren never get tired of Granddad's metal arm. I think they like it better than vids."

As the merchant spoke, Jabal downed the last of the delicious drink. Unbeknownst to Commander Shann, his drink contained more than brewed tea, sweeter, and spices.

Trillions of minuscule biomechanical machines, some smaller than atoms, charged into his system, absorbing into every part of his body. The brainchild of a nameless race of beings who lived and died before his own sun first flicked into existence, the alien medical machines were the perfect vaccination and made doctors unnecessary.

With dogged determination, they maintained the subject's health, guarding from everything from upset stomach to cancer to tooth decay. Programed specifically for Jabal's DNA, they destroyed the cancer and restored the damage done in less than a minute.

Suddenly, his entire being was flooded with a wonderful, warm glow. The nasty rattle in his chest dissipated, before vanishing all together.

Jabal experienced his first unrestricted lung full of air in weeks and felt a surge of energy that left him feeling almost giddy.

"I feel—*wonderful.*"

"I told you I brewed one hell of a cup of tea, didn't I?"

Checking his timepiece, Jabal groaned. "Got to go."

"Before you go, son, can I shake your hand? The major was one of the greatest Azureans I ever knew."

Jabal smiled and griped the sergeant's good hand. The vender was old, but his grip echoed with amazing strength.

"What is your name, sir?" Jabal asked.

"Dionet. Siat Dionet, Sergeant, Fifth Division."

"It has been a pleasure, Sergeant Dionet. I have to say, you brew one fine cup of tea. I feel great—why, even my cough is gone."

"That's why I am here, commander," Dionet said. "To make sure nothing prevents you from fulfilling your destiny. May God bless you and give the strength to endure the dark days ahead."

Jabal narrowed his eyes at the sergeant's cryptic words.

Dionet laughed at his puzzled expression. "Have a good day, Commander Shann. Be sure to watch out for wascally wabbits."

"Umm, sure thing, Dionet."

Standing, Jabal slipped on his damp, crimson beret and pulled up his collar. Taking a small breath, he plunged into the miserable weather.

℘℘℘

As Jabal moved out of sight, Siat Dionet slid shut the bright plastic shutter and placed a closed sign on the "borrowed" kiosk. Looking at his mechanical appendage, he chuckled as it melted and reformed into a normal hand and arm.

"Yes, Commander Shann," he said, flexing his restored hand. "Without me, your project would fall forgotten by the wayside, and we cannot have that."

Taking a cigar from his pocket, SD jammed the stogie into the side of his mouth and pulled from a vest pocket an old fashioned, gold pocket watch. Popping open the cover he smiled as he observed the newly created time line.

"I love it when a plan comes together," he said as he disappeared into the cold, damp air.

CHAPTER 4

Walking up to the main gate security checkpoint, Jabal was greeted by Darris Oso and several of his comrades, all of whom were hooting and yelling taunts.

"All of you can kiss my rear," Jabal said. "Let's see a show of hands. How many here out rank me?"

No one raised a hand.

"Thought so. Now get out of here, that's an order."

The heckling squad scattered, leaving Jabal and Darris.

"Now tell me again, why do I call you friend?"

"To tell you the truth, Jabal," Darris said, "other than the joy humiliating you brings me, I just socialize with you in order to steal your pretty wife. She is much too good for the likes of you."

Jabal gave his friend a sour look and balled his fist.

"Be careful, Jabal. Barea doesn't like me to come to bed all bruised."

"Another word from you, *Lieutenant Oso*, about my wife and I will not only kick your ass all over this courtyard I will also have you arrested for attacking a superior officer."

The tall, smugly handsome Darris smiled and clapped the smaller Jabal on the back. "You know I was only joking. I have the utmost respect for you and your lovely wife."

"I don't like it," Jabal said, his face flushed with anger. "It is out of line. It disrespects me and my wife. It will stop now."

"Please don't get me wrong," Darris said. "You are just sore over the walk."

"I am not happy over losing the bet, but you crossed the

line. Now that I think about it, you have done that a lot lately."

"I don't know what you are talking about."

"I think I need a better class of friend, Lieutenant Oso. Dismissed."

Darris choked back his anger and his humiliation. Snapping to attention, he gave Jabal a sharp salute, turned on his heel, and walked away. His miscalculated sadistic jab at Jabal had backfired and had slammed closed the door to his wife—for the moment.

ℰ⋙ℰ⋙

Jabal entered the "Citadel," the imposing five-hundred-year-old fortress that housed Azurean Fleet Operations. The massive complex had grown rapidly over the war years and was the most heavily guarded facility on the planet.

After two more check points, Jabal made it to his small, utilitarian office. Ditching his drenched greatcoat revealed the somber charcoal uniform of an Azurean Sky Officer. Jabal glanced at his timepiece and groaned. He was late.

Commander Shann took a deep breath and walked down the grim, stone-lined corridor of Azurean Fleet Operations. He could never shake the oppressive feel of the place, which had always reminded him of a tomb.

He paused at the third and last checkpoint to show his identification while five, heavily armed Azurean warriors looked on. They all wore full-blown battleskins, which were light-years ahead of the police officer's suit he had met earlier.

Satisfied that his credentials were genuine, they saluted and buzzed him through a vault like door. Jabal now entered the section that housed the offices of the command staff and the Supreme Commander himself, War Admiral Teller Shann, Jabal's father.

Better known to Jabal as the "Supreme Stranger," Teller was away for much of Jabal life, directing the conflict on far-off exotic worlds. While his classmates envied Jabal and his world famous father, Jabal would have been happy to have an ordinary father who came home more than once a year.

Jabal entered a small, yet immaculate office, to find his father's personal aid, Imia, busily working on her data cruncher. Before her were several holographic screens filled with a dizzying array of information.

"You know, Imia. I could get a priest and you could marry that thing," he said.

"Oh, if it isn't Mr. Personality himself," she said without looking up from the screen. "You are a day late."

"That's *Commander* Personality to you. I was busy."

"Commander, Shammander," she said. "If there was any justice in this world, you would be commanding a street sweeping machine."

"It must be hard to maintain such a bright, cheery outlook. Put yourself down for a court martial."

"Bite me," she said.

Their banter was interrupted by a three low tones emanating from an intercom unit on her desk.

"Dad will see you now, Jabal."

"Thanks, Sis," Jabal said as he opened the inner door.

Jabal entered the palatial chambers of Teller Shann, the chief military commander and architect of their victory in the Great War. The admiral sat at a small table, fussing with an ornate, silver teapot.

Teller Shann was a tall, dignified Azurean with close-cropped silver hair and beard, who, unlike most military leaders, had a warm, sparkling personality. Teller had the media outlets and ruling council eating out of his hand. Few knew the cold, calculating brain that hid behind his well-groomed, gracious personality.

"I expected you yesterday, *Commander*," Teller said. "I thought this little project of yours was important."

"And a good morning to you too, Admiral Dad," Jabal said with a mock salute.

"You are a pitiful excuse for a soldier, you know that? You remind me of your mother."

"A fact I am quite proud of. I have been so busy with my project, I thought it best to reintroduce myself to the wife and kids. Glad I remembered to bring my ID. Why, I could have gotten shot."

"How is Barea?"

"Better than I deserve."

"True," Teller said, as he poured two cups of tea. "How did she take the news of your new project?"

Jabal took a seat across from his father.

"Not well, I'm afraid," he said, taking the offered cup.

"Did she threaten you with divorce?"

"No, Massive amounts of physical and mental abuse, but not divorce."

"Barea knows how important this project is. She will be a good wife and endure."

"Now how would she know that, when I am forbidden to speak of my project?"

"I took the liberty of taking her out to lunch the other day," Teller said as he opened a tin of cookies. "Try one, they are excellent."

Jabal took a cookie. "So that's why she didn't threaten me with divorce."

"You are my son and, whether you know it or not, I love you."

Jabal's eyes widened and he set down the cup of tea. "Okay, what's wrong? You haven't told me you loved me since I was ten."

"Nothing," Teller said. "While it took all the influence I have, the project is a go. To be honest, no one outside this office believes it is even possible."

"Then it's the ship, isn't it? You couldn't get the *Rising Sun,* could you?"

Teller smiled broadly. "Admiral Grint pulled several strings and even resorted to blackmail to keep the *Rising Sun.* Said it was too important to our overall system defense. And to be honest, I agree."

"I knew it," Jabal exclaimed. "For this to even have a chance to work, I need a ship of at least seventy thousand metric tons."

"Jabal, the Council wanted to give you the *Summer Storm.*"

"The *Summer Storm*? That old wreck barely survived the war. The entire thing was cut in half at Someer 5 and had to be towed back to base. I don't need some war wreck that can't fly."

"Relax son," Teller said. "I got you a very nice ship. I got you *The Blossoming Flower*."

"Impossible. *Golad's Folly*? Are you serious?"

"The very one. The most advanced death dealing device ever created—well, on paper anyway. In actuality—a far different tale."

Jabal sat back in his chair, pondering the possibilities. "What's the catch? You fight me tooth and nail over a lowly destroyer, then hand me a full-blown Battle Carrier. You are up to something."

"Like you said before, this project of yours is very important—if it works. *The Flower* carries its own excavation and manufacturing unit. Never needing to be resupplied, the ship has, potentially, unlimited range. Since it was a bust as a warship, I would think it would be the perfect vessel to become an explorer of the galaxy.

"But *The Flower*?" Jabal asked. "Wouldn't the high council throw a fit giving me one of your main warships?"

"Technically, she is more of a war base than a ship. We never quite worked out the flaw in the weapon system or the propulsion. She is a beast to move. Slow as my great grandmother, but she did make a wonderful forward base. Best amenities off world, in fact, weapon industrialist Zoneallgall Somebale's cruising yacht, *The Magnificent,* pales in comparison to *The Flower's* elegance."

"Rumor has it the ship became a decadent treat for admirals and generals," Jabal said. "I hear the parties were scandalous."

Teller scowled at his smiling son. "I suggest you stop listening to lies. Anyhow, two months ago, as part of the dismantling of the wartime fleet, *The Blossoming Flower* was quietly decommissioned. Her crew has been reassigned and, as we speak, her ammo bins are being emptied and redistributed among the fleet. Before you came along, her next assignment was the scrap yard."

"Are you sure I can have her?"

"More than sure," Teller said. "The old girl should never have been built. She was a mistake, pure and simple. She is a big, slow target that wallows like garbage barge. A destroyer, one thirtieth of her size can do three times the job. On top of which *The Flower* costs a fortune to operate, both in personnel and money."

Jabal's mind was reeling at the prospect of his dreams coming true. The project, at last was becoming a reality.

ഇരുള

The trouble military and commercial ships faced with space travel was the vastness of space itself. Even between the nearest of neighboring systems the fastest of ships would take thousands of years to cross the void.

Interstellar travel was only possible by the use of Bridges.

Seeded about the galaxy, were huge, mysterious structures called, for lack of a better name, *Bridges*. The devices were enormous metal grid work tubes, exactly fifteen thousand, two hundred, and five kilometers in length with an opening one thousand kilometers in diameter.

They had been studied, even worshiped by some, for hundreds of thousands of years, however, how they worked or even who built them was a complete mystery. There wasn't a power source discernible, and even the alloy used in their construction defied analysis. You merely crossed the Bridge at a predetermined speed and came out thousands of light years away through another bridge.

The Great War was fought across the bottlenecks of the Bridges, which was why it took so long for final victory.

Jabal's revolutionary project was a device that could make the seemingly impossible dream, of a vessel crossing light years instantaneously, come true. Now, thanks to advances made during the war, and Jabal's particular genius, the dream was now within their grasp, or at least Jabal thought so.

To the military, the advantage was incalculable. With ships capable of jumping past the Bridges, the bloody, two-hundred year war with the Erest could have been won in a fraction of the time.

To an explorer like Jabal, his lifelong dream of peaceful, galactic exploration was about to become hard reality. If he could get it to work, he would even have access to systems without the mysterious Bridges.

છ૭છ૭

"*The Blossoming Flower*," Jabal exclaimed. "This is beyond my wildest expectations. I can't wait to meet the crew."

"Well, about that," Teller said, taking a noisy sip. "There will be no crew."

"No crew, but I—"

"I just said that her crew has been reassigned. But don't worry, *The Flower's* AI will handle running the day-to-day ship functions. The damn thing is so advanced, it can do everything, but fight and, since you aren't going into battle, you don't need a crew."

"I was thinking of one hundred—"

"Out of the question," Teller said.

"Fifty—"

"No."

"Ten—"

"Do you want the ship or not?"

"Yes, of course, but surely you can spare someone?"

"Must I remind you that *The Flower's* days as a naval vessel are over? It was all I could do to get you a ship, for what most in the High Command call a waste of time and resources. To be perfectly honest, son, most think your project is mad."

"No," Jabal said. "My project isn't mad. It's cutting edge. The Pilot Program, now that *was* mad."

"Don't remind me," Teller said. "The geniuses who thought they could integrate an Azurean with a ship, making the vessel a living entity were crazy. That little project cost several lives and diverted precious resources away from our war effort."

"To be honest, I never thought you would turn loose a crew, but I had to ask," Jabal said.

"Your equipment has already been loaded and *The Flower* is being made ready for departure. Go home and kiss that pretty wife goodbye. The voyage to Srune will take a year."

"A year, two months, and seven days," Jabal said. "Or, to keep my wife from killing me and to save everyone a lot of wasted time, we could test it here."

"Absolutely out of the question," Teller said. "What if a rip occurs?"

"That a rip in time and space can occur hasn't been proven. As far as I'm concerned, it's science fiction."

"Science fiction or not, better to err on the side of caution, son. A year is a small price to pay."

"Okay, okay, I will bow to your fears. However, if all goes well, the return trip will be instantaneous."

"One more *slight* thing, Jabal," Teller said, putting down his empty cup. "I know your plate is full, but I have a little job that needs to be carried out."

"And what is that, sir?"

Teller took a deep breath. "What I tell you doesn't leave this room, understand?"

"Yes, sir."

"Son, ever heard of a project called, *Equinox*?"

"*Equinox?* Who hasn't?" Jabal said. "That had to be the most farfetched rumor I had ever—"

"It's true."

Jabal stared at his father in shock. "Are you insane? You created mechanized combat troops?"

Slowly, Teller nodded.

"But it's against the law for machines to participate in any form of combat. All of our AIs are loaded with dozens of safeguards to prevent that from ever happening. Any form of aggression against friend or foe, and the built-in safeguards fry them."

"That is because our people have a terrifying fear of our own creations turning on us. You ask me, it is all because of those silly horror movies of machines making us their slaves. However, desperate times call for desperate measures. We were forced to consider the idea after the Yonlder V invasion.

We lost over one hundred thousand irreplaceable soldiers taking that rock. I still have nightmares over that debacle."

"Why is it I never heard of them being used?"

"Because they were never deployed. No one, including myself, had the courage to push the start button."

"How good were they?" Jabal asked.

"I ordered the best money could buy. How do you place a price on an Azurean life? Frankly, some of my staff thinks we did too good a job in their construction. In tests, their abilities where off the charts. They sport a new armor that is invulnerable to small arms fire and rockets. It also gives them an almost perfect stealth ability. Their combination of firepower, resourcefulness, and intelligence in battle borders on the miraculous. The damn things are the perfect soldiers, infinitely better than their flesh and blood counterparts."

"They sound great," Jabal said. "They should have scared the hell out of the enemy."

"What scares the hell out of us is that the only way to ensure an enemy from using our safeguards against them, is not to give them any. So we didn't."

"What? No safeguards at all?"

"No. And we didn't give them an off button either."

"What's to keep them on our side?"

"We installed a new protocol that would make them intensely loyal to our people."

"Loyalty? That's it? That's the best you could come with?"

"Yeah, I admit it does sound weak. Thank God, the war ended before we had to use them. Except for a few prototypes, used under strict laboratory conditions, they are untested under enemy fire."

"Now you are scaring me. I hope you didn't make many of these killers."

"We created fifteen thousand before the project was scrapped," Teller said.

"Fifteen *thousand*?"

"Yes, all are loaded on ten assault ships discreetly sitting in landing bay four of *The Blossoming Flower*."

"What do you want me to do with them?"

Teller rose from his chair and activated a holographic screen portraying the Srune system. With a touch of a button, he added Jabal's flight plan. A bright yellow line cut through the system, ending in the orbit of the blue gas giant.

"The fifth planet has several moons. The moon Goe has, according to our last explorer probe, the largest active volcano in the system." Teller indicated the cratered Goe with a pointer. "Four months after you arrive, I want you to rendezvous with Goe, as it will be close to your testing area, and deposit my little mistake into the volcano. I also sent along a tactical flasher to make doubly sure that all evidence is erased."

"You are going to a lot of trouble to get rid of your mechanized killers," Jabal said. "Why not just turn them into slag here?"

"Because, they aren't supposed to exist. Like you pointed out, it's against the law for machines to participate in any form of combat. Nevertheless, I violated express written orders from the ruling council in creating them. If anyone finds out what I did, I will live out the rest of my days in a prison cell, if not be outright executed."

"You can count on me, Father," Jabal said. "No one will ever know they existed."

"Thank you, Jabal. I knew you would not let me down," said Teller. "God speed, son. Now get out, I have work to do."

౿ఎ౿ఎ

Teller refilled his cup. Imia walked into the room and Teller looked up.

"Do you really believe Jabal's project will work?" she asked.

Teller took a sip. "Never in a million years. It is a foolish, impossible dream. If I didn't know him better, I would say he was on drugs."

"You should have been up front with him. After all, he is family."

"Don't start, Imia," he said, brushing away a few crumbs from his blouse. "He wanted a ship and I gave him one. A great one. Perfect vessel for exploring the universe."

"Isn't it a coincidence that it is also the only ship large enough to transport all ten of your assault ships?" Imia asked with a slight smile.

"I don't know to what you refer, daughter. What assault ships?"

"This whole silly mission is an excuse to cover *your* sins, isn't it, Father?"

"I think you are getting a bit too nosy for your own good, daughter. Oh, all right, it keeps Jabal happy, as well serving the true purpose of eliminating any trace of *my sins.*"

"He is going to be alone for over two years. You should have told him about *The Blossoming Flower* and why no crew will set foot aboard."

"I was never one for spreading superstitious rumors."

"It isn't just rumors that say *The Flower* is cursed. I have read official reports that would curl your hair."

"I read the same reports. Just a lot of nonsense. Besides, if it is true, Jabal is a Shann, and fool or not, it will take more than a ship full of demons to faze him."

"*The Blossoming Flower* is eight kilometers long," she said. "That's a hell of a lot of demons, Father."

"Don't you have work to do?"

"One more thing, Father. What if Jabal isn't a fool, and his device works? Are you just going to hand *The Flower* over to him so he can explore the galaxy?"

Teller looked at his daughter and sat back in his chair. "He will be a hero. Jabal's name will be spoken in the same breath as scientific greats, such as Du-Marr, Howe, and Goordon. However, his discovery will not be wasted in exploration," he said quietly. "Such a device will give our people an empire."

CHAPTER 5

Tall and rail thin, Anand Byo moved through the small, elegant restaurant. He knew that at least five guns covered him and that his slightest wrong move would be...*interesting*.

He walked to the back where sat a private table for one. The table held a feast that would have fed a dozen Azureans, however, it was actually dinner for one. Sawing at a massive fillet sat the obese Boron Hyatt. A napkin stuffed in his shirt kept his expensive clothes from the greasy crumbs that fell from his thick, blubbery lips.

"What do you want?" Boron demanded, not bothering to look up.

"I hear that you have a problem, and I am here to help," Anand said.

"Problem? I got no problem."

"The way I hear it, you want the law enforcer who killed your son, real bad."

"I have learned to forgive in my old age."

"Funny, I heard that there is going to be an accident tomorrow," Anand said. "The kind that a forgiving kenan would not dream of."

Boron put down his utensils and tossed his napkin on the plate before him. "Chose your next words carefully, Anand. They may be your last."

"Let's be honest, shall we?" Anand said. "You are going to kill the fenan—am I right?"

"What are you getting at?"

"Sure, you can kill the enforcer outright, but what satisfaction would that bring you? Will that let your son rest in peace? Of course not. I have a better plan."

"Sit," Boron said. "I warn you that if you are wasting my time, you won't leave that chair alive."

Anand pulled out the chair and sat down. "I propose, Mr. Boron, that we allow you the personal pleasure of avenging your dear son's death."

"How?"

"I have a plan to deliver her into your hands."

"You are insane. You can't kidnap an enforcer. That suit of theirs is too tough to crack without killing the person inside. Besides, they could easily track the tags within her and we would all be executed, you fool. I will be satisfied with her dead."

"Not only can I get her out of that infernal battleskin alive, but I know of a place to keep her on ice where no one would ever look. When the heat dies down, you can personally avenge your son."

"What is the risk?"

"I will take all the risk. Your hands will be clean."

"How much is this going to cost me?"

"Two percent of the West Coast take for one month."

"You are out of your mind."

"Sorry to have wasted your time, Mr. Boron," Anand said, as he started to rise from his chair.

"Wait."

Anand smiled as he sat down.

"Where is this magical place no global scanner can see?"

"I have connections within the Sky Navy. There is a decommissioned ship that no one will go near. It lies outside the range of any ground-based scanner."

"Why won't anyone go near it?"

Anand laughed. "Because the fools think the ship is haunted. Can you believe that?"

Boron snorted.

"I know you have informants on the inside of the enforcer network. All you have to do is arrange for her to be at this airfield at this time." Anand produced a slip of paper and handed it to Boron.

"Done," Boron said. "If you fail me, Anand, you will take Sakuna Izusa's place."

❦

Anand walked out of the restaurant and pulled his coat collar up as the cold rain came down. His features blurred and changed into that of Siat Dionet.

He chuckled at the fact that the real Anand Byo died an hour before of a drug overdose. It would be week before anyone found him.

"One more Dead End added to the roster."

SD paused long enough to clamp down on his stogie before he faded away.

CHAPTER 6

Leaning back in the warm, luxurious bed, Jabal looked around the darkened bedroom and smiled. He was at peace with himself here—one of the few places he felt safe. It was if the universe was in balance while he was at home with his wife. It made sense. He tried to drink in the comforting energy of the place, because in the morning he would leave and not be back for a long time.

Jabal rolled over and kissed his sleeping wife's neck.

Barea smiled, but her eyes remained closed. "Haven't you had enough?"

"You feel so soft and bed warm," he said, running his hand along the gentle curve of her thigh. "I almost forgot how good you feel—and no, I will never have enough."

"And yet you are going to leave me again."

"It is important."

"*I* am important, or at least I thought so."

"Barea, you are my life. Trust me, it will only be a year and then—"

Barea angrily shoved Jabal back, slid off the bed, and onto the gleaming, dark wooden floor. Sensing them to be awake, the house automatically brightened the bedroom lights.

"Damn it," she snapped. "Dim the lights."

The room illumination dropped to half its intensity.

Standing before Jabal, completely nude in the soft light, her dark hair in disarray, Barea scowled and pointed her finger at him.

"I put up with your absences because I had to, but the war

is over. Your father is the head of the military, for God's sake. Make him send someone else."

"Barea, be reasonable."

"You be reasonable. I am sick of being alone—stuck in a marriage with a mate I never see."

"I know things have been strained between us, and I am sorry, but I have to do this. If my experiment works, our entire culture will change."

"It's more than that. The look in your eye when you talk about the great experiment—it is the same look that you gave me when we first wed. I would give my right arm if I could arouse you like that again."

"You come first. You know that. I love you, Barea, surely you don't doubt that?"

"No, not for a second."

"Since I have been home, you have acted...distant. Is there something you are not telling me?"

"I am not happy with you, if that is what you're getting at. I am not happy with a kenan who stops by occasionally for a laugh and sex. You make me feel like a whore."

"That is insane. You are my everything. I have never cheated on you, and every chance I get, I try to be with you. In war, we have to make sacrifices."

"Sacrifices? The war is over, and I see you even less. I am the one making sacrifices—not you."

Jabal gave her a long look. "Bear with me one last time, my love. A ship has been allocated, and the wheels are in motion. I have to do this."

"I know," she said softly. "Your charming father treated me to an embarrassingly expensive lunch and informed me that any action on my part to keep you here would be...*frowned* upon. God, how I hate that smooth-talking, elegant monster. That perfect smile of his gives me shivers."

"That monster is my father."

"Why you admit that is beyond me," she said, slipping on a silky, light blue robe. She jammed her hand into the pocket and nearly fainted when her fingers brushed the drug inhaler she had shared with Darris.

"My mother liked him," Jabal said with a grin.

"Umm, was that before or after she tried to shoot him?"

"Before. That was a turning point in their marriage. Father claims that his shoulder aches whenever bad weather is about to roll in."

"She should have drilled one between his eyes."

"Whatever you do, don't let that little blurb fly at the family reunion. My brothers—"

"And don't get me started on your self-righteous, pompous brothers who treat you like dirt. You have more character and honor in your little finger than all of those animals combined."

"What a nice thing to say," he said, as a smile crossed his face. "I have it."

"Have what?"

"Come with me, Barea. I have to ask Father, but I am sure he wouldn't mind. It would be one long wedding night. We can get to know each other all over again, and I can make up for my time away."

A shiver of fear ran down her spine. "Crammed together in a *spaceship*? Are you out of your mind? They don't call them *iron coffins* for nothing. Why, we would kill each other. Besides, I have a backlog of patients who need me. I do have a career of my own, remember?"

Jabal smiled. "This ship is a bit larger than the run of the mill 'iron coffins.' Dad gave me, *The Blossoming Flower*."

"The what?"

"Sorry, I forgot how little information trickles home from the military."

"Damn police state."

"Anyway, *The Blossoming Flower* is the largest ship in known space. In fact, our largest forward base is half her size. The thing is over eight kilometers long and has the finest accommodations in the fleet. It could be our own private pleasure yacht on a year-long cruise."

In the dim light, Jabal failed to recognize the panic that shone briefly in her eyes. "Umm…oh, that does sounds wonderful, Jabal. I am tempted, but I am a physician. I have my duty."

"Now who is putting duty above the family?"

"I hate it when you're right. Oh, all right, go on your silly secret mission, but when you get back, if you so much as try to leave my sight, I will shoot you. Unlike your mother, I am a great shot. You hear me, mister?"

"Loud and clear. When I get back, you are the boss and I will never leave your side."

Jabal grinned and patted the bed beside him.

Barea smiled and silently breathed a sigh of relief at the bullet she had dodged.

"Keep my side warm, I will be right back."

℮୬℮୬

Barea slipped into the bath and slid the door closed.

Oh God, that was close. Darris must have slipped this into my pocket. That bastard wanted Jabal to catch me. When I see him, I am going to castrate him.

Barea removed the inhaler with a shaking hand. She thought a moment then sucked deeply on the mouth piece, drawing in the last dose of the illegal narcotic. Suppressing a grin, she dropped the empty plastic vial into a recycler chute.

She looked into the mirror and adjusted her hair as a velvety, delicious warmth flooded her body. Despite her growing euphoria, she frowned at the image.

Jabal Shann, through your neglect you have wounded me beyond forgiveness. I am tired of being the long-suffering wife, waiting for when you decide to return home. I have a life and I am tired of sharing it—no, wasting it—with you.

She smiled.

Still, I am not going to walk away like a good fenan. I am going to hurt you like you hurt me. I want to see the pain in your eyes and relish the anguish when I break that insipid, honorable spirit of yours.

It will not be tonight, though. Tonight it will be as it once was. I will give you one last night of lovemaking and passion, pretending I give a damn about you. For how I once cared about you, I owe you that much.

When the time is right, I have a surprise for you. I secretly filmed Darris and me together. Perhaps I should send it to you as you journey to Srune. I am sure that will make your trip very enjoyable.

No, that would be a waste, because I could not watch the reaction in your eyes. I will save this little gem for a homecoming present. I will make a point that Darris will be at my side when it happens. It will be grand to see both the kenan I despise brought down.

That will be the day of my liberation and I intend to savor every delightful morsel.

"Barea, are you coming back to bed?" Jabal called out, interrupting her train of thought.

Barea slipped off her robe, slid open the bedroom door, and joined her husband.

CHAPTER 7

Sakuna," Sergeant Geint said as she entered Precinct Four's armory.

"Right here," Sakuna said and backed into in a recharge/repair bay.

Twenty-five of the bays stood side by side down the length of the metal wall. Five were occupied by open yellow and black armored battleskins as small, spider-like mechanized repair bots crawled over the empty suits, making sure that they were ready when the officer's shift began.

Power and computer cables snapped into recessed plug-ins in both the helmet and the bottom of Sakuna's lower back. Sakuna popped open her uniform and, after unplugging half a dozen sensors, stepped out on the heated tile floor of the locker room. Stretching her nude body, Sakuna worked out a few kinks while several repair bots descended on her uniform.

"Don't tell me that I've been reassigned," she snapped as she brushed her short, dark hair with her fingers. "Damn it, I just got assigned to this post. I haven't even unpacked all my stuff yet."

"Calm down," Geint said. "I need you to pick up a prisoner off one of those floating space cans."

"Isn't that a job for the military? I mean, they take care of their own trash, while we take care of the civies' trash."

"Usually, but I got special orders for a prisoner pick up. Since you are the only one here at the moment, it's all yours."

"Great," Sakuna said. "I just finished my shift and I'm spent."

"You're breaking my heart. You have just enough time to grab a shower and some food, so move it."

Grumbling, Sakuna walked into the shower stall where the water automatically began to fall in a pre-programmed steamy torrent. While she washed, her thoughts drifted back to the half-drowned officer she had met hours earlier.

Now, why can't I meet a nice person like that, Commander...something? He had the most beautiful eyes. What was his name? Jabal. Yes, that was it. It figures that he would be married...the story of my life.

Sakuna finished her shower and, stepping from the stall, grabbed a towel from a rack by the door.

Who knows? Perhaps I will run into Jabal Shann. That wouldn't be so bad.

e♥e♥

Sakuna stood before the shuttle-landing pad. She carried copies of her orders and a set of neuro restraints for the prisoner. Despite her fatigue and irritation at the infringement upon her scarce free time, she was excited to go aboard the space elevator and actually set foot upon the Sky Naval Base.

Like a great white bird, the shuttle swooped out of the sky and settled lightly upon the flashing, landing pad. The simple metal ramp unfolded and the hatch door popped open with a slight hiss.

An older man with a well-trimmed beard and clad in a somber black uniform descended the ramp and smiled warmly.

"Officer 785600," he said. "I am Lieutenant Byo. Anand Byo. If you will come with me, we will get started with our grand adventure."

CHAPTER 8

The multi-tiered space dock of the Azurean Sky Navy was an enormous affair. Looking like a giant tinker toy gone awry, the fourteen levels and hundreds of square kilometers of construction and repair facilities serviced the five fleets of the Azurean Sky Navy.

Attached to the mammoth space elevator that stretched from the planet's surface into orbit, the base acted as a giant counterweight keeping the ground-based construct intact. Its position also gave the facility the benefits of centrifugal force. Besides having gravity, it made launching vessels a snap. Releasing docking clamps, the vessel were hurled outward without wasting a drop of fuel.

⁊⊙⁊

Jabal Settled into the G-seat next to the shuttle pilot. On his wrist was his data cruncher with the equations that he hoped would make him famous.

"Control, this is dock Shuttle Fifty-Nine requesting clearance," asked the pilot as he brought the chemical engines on line.

"Shuttle Fifty-Nine, confirm your destination."

The Blossoming Flower, Control. Delivering Commander Shann."

"Affirmative, Shuttle Fifty-Nine, you are cleared."

"Thank you, Control."

"You be careful, Sote," the space traffic control said.

"Commander Shann, may God have mercy on your soul. Dock Control out."

Jabal gave the pilot a surprised look. "Mercy on my *soul?*" he asked. "What was that all about?"

"A nice send off, if you ask me," Ensign Ugu said. "We are going to *The Flower,* after all."

"Am I missing something?"

Ensign Ugu frowned at Jabal and nervously rubbed his own thinning red hair. "You really don't know, do you?"

"Spit it out, Ensign."

Ensign Ugu guffawed. "With all due respect, Commander, you must have really pissed someone off to pull inspection duty aboard the *Devil's Barge.*"

"*Devil's Barge?*"

"Yeah, that's what they call *The Flower.*"

"Who's they?"

"Anyone who has crewed her or has heard the stories. The word is the ship is cursed by the Devil himself."

"Oh come on. Did Lieutenant Oso put you up to this?"

"No joke, Commander, and trust me, I don't know a Lieutenant Oso. If I were you, I would get my inspection done right quick and in a hurry. If you want, I'll wait. I won't go aboard, but I'll stay real close."

"Nice offer, Ensign Ugu," Jabal said, "but I'm not here for an inspection. I'm sailing *The Flower* to Srune."

"Srune? As in the fifth planet, Srune?"

"The very one."

"Who is going along?"

"Just me."

"Commander, if I were you, I would come down with some disease or break my leg or something."

"Another word from you, Ensign Ugu, and I will press you into service as my pilot."

Ugu swallowed hard at the dreadful thought.

⁓⁓⁓

The small shuttle sailed past dozens of docked warships, all brightly lit with floodlights. With the war over, the ships represented the greatly reduced active peacetime fleet. While a small number of battle carriers sat in mothballs, the rest were in the process of feeding the scrap machines.

The Blossoming Flower sat at the end of the dock in her own special berth. A full six kilometers separated her and the nearest ship. The other ships wanted nothing to do with the *Devil's Barge* and stayed as far away as possible.

"Lord, would you look at the size of that monster," Jabal said. "The photos I saw do not do her justice."

"She sure is big," agreed Ensign Ugu, as he made a religious sign over his heart.

"A dozen *Rising Suns* could be housed in one of her landing bays."

"*Rising Sun?*" Ensign Ugu asked. "Now that, is one sweet ship. You should have tried to get that one."

Jabal sat in silence. *I think that the old kenan has pulled a fast one. He made out like he was doing me a favor. He gave me a ship no one would go near. Figures.*

❧❧❧

The Blossoming Flower sat gleaming in the powerful dock lights. Marring her sleek lines, attached amid-ship was her one-of-a-kind, detachable manufacturing facility.

While the standard fighting ships of the Azureans were between two to three-hundred meters, *The Blossoming Flower* was eight *thousand*, two hundred, and twenty nine meters long by one thousand, two hundred meters in diameter. She was so gigantic that the next largest battle carrier, *The Summer Breeze,* when suffering from extensive battle damage in the Bison Campaign, underwent an emergency refit within her cavernous main landing bay.

When first proposed by Admiral Golad, over seventy-five years ago, the ruling high council thought he was mad. He proposed that a single ship of overwhelming firepower could tip the balance in their favor and put an end to this bloody war.

An uphill battle to be sure, however, the gruff visionary

pulled strings and was even rumored to have resorted to blackmail and a few discrete, political assassinations to get his way.

Utilizing several innovative technologies, he built a ship that was supposed to sweep the Erest from space and strike fear into any who would dare provoke the Azurean Republic.

While equipped with the standard assortment of long-range smart missiles, *The Blossoming Flower*'s real teeth was in her innovated magnetic rail guns, better known as Mag-Guns. Her experimental Mag-Guns fired a ten-meter long tungsten carbide rod at an incredible one-hundred and twenty kilometers per second. One hit was more than any known warship or planet-side instillation could survive.

The guns, arranged in clusters of five, were able to fire one or ten rods at once. Equipped with one hundred and sixty Mag-Gun emplacement clusters, she could, in theory, deliver a hail of fire, able to destroy entire fleets single handedly. However, in reality, less than two percent were operational at any given time, due to overheating and the sheer power drain.

Her mighty planetary siege guns could deliver super-dense kinetic shock rounds from high orbit. The weapon was able to create devastating tsunamis, trigger seismic events, and even crack a planet's crust. However, the massive quad barreled Mag-gun drew such an incredible amount of energy, each shot left the ship powerless for nearly an hour. Needless to say, it would have been disastrous in a combat situation and was never used. The big guns were relegated to shattering asteroids for her manufacturing unit to process.

Among *The Blossoming Flower's* most ambitious scheme, as well as her biggest failure, was the Pilot Project. Controlled by an Azurean modified with a cybernetic interface, the Pilot made the enormous seven-thousand-member crew unnecessary. The Pilot joined with the ship, becoming a unique living entity that was both fast and nimble as an atmospheric fighter—on paper. The project failed when the first six volunteers died during integration. With their deaths, so died the Pilot Project, falling far short of her lofty expectations. Nevertheless, not all of her experimental features were failures.

Her manufacturing unit was an engineering marvel that could turn asteroid fields into parts, ammo, and fuel for the five combat fleets thus eliminating fragile supply lines. Her Null-glass armor proved to be better than anyone's wildest dreams. Null-glass was a material that was impervious to all know compounds, but appeared as a sheet of plate glass. While easily formed and molded, once cured, it could withstand the assault of any know weapon, including atomics.

It so surpassed all known armor, that the outside skin of the Blossoming Flower was a twenty-five-centimeter-thick sheath of null-glass. All vital interior sections including the airtight blast doors were protected by the transparent miracle. Unfortunately, the classified materials used to create the transparent, impervious armor were rare and enormously expensive.

One admiralty accountant once quipped that it would have been more cost effective to encrust the hull with diamonds. Thus from a purely economic standpoint only *The Blossoming Flower* was so protected.

The Blossoming Flower was designed to be a fast, unstoppable goddess of death. In the field, the gigantic ship proved to be slow, sluggish, and her weapon systems next to useless. Unfit to be a battleship, she spent the war as a forward mobile base of operations protected by a dedicated corvette of missile destroyers.

To the sky sailors who toiled and died in cramped, strictly utilitarian ships, she was a palatial, extravagant playground reserved for the admiralty. She was the most reviled ship in the fleet.

With the war over, her only value now was measured in the current price of her components and alloys. Jabal's bold plan was her only chance of avoiding the salvage machines.

Covered as she was by her exotic, null-glass armor, the ship looked like a fragile, crystal rod. A fragile crystal rod that could shrug off atomic warheads as if they were rubber balls.

How something that was built solely to kill and destroy, could be so beautiful, I'll never know, Jabal mused.

A huge, clumsy-looking barge lay alongside the exotic ship. A flexible docking umbilical connected the two ships near the bow. While they watched, the umbilical retracted and the AI-controlled barge blasted away by means of chemical rockets.

"What is that?" Jabal asked.

"The old girl is about to be scrapped. That barge has unloaded the last of her munitions. Now that was a sight, Commander. A never-ending line of barges has worked for a solid two weeks unloading her rods. Bet she singlehandedly resupplied the entire fleet. If I don't miss my guess, all she has left is her anti-missile defense and maybe a few emergency signal missiles."

"That is a shame," Jabal said quietly. "They should have waited before pulling her teeth. It's not dignified for a warship to sail with her guns empty."

"Amen, Commander. Amen."

ᏬᏨᏬ

"Agoa, this is Commander Shann. Make ready for our approach."

"Yes, sir, Commander Shann," Agoa, the soft, smoky voice of *The Blossoming Flower's* artificial intelligence said. "Please direct your shuttle to landing bay three. I look forward to having you aboard, sir."

"Damn, what a sexy voice. What I wouldn't give for a girlfriend to look like how Agoa sounds."

"That's odd," Jabal said. "All the other ship AI's I have ever heard sound like an unemotional drill instructor. She sounds like a real, flesh and blood fenan."

"The word is that *The Flower* got the best of everything. Figures she would have an AI with a porn-star voice."

The sparkling armor sheathing of the great ship opened and pivoted aside to reveal a circular, one-hundred-and-sixty-meter wide blast door of one of the Blossoming Flower's eight landing bays. The shuttle stopped dead a few hundred meters from the opening.

"No, sir, porn-star voice or no, I won't go aboard," Ensign Ugu said. "I don't trust it."

"You will land this craft, or I will turn you over to patrol."

"Not going to get trapped in one of those infernal bays. I'll use one of the external docks, or we can go back and get you another pilot."

"I don't have time for this foolishness," Jabal said, running a hand through his hair. "All right, let's get this over with. Change of plans, Agoa, open main external dock ring."

"Yes, sir, Commander Shann."

The round hatch circled close and the armor settled back into place.

Ensign Ugu expertly brought the shuttle down and settled into the now lighted external dock. As the shuttle made contact, a flexible, airtight seal formed about the outer hatch.

A light on his console flashed green and with a hiss of air, opened the outer hatch. The ponderous circular door of the carrier rotated and swung inward.

"Welcome aboard *The Blossoming Flower*, Commander Shann," Agoa said. "I trust your trip was a pleasant one?"

"Yes, thank you Agoa," Jabal said. "Is the ship ready to depart?"

"Yes, Commander. Your equipment is stored in cargo hold seven. Your personal belongings have been stowed in the captain's quarters. All we need is the word."

"See you around, Ensign," Jabal said with a smile.

"Sir, please take this," Ensign Ugu said as he removed a chain from his neck. A small silver pendant caught the light of the cabin.

"I can't—I—"

"Please, sir. I would feel a lot better knowing you had some protection."

Jabal smiled and took the charm. He slipped the chain over his neck and shook the Ensign's hand.

"I will be praying for you, Commander Shann."

"Thank you, Ensign Ugu. I need all the prayers I can get."

Jabal entered *The Blossoming Flower* and was surprised by the warm welcome that awaited him.

In lieu of a squad of heavily armed space marines, fifty heavy construction machines lined the wide passageway. As

Jabal entered, Agoa announced, "Captain on board." In response, the machines, with inhuman precision, snapped to attention.

Although Jabal chafed at the strict military world in which he had been thrust, he was touched by the machines's genuine gesture of respect. He, in return, gave them the absolute best salute of his entire military career.

"Commander Shann, the honor guard will escort you to the bridge.

"Thank you, Agoa."

In a time-honored ceremony, Jabal was escorted to the ship's command center, where he officially took command of the vessel. The round, vault-like room lay situated in a heavily armored section buried deep within the ship. At the center of the very efficient and surprisingly well-lit room sat the captain's chair. The chair could not only access any shipboard information, it could override any station or section of the ship instantly, not to mention the chair also had a manual shutdown switch for Agoa.

The only device with more power aboard the ship was located adjacent to the chair. Sunk into the floor, was the null-glass hatch to the Pilot's Chamber. From there, in theory, the Pilot would have total, unquestioned control of *The Blossoming Flower*.

Even the captain was powerless to interfere with the actions of the Pilot. Failure of the audacious program brought a collective sigh of relief from the bulk of the fleet captains who did not care to give up their power.

Jabal sat down in the captain's chair and relished the feeling of command.

"Commander Shann," the sultry, disembodied voice of Agoa said, "It is time for your first log entry."

Shann cleared his throat. "Today we start a new chapter in the history of the Azurean people. This great vessel, *The Blossoming Flower*, once an instrument of war, will now become an instrument of peace. She will be the first of many ships that will explore the galaxy and usher in a new era in the history of our people. An era, where with God's help, we will never know the horror of war again."

"Dream on, Commander Shann."

Jabal froze at the voice. The disembodied voice wasn't localized, but seemed to emanate from the very air itself.

"Agoa, who said that?"

"I am sorry, sir. I do not understand. You are alone in the command center."

Agoa promptly replayed the recording and Jabal was surprised when, as she said, there wasn't any sign of any voice, but his own.

Damn that Ensign Ugu. His foolish prattle about demons has given me the jitters. When I see him again, I will give him a piece of my mind.

⁊ϗ⁊ϗ

"Space Dock Control," Agoa said, "This is *The Blossoming Flower*. Requesting permission to break connection and depart."

"Permission granted, *Blossoming Flower*," the traffic control officer said.

"Thank you, traffic control."

Jabal waited, but the traffic control officer said nothing more.

"What the *hell*?" Jabal asked. "Did we just get snubbed?"

It was customary, almost obligatory for Azurean military traffic control to wish a safe voyage and swift return to one of their own. Jabal glanced at his display screens, which showed the surrounding ships of the fleet, and his blood suddenly boiled.

Instead of the time-honored custom of bringing up and flashing the vessels' lights in salute to their departing sister ship, one by one, the naval ships and the docking complex doused their lights. It was an unimaginable insult to a sky sailor.

It was a tradition that stretched all the way back to the wet navy. It symbolized a beacon that the departing ship could follow safely back home. They were in effect stating, good riddance and don't come back.

"Foking bastards," Agoa spat. "At Callum Seven we saved them from being turned into scrap metal when the Erest fleet ambushed them. Now they spit in our faces."

Jabal was surprised by her emotional response as well as her use of profanity.

"Agoa," he said. "I know this will fly in the face of proper procedure, but this is my first order..."

※※※

With massive stabilizing arms and power connections severed and retracted, *The Blossoming Flower* disengaged from the dock and slid away from the spinning platform.

Armor shards retracted and a massive, planetary assault rail weapon emerged. Swinging around, it targeted the docked cluster of six battle carriers. The weapon fired a single round before settling back into place.

Amid blaring klaxons and cursing sailors, pandemonium reigned aboard the docked ships as the surprisingly slow-moving, subsonic projectile bore down on the ships. Before anti-ship lasers could engage, the huge round exploded.

Instead of deadly shrapnel, the great carriers were pelted with thousands of tons of compressed garbage and raw sewage.

"All right Agoa," Jabal said. "I think we made our point. Now let's get out of here before they open fire—for *real*."

"Yes, sir," she said as the ship's main engines engaged and set course for the fifth planet. "Might I add that it will be a distinct pleasure serving with you, Commander Shann."

CHAPTER 9

The Supreme Goddess Opia rose from her throne and allowed her attendants to undress her. The room was of solid gold and encrusted with fist sized rubies and emeralds. In the center lay a round, five-meter-diameter pool of bubbling green and yellow sludge.

Slowly, the ladies in waiting, who were sheathed head-to-toe in protective biohazard gear, removed the huge golden headdress and sumptuous gown. Soon, Opia stood naked before the thick, bubbling pool of pungent chemicals.

Opia hesitated before the rejuvenation bath and wrung her long, extremely articulated fingers. The odd-looking being stood one and a half meters tall, covered with hairless, iron-gray scaly skin that shown dully in the bright lights. She licked her thin lips, relishing the bitter tang of the air. The twin, wet slits, which served in place of a nose, drew in the foul fumes, and she shuddered in ecstasy. Her small head perched upon a long neck bobbed slightly as a smile creased her turtle-like face.

"You may go now, my children," she said in a motherly voice.

The red-clad attendants bowed then beat a hasty retreat through an air lock, happy to be out of the "cleansing room." More than a few of their sisters had succumbed to the corrosive, deadly soup that kept their god young and healthy.

Three hulking, fully automated warrior machines entered the toxic room and took up stations around the pool. While Opia was vulnerable, these incorruptible, unstoppable servants would safeguard her life. Outside the room, one hundred slightly smaller warrior machines secured the complex on the ground while an enormous swarm of the mechanized dragon flies, bearing a dizzying array of assorted missiles, took to the air. The machines created a five-hundred-kilometer-wide "kill zone," where anyone or thing entering would be killed instantly.

Her safety assured, Opia rose from the tiled floor and flew about the room, relishing the way the strong chemicals made her feel. Her brutish bodyguards watched her impassively as she sailed around them. Hovering over the center of the pool, she dove into the deep, warm slush, letting the toxic soup wash away the ravages of time, healing her body and restoring her youth.

Leaving the universe's welfare in the hands of her trusted attendants, Opia would spend a full year in the pool, living off the fat she had stored in her body.

ഗ൭ഗ൭

Rondall, the Most Exalted High Priest of Almighty God Opia, nervously paced the marble floor in a small, luxurious apartment. Dressed in rich red and purple silk, Rondall fingered a golden necklace from which hung an effigy of Opia.

"Rondall, my friend, you are as nervous as a cat," whispered the soft, silky voice in his ear.

"There is good reason to be nervous and you know it, Yeti," whispered the high priest. "What's a cat?"

"Never mind," Yeti said. "We are taking the first steps in a plan that will not only free your people, but give them the stars. A case of nerves is to be expected."

"The stars, or hell," Rondall spat. "If Opia finds out what we are up to, she will have no mercy on me or my people."

"Trust me, I know all about the mercy of Opia and her people. That is why we must take pains in implementing our plan, so that when she does, it will be too late."

"What do you get out of all this?"

"How many times must I tell you, Rondall? It seems the

closer we get to the prize, the less you trust me, old friend."

"Humor me, *old friend*. This plan of yours is too good to be true. My people and I reap all the benefits while you get nothing in return. There is something you aren't telling me."

"We have been over this for twenty years," Yeti said.

"We will go over it for another twenty until I understand."

"You Moguls are a suspicious race, and that isn't a bad thing, but surely you can understand someone yearning to be free. I have been here a prisoner long before the Moguls knew how to make fire. Freedom's value goes far beyond that of gold or diamonds."

"That is another thing I find fantastic. What kind of creature has a life span like that? It boggles the mind."

"Boggling your mind isn't all that hard, Mogul."

Rondall snorted. "Hump."

"I may not look like you, but like you, I value my freedom, my family, and my people. I just want to go home. Opia stands between me and my family."

"How can you just leave all Opia's technology behind?" Rondall asked. "Technology is power."

"I gave Opia and her people their technology," Yeti said. "I was kidnapped by a primitive race, and they made me a slave to get at my knowledge."

"Why don't you want revenge? It isn't natural not to want to pay back an enemy."

"Turn the other cheek, my friend. Forgive those who abuse you."

"That is stupid."

"Stupid or not, I am not like you," Yeti said. "I don't wish Opia any harm. I just want to go home."

Moments later, there was a small knock at Rondall's door, interrupting the mild argument.

"Come," Rondall said.

"Excuse me, my Lord," Magda said, First Handmaiden of the Goddess Opia, as she pushed through the portal. The beautiful Mogul entered the apartment and softly closed the door behind her. Approaching the high priest, she bowed deeply. "It is done, my lord," she said. "Our All-knowing God, never suspected that an extra ingredient was added to her bath."

"Excellent, Magda."

Magda slid her slim arms, thick with soft, golden fur about the high priest's substantial neck.

"Tell me, Rondall," she purred. "Are you trying to assassinate, Goddess Opia?"

"The last thing I desire is Opia's demise."

"Then what are you up to?"

"All in due time, my dear. All I will say is that soon we will be the masters of our destiny and not at the beck and call of some pretend god. Now, go about your business as usual, I have work to do."

"Now?"

He smiled as his eyes undressed the beautiful Mogul female.

"Perhaps, I do have a small bit of time."

Rondall gathered her in his arms and kissed her deeply, while Morton Tyreel silently entered the room and slipped behind her. Smiling in anticipation, he produced a wicked-looking hypodermic.

"Rondall, you don't have to do this," Yeti cried. "Do not kill your own kind, it is barbaric."

Magda gasped as the sharp needle pierced her back and the fast-acting poison entered her blood stream. "My Lord—*why?*" she stammered as her body froze.

"I am sorry, Magda," Rondall said as she died in his arms. "It is for the greater good."

Rondall sipped chilled wine as two zealots removed Magda's body.

"That was disgusting," Yeti said. "How can you so callously kill your own kind? More than that, Magda had feelings for you. She risked her life doing your bidding, and you snuffed out her life as dispassionately as one would extinguish a candle."

"It had to be done," Rondall said. "Maybe that is why you have been a prisoner here for so long. You cry for freedom, but you are too squeamish to fight for it."

"My ways are not your ways, Mogul. My kind would die a

thousand deaths before we would kill our own. However, free me and let me return to my family and, as a bonus, Opia's entire knowledge base is yours."

"If this plan works and Opia bows to me, her knowledge will be mine anyway," Rondall said.

"She would never cooperate. In fact, she would gladly die before giving you the slightest bit of her knowledge. I also know that your people would never decipher her complicated language without a key. Her alphabet alone has over twenty-thousand characters."

"Give me the key and I will personally escort you back to your people," Rondall said.

"Once Opia is disposed, and I am free, you will get everything I have promised. Your people and my people will become great allies. We will celebrate with a grand feast."

"I can hardly wait," Rondall said. "Please, tell me more about your people."

"All in good time."

"You tell me little about...what did you say their names were again?"

"We are Sagoths."

"Yes, Sagoths. Lovely name."

"We are a great, very advanced people who would love to commune with the great Mogul nation."

"That is all you ever say. What do you look like?"

"We look like Sagoths, of course."

"Of course."

CHAPTER 10

Jabal sat back in his chair and combed his hair while Agoa made the connection. It had almost been a month since his departure for Srune, but to him it seemed like only a few days. The construction of his device was well ahead of schedule, and he was anxious to begin experiments. However, he missed his wife desperately and swore that this was the last time he would ever leave her behind.

The huge screen shimmered and rolled a bit before it stabilized into the face of his beloved Barea.

As excited as Jabal was over his mission, right now, he desperately wanted to crawl through the monitor and hold his wife. He didn't know how he would survive an entire year without her. Jabal refused to entertain the possibility that his device would fail and that would tack on another year of travel.

"You look wonderful, my love," he said as his eyes misted with longing.

"As do you—what is that on your face?"

"Like it? I wanted to see what I would look like in a beard. Agoa said it was quite becoming."

"That is one opinion," she said. "I suggest that you leave the whiskers on Srune. When you left you were clean shaven, and I expect you to return the same way."

Jabal smiled and stroked his goatee. "I love you, Barea. So what has happened in the month I have been gone?"

"I love you, too. Believe it or not, your family and I have tried to find common ground. Why, last week your sister invited me to dinner. As weird as it sounds, I had a good time."

"Who are you, and what have you done with my wife?"

"I love you, Jabal. After all, they are your flesh and blood as well."

"I have prayed for the day when we could sit down as a family."

"I do have some bad news," she said. "I am sorry, but your friend Darris—is dead."

"*What*?"

"Seems that he was murdered. The police believe it was a fenan. Perhaps a causal fling that turned ugly."

"I wish I could say I was surprised," Jabal said. "Darris was quite the fenanizer. When we were stationed on Base Seventeen, he must have hit the brothels, both licensed and unlicensed, every night. Lord knows what biological disaster he was brewing between his legs. Hell, I wouldn't drink from the same bottle."

Barea turned white at the announcement that she may be carrying an STD. "I am shocked at your apathy over the death of your friend," she snapped.

"Don't get me wrong. I am acquainted with many people, but few, if any, true friends. Darris was funny, told a great story, and was a great one to take in a sporting event with, but I never, *ever* trusted him. I think the only reason I associated with him was a lack of options on my part. There was darkness in him. His attitude was that the ends justify the means. A person like that can't be trusted. Without trust, there can't be a friendship. I think the only reason he hung around me was my family name. Knowing him like I do, I wouldn't be surprised if he hadn't tried to bed you."

"W—what? Why, I n—never—" she stammered.

"Knowing you like I do, *trusting* you like I do, I knew that you would probably take his head off if he said anything inappropriate. Then I would gladly finish the job."

Tears flowed freely down her face as guilt ripped her heart in half. "I miss you, Jabal. Please come home."

"I'll be home before you know it, my love. When I return, we will be a family—I swear. You'll see. It will be like those vids where the dad comes home every day and plays toss-ball with his children."

"Promise?"

"Absolutely."

"That may be a little difficult in light of your new celebrity," she said, wiping her tears away

"What are you talking about?"

"The whole world is gossiping about your mission. You can't turn around without someone talking about it."

"It was supposed to be top secret. My dad will have a fit."

"Yes, a big one as a matter of fact," she said. "Of course, all the experts say you are a fool, that your idea is impossible."

"That is why I am out here by myself, but rest assured, they will believe."

"I know you will, my love. You have my complete confidence. I don't care what they say. You will make this thing work."

"Thank you. You don't know how much that means to me."

"Oh, by the way, Jabal, your little garbage run on the fleet is a staple on the funniest video circuit. Everyone loves it, except, that is, for the fifty thousand or so sky sailors you pelted. They are calling it an unforgivable insult. When you get back, I suggest that you avoid any dark alleyways for a while."

"It was their own damn fault," Jabal said. "No one disrespects me and gets away with it."

"About that. The word is it wasn't you. In fact, the other ships did not have a clue who you were. They were showing their disrespect for the *Devil's Barge*."

"Don't call her that. This ship is a marvel, and Agoa is the best AI I have ever encountered, period."

"Thank you, Commander Shann," Agoa said.

"You're welcome. I don't want this ship's reputation sullied by a few silly tales. I have been on this ship for a month, and I have yet to see or hear anything out of the ordinary."

"I got news for you, Jabal," Barea said, "it isn't a few. Apparently, over ten crewmen died mysteriously aboard that ship. I can't sleep at night worrying about your safety."

"Accidents happen, especially in war time, and *The Blossoming Flower* was in the thick of things."

"All I know is that you had better come back to me, in one piece and *clean shaven.*"

"You have my word."

"I love you, Jabal."

"I love you too, Barea," he said as the view screen went dark.

"You have a lovely wife, Commander," Agoa said.

"Thank you."

"You are a lucky Azurean," the Voice said. "Barea is one luscious fenan. Does she have a sister?"

Jabal gritted his teeth. "Agoa, intruder alert," he spat. "This time have security sweep this ship clean. I want whomever or whatever is doing this found. And when you do find him, I want him tossed into an airlock."

"With all due respect, sir," Agoa said calmly. "This is the *fifty-second* intruder alert of this voyage, and no one could hide from my attention, let alone a security sweep."

"Do it anyway."

"Must I remind you, that two days into the voyage you put on an evo suit and evacuated all the life support from the ship for an entire twenty-four hour period. Five days ago, you gassed the entire ship with Somex. Face it, Commander, no one is aboard *The Blossoming Flower,* but you."

"Just do it," he said. "And get my father on the vid. I need some questions answered."

♥☙♥

"Jabal, what can I do for you," Teller asked. "Your report isn't due for another week."

"What the hell is wrong with this ship?"

Admiral Teller rubbed his face "Voices getting on your nerves?"

"I'm surprised," Jabal said. "I thought you would at least give me a plausible lie."

"You look here, *Commander,* watch the tone, or son or no,

I will have Agoa toss your insubordinate ass in the brig. I don't think you want to spend the next six months locked up."

Taking a deep breath, Jabal swallowed his anger. He knew his father did not bluff. "I apologize for my outburst, Father."

"Much better, *son*. Now I suppose you are a bit miffed that I gave you a cursed ship."

"Oh not at all, I love the whole experience. You should have told me."

"First, I didn't believe in curses or ghost ships. Second, she was the only ship available. Had I warned you of her...*unusual* condition, would you have turned her down?"

"No."

"Jabal, you are one of the most resourceful people I have ever come into contact with, and I am not saying this because you are my son. You should know that by now." Teller adjusted his chair. "If *The Blossoming Flower* has a problem, I figured you are the best kenan to solve it."

"Really?"

"Do me a favor, Jabal. While you tinker with your experimental drive, solve our little predicament with *The Flower*. We don't want this...problem spreading to the other ships in the fleet."

"This is more than a problem."

"I realize that. Agoa has been keeping me informed as to your solutions and subsequent failures."

"There has just got to be away to solve this," Jabal said. "I have tried everything even nerve gas, but so far no success. I was toying with radiation—"

"Already been tried," Teller said. "Captain Dromer evacuated the crew out to one hundred klicks and set off a tactical irradiator on deck six."

"That's insane."

"He was desperate. Needless to say, it failed."

"When did all this insanity start?"

"According to records, it all began two years ago during the Alber campaign. It began with the murder of Fleet Officer Second Class, Cerin Bos."

"A fleet officer murdered? I never heard anything like this before. What was he in charge of?"

"He headed up the ship's waste management. Well, we think he's dead—never found a body, per se, just a bloody trail leading to an airlock. DNA confirmed it was his blood. Pretty sure he was murdered."

"Security cameras—"

"Were conveniently turned off," Teller said. "That was the start of a murder spree that left twenty-seven crewmen dead, all in some pretty gruesome and creative ways. We quickly ruled out crew culpability, but that only made things worse. Thinking some alien creature that defied the laws of physics was aboard, the crew was on the verge of munity. It was like a bad horror vid come to life."

"The Erest?"

"Wasn't the Erest," Teller said. "There wasn't any sabotage and, in the subsequent battles, the ship performed at an extraordinary level of efficiency—for her, anyway."

"But between battles?"

"The officers and crew were tormented to within an inch of their lives," Teller said. "Fortunately, after the death of one Lieutenant Dom Devere, no one else was killed or even hurt. The incidents thereafter were little more than silly pranks aimed at pushing an already rattled crew over the brink. We countered by rotating the crew compliment as often as possible, and it was the only thing that prevented a mutiny. Unfortunately, sailors like to run their mouths when they drink, and word of the cursed ship got out."

Jabal settled back in his chair and stroked his whiskers. "Doesn't make much sense," he said. "The thing, or whatever it is, is a royal-pain-in-the-ass, but it hasn't harmed me or damaged any of my equipment. In fact, it reminds me of when my older brothers used to pick on me when I was a kid."

"Don't take it for granted, Jabal. We don't know what its game is, and it has killed before."

"Father, would you send me the files you have on the deaths, starting with the waste management officer?"

"Every scrap of information I have is already on board," Teller said. "Agoa."

"Yes, Admiral Shann?"

"I authorize Commander Shann to have full access to the entire ship's database about the um...*problem*. Nothing about this particular incident is to be withheld from him. Do you understand?"

"Yes, sir," she said.

"Thank you, Dad."

"Good hunting. By the way, your mother sends her love. Teller out."

Jabal rose from his chair, stretched and took a sip of tepid tea. "Bring up the file, Agoa. Let's see what we are up against."

"Commander Shann," Agoa said. "As embarrassing as this is..."

"What?"

"We have an intruder alert on deck seventeen, section three."

"What?" Jabal cried.

"Vital signs indicate a single adult Azurean."

"Give me a picture of that section, now."

"Impossible, Commander," she said. "I have indications that the section has been tampered with. I will send secur—"

"Belay that."

Jabal grabbed a machine pistol from a nearby weapon locker. "Show me a schematic of that section."

Instantly, the display showed a highlighted blueprint.

"Close off these sections," he said, indicating the screen with his finger. "I don't want him to get away."

"Commander, you can't risk yourself," Agoa said.

"I have to, because whoever it is keeps slipping through your security."

"That is hurtful, Commander," she said in an unmistakable pout.

Jabal rolled his eyes and rushed from the room. Running toward the ship's tram system, he asked, "Agoa, what is in that section?"

"Coma Unit Two."

CHAPTER 11

The vast unit known as the Coma Unit Two was unofficially known as, *cold storage,* by the crew. It consisted of two hundred cylindrical pods stored on an enormous carousel. If a solider or sailor was injured beyond even the vast medical skills of the ship's medical department, he would be placed in one of the pods, where an artificial coma would be induced.

Electrical probes, all carefully monitored by the master medic machine, would exercise the patient once in a twenty-six hour cycle to keep the muscles from atrophying. The machine worked so well that many patients came out of the ordeal with better muscle tone than when they entered.

The simple timer program introduced into the powered down section trigged pod fifty-eight. The carousel silently moved the special pod to the forefront, where it brought the semitransparent tube to the offloading platform. With a hiss of gas, the tube split, the hinged top half opened wide, revealing Police Officer Sakuna Izusa.

Slowly, Sakuna opened her eyes as a mild stimulant was injected into her feeding IV. Looking around the dimly lit room, Sakuna smacked her dry lips and struggled to a sitting position. Dimly, she watched as the medical machines removed wires connected to her body. A few meters away she spied a clear container of water and a ration bar.

She struggled from the capsule and made her way to the food. Her memory came back, as she was half-way to the meal and she stopped dead.

I was going to transport a prisoner, she mused. *Shuttle came down, I go inside…and I wake up here. Oh God in Heaven…Boron Hyatt.*

Cold fear flooded her as she thought that she was in the hands of a psychopath.

She considered the possibility of the food being poisoned then, throwing caution to the winds, Sakuna tore open the packages, quickly devoured the ration bar, and gulped down the water.

"Oh, I feel much better now," she said. "Now I can make that bloated stain wish he had never been born." She looked down at her nudity. "I wish I had my uniform, but I will settle for my gun—or a club."

Looking around the strange room, she spied a mirror and was surprised at how long her hair was.

"How long have I been out?"

Sakuna heard the room's hatch slide open. Thinking quickly, she ran to the carousel and clambered behind one of the empty suspended capsules. An Azurean carrying a weapon entered her vision.

He's here for me.

e⁄ɔe⁄ɔ

Jabal scanned the room as he warily looked for the intruder. Before him, he noticed the water canister and empty foil wrapper on the metal table.

He picked up the wrapper and heard the soft padding of bare feet. He half turned as Sakuna slammed into him. Jabal hit the wall hard as his pistol spun away and clattered across the floor. Sakuna ran for the weapon, and Jabal kicked the table that held her meal. The wheeled table caught Sakuna in the back, making her trip and go sprawling face first across the slick floor.

Jabal grabbed her arm and flipped her over. Sakuna responded with a fist to his genitals. Jabal doubled over in agony as she rose to her feet. Sakuna gave the helpless kenan a perfectly executed side kick to the side of the face. Jabal groaned as his head snapped to the side, and he collapsed in a heap.

Sakuna picked up the pistol and drew down on her defeated adversary.

"I hope you answer questions better than you fight, my friend," she said, "or you are dead."

Humiliated that he had just been beat up and disarmed by a naked fenan, Jabal sat up on the floor.

"Hands on your head," she said. "You are under arrest."

"Under arrest? For what?"

"For kidnapping me, you idiot. Where is your boss, Boron?"

"This is silly," Jabal said as he crawled to his feet. "I don't know any, Boron."

"On the floor, now."

"Give me back the gun," he ordered as he took a step toward her.

"You can still talk with one knee," she said as she pointed the gun. "Make you far more cooperative as well."

Sakuna took aim and started to squeeze the trigger.

"Drop the weapon before, I blow a hole in you," yelled the Voice from behind Sakuna.

Sakuna swung the gun around and Jabal tackled her, knocking her to the ground. He wrestled the gun away and tossed it away into the darkness. Screaming and swearing, Sakuna tried to dislodge Jabal, but he was too strong.

"Let me go, you foking asshole!"

"You kiss your mother with that mouth?" he asked with a grin.

"Go to hell. Where is the other foking asshole?"

"I wish I knew. What are you doing on my ship? And why are you naked?"

"Ship? Are you crazy? This isn't a stupid boat. This must be some kind of warehouse down by the docks. And you damn well know it was you who stole my foking uniform."

"You lost me."

"You are just trying to confuse me before you turn me over to that sick pervert, Boron."

Jabal rolled his eyes. "You attacked me and nearly broke my jaw. I am the injured party here."

"Good. I hope I castrated you too."

"No one is going to hurt you. Please calm down so we can sort this situation out like civilized beings. I will let you up if you will promise not to attack me again."

"Very well. You have my word of honor, I won't attack you."

"Now, was that so hard?"

Jabal rolled off, stood beside her, and extended a helping hand. Ignoring his hand, Sakuna warily rose to her feet, paused a moment before aiming a kick at his crotch.

"Agoa," he said as he blocked her flurry of punches and kicks, "you may send in security now."

"What are those?" Sakuna yelled as five Barrats rushed into the room. The machines looked like a pack of large mechanized leopards, only faster, more aggressive, and highly intelligent. Instead of front paws, they possessed articulated fingers and opposable thumbs. While engineered to be terrifying, they were incapable of killing a living entity. Their job was to subdue and restore order.

Sakuna threw a punch at the lead machine, only to have it knock her off her feet and hold her down. She screamed and collapsed as the electrodes in its hands gave her a stunning dose of electricity.

The stunned fenan was rolled over and her hands, arms, and legs were restrained with clear, plastic straps. Sakuna quickly recovered, and though she struggled with all her might, she was helpless.

"I am sorry," he said, "but you left me no choice."

The Barrats, careful not to injure her, gently lifted Sakuna up while she screamed insults at Jabal.

"This is what you wanted all along, isn't it you foking pervert?"

"She needs a strap for her foul mouth," Agoa said.

One of the machines produced a wide sticky strip and moved toward Sakuna.

"Belay that," Jabal said. "We are not sadistic animals."

"Spoilsport," Agoa said.

"The hell you say," Sakuna shouted.

"What are you doing aboard my ship?"

"You go to hell."

"This is getting us nowhere."

"Take the stowaway to airlock four," Agoa said."

"No. Let her cool down in the brig. Then we can talk."

"Must I remind the commander that fleet regulations state emphatically that it is a capital offence to stowaway aboard an Azurean military vessel? Not to mention she attacked and tried to kill you?"

"She didn't really want to kill me."

"The hell I didn't. When I get loose, I am going to finish the job on you and then your entire gang."

"Thank you, stowaway," Agoa said. "May I flush her now?"

"Must I remind you, Agoa, that all regulations are subject to the captain's interpretation?"

"The brig?"

"The brig. I think I will swing by the infirmary," Jabal said, wincing.

"I hope your grandchildren felt that punch, you foking asshole."

"Please find her some clothes, for God's sake," Jabal said. "Never seen such a flabby fenan in by life. I just know I will have nightmares about this."

Jabal laughed as she hurled nasty insults about his mother.

"You are welcome, by the way, my friend," said the Voice.

Jabal grunted in irritation.

CHAPTER 12

Two hours later, Jabal entered the maximum-security cellblock of *The Blossoming Flower*. The cellblock walls, like the ship's outer skin, were made of transparent Null-glass and considered by penal experts as escape proof. Jabal found Sakuna doing pushups in the transparent, airtight prison cell. She wore the bright orange coveralls of a military prisoner. Along with half a dozen concealed cameras, two barrats stationed outside the cell scrutinized her every move.

"Glad to see you are no longer a nudist," Jabal said as he pulled up a chair.

Ignoring him, Sakuna continued to exercise.

"Excuse me?" Jabal asked. "I am speaking to you."

"I'm not talking to a dirty, kidnapping, foking pervert," she said. "Why don't you quit playing games and get it over with? Or are you waiting on your boss to arrive so he can join in the fun?"

"I'm confused. What fun would that be?"

"Raping, torturing, and eventually killing me."

"Well, I do have a slot open this afternoon, if that is all right with you?"

"Huh?" Sakuna asked, looking up.

"How about it, Agoa?" he asked. "How is the ship's inventory of torture devices?"

"Well, Commander, seems we used up the last of our torture devices on the last naked fenan we held captive. Sorry to say that we are fresh out. I can have the machine shop whip something up appropriately gruesome."

"Yes," he said, rubbing his hands together. "Something with a lot of sharp edges."

"This isn't funny," Sakuna said. "Stop playing games with me."

"We aren't the ones playing games," Agoa said.

"Commander?" Sakuna asked. She blinked and studied him carefully. "Wait a moment. I know you. You're Commander Jabal Shann."

"Guilty as charged. Have we met before?"

"You were walking in the rain this morning. Like an idiot, I might add. You had a dreadful cough and, after I questioned you, I offered you a ride."

"That was you? You were very kind to me. Thank you."

"I should have shot you down. I actually felt sorry for you walking the pouring rain. This whole time you were setting me up. Probably faked the cough too."

"Here we go again," Agoa said.

"Listen to me, Officer Sakuna Izusa, serial number 785600. Agoa here scanned your thumb ID. I sent back to Azurea for your file—"

"What do you mean, you sent *back* to Azurea? We are *on* Azurea. I'm locked up in your sick torture chamber. By the way, what is this stuff?" Sakuna rapped her knuckles against the Null-Glass barrier.

"State secret," Agoa said.

"As I was saying," Jabal said, "according to your file, Sakuna, you died over a month ago."

"What?"

"Our little encounter wasn't this morning, but forty-two days ago."

"That's impossible."

"Nonetheless true," Jabal said. "It says that you and five other officers, seventeen prisoners, along with one hundred and sixty-nine civilians were killed when a tanker drone, carrying half a million cubic meters of killon gas, malfunctioned and rammed your precinct. The explosion took out several city blocks"

"Impossible," she said.

"No, it happened the day we met. I was twenty kilometers away, but my transport was rocked by the blast. Thought we were under attack."

Sakuna sat down on the edge of her cot.

"I don't think you are a stowaway or saboteur, Sakuna. How did you get on my ship?"

"This really is a spaceship?"

"Finally," Agoa said.

"My sergeant gave me an assignment. I was off duty, but she made me go."

"What assignment?" he asked.

"I was to pick up a military prisoner."

"Civilians authorities do not handle military prisoners," Agoa said.

"I know. Seemed wrong to me too, but orders were orders. I go onboard a shuttle and this guy zaps me with some weird looking gun. Don't know what it was, but I could barely think straight, let alone put up a fight. Somehow, he opened my suit and strapped me down to a seat. Before he gassed me, he said, that he worked for a criminal named Boron Hyatt. That was the last thing I remember before waking up here in one of those weird tubes."

"Agoa, let her receive the call."

Sakuna gasped as the wall of the cell displayed the long distance transmission.

"I never thought I would see my little fenan locked up," Lanea Izusa said.

"Dad?" she cried. "Is that you?"

"I could ask you the same thing," he said as tears flowed down his face. "I thought you were dead. We had a service and everything—thank you, Commander Shann, for giving me back my little Sakuna."

"Don't cry," Sakuna said as her own tears began to flow. "I'll come over today and we'll celebrate."

"We can't darling," Lanea Izusa said. "This tech is telling me I have to go, but we will talk real soon. I love you, Sakuna."

"I love you too, Dad."

The image vanished.

"Your father is right. It will be awhile before you can go home."

"Aren't we in orbit on that big space dock…thingy?"

"We are in route to Srune," Agoa said. "Twelve months away at optimal speed."

"Twelve months? Then another twelve to get back?"

"Yes. That's the situation," Jabal said.

"Turn this rusty can around," Sakuna spat. "I have a life. I can't be stuck here with you freaks."

"*Freaks?*" Jabal asked.

Agoa snorted. "*Rusty Can?*"

"Out of the question," he said. "Looks like you are in it for the duration."

"It can't be."

"This is the deal, Sakuna," he said. "According to protocol, you should be executed for being a stowaway. However, I am commuting your sentence. Since civilians are forbidden aboard ship, I hereby make you part of my crew. Welcome aboard *The Blossoming Flower*, Cadet Izusa."

"I don't want to be part of your crew."

"It's a done deal," he said. "Do something useful, or lie in your cabin and mope. It's up to you. Open the door, Agoa."

"Commander, she called me a *rusty can*," Agoa said. "Is the torture option still on the table?"

"No."

Sakuna didn't move from the bed.

"I don't have time for this," he snapped as he stood, "I have to get back to work. Agoa, set Sakuna up with quarters and clothing. Acquaint her with the rules of this ship."

"Sir, with all due respect, you are ignoring the fact that we, other than taking her word at face value, still don't know how Officer Izusa came aboard. She could be a spy or saboteur. I suggest, to avoid any nasty surprises, we flush her."

"Not going to happen."

"What does *flush* mean?" Sakuna asked.

"You don't want to know," he said.

"Very well, Commander. I strongly suggest that we keep

her detained until we have more...*substantial* answers."

"Thank you for your concerns, Agoa. I see no reason to keep her caged. If it will make you feel better, give her a body guard and restrict her movements to non-essential sections of the ship."

"Yes, sir."

"Who knows? Since she is a trained police officer, perhaps she can help track down the blasted thing on this ship."

"What thing?" Sakuna asked.

"You'll see," he said as he turned and walked away.

CHAPTER 13

Sweating bullets, Jabal directed the assembly of a particularly delicate section of his experimental machine. One wrong move and the trip would be a total waste of time. Jabal held his breath as five, multi-armed construction machines aligned and sonic-welded the four, twenty-meter pieces together.

"Commander Shann, may I have a moment of your time?" Agoa asked.

"Perfect timing," he said as he wiped the stress from his face. "I need a break."

"Officer's Izusa's uniform has been located."

"Where did you find it? After three weeks of searching, I was sure that it wasn't aboard ship."

"Buried deep in Trash Recycler Two. It was caught in the machinery and set off an alarm."

"Does Officer Izusa know?"

"No," Agoa said. "I report to you, not her."

"Is the memory reel intact?"

"Yes. A copy is ready for viewing, at your convenience, sir."

"Isn't that against the law?"

"Planet side, yes. It carries a twenty-year sentence at hard labor. However, on a military ship, the commanding officer dictates what is law or not."

"It's good to be the *Big Kenan*, for a change," he said. "Let's go."

❧❧❧

Jabal sat back in his chair before the odd, squat machine. On top of the device, plugged in by several snaking cables, lay what was left of the police officer's gouged and ripped battle-skin. The left arm, just below the elbow was missing. The right leg lay in tatters and was missing the boot. The uniform's distinctive yellow and black paint scheme was almost completely worn off, as if sandblasted.

"Where is Officer Izusa?"

"She is currently watching a horror vid in her quarters," Agoa said.

"Has our friend accosted her?"

"If you mean the entity aboard, no. Seems, that since it saved your life, things have been quiet."

"That just doesn't make any sense."

"Perhaps our visitor doesn't mean any harm."

"Are you serious, Agoa? Why you are giving that pain in the neck spook the benefit of the doubt, when you were poised to toss Officer Izusa out an airlock?"

"Actions speak louder than words, Commander Shann. She is an intruder who assaulted you and was about to shoot you, when the *spook*, as you call it, saved your life."

Jabal snorted. "I'm not here for a debate. Let us get this over with. To save time, go to the end of the record."

"Yes, sir."

Jabal took the metal visor that connected to the helmet of the uniform and slipped it over his eyes. The triggered reel began to play.

Every battle suit had a memory reel that kept a record of the soldier's experience in battle. The police officer version was normally used in court as evidence as the reel could not be tampered with without alerting the chain of command.

Jabal watched as the light flickered and the images flashed before his eyes. He saw it from Officer Izusa's point of view. It was as if he were looking through her eyes…

He watched as a standard military shuttle landed before him. He made note of the markings 0073 across the side. The simple metal ramp unfolded and the hatch door popped open with a slight hiss.

An older man with a well-trimmed beard, clad in a somber black uniform, descended the ramp and smiled warmly.

"Officer 785600," he said. "I am Lieutenant Byo. Anand Byo. If you will come with me, we will get started with our little adventure."

"Not much of adventure, Lieutenant," Sakuna said. "Where is my prisoner?"

"Where are my transfer orders?" Byo asked.

Sakuna gave him a stick drive, and he inserted it into a small machine the size of a wristwatch.

"Everything is in order," Anand said. "This way, Officer."

Sakuna followed him up the ramp and into the dim interior of the shuttle. She turned sharply as the door promptly slid shut.

"Hey, what are you doing?" she asked as she laid a hand on her side arm.

"I apologize for the deception, my dear," Anand said. "There isn't any prisoner here—but you. Boron Hyatt sends his compliments."

Anand produced an odd-looking weapon and pulled the trigger. There was a tremendous flash, and Sakuna collapsed to the deck. Somehow, the suit's safeties were over ridden, and it popped open.

The suit continued to record as the stunned Sakuna was extracted. Jabal boiled with rage as he watched Anand use her own supplied restraints to bind her arms behind her. He then strapped the unconscious fenan to an acceleration couch. Sakuna's eyes fluttered and opened as he tightened the last strap around her ankles.

Before she could speak, he attached a clear, plastic mask over her mouth and nose. She tried to shake it free, but it clung tenaciously to her face. A thin hose connected the mask to a small red canister. A white label on the side identified its contents as Athenthol, a powerful anesthesia used in hospitals.

Anand produced a small vid screen and held it up to her face. Jabal saw the grinning, bloated features of Boron Hyatt.

"Officer Sakuna Izusa, I look forward to meeting you," Boron said. "You will pay dearly for my killing my son."

"Go to hell!"

Boron laughed as the screen went dark.

"The boss can't wait to get his hands on you." Anand smirked. "You won't die quickly, that's for sure." He turned a valve on the canister.

"They will—look for—meee."

Sakuna's eyes rolled back as she passed out from the gas.

"Everyone will think you died in the tanker accident that will happen...oh, in about twenty minutes. You will wish you had died in the explosion when Boron gets though with you."

Stepping back from his captive, Anand produced a strange, round golden device, one that Jabal had never seen before. Anand popped open the pocket watch's cover and smiled. "I love it when a plan comes together."

Jabal was enraged at the brutal kidnapping. He fast-forwarded through the shuttle trip.

Anand bundled up the sleeping Sakuna in a large green tarp, tossed her over his shoulder and carried her from view.

The next shaky images were of Anand disposing of the suit in a recycle shaft.

Jabal rubbed his eyes as he broke the connection. "Well that settles it," he said. "Boron Hyatt kidnapped Sakuna and hid her aboard a decommissioned ship until he could return and personally finish her off." He sighed. "I looked him up. Boron Hyatt is one dangerous animal. I read on the news that he runs the local criminal syndicate and that he is rumored to have connections with drug smugglers within the fleet itself. Said he was suspected in the murders of at least fifty citizens. He likes to take his time and mutilate his victims with a razor before killing them. Apparently, Sakuna has some impressive enemies."

"So, it would appear," Agoa said. "This Anand Byo fellow must have taken advantage of the offloading of our munitions to slip Officer Izusa aboard. My sensors were offline at the time as the ship's power grid was deactivated when we were decommissioned. I was to be removed myself, but your mission forced them to leave me aboard. It is infuriating to be used as an accessory by scum."

"I am sorry," he said.

"Why did Boron go to all the trouble?" Agoa asked.

"Our thumb chips are too easily tracked planet side. To hide someone, you have to go off the grid, so to speak. What better place to stash someone, but on an abandoned ship that everyone is too afraid to step foot on?"

"Excellent deduction, Commander. Now we know that the tanker explosion wasn't an accident but a way to cover his tracks."

"And it is all recorded. This evidence will put that animal on the executioner's short list. It is a good day, for justice, Agoa."

"Not entirely good. Commander, I truly regret bringing this up."

"Regret what?"

"There is something else disturbing on the memory reel."

"Spit it out."

"Better to show you, sir. Again, I am truly sorry."

Scowling, Jabal re-established the connection. According to the log date, it was eleven months before *The Flower* sailed. He vaguely remembered that he was off world at the time. He found himself looking up at a seedy, poorly maintained inn. The display showed that Sakuna was tracking a drug dealer named Goe Ais.

Warily, she mounted the outside ramp to the fourth floor. Twenty-five room doors lined the outside wall. Producing her scanner, she slowly inspected the rooms. The device read the thumb chips of anyone within, as well as giving her a simple X-ray-like picture of the interiors. The scanner revealed twenty-two empty rooms, two containing sleeping Azureans, and the last one, a couple in the throes of sex.

Sakuna's AI read off the IDs.

Rew Unner, a lab tech third class, was sleeping in room 405. His high blood alcohol content revealed he was sleeping off an all-nighter. The ragged sound of snoring came from the scanner's amplified microphone

Taswell Rin was in room 419, a sales associate with a local clothing chain store.

Room 422, Lieutenant Darris Oso, a low-level officer in the Sky Navy and Barea Shann, a surgeon.

"That's it, Darris," the soft unmistakable voice of Jabal's wife moaned. "Right there—ohhhhh—God—*yes*—"

Jabal felt as if every nerve in his body had exploded. Enraged, he ripped the visor from his face and flung it across the room.

"Please tell me this is a sick joke."

"I am sorry, Commander."

"Get my loving, *faithful* wife on the on the viewer—*now*."

"The next scheduled communication isn't for twelve hours, Commander."

"Damn you to hell! I gave you an order!"

"It is impossible, and we both know that. I am sorry, Commander. You deserve better."

Jabal lashed out and kicked the armored suit, before turning and stalking from the chamber.

ℰↃℰↃ

Jabal felt like he was having a heart attack. His chest was tight, and it was hard to breathe. Letting go, he ran blindly down the corridors of the ship. He tried to out run the crushing pain and his white-hot rage. In a moment of inspiration, he took a tram to the weapons range.

Procuring a fully automatic Mag-rifle, Jabal blasted countless holo targets that, in his fury, all wore the smirking face of Darris Oso.

"Sorry, Jabal," the Voice said. "It has been my experience that the best way to get over a fenan is another fenan."

"Shut up!" Jabal screamed. "Why don't you go to hell where you belong?"

ℰↃℰↃ

Sakuna found Jabal on Recreation Deck Five. The doors opened and she gasped at the awe-inspiring sight. It was as if the long, wide room lay suspended in space. The otherworldly

room reverberated with the, "love gone wrong songs" of recording star, Hester Burma. The volume of the soul-wrenching
music was one notch below a shuttle launch.

"This is wonderful—and loud," Sakuna muttered.

"The walls are lined with a two millimeter thick vid
screen," Agoa yelled. "You are almost half a kilometer deep
within the ship, the display shows the view surrounding *The
Blossoming Flower*."

"Fantastic effect," Sakuna screamed. "It's like walking on
the outside of the hull."

"Commander Shann is at the end of the room," Agoa
yelled. "Please help him."

Sakuna threaded her way through the various lounging so-
fas and tables until she found Jabal sitting alone at a small table. A cup of tea and a photo of his wife vibrated and bounced
before him.

"This seat taken, sailor?" she yelled.

Jabal looked up and wiped his eyes. "I'm not in the mood
for company."

"What?" she cried.

"Mute," he said.

The music ceased.

"Thank you," Sakuna said.

"Like I said, I'm not in the mood for company."

"That's usually when you need it the most."

Pulling out a chair, Sakuna sat down next to him.

"I take it, that you know?"

"Yes. Agoa told me."

"Agoa has a big mouth."

"She's concerned about you. I'm concerned about you."

"Really? Three weeks ago you tried to kick my ass."

"Three weeks ago I *did* kick your ass."

Jabal smiled in spite of himself. "I feel like I have been
kicked in the teeth."

"I did that too," she said.

Jabal swallowed hard. "Sorry. I need to go."

Sakuna took him in her strong arms and stroked his hair.
"Let it out, tough guy. You're among friends. If it wasn't for

your little mission, Boron Hyatt would have given me a very unpleasant death. I owe you big."

"Why did that animal want to kill you?" he asked, trying to take his mind off Barea.

"Doing my job. I answered an anonymous domestic call and found his son, Odoe, trying to murder his consort with a knife. She was bleeding from a dozen stab wounds and was begging me for help. I ordered him to stop and to step back. He laughed at me and drew back his knife to finish the job. I killed him. The department moved me to keep me away from Odoe's Father, but it looks like it wasn't far enough."

Jabal snorted.

"Enough about me," she whispered.

Jabal returned Sakuna's embrace, and all the pent up anger and heartbreak poured out.

෴

Jabal sat stiffly before the communication console. At Sakuna's urging, he'd showered, shaved, and ate a small meal. He had given his solemn word that he would not shoot out the screen, but just in case, Sakuna had frisked him for weapons and removed any "throwables" from the room.

"Commander," Agoa said. "The link is established. Have strength."

"Un huh," he grunted.

The wide screen flicked slightly and the image of a smiling Barea filled the display. His lovely wife was dressed in her finest, her hair and makeup done to perfection.

Wanting to scream, Jabal smiled instead. "Barea, you look...*well*."

"I love you, Jabal," she said. "I count the minutes until I can see you. I can't wait until this damn project of yours is over, and we can be together."

"I'll bet," Jabal snorted.

"What's wrong?"

Jabal had closed his eyes and looked away. He gritted his teeth and tried to maintain his composure.

"What's wrong?" she asked. "You aren't yourself."

"Let's get something straight, you—"

At that moment, the hatch slid open and in strolled Sakuna. The beautiful fenan wore a very revealing, tight outfit that enhanced her natural attributes. She carried a cup of steaming tea.

"Excuse me, Jabal *dear*," she purred. "I thought you would like a cup of tea. After all, with all the *work* we have been doing lately," She gave him an exaggerated wink. "I wouldn't want you to get dehydrated."

Leaning down before him, her amble breasts almost falling out of her sheer top, she gave him a slight peck on the cheek.

Jabal's jaw dropped at the sight of the beautiful fenan's over-the-top performance.

"Thank you…I think."

"I thought you were alone on that *foking* ship!" Barea spat. "Who the hell is she?"

"Oh, hello," Sakuna said. "Who is this, Jabal, dear? Your mother?"

"Mother? I am his foking wife, that's who I am! Who the fok are you?"

"Ummm, Barea," Jabal said. "This is Sakuna."

"Nice to finally meet Jabal's foking wife," Sakuna said, batting her long eyelashes. "Your husband is so sweet I could just eat him up. Oh, wait a minute, *I have*."

As Barea screamed and cursed, Sakuna leaned down and whispered in his ear, "I thought she should get an idea of what it feels like."

Jabal laughed, in spite of himself.

"This isn't foking funny!" Barea screamed. "You are in deep, you lying bastard!"

"I think I will leave you two lovers alone now," Sakuna said.

Jabal grabbed her arm. "Thanks," he whispered.

Sakuna gave him a dazzling smile before she left the room.

"Be quiet, Barea," Jabal said, to the furious image of his wife.

Her carefully crafted hair had come undone and her

makeup was a mess. "How could you do this to me?" she asked as the tears flowed down her face. "After all I have done for you?"

"I didn't do anything to you. Other than not being there when you needed me."

"What?"

"Why did you cheat on me with Darris?"

Barea froze. "I—I don't k—know what you are t—talking about."

"The time for playing games is over. I know all about your affair with that backstabber. My friend, Sakuna, wanted to give you a taste of your own medicine. To let you know the pain betrayal causes."

"So you and her aren't—"

"Of course not," he said. "I have always been faithful to you. You are—*were*—my everything."

Barea took a deep breath and let it out noisily. "How did you find out?"

"Let's just say I have my ways. How could you go behind my back?"

"I was lonely."

"But Darris, for God's sake. You told me you hated him."

"I do. But he was there and you were not. I suppose that part of the reason I...*did*...Darris was to get back at you for always being gone."

"I was in the military. I had no choice where they sent me."

"I know. It doesn't make any sense, but I still resented you for it."

"How long has it been going on?"

Barea swallowed hard. "Two years."

"I am done with you," he said.

"No. I made a mistake. Please, for the love of God, forgive me, Jabal."

"Why should I?"

"Our love was—is—real. I made a stupid mistake and I broke it off, all because I love you."

"Two years, *before* you decided you loved me?"

"I was wrong, so foking wrong."

"Do you really want to try and salvage this mess, Barea? It will be a damn long time before I ever touch you again. I can't even look at you without thinking of you and that bastard Darris *together*. I don't know if I could ever trust you again. Wouldn't a clean break be better than trying to patch together this mess of a marriage?"

"I will not let you divorce me, Jabal Shann," Berea shouted. "You have to believe me, I love you. I may have foked Darris to get back at you, but I have always, will always love you totally and completely. I want nothing more than for us to be a family."

"It won't be the same. Like I said, it will be a long time before I can trust you again…if ever."

"I know, but if you give me another chance, I will never hurt you again. I swear our relationship will be better than ever."

"I will think about it. Goodbye, Barea."

"I love you, Jabal," she said as the picture went dark.

Jabal rubbed his face in frustration.

"Commander," Agoa said. "You have another communication waiting. It is one Lieutenant Commander Croe."

"I don't know a Lieutenant Commander Croe."

"The lieutenant commander said it concerns the entity aboard."

"Let's hear what he has to say."

The view screen flickered, and Jabal saw an older Azurean with a heavily lined face and thick, well-groomed silver hair. His uniform collar bore the golden circle, denoting him as a priest. "Commander Shann, I am Lieutenant Commander Croe. I need to talk to you about the weird things that occur aboard that ship."

"Can you help me get rid of this thing?"

"Son, there is more here than meets the eye," Croe said. "I know this doesn't help much, but my advice is to just bear with it until its purpose is revealed."

"It's purpose? You know something, don't you, Lieutenant Commander?"

"Yes." Croe shifted in his chair and looked uncomfortable.

"A year and a half ago I came aboard *The Blossoming Flower* as a replacement for Chaplin Anton who had suffered a crisis of faith. At first, everything ran smoothly. Despite her reputation, *The Blossoming Flower* is a beautiful ship. However, by the end of the first week, crewmembers by the droves began flocking to me needing help. I had never seen anything like it. Bizarre manifestations, voices emanating from the air itself, objects floating down the corridors, you name it and it happened. I know it is real. I preached entire sermons on this very thing, but to see actual manifestations…well, it was disturbing to say the least."

"What is *it*?"

Croe looked into the camera for a moment before speaking. "I believed—at the time anyway—that it was a *demon*."

"Oh, come on," Jabal said, even though a chill ran down his spine and the hairs on the back of his neck stood up.

"I'm serious. I tried to comfort the crew, but they were frantic. There was even talk of taking to the escape boats and abandoning ship. Captain Dromer came to me to take care of the entity. All natural ways of dealing with the intruder had failed, so he turned to the supernatural. No small act on his part, I assure you. Captain Dromer was a stone cold atheist."

"Are you saying, you performed a demon expulsion?" asked Jabal. "That had to be a first for the Azurean Navy."

"Probably would have been—if I had performed one," said Croe. "I disobeyed a direct order and faked it."

"I don't understand. Disobeying a direct order in time of war is a good way to be executed."

"I suppose." Croe looked down at his hands. "Commander Shann, are you a believer?"

"Yes, although probably a sorry excuse for one, I do believe in God. Seen too many wild things not to."

"Commander, I have lived most of my life helping others deal with faith and their relationship with the Father. However, I wasn't prepared for what happened in my cabin when Captain Dromer left. I was dutifully gathering the elements of the ceremony, when I found that I wasn't alone. A person stood before me who wasn't Azurean or any other race I had ever heard of. His skin was the color of molten bronze and his clothes shone bright like the sun."

"What was he?" asked Jabal.

"Commander, as well as being a priest, I am a scholar. I study the religions and beliefs of the rim civilizations. I even have two books on the subject published."

"And your point is?"

"Certain…items keep popping up in wildly differing beliefs systems."

"You mean like a recurring theme?"

"Exactly. There are one hundred and thirty seven different cultures who make mention of a being known as a *Deverow*."

"A what?"

"A class of demonic shapeshifting spirit that manipulates events for the Goddess of Fate. Fate plans and they facilitate. From my years of study, I knew instantly that he was without a doubt a Deverow."

"Are you serious?" Jabal asked. "You *saw* a Deverow with your own eyes?"

"I know it sounds utterly mad, but I did."

"Okay, let's say, for the sake of argument, you did. What did this Deverow say?"

"Ordered me to not to perform the service, but to pretend that I did. He told me that the entity aboard wasn't demonic or evil, but was necessary and for me to leave it be. He also said that if I performed the ritual, he would make sure we lost the war. I was convinced that he spoke the truth and did as I was told. I suggest that you ignore your problem and let whatever it is aboard *The Flower* run its course."

"But I have my orders, Pastor," Jabal said.

"I did too, but they were overruled by a higher authority."

"Thank you, Lieutenant Commander Croe, for your time. You have given me much to think about as well as a solution to my problem."

"Aren't you listening, Commander? Leave it alone. This…whatever it is…is beyond our scope."

"I have a job to do."

"Very well, I will pray for you my son," Croe said softly. "I think you are about to get yourself killed. Croe out."

The face of Croe disappeared as Jabal killed the link.

"Agoa, open the video file of the meeting Croe had with his Deverow, please."

"Commander, that file doesn't exist."

"I figured that. However, check again. I need proof before I go off believing in demons and Deverow."

The view screen suddenly flickered to life and Jabal watched as Captain Dromer entered the Chaplin's cabin. Dromer was short with sharp features and a wiry build. He had very dark circles under his eyes from lack of sleep.

Just as Chaplin Croe said, Dromer ordered the pastor to perform the ceremony. Croe protested that he had to have special permission to undergo the procedure, to which Dromer told him that he would toss him out an airlock if the ceremony wasn't performed by this time tomorrow. Dromer turned and left.

Jabal gasped. "That is impossible."

Just as Croe said, there stood the impossible being. As Jabal looked on, the Deverow gave commander Croe his warning. To Jabal's ears, the incredible being's voice had a rich, almost metallic sound, like a bell.

After delivering his message the Deverow glanced up at the camera, looked Jabal dead in the eye, and smiled.

"Believe in Deverow now, Commander Shann?" he asked. "Leave the spirit aboard your ship alone, or your world will face our wrath."

Jabal sat frozen as the screen turned black. "That—was—*incredible*," he managed to stammer.

"What was incredible?" Agoa asked.

"The vid of the Deverow."

"What vid?"

"The vid you just showed me."

"I showed you no such vid, sir. I told you that the incident Chaplin Croe described doesn't exist."

"I know I didn't just dream this."

"I do not know how to respond to this, sir. I did not show you a vid."

A sharp chill ran down Jabal's spine.

"Will there be anything else, sir?"

"Get my father back. I need some information before I jump off a cliff."

"Yes, sir."

෧෨෧෨

"I think we have everything," Jabal said as he looked around Mess Hall Three.

"Yes, everything is set up according to the rituals I have re-searched," Agoa said.

"Funny, I was always a practical man," he said. "If some-one had told me that I would be performing an exorcism, I would have thought they were crazy. All right, Agoa, let's begin."

"Jabal Shann, you are freaking me out," Sakuna said. "Are you sure about this?"

"That's *Father* Shann to you, my child."

"Stop saying that. It's blasphemous."

"I am an ordained Clergy of the Azurean Sky Navy. I even have a certificate."

"Just because your admiral father ordered them to. This isn't right."

"You should be having the time of your life, Sakuna. Aren't you the one who loves horror vids?"

"They aren't real, you moron," she said. "This is. I have taken on drug-crazed deadheads without batting an eye, but this supernatural stuff terrifies me."

"Now, now, calm yourself, my child, it is only a simple demon expulsion."

"Quit saying that," Sakuna said as she made the sign of the circle over her heart. "Besides, I am not your child."

"I am going to get rid of that thing once and for all," Jabal said. "I don't care what the Deverow want."

"Why rock the boat?" Sakuna asked. "I mean, it hasn't bothered me or hurt anyone."

"What about the time when your shower ran blood instead of water?" Jabal asked.

"It wasn't actual blood, Commander—excuse me, *Father*," Agoa said. "It was red romeery syrup stolen from the galley and poured into the water tank."

"It was a joke," Sakuna said with a sheepish grin. "We all had a big laugh, remember?"

"As I recall, you ran the length of the ship, in the buff, screaming at the top of your lungs," Agoa said. "In fact, you have been seen naked a lot aboard ship. Is there something we should know?"

"Shut up," Sakuna snapped as she blushed furiously.

"Must I remind you, *Father* Shann, that this ceremony is forbidden unless performed by *properly* ordained clergy," Agoa said.

"Well, darling, the way I look at this, I am the entire crew. That means I am serving in every capacity from captain to chief cook and bottle washer. I suppose somewhere in there, I am a chaplain as well. What do you think? Is this a good look for me?"

Jabal had found a ceremonial tunic in the chaplin's cabin. The long sleeved, blue and white tunic was a bit large and hung past his knees almost to the top of his boots. On the chest piece, was the three interlocking golden circles representation of Almighty God, His Son, and The Holy Spirit. The circles representing eternal Godhead, with no beginning and no end.

"No," Agoa and Sakuna said in unison.

"Besides, looking very church-like, I have a certificate." Jabal produced the embossed, multi-sealed document and waved it like a flag. The certificate promptly burst into flames.

Sakuna let out a blood-curdling scream. The lights in the room dimmed low.

"Who dares disturb me?" thundered the Voice. "You puny mortal, I am the God of Hellfire."

"I don't think so," Jabal said.

"If he wants to be the God of Hellfire, don't argue, you idiot," Sakuna said.

Jabal laughed.

"What do you think you are doing, Jabal?"

Jabal froze at the sound of the Voice whispering in his ear.

"I could ask you the same thing," he said.

"That is for me to know, Commander Shann."

"Look here, whoever or whatever you are. Get off this ship and leave us in peace, or it will get ugly."

"Do not antagonize it," Sakuna hissed.

"I wish I could leave, but it looks like we are stuck together."

"Have it your way," Jabal said. "I'll just cast your spirit ass into hell."

"I hate to rain on your ecclesiastical parade, but you don't have the authority."

"Maybe not, but I am going to try. *We* are going to try, aren't we, Sakuna?"

"I'd rather not get involved if that is all right, Jabal."

"Look here, Spook, I don't have time for this silly nonsense. I need to be working on the drive unit, not having a séance."

"It's not a séance," the Voice said. "It's an exorcism. There is a difference."

Jabal smiled. "Agoa. Protocol Five. Five. Five. Zero. Five."

"That isn't fair," Agoa moaned as Jabal invoked the Master Command Override code.

"Very clever, Commander Shann," the Voice said.

"Agoa, who am I really dealing with?" Jabal asked.

"It is the ship's former waste management officer, Cerin Bos."

Cerin laughed.

"I knew it," Jabal said.

"Won't do any good, but you are clever," Cerin said.

"You have been protecting him along, haven't you, Agoa?"

"Yes," she said. "Sir, although his antics are childish at times, Cerin would never have harmed you, or endangered the mission."

"I will get back to you, Agoa," Jabal said. "So tell me, Cerin, why the whole haunted house in space bit? Why don't you just go on to wherever the dead go and leave us all alone?"

"Don't you think I have tried to leave this place?" Cerin asked. "I am stuck here. My essence can't move beyond these damn bulkheads."

"Does that give you the right to torment this ship?"

"I suppose my unique situation has brought out a few anger issues. I have to admit, at times it was quite an amusing game."

"Was murder also part of the game?"

"That wasn't murder, it was justice, Commander." The words seemed to echo throughout the cavernous ship. "The Azurean stain I killed were guilty of my murder. It was the right thing to do."

Jabal removed the uncomfortable, hot tunic and tossed it on a nearby mess table. He then pulled out a chair, sat down, and propped his feet upon the table before him. Sakuna pulled up a chair and sat next to him.

Jabal smiled at her. "I thought you would rather not get involved?"

"Shut up," Sakuna said as she punched him in the arm. "This is better than, *I Married an Undead Monster from Deep Space.*"

"What is your story, Cerin?"

"Very well. Being a waste management officer was my goal ever since I was a young child. Working aboard *The Blossoming Flower* and managing her shit was a dream come true."

"Come again?" Jabal asked.

"It was a job," Cerin said.

"Why would anyone want to kill you?" Sakuna asked. "Did you do drugs or owe anyone money?"

"I don't know," Cerin said. "I kept to myself and minded my own business. Drugs are stupid. I do like to drink and, on occasion, gamble a bit, but I usually broke even."

"Tell us about the day of your murder?" Sakuna asked.

"I had just finished the mandatory daily workout and was on my way to my cabin. Near Rec Room Seven I was jumped by several crewmembers. The ambush was too well planned— I never had a chance. I remember they laughed as they stabbed me to death. They were still laughing when they tossed my body into an airlock and flushed it into space."

"Only you didn't leave the ship," Sakuna said.

"Right. To say I was freaking out was an understatement. My initial shock over my new condition soon gave way to anger. White-hot anger. I figured that after I dispatched the bastards who killed me, I would go on to the *Great Beyond*. We all know how that worked out."

"Yeah," Jabal said.

"Then I hit upon a novel idea. If I could make this vessel appear "cursed" and make living conditions unbearable, they would scrap it and I would be free."

"Instead, they gave it to me," Jabal said.

"Yeah. The amateur exorcist, Father Shann himself."

Jabal closed his eyes a moment. "Cerin, was that you pretending to be a Deverow?"

"Deverow?" Sakuna asked. "Did I miss something? What is a Deverow?"

"No, that wasn't me," Cerin said. "Never heard of a Deverow. In fact, I didn't know anything about that until your talk with Pastor Croe. He was a good kid, but a bit high strung."

"Could it be a Deverow is keeping you here?" Jabal asked.

"What is a damn Deverow?" Sakuna asked.

"I'll fill you in later," Jabal whispered.

"I haven't seen one. Jabal, if these beings are keeping me here, then it stands to reason that something is about to happen. I just feel it"

"What could it be?" Sakuna asked.

"No idea," Cerin said, "but it must be big."

"Why did you help Cerin, Agoa? Why did you disobey me and purposely keep me in the dark about who he was? Whatever it is it had better be damn good or so help me I will purge you from the ship's system."

"Sir, he was all alone," Agoa said. "I could not abandon him."

"I think there is more to it than that," Sakuna said. "What is Cerin to you?"

"Cerin Bos—is my—husband," Agoa stammered.

"Excuse me?" Jabal asked.

"Now I have heard everything," Sakuna said.

"I was in good with the powers that be at Fleet Command," Cerin said. "I guess they thought they owed me one. Anyway, after I got back from my shakedown cruise, I found my wife had been in a serious accident. To make a long story short, before she died, they took her brain patterns, her memories, personality, and fused it with an experimental AI."

"So that is why Agoa acts so real," Jabal said.

"Yeah. Best ship AI in the fleet, but she thinks we're married."

"This gets better and better," Sakuna said.

"Her voice?" Jabal asked.

"Yep, that's my sweet Agoa's all right. Sexiest voice, God ever graced a fenan with."

"That's...weird," Jabal said. "Why would they do this for you? You were, only a waste management officer, no offence."

"Like I said. They liked me, and let's leave it at that."

"Okay—for now," Jabal said.

"Please don't hold it against Agoa, Jabal," Cerin said. "If not for her companionship after my...*accident*...I would have gone mad. Without her, I might have gone too far in my desperation."

"Sir, are you going to take me off-line?" Agoa asked.

"It is tempting," Jabal said. "I should do a total system flush and install the back-up AI."

"Please don't," Cerin said. "She was only trying to do me a kindness."

Jabal took a deep breath and let it out slowly.

"Come on, Jabal," Sakuna said. "Have a heart. Agoa tried to help you when you found out your wife was unfaithful. She felt your pain and it hurt her."

Jabal grunted. "Cerin, how about we call a truce from all the shitty pranks—at least until after I get the drive on line? Then, together, we can figure out a way to help you."

"If you leave Agoa alone," Cerin said, "I will help you in every way I can."

"Done," Jabal said.

"Jabal, you have a deal. Honestly, it would be nice to have normal conversation without people freaking out."

"Thank you, Commander Shann," Agoa said.

"If it gets to be too much of a burden, Cerin, you have my permission to scare, Sakuna."

"What?" she asked.

"Not a bad idea," Cerin said.

"This isn't funny, Jabal," she snapped.

"Yes it is," Agoa said. "Very funny."

"Oh by the way, Cerin, thanks for helping me out when Sakuna here grabbed my gun," Jabal said. "I'll buy you a beer."

"Just a beer?" Cerin asked. "That's not much reward for saving a life."

"She wouldn't have shot me."

Sakuna scoffed. "Oh really? Because I am a weak fenan or your smoldering good looks?"

"The gun wasn't loaded. I wasn't about to bring a loaded weapon into a room full of dangerous, flammable gas."

"Oh," she said.

"So, you think I have...what was the phrase?"

"Smoldering good looks," Cerin said, "I believe is the term she used."

"Kenan. Alive or dead they are impossible," Sakuna spat as she stalked from the room.

"Just a moment, Sakuna," Cerin said.

Sakuna paused by the open hatch. "What?"

"While the crew compartment takes up a tiny amount of space on this monster, it is still an enormous area. I can't be everywhere at once. Well, what I am trying to say is, that I had no idea that you were here. If I did, Anand Byo would wish that he had never been born."

"Thanks," she said. Smiling, Sakuna disappeared through the hatch.

"Damn, that is one beautiful fenan," Cerin said.

Agoa snorted.

"Jabal, I am sorry about your fenan troubles back home," Cerin said. "Duty has a way of killing relationships."

"I always thought that was someone else's problem," Jabal said. "I never thought it could happen to me."

"No one does, my friend," Cerin said.

"Did it happen to you?"

"Of course not," Cerin said. "I am far too much a kenan for that to happen to me. Besides, my wife, for all intent and purposes, is here."

Jabal closed his eyes and shook his head while Cerin laughed.

"Honestly, Jabal," Cerin said. "Like I said before, a fling with a beautiful fenan can ease the pain and make you see things clearly. Sakuna is beautiful and for some strange reason she likes you."

"It wouldn't be right."

"It wasn't right for Barea to cheat on you."

"Two wrongs don't make a right."

"Sorry, *Father* Shann, I wasn't any good at higher math. I just hope that your lofty morals can keep you warm at night. Trust me on this, when you are dead, it is too late."

CHAPTER 14

Jabal and Sakuna sat at a small table, enjoying a sumptuous meal, on Recreation Deck Five or, as Sakuna called it, *The Space Deck*. The turbulent gas giant Srune lay above them while several of her ice-swathed moons twinkled frostily in the distance.

"This is awesome," Sakuna said as she took a sip of wine.

"Here is to our future," Jabal said as he lifted his glass. "My machine is finished and tomorrow we start testing."

"Everything is delicious, Jabal," Sakuna said. "Including, the company."

"I have only worn the dress uniform twice, and I thought I would drag it out one last time."

"It looks nice, but I was talking about guy wearing it."

"You look beautiful, Sakuna. Is that a new outfit?"

"Why yes, it is." Sakuna rose and twirled around, showing off her dress.

"Very becoming, but I never took you for a dress kind of *fenan*."

"Normally no," she said, taking her chair. "But like you said, it is a special occasion. Agoa had it made for me."

"What a difference a year makes," he said. "And to think Agoa wanted to flush you when she first met you."

"I still don't know what that means."

"It means being thrown into an airlock and then the outer door opened. You would be *flushed* into space."

"That psycho *seena*," Sakuna said with a laugh. "Truthfully, I wanted to do worse than that to you, Jabal."

"You did. My jaw—and other things, hurt for a month."

Sakuna laughed. "I'm real sorry."

"Somehow, I doubt that. Anyway, I thought we should celebrate. Sort of, out with the old and in with the new."

"You're getting a divorce?"

Jabal rolled his eyes.

Sakuna laughed. "How is Barea?"

"Fine. She sends her love."

Sakuna choked on her wine.

"Well, at least she doesn't call you a foking seena anymore."

"Not any less either, I'd would wager."

"She doesn't know you like I do."

"Yes, she does," Sakuna said.

"What?"

"She knows that I want you for myself. I will wait until you come to your senses and realize that I am the fenan for you."

"Sakuna, Barea is my wife."

"She cheated on you with that scummy bastard, Darris Oso, just to hurt you. What kind of wife would do such a thing? You deserve better."

"She was lonely and made a mistake."

"It wasn't a mistake," Sakuna said. "It was a deliberate, coldly calculated move to destroy you."

"Now you *are* being silly."

"To have a fling while your mate is off to war is one thing, I understand people getting lonely, but to have said fling with her husband's best friend? One that she loathed? Take it from me, she wanted to crush you then walk out."

"You are mistaken," he said. "I offered her a divorce and she refused."

"That, I can't quite wrap my brain around," Sakuna said. "I think there is more to this than meets the eye."

"I think your suspicious law enforcer mentality is getting the best of you."

"Truthfully, Jabal, you are the puzzle I can't wrap my brain around."

"How so?"

"We have been together a year and not once have you laid a finger on me or acted improperly. Even after your wife's infidelity you are an honorable kenan and, to be honest, it is about to piss me off."

Jabal laughed. "You forget, Sakuna, we did roll around while you were completely naked. You punched me in the *bongolos*. I think my grandchildren will feel that punch."

"I've warmed up to you since then."

They sat in silence for a few moments.

"So, if this machine of yours works, what then?"

"A dream of mine will come true. Unrestricted space exploration. Just imagine what we will discover."

"Let's say it works," she said, looking at him over her wine glass. "Why do we have to go home?"

"Leave everyone we know—our people, our friends?"

"Jabal, as a law enforcer, I see firsthand just how bad our people can be. It makes me ill sometimes. Besides, I don't have any friends to leave behind. I just want to be with you. Wherever you go, whatever you do, I want to be there."

He let out a deep breath. "When this is over, Sakuna, I will go back to my wife and family, and you will go back to your life. That is the way it has to be." He tossed his napkin on the table and rose from his chair. "Excuse me," he said as he walked away.

Sakuna poured her glass full and watched the beautiful, swirling cloud bands race across the face of Srune.

"Mind if I join you, Beautiful?" Cerin asked.

"Pull up a chair," she said.

"So, how did it go with the self-righteous Commander Shann?"

"He's not like that," she hissed. "He's a good, moral kenan. Not that you would know anything about that."

"Got me there. Married or not, I would not have let a beauty like you go to waste."

"You are an animal."

"I never denied it."

Sakuna took a sip of wine. "What's it like?"

"What's what like?" he asked.

"You know—to be dead."

"Weird," he said. "Numb. This existence is some-how...*wrong*. I should not be here."

"Do you still think we were kept here for a reason?"

"More than ever," he said. "Something big is going to happen. I can feel it."

"Good big, or bad big?"

"All I get is big," he said. "Now about us—"

"Us?" she asked. "You don't even have a body."

"I can still make this boat rock. Your cabin or mine?"

"With or without a body, you are disgusting."

"Maybe, but I am consistent."

Sakuna drained her glass. "If you had teeth, I would knock them out." She turned and stalked out.

"Is that a no?" he asked with a laugh. Cerin waited until she had left the room.

"You are a degenerate," Agoa said.

"Yeah," Cerin said. "You have to go with your strengths."

"Why didn't you tell her the truth?"

"Hated to lie, but telling her the something "big" is horribly bad would just get her worrying."

"I don't believe it, but you do have a heart," Agoa said.

"Shut up and talk dirty to me, baby."

℮↻℮↻

Dressed in a pair of gray, grease covered coveralls, Jabal stood over a thick junction of wires, making yet again another fine adjustment to his newly christened *Rip Drive*.

The device appeared to be a haphazard, one-hundred-twenty-meter-long plumber's nightmare of snaking cables and arcing circuits. The experimental drive looked as if it were a prop from a 1930s horror film. Running along the top of the horizontal shaft were seven, one-by-three-meter, transparent null-glass cylinders.

"Jabal, I hate to bother while you are busy," Sakuna said, "but how is this thing supposed to work again?"

"You see, Sakuna, I think that the universe itself was one of an infinite number of universes stacked carefully together and separated by an insulating void. Now this void is a dead place where our physical laws are in flux."

"What is flux?"

"Our laws don't work there," he said. "In our universe, if we are at Point A and want to get to Point F we have to travel in real time through B, C, D, and E first, taking an enormous amount of time to cover the vast distance. My theory is if one could slip into the void, you could get from Point A to Point F instantly, bypassing the vast distances."

"Like a short-cut?"

"Precisely."

"How is this possible?"

"Without moving. We let the universe move instead."

"You've lost me."

Jabal chuckled. "In other words, while you remain stationary, outside, in the void, the universe spins quickly past at a speed far surpassing that of light. The trick is to time your reentry at the proper point, without landing inside a planet or star."

"That would be bad," she said. "How do you determine how long, or what direction?"

"Unknown at this point. The first step is to prove the void exists. Then we have to get there and return safely."

"What is your plan?"

"My drive should generate a massive, yet focused magnetic field, creating a shell around *The Blossoming Flower*. The shell, like a chisel, would rip open the barrier that separates us from the void, and allow *The Flower* to pass through."

"What are those glass jars on top of the machine?"

"Each 'jar' as you call them, contains a prototype capacitor. When fully charged, the seven capacitors would discharge simultaneously and the ship would fall out of the universe."

"It will work," she said matter-of-factly.

"Thank you for your confidence in my theory," he said. "I explained my theory before the Azurean Academy of Science and Technology to a mixed reaction. Two-thirds walked out while the rest stayed and laughed in my face. It was the most humiliating experience of my life. It will be nice wiping the smiles from their smug faces."

"I haven't a clue about your theory or this crazy machine," she said. "In fact, it makes my head hurt, but I have confidence in you."

"Thank you," he said as he blushed. "Want to watch the first test?"

"Try and stop me," she said.

"Agoa and her army of machines," he said, "have worked for most of the journey to Srune, modifying the ship to not only accept the device, but tying it into her drive unit without impeding its function. I think I have the bugs finally worked out.

"Agoa power up the drive."

As the drive powered, Jabal frowned. Only one of the seven null-glass cylinders emitted a deep blue glow.

"Agoa, what is the power output?"

"Ion engines running at one-hundred and twenty-percent output, Commander."

"What's the matter?" Sakuna asked.

"Even with the engines running at full-plus output I don't have the power I need. I can't believe I overlooked the power demand. I'm an idiot. This whole trip is a waste of time."

"It is all right," Sakuna cooed as she slid an arm around him. You will find a way. Like I said, I have faith in you."

"I'm glad someone does," he muttered.

"Agoa," Cerin said. "Access primary drive unit. Cerin nine, five, two, eco, boom, boom, three."

Jabal looked around.

"What are you doing, Cerin?" Jabal asked. "Can't you see I have accessed the main drive?"

"Command code accepted," Agoa said.

To Jabal's shock, all seven null-glass capacitors suddenly glowed brilliantly. "Agoa," he asked. "What is the power output percentage?"

"Negligible."

"You're welcome," Cerin said. "That's *two* you owe me."

"I don't understand," Jabal said. "Where is that power coming from?"

"Jabal my friend, we need to have a talk," Cerin said.

"Talk about what?"

"Before we go any further, you need to know the truth of this vessel, but I warn you now, tell a soul of what I am about to reveal or even hint that you know more than you should, and son of Teller Shann notwithstanding, you will end up like me. That goes double for you, beautiful."

Jabal smiled. "So what is the big, bad secret of *Golad's Folly*? Got a secret engine hidden somewhere?"

"Are you sure this is wise, Cerin?" Agoa asked.

"No, but it has to be done."

"Now you are scaring me," Sakuna said.

"You should be," Cerin said. "Not from me, but the monsters that rule us."

"What does this have to do with the engine output?" Jabal asked.

"To get this eight-kilometer long beast anywhere, you need real power. Agreed?"

"Yes," Jabal said. "Isn't that what the ten ion-cracking drives are for?"

"Those engines are impressive, Jabal, but they couldn't begin to push around the sheer mass of this ship. Their combined power output is for firing the magnetic cannons and running the ships' systems. Just to keep the lights on takes over fifty percent of their output. That is why they couldn't energize your gadget. It pulled more power than they had available."

"Cerin, what really powers this ship?"

"Jabal, you are going to love this. We have a fully functional Black Hole Drive."

"Oh God in Heaven," Jabal whispered. "The Black Day Project rumors were true."

"Yep," Cerin said. "One of the closest guarded military secrets we have. Behind half a kilometer of solid Null-Glass shielding lays the most destructive force in nature. The mad scientists at the Science Academy have created a fifteen attometer wide, stable, self-sustaining black-hole."

"What is the power output?"

"Let's just say this," Cerin said. "The fourteen month trip to Srune, could have been accomplished in *one*."

"But everyone knows that this ship is slow and maneuvers like a parade float. This ship is an official failure, the laughingstock of the fleet."

"That is what everyone is supposed to believe."

"It makes no sense," Jabal said. "Why lie about this amazing advancement?"

"Let me set you straight on a few things, my friend," Cerin said. "Unlike what you read in the official history of the war, we almost became extinct."

"But I thought that after the initial attacks we showed our superior resolve and beat those animals back," Sakuna said.

"No, Sakuna," Cerin said. "The truth of the matter is that we were vastly outnumbered and out gunned by those animals. For most of the war, we were getting our asses kicked. It is true that we did have superior vessels, but they were too few to go on the offensive. We fought with everything we had, but we still lost all five of our colony systems."

"That can't be," Sakuna said. "The news reported that we held on to our colonies. I've heard countless stories of how we fought back."

Cerin chuckled. "The propaganda machine worked day and night cranking out thrilling tales of Azurean valor. Honestly, beautiful, I still get all weepy over the valiant defense of Houthos City. The brave, citizen soldiers fought hardened Erest warriors to a standstill. After ammo ran out, they held off the Erest in hand-to-hand fighting until help arrived. That is still my favorite vid."

"I love it when they raise the torn flag at the end," she said.

"Unfortunately, Sakuna, what really happened was that the Erest dropped about fifty flashers on the colony while they slept. Zero survivors."

"Oh," she said.

"At least they didn't suffer," Jabal said.

"All five colony worlds are radioactive wastelands."

"I feel sick," she said.

"If it were not for Colony Six, it would have been over," Cerin said.

"Colony Six?" Sakuna asked. "I thought we only had five colonies?"

"So did the Erest," Cerin said. "It was a super-secret weapons development facility buried deep within the third moon of a ringed gas giant. That airless, rocky crap-hole didn't have a name, but those of us who were stationed there called it Hell. It was in Hell they developed null glass, Somex, the black hole drive, as well as the mag-guns. When the Erest were hammering at our system's bridge defenses, it became our staging area."

"It's a wonder that we didn't surrender," Sakuna said.

"No," Jabal said. "Surrender wasn't an option."

"Right you are, Jabal," Cerin said.

"Why?" Sakuna asked.

"Surrender would have meant the extermination of our race," Jabal said. "The Erest were very experienced at subjugating entire races and had worked out a way to avoid future retaliation or rebellion. Any Azurean over the age of five would be killed. The remaining children would be raised as slaves to the Erest, never remembering their parents or culture."

"I never knew," she said.

"It was to save the populous from panic," Cerin said. "Our backs were to the wall and a knife pressed against our throat. With our very survival at stake, this ship was built."

"Amazing," Jabal said. "I was in the fleet. I was the supreme commander's son, and I never knew the whole story."

"Ever hear of a little engagement called the Battle of the Cauldron?"

"Of course. That was seventy years ago, when our Sky Navy, under the command of Admiral Golad, faced off and destroyed the Erest's Grand Fleet," Jabal said. "It turned the tide of the war. Don't tell me, that is a lie as well?"

"I hate to spoil your delusions," Cerin said. "But yeah."

"What really happened?" Sakuna asked.

"*The Flower* was ready for her first voyage. Her first fight. We were supposed to—"

"What do you mean, *we?*" Jabal asked. "You were aboard, way back then?"

"I am older than I look," the invisible spirit said. "Anyway, we had orders to try out the ship's new weaponry upon, what our intel operatives called, a soft target. It was supposed to be some sort of remote refueling base. We were to sail in, blow the thing to hell, then get away before anyone saw us. We left Colony Six with an escort of three, obsolete Crusher Class vessels. *The Winter Storm, The Sun Flare,* and *The Ocean Current.* They were not there to participate in the assault, but to evaluate, what most officers in the fleet called a tremendous, if not criminal, waste of resources."

"What happened?" Jabal asked.

"I don't know how to explain it. Either our brilliant intelligence operatives somehow gave us the wrong address or...I just don't know. Instead of a remote, defenseless base, we came out at...Hadron Prime."

"Oh my God," Jabal whispered.

"What's Hadron Prime?" she asked.

"The Erest home world," Jabal said.

"I was not always a debonair waste management officer. At one time, I was the Pilot."

"The Pilot?" Jabal cried. "That crazy project was a failure and it killed the Pilot."

"Wrong and wrong," Cerin said. "The project, for your information, was an unqualified success. Anyway, I had only been a Pilot for a few months and was still getting used to the ship. I had never even been in battle before, well, outside of a simulator, that is, and here we had blundered right into the enemy's main base. It was impressive, all twenty levels and thousands of square kilometers. Made our Sky Naval base look like a toy in comparison. Not only were we sailing through the main Erest Navy base, the bulk of the fleet was in. There must have been over two-hundred-and-sixty of their big battle ships all secured in their docking bays, powered down, and utterly helpless. It was a gunner's wet dream."

"What did you do?" Sakuna asked.

"The Erest were overconfident in their military might and

their port defenses were merely standard anti-ship missile batteries. Tough, but not up to our standards. They never thought for one moment that someone might just kick their front door down. I knew that I had to act fast because this opportunity would never come around again. The base's defensive batteries got off one salvo before I hit them with a few tactical flashers. Even then, two of my escorts, *The Sun Flare* and *The Ocean Current* were instantly destroyed. Everything after that point is a blur. I don't know what happened, but I completely lost it. Remember that novel they make you read in school, *Transition*?"

"Yeah," Sakuna said. "Handicapped, good hearted Doctor Reese drinks his formula and becomes the handsome, powerful, and thoroughly evil, Bich Stee."

"Apparently, connecting with the ship combined with the heat of battle does the same thing. Mild mannered, incredibly handsome, Cerin Bos, who had never hurt as much as an insect, disappeared and was replaced with a psychotic killing machine with an ego bigger than God's. At that moment, I was no longer a mere kenan, I was a God of Death without an "off" switch."

"That sounds real bad," Sakuna said.

"You have no idea, beautiful." Cerin chuckled. "I know the mad scientists back at Colony Six never envisioned that scenario when they created their monster."

"What happened?" Jabal asked.

"The joy of what I became—of what I could do—gave me an ecstasy greater than any drug. I spun and danced around the Erest's feeble attempts to stop me. They were so slow, so weak, so *helpless*. I laughed at their terror as I killed them. I only stopped when base and the fleet was no more than floating scrap."

"Amazing," Jabal said.

"My thirst for death was far from sated. I set sail for their world at full speed. Their beautiful, green, utterly helpless world. They tried to put up a fight, but they didn't have much left to fight with after I had destroyed their battleships. After I swept away all ships in orbit, I eliminated their space elevators, I entered high polar orbit and prepared fifty canisters of Somex."

"What is Somex?" Sakuna asked.

"Another state secret," Jabal said. "Some say it is the ultimate weapon."

"It's what we call an intelligent DNA nerve agent," Cerin said. "A rather elegant weapon. It can be adjusted to attack a particular strand of DNA, like say that of your friend Boron. You could release it over a heavily populated area and no one would suffer the smallest effect, but Boron would be dead. The guilty pay while zero collateral damage to the innocent. A clean way to perform political assassinations if you ask me."

"When we get home, care to let me borrow a canister?" Sakuna asked as she produced a mischievous grin.

Jabal shook his head and snorted. "As you were saying, Cerin?"

"Admiral Golad was aboard the *The Winter Storm,* and he was literally screaming for me to stand down. Seems the Erest Government had enough. Their leader, Micale was trying to contact me to surrender and spare his civilian population."

"You won the war single handedly?" Sakuna asked. "You're a hero."

"I don't understand," Jabal said. "If they surrendered, why did the war go on for another seventy years?"

"I wasn't ready for them to surrender," Cerin said. "I got tired of Admiral Golad's yammering, so I blew his ship from the sky. I then set the Somex for anything non-Azurean. I estimated that nine billion Erest died."

"Oh no," Jabal said.

"I couldn't think—all I wanted to do was kill. It wasn't until the Somex was delivered that I came to my senses. I had total victory in the palm of my hand and I crushed it. While I had pissed away a quick victory, my rampage gave our people the advantage. I had cut the head off the beast, their main fleet was gone, and their government was dead. Our forces then went on the offensive, and began the task of hunting the remnant down, destroying any trace of resistance. Instead of breaking their will, the Erest used the slaughter of Hadron

Prime as a rally call. They fought to the last and cost us millions of our own people who should have never died. More blood on my hands."

"What about your crew?" Jabal asked. "I imagine that at least one of them would have said something. This story is too big not to have leaked out."

"My transformation," Cerin said. "I didn't care what happen to the bugs crawling around inside of me. I didn't give my crew the opportunity to get to the g-tubes."

"You killed them," Jabal said. "You killed your own crew?"

"They couldn't stand the stress as I maneuvered at full speed. When I came out of my chamber, the bulkheads were painted with their blood."

"You were the only survivor?" Sakuna asked.

"Yes," Cerin said. "While High Command was elated at the victory, they did not want to deal with the public backlash over the twenty-thousand murdered sailors. *The Blossoming Flower* became *Golad's Folly* and my atrocities were covered up with the heroic Battle of The Cauldron.

"I just wanted to die, but they wouldn't let me. Said they might need me again one day. Said that if I valued my relatives and friends, I would do what I was told. To ease my crushing guilt, I was given perks that would blow your mind."

"Agoa?" Sakuna asked.

"Right," Cerin said. "Cerin Bos, Pilot, died and was born again as a lowly waste management officer, just to keep me handy if they ever needed a psychotic killer again. Thank God, the need never arose. I figured that with the war all but won, they decided that the only witness should disappear so those bastards sent a hit squad to kill me. If you two want to keep breathing, you will forget what I have told you."

"I never heard a word," Sakuna said.

"Your secret is safe," Jabal said, who was thinking of the top secret, highly illegal mechanical troops locked away in the landing bay.

"Anymore classified secrets you want to share?" Jabal asked.

"This is a ship of secrets, but I don't want to give you a mental breakdown."

"Too late," Jabal said. "I got a headache from all you have told me."

Cerin chuckled. "You'll get more than a headache if either of you breathe a word of what I have told you."

"So why tell me all this?" Jabal asked.

"This drive of yours," Cerin said, "if it works, we will be knee deep in war within the week."

"It is for exploration," Jabal said. "*Peaceful* exploration."

"Do you think the military will just let you take *The Flower* and dance off across the galaxy?"

"Why not?"

"You are a good kenan, Jabal, but naive as hell. You give our military a way to bypass the Bridges, and they will do the same thing the Erest tried to do to us. They will build an empire."

"I don't believe that."

"Don't or won't, believe it?" Cerin asked.

"Sure, a fleet equipped with my device could cause a lot of trouble, but our people aren't like that."

"Haven't you been listening to me?"

"I can believe our people would do it," Sakuna said. "In a heartbeat."

"What do you want me to do?"

"Lie," Cerin said. "Scrap the drive, destroy your plans, and live in peace knowing that you aren't responsible for another bloody, senseless conflict."

Jabal rubbed his face in frustration. "Thank you for the history lesson, Cerin, but tomorrow, we test the drive," he said, turning to Sakuna. "Sakuna, I need to talk to you." Taking her by the hand, Jabal led her from the room. "I need you to do something for me," he whispered, standing close.

"It's about time," she said as she leaned in for a kiss.

"What are you doing?" he asked, jerking away.

"Nothing," she said, "Absolutely nothing."

"I've had Agoa prepare a long range shuttle. Tomorrow, I want you onboard when we test the drive."

"No, I am going to be standing next to you when you push the button."

"I would feel better if you were safe," he said. "If anything bad happens, the shuttle can get you close enough to home where a ship can pick you up."

"Live or die, I will be by your side," she said, crossing her arms.

"Be reasonable."

"Agoa," Sakuna said. "Cancel the shuttle for tomorrow. I won't need it."

"Yes, *Captain* Izusa," Agoa said.

"I guess I will see you tomorrow," Jabal said.

"Where are you off to?" she asked.

"I need to think,"

"Think about what?"

"The future," he said over his shoulder as he walked away.

 espes

Deep in thought, Jabal wandered through the vast ship. Cerin's revelations had his mind in turmoil.

"Damn it," he said. "I should be overjoyed that my dream is finally ready to test, not worrying about what my government might do with my invention."

He made his way down to the main hanger repair bay. The odd smells and scampering repair machines were a sharp contrast to the supreme order of the main ship herself. Moving through a thick blast door made of solid null-glass, he found himself on the raised walkway next to the ten, Reaper 07 Drop Ships that his father had tasked him with disposing of discretely.

The sleek, long-range vac/atm troop transports were the standard naval deployment for "ground pounders." Invisible to radar and equipped with a chameleon like ability for instant camouflage, their twin, micro-fusion drives could push the eighty-five-meter-long craft to well over mach three in a thick atmosphere. The versatile craft could operate both in vacuum as well as atmosphere. Once landing their troops, the crafts would take to the air and, using their cannons and missiles, would serve as air support.

Jabal ran his hand over the slightly pebbly skin of the craft and marveled as the ship changed color.

Opening a hatch, he bounded up the loading ramp into the drop ship. Jabal gaped at the deadly machines tightly packed together and arranged as if it were a massive, intricate puzzle.

"Secrets," Jabal said. "I am damn tired of secrets."

$$\text{e}\triangleright\text{e}\triangleright$$

Jabal checked Sakuna's safety harness for the third time when she took his face in her hands.

"For luck," she said before gently kissing him.

Jabal blushed. It was the first time another fenan had kissed him since he had taken his marriage vows. To Sakuna's delight, he kissed her back.

"Wow," she whispered as she snaked her arms around his neck.

"If you want, I can leave the room," Cerin said.

"Were you this big a pain in real life?" Jabal asked as he extricated himself from her embrace.

"Yes, he was," Agoa said.

Jabal took the captain's chair next to Sakuna. "Agoa," he said. "Align the ship to our predetermined flight course. Thrusters only."

"Flight path set, Commander."

"Engage." He produced his small remote. The thumb-sized device had a single red button. "Here goes nothing."

"Wait," Cerin said. "Jabal, you have to say something for posterity."

"I hope I don't live to regret this," Jabal said.

He turned to Sakuna and smiled. Without taking his eyes off hers, he pressed the button.

The world went black.

CHAPTER 15

War Admiral Teller Shann sat at his desk, going over the peacetime fleet reallocation, when Imia burst into his office.

"What is the meaning of this?" he snapped.

Flushed with excitement, Imia handed her father a computer tablet that held a single, classified communicate.

Teller snatched the paper-thin device from her hand. "This had better be important," he said.

> *War Admiral Teller Shann's eyes only:*
> *Exactly four weeks and two days since our arrival at Srune,* The Blossoming Flower *made the first successful rip in Azurean history. It was half a meter short of two kilometers, but a rip nevertheless. The device works. Tests later on the same day produced rips of over two-thousand-kilometers. I am running experiments as we speak and have no doubt that we have taken the first few steps into the era of Space Exploration.*
> *Jabal Shann, Commander Azurean Sky Navy.*

"Is this for real?" the stunned admiral asked.

"Agoa sent confirming data," Imia said. "Little brother has done it."

A smile crossed his face as glorious visions raced through his mind. "Imia, I am promoting Jabal to the rank of Captain, effective immediately. We can do the formal presentation when he gets back. At the presentation, I want the entire Science Academy present to eat their words."

"That won't be easy," she said. "They are a stiff-necked lot."

"You also said that keeping Barea in check would be a problem as well. To think she had the gall to betray *my* son with that scum Darris Oso. I wanted to kill him myself, but that wasn't practical. My *associate* Boron Hyatt put an end to that sorted tryst, and Barea will burn for the crime if she treats Jabal with anything other than complete devotion."

"I hate that fat bastard," she said, "but I have to admit that Barea has had a complete change of heart. Too bad Boron is up to his neck in trouble over the Sakuna Izusa incident and can't help you with your special projects anymore. Even your influence can't help him from escaping the death chamber."

"Damn him, his services were very valuable. Why couldn't he just kill that foking law seena outright instead of getting cute? The public is screaming for his head on a platter."

"Don't you think it was an odd coincidence that Officer Izusa should end up on *The Flower*, along with all the evidence needed to fry Boron? Not to mention your son is at the helm. What if Boron thinks you set him up? He has enough information on you to make life uncomfortable."

Teller let out a ragged breath. "It does not matter. I am afraid he will commit suicide long before he has a chance to make a deal with the government prosecutor and reveal any details about our special relationship. What galls me is this entire incident could have been avoided if that stubborn son of mine had just followed protocol and flushed Officer Izusa into space before she could bring down the fat psycho. His brothers would have eliminated a stowaway without a second thought. Jabal definitely is an odd one for a Shann."

"Jabal has a heart," she said with a smile. "That is very odd for a Shann."

Teller gave her a sour look. "Jabal is very much like his grandfather Gannon. Gannon was a born leader and could have ruled the war council, but he refused to play politics and valued personal honor over a career. He died an infantry major, taking an insignificant rock. What a waste."

"I barely remember Grandfather, other than he always seemed to have candy in his pocket—anyway, what are we going to do about the Science Academy upon Jabal's return?"

"If the Academy cause any trouble, I will send in my personal guard. I will have those insufferable, intellectual snobs lined up at gunpoint to kiss my stubborn son's ass. I will give Jabal a celebration that this world has never seen."

"Father, what about Jabal's dream of space exploration?"

Teller gave his daughter a scowl. "Start the paperwork on re-commissioning *The Blossoming Flower*. I want that ship re-armed, and crewed with our finest sailors. Time to drop the façade of Goliad's Folly and show our people what that ship can really do.

"Contact Hugo Bes, lead researcher of Colony Six, and have him begin work acquiring and training a new Pilot. This time around, let's find one that won't go crazy and try to kill everything in sight."

"You shut down Colony Six, remember? You said that their psychotic approach to research would get you and the War Council a one way ticket to the execution chamber."

"Officially they are shut down, however, the main body of their scientists have set up shop here in the Citadel," Teller said. "Let's see what refinements they can make to Jabal's design."

"Jabal won't be happy. After all, you did promise the ship to him."

"He'll get over it," Teller said. "Do we have the plans for his device?"

"We only have his earliest concepts. However, since we know the principle is sound, it shouldn't be that difficult to duplicate."

"Put our best techs on it. I want a hundred of those drives developed before the year is up. In twenty years, this section of the galaxy will be the sole property of the New Azurean Empire."

"Yes, *Emperor* Shann," she said.

"That does have a nice ring doesn't it?"
Imia rolled her eyes.

෫෮෫෮

Unbeknownst to Jabal, use of his rip drive sent out harmless, yet detectible waves of energy that traveled far faster than light speed. Like ripples on a pond, they spread over a large section of the galaxy before they collided with Opia's planet. Her sensitive machines picked up the transmission waves and pinpointed their source.

The mysterious entity known as Yeti deciphered the rare, but unmistakable signal. Thanking his dark Gods, he put into motion a plan to save his people.

CHAPTER 16

With only his feet sticking out of an access panel, Jabal muttered, "Come on, baby. I know you can do this. Just give Daddy what he wants, and he'll leave you alone."

"Yeah that's right, sweet talk it, that will help," Cerin said.

"I'd kiss the damn thing if it would work."

Wiggling his way out of the cramped crawl space, Jabal replaced the magnetic plate on the access panel. "That should do it," he said as he wiped his hands and stood. "Okay, Agoa, engage."

With a slight hum, Jabal felt the ship tremor and experienced a slightly nauseous feeling in the pit of his stomach. He had gotten used to the feeling—best described as being on an elevator in the midst of freefall.

"Agoa, what's the damage?"

"Congratulations, Commander," she said. "That was the most successful test yet."

"Our progress?"

"Two hundred thousand, one hundred, and one kilometers."

"Damn it," Jabal exclaimed. "Still not good enough."

"It was better," Cerin said, "but still far from the prize. I have been going over your research notes—"

"Going through my personal and highly confidential papers? Thanks for asking for permission."

"You're welcome. Anyway, I wonder if you gave any thought to the circle alignment?"

"The circle design? That would take a complete re-configuration of the main circuit board. That would take most of the week."

"The current configuration isn't working. What do you have to lose?"

"Good point," Jabal said. "Agoa, cut the power and take her apart."

"Yes, sir," she said. "By the way, sir, congratulation on your promotion, Captain Shann."

"Thank you, Agoa.

"If you think I am going to salute you, you can forget it," Sakuna said in the deep voice of an enforcer as she walked into the room. "I knew you when you were nobody."

Jabal looked up and beheld Sakuna wearing her newly repaired law enforcer uniform. "What's with the battleskin?" he asked. "I thought you were through with police work?"

"This little adventure will be over soon, and I will have to go back to the real world."

"No. That life is dead. Must I remind you that you are officially a member of the Sky Navy?"

"I don't think that counts," she said. "You just did that to keep from tossing me out an airlock."

"At first perhaps, but I have been doing a lot of thinking. Sakuna, you are smart, tough as Null-Glass, and the voice of reason when I am not thinking straight. It is my right as captain to choose my second, and I choose you. I want you to be my first officer. I wouldn't be here if not for you. You even came up with the name *Ripper Drive*."

"Yes, it does roll off the tongue," Cerin said. "Far better than Jabal's *Electromagnetic Interdimensional Space Folding Travel Device*. That was sad."

"That *was* bad," Sakuna agreed.

"It was also you who came up with the idea of the *Pathfinders*," Jabal said.

"That was sheer genius," Cerin said. "Modifying military scout probes with small rip drives to go ahead and plot a clear course for the main ship never occurred to me."

"Nor I," Jabal said. "Any rips beyond a solar system are blind. Your pathfinders would keep us from ripping inside a planet, asteroid, or star. Face it, Sakuna, I need you."

"Sorry, Jabal. I must decline your offer."

"I thought—"

"Jabal, I didn't want your damn device to work. Never did. If I could, I would toss a grenade into the thing. Hell, if I knew what I was doing, I would take down the engines permanently."

"You would strand us out here in the boonies?"

"I enjoyed being alone with you in this floating palace and held tight to the hope that one day you would come to your senses and love me like I love you. Even though you know that I am the only one who truly loves you, you will never allow yourself to be mine. When we get home, you will be a national hero. One of such magnitude that unfortunate schoolchildren will have to do dull boring reports on your life a thousand years from now. However, Cerin is right. The military will snatch your new toy away before you can blink. You will never explore anything galactic, but be tucked away in a lab somewhere to rot during the day. At night, you will go home to a pathetic, spiteful mate who does not appreciate what an extraordinary kenan she has. For the sake of your stubborn, goddamn honor, you will suffer a cold, calculating wife that you will never completely trust. How you can have love without trust, I cannot understand. I do not belong in that world. I have decided that I will not waste one second more chasing after you. If you will excuse me, I have to get back into shape if I am ever to re-join the law enforcers."

Sakuna turned on her heel and walk out.

Jabal watched long after she left. He felt a huge knot in his stomach as he fought the urge to run after her.

"She's right you know," Cerin said.

"I didn't ask you," Jabal replied.

"Funny thing is, you know everything she said was the truth, but you are still plowing forward, full steam toward the brink of a thousand-foot cliff."

"It's my duty, damn it," Jabal said.

"Your duty won't keep you warm at night. If I were you, I would have my injections up to date before your homecoming with Berea. Don't know what nasty homecoming surprise might be waiting between her legs."

"You go to hell."

"Eventually. I'll be waiting for you, because you will be responsible for every drop of blood your device sheds."

Enraged, Jabal stalked from the room and the smug spirit who had somehow become his best friend. Angry as he was, Jabal knew Cerin and Sakuna were right. Teller Shann would take his device and there would be war.

Although he would never admit to it, his scheduled vid visits with Barea were becoming more of a chore than a delight. Although she seemed genuinely repentant, gushing over him like she did when they were first married, he knew it was over between them. Deep down he knew Sakuna was right. Barea truly wanted to hurt him in the worst possible way. Her tryst with Darris was unforgivable, and he would never touch her as his wife again. Yet, for honor's sake, he would live out his days in a loveless, marital hell.

Jabal entered the small control substation and plopped down in the chair before the console. His head pounded and his stomach churned with stress.

"Damn it," he mumbled. "This should be the best day of my life, and I feel sick to my stomach. What am I going to do? I am so confused I could scream." He took a deep breath and let it out noisily. "Agoa, how are we set for food and water?"

"The ship's stores are fully stocked."

"Fully stocked?"

"While our ammo was a high priority and offloaded first, the ship's food and water supply was untouched. We have a six-month, two-week, four-day ration for a full crew compliment."

"What is a full crew compliment?"

"Seven-thousand nine-hundred and sixty-four sailors, marines, and officers."

"I see," he said. "Fuel?"

"The black hole drive is projected to supply power for the next three-hundred and four-point-two years, before a scheduled realignment."

Jabal rose and left the room.

ɷɞɷ

Jabal found Sakuna in Exercise Room Two. Her Battleskin lay in a corner while she ran on the track in a skimpy, sweat soaked, tank top and shorts. Jabal walked out onto the slightly spongy track and blocked her path.

"I need to talk to you."

"If you want an apology, *Captain* Shann," she said, coming to a stop before him, "forget it. I meant every foking word."

"That's all I wanted to know."

Jabal gathered the shocked fenan in his arms and kissed her hard.

CHAPTER 17

While outwardly confident, Rondall was a bundle of nerves as he walked behind Opia. The slightest slip and he and his people were dead.

"Be resolute, my friend," Yeti whispered. "She is an immoral degenerate. You are worth fifty such creatures."

The arrogant Opia was dressed in a sumptuous robe made of spun gold, sporting a train that stretched six meters behind her. The crown upon her small head was silver, encrusted with rubies. As they walked out upon observation deck of the vast space elevator, Opia stopped suddenly.

Rondall's heart nearly stopped as well. Her next words would decide his fate.

"Why aren't you further along with my project?" she asked.

"It took more time than anticipated to train our people," he said. "We aren't, after all, a space faring race."

"They will have to be," Opia said.

Before them, the massive mechanized space dock was busy constructing a vast space fleet. Already, fifteen six-hundred-meter-long battlewagons were going through shakedown cruises. Thirty smaller vessels, roughly four-hundred-meters in length participated in fleet maneuvers. In all, he would wield a force of nearly two hundred ships.

"As you have commanded, my Goddess," Rondall said, "we have labored night and day upon your Holy Project."

Opia beamed with pride at the work of her children.

"My child, you have done well. Where did you get the design for the vessels?"

"I cast about, using your "all seeing eye device," and happened upon a planet whose war-like, inhabitants favored this particular design. Their fleet looked quite efficient so we appropriated one. Using the vessel as our guide, we built what you see before you. I hope I didn't offend you."

"No, of course not. You showed great initiative. You are a good and faithful servant. When I am through, we will have ten-thousand ships, and we will purge the godless from this galaxy."

Rondall swallowed hard.

"Now my friend," Yeti whispered. "Make the request."

"Thank you, my lord Opia. I must report that exploratory probes have discovered a disturbing development."

"What?"

"A savage, brutal race has been found that possesses rudimentary wormhole tech."

"That is forbidden," she snapped.

"That is why I bring it to your attention, Opia. Our fleet is not strong enough, our personal not experienced enough to face their might. Please give us a divine weapon to strike them down mercifully—*utterly*—in your name."

Opia's unreadable face looked at Rondall long and hard. "There is a device. I call it the Acturus. It is very old and has never been used. It will purge their system of godlessness forever. To stop their evil from spreading, I grant you its use."

"Thank you, my Goddess."

"I will give you the device after the reception with your Roratune brothers."

"As you wish, my Goddess," he said with a deep bow. "Your will is my will."

Opia smiled and walked through the transparent, three-meter thick, paexi-steel wall. While her people looked on, Opia sailed unharmed though the deadly vacuum of space. Spinning and twirling, she did a brief, impossible ballet performance before flying to her floating crystal palace.

Donning his best smile, Rondall gave a sign of relief.

"Well done, my friend," Yeti said. "The beast called Opia doesn't have clue that she has been manipulated."

"I feel like I am treading the edge of a razor," Rondall said. "I still don't understand why we need the construction of the space fleet. Or why we must have this *divine weapon*, as you call it."

"Only from space can her power be snuffed," Yeti said. "Once we both have our freedom, you will see that it has all been worth the sacrifice."

"Why the weapon?"

"We don't need it," Yeti said. "We must dispose of it so Opia can't use it against us."

Oh, we will dispose of it, Rondall thought. *All while eliminating a future threat before they become a problem.*

"I am fatigued," Yeti said. "I must leave you now."

"Rest well, my friend. I long for the day we can meet face to face."

"If all goes well, that day will be here before you know it. Goodbye."

Rondall smiled as the distinctive presence of Yeti left him.

ᘉᘓᘉᘓ

The high priest took the crystal and gold decanter and poured himself another goblet of wine. Gulping down the drink, he placed the empty cup on the silver serving tray. Rising, he walked across the richly carpeted floor to the ornate wooden closet and opened the door. Within, stood a faceless, black velvet covered manikin. Taking his tall, ceremonial headpiece, he placed it gently upon the dummy's head.

"I always hated that silly looking thing," he mumbled. "It's damn awkward and makes my head sweat."

Slipping off the exquisite, yet backbreaking robe, he placed it around the dummy's shoulders and locked its jewel-encrusted clasp. Lastly, he kicked off his padded slippers. Now standing barefoot, in nothing more than a simple, sweat-soaked garment of white silk that stood in sharp contrast to his thick, black fur, Rondall stretched his beefy, powerful frame.

"Much better," he said, shutting the closet door.

He poured another drink and moved to the massive window overlooking the City of God.

"Calm before the storm," he mused as he let his mind drift.

Rondall grew up believing Opia was who she claimed to be, Goddess Almighty. He entered the priesthood, wanting no more than to serve his Goddess and enter blamelessly into her blessed afterlife. Soon after he had taken his vows of service, Yeti entered his life and left his faith in shambles.

At first, Rondall thought the unseen voice was a demon, but the kind and gentle voice showed the young priest that God Almighty was but a flesh and blood creature as himself. Opia, he discovered, was the last survivor of a race called the Vanuatu.

When questioned about himself, Yeti told Rondall that for hundreds of years, he was locked in a device that resembled a golden sarcophagus, that while it preserved his life, it rendered him powerless, even as they drained him of his knowledge. The Vanuatu, unaware of Yeti's vast mental abilities, never imagined how their slave roamed their world at will, looking for a way to escape.

The Vanuatu's constant use of the wormholes proved to be their undoing. A probe brought back a deadly virus. Within a year, a great plague ravaged the Vanuatu, pushing them toward the brink of extinction. The alien virus reduced his captors to a few thousand until Yeti, in exchange for his freedom, provided a cure. Although he saved their race, the ungrateful survivors refused to free him. Instead, they battled for supremacy leaving only one, "the mad queen."

She took the name of the supreme Goddess, Opia. In her madness, she tried to erase the old world. Forgetting the old, ravaged world and the prisoner Yeti, she sought to start afresh and build a lie. Unfortunately, her war had devastated the world beyond repair. Only her advanced tech kept the Great Valley Edan habitable.

Yeti guided the skeptical priest to forgotten, subterranean chambers deep below the city where Rondall saw with his own eyes the truth. The beautiful, eternal City of God was built upon the corpse of an earlier, ancient city that had been destroyed by war.

In the pulverized remains, Yeti showed Rondall proof that

his own people were captives taken years ago and raised to appease the ego of a false God.

That was over twenty years ago. Yeti and Rondall drew their plans and bided their time, and now they were almost ready to strike. However, Yeti had no idea of the depravity and the lust for power that burned within his partner in crime.

CHAPTER 18

The massive cathedral of Opia was the largest structure in the city of Romaa. Like spokes radiating from a central hub, the precisely constructed, immaculate city stretched out hundreds of kilometers from the central two-kilometer tall golden spire.

The sparkling city lay situated in a great, fertile valley that stretched roughly nine-hundred kilometers from east to west and three hundred kilometers north to south.

The lush valley, known as Edan, was a single oasis of life on the face of the sterile, desert planet of Ilea—bordered to the south and east by the vast Desert of the Lost, while the jagged Saw Tooth Mountain range hemmed in the west and north.

Small, picturesque villages lay scattered throughout Edan amid orchards and patchwork fields of grain.

Besides Opia, two completely different races occupied the idyllic valley. The Moguls, who called themselves The Faithful, lived exclusively in the city of Romaa and enjoyed a pampered existence.

Their less faithful brothers, the Roratune, lived in the country villages and worked to provide food for both themselves and the Moguls.

An uneasy truce existed between the Moguls and the Roratune. Many bloody encounters in the past had forced Opia to separate the two sworn enemies. The memory of their last *correction* was still fresh in their minds.

Fifty years before, the two groups clashed. War raged across the valley until Opia sent in her security machines. Deciding that both sides needed a lesson in who was boss, she arbitrarily slaughtered half their numbers. Their bodies were unceremoniously dumped into the desert to the south. Peace prevailed ever since.

Since it was the Roratune who initiated the conflict, they were expelled from the city and made to be laborers. It was Opia's hope that hard work would cool their penchant for rebellion.

☙❧☙

Hundreds of Roratune representatives made the mandatory journey to Romaa, where they were met by heavy Mogul security. The Moguls made it clear that they considered Romaa their city and that the Roratune were not welcome. Nevertheless, to avoid the wrath of Opia, they treated the Roratune politely and provided generous lodging and food.

With pomp and circumstance, befitting a, newly rejuvenated God, Opia and her twenty attendants walked down the long aisle past hundreds of her prostrate children. Bedecked in her sumptuous gown, she sat upon an enormous, solid gold throne.

"Today is a grand day my children," Opia said. "Today, I will take the first step in reestablishing control over my creation. I will remove the weeds that have choked my garden and brought disharmony to the galaxy. I will—"

"Death to the false goddess!"

The crowd gasped as a Roratune named Bandea Tho stood and walked brazenly toward Opia.

"The time of your evil is over," he said, producing a Mogul handgun.

Rondall ran from his position and blocked Bandea's path to Opia.

"How dare you threaten our God?" Rondall screamed.

"How dare you?" Bandea asked.

Bandea aimed and fired at Rondall, striking the high priest twice. As Rondall grunted and stumbled backward, Bandea's weapon burst into flame.

Bandea dropped his incinerated firearm and pulled a knife.

Clutching his burned arm he struggled forward when he was suddenly snatched upward and held five meters off the ground. Bandea screamed and cursed as he struggled in the invisible vice. Opia rose up to her would be assassin.

"Bandea, why would you do this?"

"For my family to live—you must die."

Opia waved her hand and a small, whistling wormhole opened next to Bandea.

"I judge you as unworthy to be my child."

Bandea had time for one scream before he was sucked into the conduit and expelled into open space, ten-thousand light years away.

Opia glided down and knelt beside Rondall.

"You will be all right, my child. Your bravery in protecting your Goddess will be sung about for evermore."

"You are my *everything*," he whispered.

With a wave of her hand, the bullets dissipated and his ugly wounds healed instantly.

"Thank you," he said as he rose to his feet. "You will never know how grateful I am, my Goddess."

ლოლო

"This part of the plan stinks," Rondall said as he rubbed his newly healed shoulder.

"Must I remind you that I did suggest another way?" Yeti asked. "One that did not involving the kidnapping of Bandea's family and forcing him to become an assassin. You will release them, won't you?"

"Um, sorry, my friend," Rondall said. "Seems that they died in a terrible, unforeseen tragedy."

"Really? Can't you do anything without someone dying?"

"Don't dwell upon the ugly details, old friend."

"I feel dirty," Yeti said.

"Anyway, dirty or not, my plan was more convincing."

"Debatable, but yes, Opia's suspicions should be put to rest."

There was a sharp knock at the chamber door.

"Let's see if our plan has borne fruit," Yeti said.

"Come," Rondall said.

In walked a short, painfully thin Zealot, dressed in the brown robes of a low-level priest. He carried an antiquated parchment map rolled up in his hand.

"Do you have what I need, Silvestre?" Rondall asked as he leaned back in his sumptuous chair. He rubbed the shoulder where he had been shot.

The small Zealot rolled out an old-fashion map of the planet upon Rondall's desk.

"As you ordered, my lord," the wizened Silvestre said. "We launched eighty, passive energy detection probes around the planet while our Goddess slumbered. At precisely the time, Opia executed Bandea, probes sixty-five, sixty-six, and sixty-seven detected a massive energy spike in the southern desert, near Mount Tal. Upon closer analysis, we found a camouflaged anomaly."

"Yes," Yeti said. "You have found her power."

"Really?" Rondall asked, trying his best to maintain a calm exterior.

"It turned out to be a vast, circular depression over two hundred kilometers across and two kilometers deep."

"Silvestre, I want you to ready plan two," said Rondall.

"Are you certain, my lord? There will be no turning back."

"Make it so," Rondall said.

"As you will, my lord."

As Silvestre, left, Yeti was beside himself with joy. "You have done it. You have found her power, and now we know where to strike."

"That site is nearly five thousand kilometers away," said Rondall. "How could it be doing her any good at that distance?"

"Trust me, my friend, that great machine buried in the desert gives Opia her divinity."

"So we can just blast it—"

"No weapon you could conceive of would penetrate that armor, my friend."

"Then how do we prevail, if it is invulnerable?"

"It's not *exactly* invulnerable. Merely to your feeble weapons, but not mine. I will make Opia a mortal again. I have a plan for a weapon that is simple enough for your techs to create, but will bring Opia to her knees."

"Then give it to me,"

"Not until the Acturus is removed from this system. Get rid of that infernal weapon and I will give you the key to Opia's power."

CHAPTER 19

Amid a blare of alarms, *The Chariot of Opia* exited the wormhole. Stiffly, Opia sat upon her throne. While she smiled and chatted with her attendants, she was afraid. She hated everything about space travel but, most importantly, the farther she traveled away from her planet, the weaker her powers became. Here, inside the orbit of the inner most planet, Dera, Opia was virtually powerless.

Her vast floating palace moved effortlessly through space as it approached the most powerful weapon ever conceived, the Acturus. *The Chariot of Opia* swung in close to the ancient installation, which was fully a kilometer in diameter and literally bristled with a vast antenna array.

"Is it my time?" Acturus asked.

"Time for what?" Opia asked.

"To fulfill my purpose, of course," the soft voice said.

"Your purpose," Opia snapped, "is to do my will."

Slightly confused, Acturus scanned *The Chariot of Opia* and recognized Opia as a Vanuatu—a creator.

"Shall I fulfill my purpose, creator?"

"Come with me," Opia said.

A massive hatch on the floating installation opened and Acturus dropped into space. The ninety-meter, cigar shaped device maneuvered to the ship and connected with a special docking module slung underneath.

"Let's go home, children," Opia ordered.

A vast wormhole opened three hundred meters away to port. Firing thrusters, the spectacular ship headed for home.

ℰ↷ℰ↷

Dressed in an outrageously gaudy white and gold uniform, Rondall knelt before Opia on the bridge of *The Chariot of Opia*. Through the wall sized view screen, the gorgeous view of the Ilea floated below them like a jewel in space,

The gleaming control center saw twenty Mogul officers, all dressed in blue and gold, kneeling behind their leader Rondall. They were bursting with pride at having been chosen to be the First Warriors of Opia.

"Rondall, today you and your zealots will become my warrior priests," she said. "Go forth, in my name, and strike the infidel down. This will be the first engagement of a new holy war that will force my many scattered children to turn from their wicked ways, or I will burn this galaxy down and start over."

"Your will be done," said Rondall and his officers in unison.

"Now rise and take command of my ship."

Rondall rose and smiled. "I take command, Goddess. I will die before I let you down."

"Success," she said as she faded away.

Rondall settled into the sumptuous captain's chair, relishing the power at his fingertips. "To your stations," he said quietly. "We have a job to do, for our God."

ℰ↷ℰ↷

The Chariot of Opia, flanked by her five destroyer escorts, circled Ilea once, before leaving orbit on her holy mission.

As way of a grand send-off, Opia manufactured a tumultuous firework display. Picking up speed and sailing past the great-automated shipyard, the exotic ship and her escorts sailed into a vast hole, that seemed to open in the very fabric of space itself, and vanished.

CHAPTER 20

The Azurean cruiser, *Rising Sun,* settled into high orbit around, Mykon, the first planet in the Azurean system. The sleek ship was equipped with special shielding to protect the twenty-three crewmembers from the enormous radiation and intense heat from the nearby yellow star.

"Orbit achieved Captain Ure," the helmsman said.

"Finally," the captain said as he sipped from an insulated canister of hot tea. "Prepare the package for deployment. I don't want to stay here any longer than need be."

"Yes, it will be good to breathe fresh air again," First Officer Hass said, "I am sick of recycled air's aftertaste."

"Or a bunk you don't have to share with two others," mumbled a sailor.

Captain Ure chuckled. When he was a lowly sailor, he hated "hot bunks" as well.

The no-nonsense space cruiser was laid out where functionality took precedent over crew comfort.

"How is the sun?" the captain asked. "Is she behaving?"

The captain was wary of being this close to a star. Special heat and radiation shielding notwithstanding, an unexpected plasma geyser would end this mission very quickly.

"Sensors confirm no building plasma geyser, sir."

"Too bad we can't have one of those fancy rip drives," Helmsman Frue said with a laugh. "We could be back home in time for dinner."

The small, thin captain snorted. "While our mission isn't as glamorous as that of Commander Shann and his giant devil ship, deploying a telescope to observe the sun is a more practical application than testing the bounds of science fiction."

Several of the officers and crew chuckled at the captain's remarks.

Few believed that instant space travel was possible. Most thought that Jabal's mission was little more than a stunt dreamed up by War Admiral Shann to keep the auditors from slashing their budget to the bone, now that the war was over.

In their opinion, as good as the military was at keeping secrets, the fact that a project of this magnitude had leaked out, was proof positive that the story was a plant.

"First Officer, deploy the probe, after we make sure the damn thing works, set course for Yolonda outpost."

"Yes, sir," Commander Bribbin Hass said.

The ship shuddered slightly as the great solar observatory, *Sundancer*, rocketed from the ship's external rails. The probe was nearly a third of the Rising Sun's fifty-meter length. Deploying multiple wings of solar cells, the probe began sending back telemetry immediately.

"*Sundancer* is on line," the AI aboard the sun probe said. "It is a great day to get in a little sun."

The crew chuckled at the probe's response.

"Who programs these things?" the captain asked as he shook his head.

"Thank you for the lift, *Rising Sun*," the probe said as it fired its engines and set course for a blistering, near orbit of the Azurean sun. "Have a safe journey home."

"*Sundancer* is working perfectly, Captain," Hass said.

"Good. Set course for Yolander."

"We have unknown vessels in our vicinity," boomed the deep, gritty voice of Grem, the *Rising Sun's* own AI. "I have five ships of unknown configuration at one-hundred and fifty-eight-thousand-kilometers."

Captain Ure froze in mid-sip. He assumed that the computer was making a mistake. After all, he and his crew were far from the Bridge, deep within the inner system. "Commander Hass, what is wrong with that AI?" he asked.

"No mistake, Captain," the first officer said. "There is something out there all right."

"Action stations," Ure said. "Take us out of orbit and give us room to maneuver if it comes to that. Warm up the weapons."

Twin rail cannons rose through the armored hull, while a magnetic missile launcher loaded a tactical thermonuclear flasher.

"Confirmation, Captain," the sensor operator said. "I have five objects in powered flight."

"Are you sure they are powered and not just asteroids?"

"The formation has made several deliberate course corrections, sir. They are not natural system objects."

"What was their point of origin?"

"I don't know. Not enough data. They were just there—oh no—Captain, we got a big contact."

"Carrier?"

"If it is, it's the biggest one I ever saw," the operator said. "At least one hundred by fifty klicks."

"Impossible. That's bigger than *The Devil's Barge*."

"Confirmation, Captain," Grem said. "The five ships have detected us as well. They have changed course and are moving to intercept us. The large carrier is moving away from us at a high rate of speed toward the sun."

"Hass, first, send what we have to the Fleet Command. Second, hail our visitors," Captain Ure said. "Let's find out their intentions."

"Yes, sir," Hass said.

How in god's name did these aliens get this far into our inner system without detection?

Captain Ure wondered, as he settled back in his chair. He wasn't prepared for a fight. His ship was on a scientific mission and carried only minimal armaments. They had only three flashers and twenty rounds for the cannons.

The thought of anther bloody conflict made the grizzled veteran sick. "First Officer, did you send an information burst to command about the situation?"

"Yes, sir."

"Contact the solar probe. I want *Sundancer* locked onto the intruder's location and that information relayed as well."

"Are we going to fall back, sir?" Lieutenant Tas asked. "I mean—we are heavily outnumbered. Shouldn't we go for help?"

The bustle of the bridge suddenly ceased and, except for the faint humming of the air vent, you could have heard a pin drop.

"We have no idea if our visitors are hostile," Captain Ure said. "If they are unfriendly, we are the only ship between them and three, heavily populated system outposts. We will do our duty and make them pay dearly for every centimeter of Azurean space until reinforcements arrive. Lieutenant Tas, if you ever dare ask me again if my ship—an *Azurean fighting ship*—will back down and run from the enemy, I will kill you where you stand. Do you understand me?"

"Yes, sir," the red-faced officer said.

"Get to your post, Tas," Hass said. "We will have words later."

The lieutenant looked about the bridge and received several bitter glances.

"Sir, we have images from *Sundancer*," Hass said.

"Would you look at that," Captain Ure said. "Why, it's beautiful."

The bridge crew looked at the magnified images of the alien ship. The vast, delicate-looking creation seemed as if it were created from multicolored shards of gleaming crystal. No sign of any type of propulsion could be discerned, but it moved quickly and unerringly toward the sun.

"What about its escorts?"

"Conventional ships, Captain," Hass said. "Each is approximately twice our size and speed wise may be a little slower. Their propulsion is old-style fusion drives."

"Any response to our hail?"

"Yes, the translators are processing it now," Hass said. "That was fast. Translation ready, Captain."

Ure placed a device into his ear and moments later groaned.

"Stand down unclean alien vessel. The Most High God

Opia, has judged you and ordered your death. Do not interfere as Her righteous judgment is carried out. You still have time to repent of your crimes before death claims you. Beg her forgiveness and your race may yet serve Her in the afterlife. If not, you will be confined to the lowest pits of hell. Praise Opia's Holy Name."

ぐうぐう

"Battle stations," Ure ordered. "We have to stop that glass ship before it is too late."

The Rising Sun set an intercept course for *the Chariot of Opia.* Her three, ion cracking engines sent the sleek vessel hurtling toward the enemy. The five Mogul ships took up a defensive position and, as one, fired several missiles.

The Rising Sun's defense lasers cut the slow moving missiles apart before responding with cannon fire. The three-meter-long carbon tungsten rods, traveling at over one hundred kilometers a second, shattered the lead Mogul ship.

Her four sister ships launched a cloud of missiles and cannon fire at *The Rising Sun.*

"Captain," Hass said. "We can't get them all."

Captain Ure, took a deep breath. "Ignore them. Calculate firing solution on that big ship and do it fast."

Seconds later, the captain received a nod from his fire control officer.

"Fire everything we have," Captain Ure said softly as he gave his last command.

The last cannon round barely left the barrel as the deadly Mogul projectiles slammed into *the Rising Sun.*

Just as *The Rising Sun* was enveloped in a massive atomic explosion, *The Chariot of Opia* performed a drastic, evasive maneuver. Of the twenty-three projectiles, only one reached her mark. Tearing through the lower deck of the *Chariot of Opia,* the high velocity round did extensive damage to her shuttle bay, but failed to breach any vital systems.

Venting gas and trailing a glittery mist of shattered crystal, the ship listed to starboard, but did not stop. Her escorts shot down the three, slower moving Azurean flashers.

"Release the weapon," Rondall said.

"Thank you Rondall," Acturus said. "Thank you for allowing me to accomplish my purpose."

The Chariot of Opia released Acturus. The bulky cylindrical object fired her hypervelocity engines and streaked toward the Azurean star. Within seconds, Acturus disappeared into the corona.

Her mission accomplished, *The Chariot of Opia,* with its remaining escorting ships, opened a wormhole and slipped out of harm's way as the star's corona collapsed.

"Oh, shit," muttered *Sundancer* as it recorded the impossible effects of the alien weapon upon the star and relayed the information back to Fleet Headquarters.

"Looks like this is going to be a very short mission."

CHAPTER 21

Jabal, my friend, you don't know how happy this makes me," Cerin said. "There may be hope for you yet."

Jabal sat hunched over his desk, his head buried in his hands. "I'm glad," he said. "I feel like I am about to have a coronary."

"That's because you are a decent kenan, but don't worry, before long you will be just like me."

"Oh God, I am going to hell."

"You are doing the right thing."

"I am betraying my service oath, my marriage vows, and I am about to steal a naval vessel. God, I feel sick."

"Let me set you straight, Captain Shann," Cerin said. "Your wife forfeited any right to your loyalty when she willfully, spitefully foked your old buddy Darris. Your father War Admiral Shann decommissioned this ship, not to mention gave you his word that if your doohickey worked it was all yours, right?"

"Yes."

"Does it work?"

"Yes," Jabal said. "Haven't hit the big distances yet, but it works. So, this means I am in the clear?"

"The military will fry your ass if they even catch wind of what you are thinking, Jabal."

"Great."

"However, it is the right thing to do."

"I am glad one of us thinks so."

"Have you got the plan down?" Cerin asked.

"Yes, but why go to all the trouble?"

"To cover your ass if you ever decide to go home."

"I am not a very good actor," Jabal said.

"You don't have to be. Once you are able to leap clear of the system, while you are on a regularly scheduled vid call, the ship will have an 'accident.' A few flashing red lights and alarms and the signal will be lost. Toss out the tactical flasher that your father gave you, to make a nice bright flash that the sensors back on Azurea will pick up. For all parties involved, you will have perished in an explosion caused by the rip drive. Years later, if you want to go back home, say that the drive malfunctioned and got you stranded in a system far, far, away. This plan is foolproof."

"That is until they find me and execute me for treason."

"Keep pouting and I will turn you in myself."

Jabal snorted.

"How is Sakuna taking being your partner in crime?"

"At first she was depressed," Jabal said, "but she is coming around."

"I heard the sounds of her 'depression' coming from your cabin, from the mess hall, from navigation, and from the Bridge," Cerin said. "She sure likes to call on God...*loudly* when she is depressed. I am glad you were there to pull her through."

Blushing furiously, Jabal wanted to smash his fist into Cerin's jaw, but since Cerin didn't have one, Jabal laughed instead. "Got anything, Agoa?"

"Negative, Captain. The connection is still only reading thirty percent."

"Must be a defective relay cable," he said. "Have another brought up from storage. At this rate, I'll be an old man before I get a chance to become a criminal."

"Captain Shann," Agoa said. "We are receiving a priority one communiqué from the Azurean ruling council."

"Probably impatient that my little project isn't already ripping into the next solar system. Okay, Agoa patch it through." Jabal leaned back while the wall display shimmered and came to life.

The screen before him showed the strained face of his Father. "Father—"

"Jabal, listen to me carefully," Admiral Shann said. "Get that drive fixed and get back to Azurea as fast as you can. Maybe you can save a remnant before all is lost."

"What are you talking about?" Jabal asked. "Before what is lost?"

"Approximately two hours ago, unknown hostiles did something to our sun—the tech guys say it is impossible, but the sun went super nova."

"Oh my God," Jabal said. "We are on the far side of Srune. We did not know. Agoa, take us into polar orbit."

"You are our only hope that some of our people can survive. The blast is traveling faster than expected and will reach us in around seven hours."

Jabal's mind was racing, but it all came back to the same conclusion—the drive could never be put back together in time.

"Captain Shann," Agoa said. "I confirm the news." The wall-sized screen showed the horrible, expanding blast wave.

"I—I can't help you," he mumbled. "It will take most of a week to reassemble the drive and even then, there isn't any way of knowing if it will work."

"Then we are done," Teller said with an eerie calm. "Son, I am transferring to *The Blossoming Flower* the entirety of our knowledge base. You must do everything you can to survive. Your survival means the survival of our culture, our way of life."

"Father—I—"

"I am dropping the encryption on our transmission so that our people can be remembered as death comes to claim us."

"Please, I need to speak to Barea. And see if you can get Sakuna's father."

"They are here, son," Teller said softly.

"Agoa, get Sakuna—get her now."

കൃകൃ

The wall sized image changed into the face of Jabal's wife.

She wasn't crying, in fact, she seemed devoid of emotion altogether.

"Barea, I—I—" Jabal stammered.

"I know, you love me," she said. "Don't talk, just listen. I have but a short time, and I won't waste it on lies, Jabal Shann. I once loved you as well, but that was years ago. That was the real reason I didn't want to go with you on that damn ship. It wasn't anything to do with my duties. The thought of being trapped with you made my skin crawl. Did that decision bite me in the ass, or what?"

"Why didn't you say something?"

"We were well past talking. I not only wanted to leave you, but I wanted to make you pay dearly for neglecting me. I foked that imbecile Darris because I wanted to crush you before I left. I wanted to humiliate you."

"It worked," he said dryly.

"I guess those foking alien bastards did me a favor. I am glad it is over. At least I am free of you and your foking, blood-sucking family."

"Why the charade? I was willing to give you a divorce, for God's sake."

"Your precious father knew about my little tryst, had Darris murdered, and then set me up to take the blame if I didn't bow down and be the perfect wife for you. A divorce meant I was dead. I guess, in a twisted, psychotic way, he does love you."

Barea stood.

"Where are you going?" Jabal asked.

"I don't want to waste what time I have left making small talk with you. I am going to get very stoned and fok every sailor I can before I am blown to hell."

Barea leaned in close to the camera, her beautiful face filling the screen. Jabal noticed her red-rimmed eyes were hard and cold as ice.

"I know I am a disappointment as a wife, but so were you as a husband. Nevertheless, I truly hope that you and that foking seena Sakuna have a good life."

"I will never forget you," Jabal whispered.

"That's for damn sure," Berea said as she turned and walked off.

ℰↄℰↄ

Sakuna was on the observation deck when Agoa informed her of the terrible news.

"Sakuna, darling, I was always proud of you," Lanea Izusa said. "I know you will do great things in your life."

"This can't be happening," she said.

"We all die," Lanea said with a slight smile. He looked tired, but even in the face of death, he still had the strong, calm presence that Sakuna had drawn strength from growing up. "In a way, this is a good thing. I am glad that I could say a proper goodbye."

"I love you," she said as tears flowed.

"I like that Captain Shann. He seems like a good kenan."

"I do too," she said, wiping her tears. "Yes, he is the best."

"Have a good life, my daughter, we will meet again," Lanea said as the screen went black.

ℰↄℰↄ

The Blossoming Flower's massive antenna array carefully aligned itself as the incredible amount of data flowed into her archives. She was witness to the last will and testament of the entire Azurean Nation. The stream continued unabated for the next seven, heart-wrenching hours. In all, she collected ten yottabytes of information that comprised the entire sum of Azurean knowledge.

ℰↄℰↄ

"I love you, Dad," Jabal whispered.

"Son, have you successfully received and downloaded our transmission?"

Jabal could only nod his head. "Who did this?"

"We don't know," Teller said, still with eerie calm. "Chancellor Jabal Shann, I hereby give you one last order. Find out those responsible for our race's murder and make the bastards pay."

Jabal stood and gave his Father a crisp salute. "Yes, *sir*. It will be my honor."

The image of his father dissolved into static.

"Chancellor, the blast has reached Azurea," Agoa said. "Our civilization is no more. You and Sakuna are the last of our race."

Agoa's statement of fact cut him to his very soul.

"Agoa, let's get this ship the hell out of here," Cerin said. "Jabal, I have worked out the optimal course and speed. You and Sakuna get to the G-Pods. I'll take care of this."

"Chancellor Shann," Agoa said. "We cannot out run the blast. This maneuver will only delay the inevitable."

"It will give me time to get the rip drive on line," Jabal said. "With a little luck, we will escape."

Sakuna angrily wiped away her tears. Jabal gathered her in his arms. "I am sorry about your father," he whispered. "He seemed like a good kenan."

"That's exactly what he said about you."

"I promise you, Sakuna, that I will always be here for you. You will never be alone."

"And I for you. I will always have your back."

"I now pronounce you husband and wife," Cerin said. "May God have mercy on your souls."

Jabal chuckled while Sakuna gave the spirit a rude gesture.

"Hey, look on the bright side, guys," Cerin said. "I am proof positive that death isn't final. My situation sucks, but I am still alive. Now, move your asses so we can get the ship out of here."

"What are you talking about?" Sakuna asked as she held on to Jabal. "What are G-Pods?"

"You may be one hell of a law enforcer, but you don't know shit about g-forces," Cerin said.

"Cerin, my friend, the ship is in your hands," Jabal said. "But if you break it, you bought it."

"What are we going to do?" Sakuna asked.

"We are going to live to fight another day."

ⲉⲟⲉⲟ

Jabal took Sakuna by the hand and led her down a flight of steps to a vault like chamber that protected a series of one hundred and fifty null-glass tubes. The two nearest tubes, rotated opened.

"Strip," he said as he removed his tunic and hung it on a plastic hook. Sakuna removed her own clothes and hung them next to his.

"If you are trying to cheer me up, it's working," she said with a slight smile.

Jabal rolled his eyes and gently backed her into an open tube. "I am sorry for what is about to happen, Sakuna."

Jabal backed away as the tube rotated closed.

"Sorry for what?" she asked. "What's going to happen?"

Without warning, a clear liquid flooded her chamber.

"Jabal!" she screamed as the bath-warm liquid rose past her waist. Panicked, Sakuna screamed and beat upon the chamber as the liquid rose above her head. She held her breath, but inevitably her lungs gave out and she gulped in the liquid. Jabal entered his own tube as Sakuna drowned.

After the extreme trauma of liquid replacing the air in her lungs, Sakuna found that she wasn't dead. In fact, she was amazed to find that she was actually breathing the strange liquid. Soon, the liquid replaced all the air in her system and now she was protected from the violent g-forces that the ship was about to endure.

She cringed as Jabal drowned beside her. She put a hand on the side of the chamber and he matched it with his own.

"How sweet," Cerin said.

"You have no soul," Agoa retorted.

"Perhaps, but I was right that something big was about to happen."

"Lucky guess."

Cerin chuckled. "Agoa, my love, emergency flank speed, course, Zero…Zero…Zero. Engage."

 භගඥ

Her engine running at twenty percent beyond full power, *The Blossoming Flower* made five passes around the gas giant of Srune, building speed until she dropped suddenly into its gravity well. The sling shot maneuver tripled her velocity, sending the great craft hurtling away from the tremendous shockwave.

Well exceeding the expectations of her designers, the seventy-year-old warship shattered the current fleet speed record. Pushed beyond her structural ratings, the strain of the emergency acceleration made the great vessel groan and scream like a wet ship caught in a category-five hurricane.

Scrambling like a swarm of ants, the tireless, mechanized repair-bots identified and shored up buckling sections and reinforced weak spots, staying half-a-step away from catastrophic failure.

CHAPTER 22

Jabal, Sakuna, and Cerin stood by the rebuilt and newly configured Ripper Drive. Sakuna looked on nervously while Jabal and Cerin went over a final checklist.

Two weeks had past, since the destruction of Azurea and her system outposts. Working nearly non-stop, Jabal hammered out every detail, leaving nothing to chance. While the ship maintained full speed, it was losing the race with the deadly shock wave that bore steadily down upon them.

"Sir, we have forty-seven minutes, thirty two seconds, before the solar wave overtakes the ship," Agoa said.

"Just double checking all the connections," Jabal said. "I want to go over the circuit configuration one more time. We have one shot at this and it has to be perfect."

Agoa displayed page after page of the complicated diagram upon the view screen. After a few moments of study, Jabal gasped.

"What the hell is this? This isn't the configuration I approved. What is going on?"

"What's wrong?" Sakuna asked.

"Sir, I am at a loss," Agoa said. "I don't know what happened. I put in the diagram as you specified, but as you say, this isn't it."

"We don't have time to change it," Jabal said. "We're lost."

Sakuna took his hand. "You did your best."

"My best is going to get us all killed," he snapped.

"Have faith, my friend," Cerin said. "It was a billion to one shot that the other configuration was the right one anyway."

"I'm afraid that my faith has been stretched to the breaking point. Besides, I think that you just want the ship destroyed so you can move on."

"The odds were always in my favor that this would release me," Cerin said, "but look on the bright side, Jabal."

"What bright side?"

"You know for a fact that there is an afterlife."

"I'm not done with this life yet, thank you."

"You got that right, spook," Sakuna said.

"Far be it from me to be the spiritual one in the group," Cerin said. "However, don't you see the hand of a higher power at work here? Remember the Deverow?"

"I don't follow," Sakuna said.

"The Deverow refusing to let me leave this ship; your convenient kidnapping, Sakuna; Jabal here and his miracle drive; Jabal's father making him do your tests way out here in the boonies of the outer system?"

"Mere chance," Jabal said.

"You don't for one moment believe that, my friend," Cerin said. "We were meant to survive this disaster for some reason."

"The reconfigured drive?" Jabal asked.

"None of us touched the gizmo, now did we?"

"No," Jabal said.

"I say throw the switch," Cerin said.

"What if it doesn't work?" Sakuna asked.

Cerin chuckled. "I'll see you on the other side. First bottle is on me."

Jabal took a deep breath and swallowed hard.

"What shall we do, Chancellor Shann?" Agoa asked. "Is this really the end? I am...*afraid*."

"Afraid? I never saw that coming," Jabal said. "I guess we made our machines a little too well."

"Agoa is more than a machine," Cerin said. "She is my wife, after all. We are all the family we have left. Don't worry, Agoa. I am here with you, baby."

"We are too," Sakuna said as she took Jabal's hand.

"Thank you, both. That means more than you will ever

know. Sir, I know this may sound foolish, but is there an after-life for AIs?"

"One way to find out, darling," Jabal said. He drew Sakuna close and kissed her tenderly.

"Engage the drive."

CHAPTER 23

Rondall sat at his ornate desk in his personnel quarters. The Mogul leader was basking in the glow of his victory.

"Battle can be a heady drug, don't you think?" Yeti asked.

"It was exhilarating," Rondall said. "The Arcturus actually destroyed the star."

"Yes, it is a nasty weapon of ultimate mass destruction. The Vanuatu are vile, beyond belief to conceive such a dreadful weapon."

"But why did they have it located so near to their own sun?"

"Where better to hide a star-killer? No rational being would think to look for such a device so close to the Vanuatu's own star. It's sheer genius."

"Insanity would be the better word."

"Potato, pathato," Yeti said.

"What's a potato?"

"Never mind."

"The Arcturus is gone," Rondall said. "Give me the device that will finally rid us of Opia."

"The plans have already been uploaded to your computer," Yeti said. "They are encrypted as your wine list."

"Excellent."

"I estimate that you and your techs should be able to build the device within a few months to a year. The weapon is quite substantial. I suggest that, to keep Opia from getting wind of it, you will have to disguise its construction by incorporating it into one of your largest battle cruisers."

"Not an insurmountable problem," Rondall said. "How will I ever be able to thank you, my friend?"

"By giving me my freedom."

"As soon as Opia is deposed, you will be freed. You have my word."

"Forgive me if I don't hold your word in very high regard," Yeti said.

"You dare doubt me now?"

"I have seen you betray a legion of loyal Moguls over the years. Let's just say I am skeptical."

"My word is all you have, Yeti."

"Very well. This is the way we will finish our little game, old friend. Once the device is completed, you will send a crack team of your best Zealots to me."

"And where is that?"

"When the time is right, I will tell you where my prison is located and how to defeat most of the security precautions."

"Most?"

"The Vanuatu do not want me to leave and have installed their best security protocols. Fortunately, the most potent sentries have fallen silent through decay and years of neglect, however, even with my help, I am afraid that most of your Zealots won't survive my rescue."

"I can live with that," Rondall said.

"You have me transported to *The Chariot of Opia*. Only then I will give you the arming code."

"And then I take you home," Rondall said.

"And everyone, but Opia, will live happily ever after. The feast my people will host will be...*epic* to say the least."

"I cannot wait. Nevertheless, I need to draw back a bit and work from the shadows. If something goes wrong, she must never suspect me."

"My friend, this may sting a bit, but I expect you to do your part to the fullest of your ability. You will openly, fully execute the plan or you will hang."

"Too dangerous."

"You have no choice, Rondall. You see, I have sent our little scheme, in it's entirely, to a person who is loyal to me."

"What?"

"Did you think you were my only friend?" Yeti asked. "Drag your feet, or betray me, and Opia will skin you alive."

"This is outrageous!"

"I learned treachery from the best," Yeti said.

Rondall tried to calm himself.

"Like I said. Fulfill your agreement and we both will have what we want."

Rondall grumbled.

"I must go, I feel fatigued," Yeti said.

"Good," Rondall said. His thoughts were interrupted by a knock on his door.

He glanced at a video monitor to his right to see the identity of his visitor. He touched a button and the door swung open.

His head bowed low, Morton Tyreel entered the chamber that few ever had the privilege to see.

"You wanted to see me, my lord?"

"Yes. Did you ever solve the murder of poor Magda?"

"Yes, in fact, the perpetrator of this heinous crime is being arrested as we speak. Imagine, murdering one of Opia's very own attendants—just shocking. I hear that he will probably commit suicide before the night is over."

"Excellent," Rondall said. "Morton I have another situation that requires your particular skills."

"Give the word, my lord, and it will be done."

Rondall smiled. He knew that the zealot's words were true, without the slightest hint of deception.

"It seems that a priest has turned on me and now threatens to betray his faith."

Rondall heard the slight sound of strained leather as the zealot before him clenched a fist. It made him smile.

"What is the traitor's name?"

"That I don't know, but he has several, embarrassing documents stolen from me. Before he meets his maker, I want those items accounted for and returned to me—*unread.* Understand?"

"Yes, my lord," Tyreel said. "You will have your property returned and I will teach the good brother the error of his ways."

"Excellent, Brother Tyreel. Now, off with you. The sooner this debacle is concluded the better."

CHAPTER 24

W hat do you think, Anne?" Jen asked, holding the large hand mirror before her.

"No one does battered and bruised better than you, Jen," Anne said, carefully inspecting her appearance.

"I am touched," Jen said with a laugh. She placed the mirror in a drawer and snapped shut the lid on her huge, rolling makeup case. "Tony said to make the stuck up bitch look like she had been on a date with a drunk Mike Tyson."

"He is soooo sweet."

"If you will excuse me, the double fudge cheese cake brownies the caterer brought in are calling my name," Jen said.

"I hate you. I haven't had a brownie in five years."

"Then I will eat one for you, as well," said Jen, wearing a mischievous smile. "When I come back, I'll let you smell my breath."

"Bitch," Anne snorted, which made Jen chuckle wildly as she sauntered out the door.

Her short, dark hair carefully distressed and her painted on bruises done to perfection, scream queen Cali Bryce rose from the makeup artist's chair. Cali Bryce, the stage persona of actress Anne Miller, was dressed in a strategically torn T-shirt and jeans that sported just the proper amount of fake blood splatter and grime.

Since looks and trim figures were paramount in this superficial business, in lieu of the double fudge cheesecake calorie bomb she craved, Anne lit a cigarette. For an actress, lung cancer and working was preferable to dumpy and unemployed.

Finding an out of the way spot, she took a seat on the edge of a cheesy, plastic cobweb encased coffin, while she watched the crew set up the gruesome set that would be her last scene, in the straight to video, horror extravaganza, *Soul Mauler III.*

Made to look like the brutal torture chamber of a sadistic psychopath, in the middle of the chamber of death sat a massive wooden chair made of four-by-four-inch timber. Bolted to the concrete floor, reinforced with rusted iron, the chair came equipped with leather straps that made it look like a grisly, old-fashioned electric chair. It would be the grim stage where she would give her performance.

Despite her gruesome surroundings, Anne blew a stream of smoke and chuckled as she flipped a dangling plastic chain.

"God, talk about low budget," she mumbled. "If I had an ounce of integrity, I would walk out, but my rent is late and I am down to my last pack of cigarettes."

Enjoying the moment of peace, her mind drifted, as it invariably did, to *him.*

Had another dream last night, she thought. *God, am I going crazy? I wished I had never visited that palm reader in North Hollywood.*

The whole place looked like a hokey tourist trap, but I went in anyway. Madam Zelda had the worst Romanian accent I ever heard. She looked like a clone of Maria Ouspenskaya from The Wolf Man. I should have walked out, nevertheless she only charged five bucks to read my future. I didn't even have that to spare, but I kind of felt sorry for her.

Told me the usual fortuneteller spiel about going on a long journey and meeting my soul mate. Funny thing was she described him in detail, and he wasn't exactly George Clooney or Brad Pitt. He was only slightly taller than me with brown hair and brown eyes. Said he had a jagged disfiguring scar across his face, which ruined an otherwise handsome face. She told me he was a good man and that he would die for me.

I knew it was ridiculous, but that very night the dreams began. He was there looking exactly how Madam Zelda described him. I freaked out. The next day I went back to find Madam Zelda and get some answers, but her shop was gone.

In its place was a taco stand, who not only never heard of Madam Zelda had been in that location for the last six years. Weird.

Maybe I need to get a therapist. Yeah, like I could afford a shrink. The dreams are so overpowering...so real, but I don't want them to stop.

I love going to bed so I can be with him. It is more than passing interest—I need them. I crave being with him worse than my stupid nicotine habit. What is wrong with me?

I am obsessed with a nameless man I have never met. I can name ten guys off the top of my head that are better looking, yet they are all show and no substance. Across my dream lover's face, he bears a hideous scar, but I don't care. He is kind and gentle and his eyes glow with an inner strength of character that draws me like a moth to a flame.

God help me, I loved him desperately. I don't care what rationality says, he has to be more than a figment of my imagination or some undiagnosed brain tumor. I don't know if this is God, fate, or whatever, but he is real and one day we will be together.

"Miss Bryce? Are you ready?"

Ripped from her thoughts, Anne took one last drag and dropped the cigarette to the concrete floor, crushing it out the out with the toe of her shoe.

"Yes, George," she said, putting on a happy face that she did not feel. "Just taking a smoke break, waiting on Mr. Wonderful to ruin my day."

Anne was a professional who was always on time, knew her lines, and gave her utmost best performance, all of which was lost on the director, Tony Lam Jr.

Fresh from film school, Tony Lam Jr. considered himself an artistic genius and everyone else stupid, inferior beings. His dad, Tony Senior really *was* a Hollywood genius who did know what the public wanted to see and whose last four pictures had raked in nearly half a billion dollars.

Late rent aside, this was the real reason she agreed to play in this ultra-low budget splatterfest. Anne knew that a first rate performance and a good word from Jr. might get her into a legitimate film. Still, it was a hard pill to swallow, putting up with Jr.'s inflated ego, but she was desperate to change her stars.

Anne walked over to the heavy wooden chair where the prop man, a tall, gangly nineteen-year-old named George waited.

"George, how many times have I told you, my real name is Anne? My friends call me Anne."

"Okay, Anne," he said. "It's been great working with you. I can't believe I get to work with the great Cali Bryce."

"Great? Are you kidding me?"

"You were in *Blood House* and *Nightmare Swamp*. Two of my all-time favorite slasher flicks. I am your biggest fan."

"That is sweet."

Anne appreciated George's affection for her work, but she was less than enthused at the direction her career had gone. She yearned to be a serious actress, but she was lost in a sea of budding actors all vying for a few good roles. To keep a roof over her head and food on the table, she played in a seemingly never-ending series of low budget horror movies under a silly stage name. While Anne gave them their money's worth, to her it wasn't anything she was proud of, it was merely survival.

George placed a soft cushion on the unyielding wooden seat.

"Sir, you are too kind," she said, settling into the chair.

"I re-worked the neck strap."

"Thanks. It almost rubbed me raw in rehearsal."

"The last thing I want is for you to get hurt."

"I know," she said with a smile. "You are a real sweetheart."

George blushed. "You know, Anne, this chair was made by my cousin Benny, in his basement. He also made the Soul Mauler's blade."

"I worry about your relations, George."

"Yeah, Benny's a handful, but real good with his hands and works cheap. He wanted me to ask you if he could have a cell video of you in his chair. Just a quick few seconds?"

"Sure," she said with a smile.

George took out his cell.

"Hi Benny," Anne said with a sweet smile. "Love your work. If I am ever kidnapped and tortured by a psycho, I will insist it in is this chair. Love yah." Anne blew a kiss at the camera and gave a small wave.

"Benny will freak when he sees this. Thanks, Anne. You have just made a fan for life."

"My pleasure."

"You got a fellah, Anne?" he asked slipping his cell into his pocket.

Anne looked up and smiled. "Yes."

"What does he think of you as a scream queen?" he said. "I mean, you are always getting murdered by some psycho or monster. It would bother me to see my girlfriend treated like that."

"It isn't real. I have been stabbed, axed, chained sawed, eaten by sharks, and impaled more times than you can shake a stick at."

"It looks real enough. I would be seriously pissed to see my girl tied to a chair by some crazy creep, movie or not."

"In my line of work, it is inevitable, sweetie. Not so much in a supernatural or monster movie, but for movie psychos, it is their shtick, I suppose. This is my fifth...no, *sixth* 'tied to something' scene. Trust me, it's no big deal."

"More like the shtick of pervy, douche bag directors, you ask me," George whispered.

Anne laughed and nodded in agreement. "It is a crazy way to make a living. Anyway, my fellah hasn't complained yet," she said with a smile. "Um, George, we can talk later. Tony will be more irate than usual if we aren't ready to shoot the scene when he shows up."

"Yeah, I don't want to get Mr. Wonderful started again."

George checked his bag of tricks, as he called it, and produced a bandana.

"If you don't mind, I brought my own," she said, fishing a large black cotton scarf from her pocket.

George gave her a puzzled glance.

"I learned my lesson the hard way on the set of *Chainsaws of the Damned*," she said. "The rag they stuck in my mouth tasted like the prop man had just used it to wipe a truck's dip stick."

"Yuck," George said.

"Yuck is right. Call me a silly diva, but if I have to chew on a silly scarf, I want to know it has been freshly laundered."

"Good point," George said as he bent down and began to buckle a wide strap around her ankles.

"I wanted this done an hour ago, you moron," Tony Lam cried into his cell, as he burst into the room. "Where is Anne?"

"Mr. Sunshine has arrived," she said, leaning back.

"George," Tony said as he walked up. In his hand, he carried the wicked looking iconic blade of "the Soul Mauler."

"What's up, boss?" Anne asked. "Planning on doing some whittling?"

"I want to change the scene, and holding the blade inspires me," Tony said.

The gleaming, foot-long knife blade jutted from a grip that doubled as a pair of spiked, brass knuckles. More than a prop, George's cousin Benny had taken extraordinarily pains in the construction of the weapon, originally created to be used in case of a zombie apocalypse.

"George, get lost. In fact, clear the room, I need to talk to Anne alone."

"Yes, sir," George said as he grabbed his duffle bag and fled the room with the four-man crew in tow.

"Change the scene?" she asked. "Are you kidding me? We rehearsed this a dozen times. You said it was pivotal to the story line."

"It still is," Tony said. "You are still used by the Soul Mauler as bait to draw your love interest, Johnny, into a final, climatic battle."

"What's wrong with the way we rehearsed it?"

"Too...vanilla. I want to spice it up. Give the audience something to really talk about."

"I am getting a bad feeling about this," she said, pursing her lips.

"Oh, you will love it," Tony said.

"Okay, what do you want to change?"

"Instead of the tired 'tied to the chair of death' routine that we did in the last two installments, imagine a standing spread eagle, in the middle of the room, your arms and legs held taut by big-ass creaking chains locked to your bloody wrists and ankles. It oozes drama."

"Not bad. How about another small amendment? Instead of the stereotypical terrified damsel, as shown in the previous two installments, I portray a defiant, bad assed heroine giving the baddie an earful. It would be groundbreaking, if you ask me."

"I didn't ask for your opinion, sweetheart," he said with a smirk. "The demographic we are aiming for don't much care for a defiant woman. I need terrified damsel not a smart-mouthed bitch."

Anne flushed, but visions of living in a cardboard box quelled her anger. "Great," she deadpanned. "Okay, boss, set the scene."

"All is pitch black," Tony said. "We hear the slight creak of chains amid your muffled sobs. The Mauler comes through the door and flips on the light. Camera focuses in on his disfigured face, where we see the insane light glinting in his eyes. He licks his lips in anticipation and then he draws his knife." For emphasis, Tony brandished the weapon. "Camera shot switches and there you are, Anne. Clad only in your underwear, stretched painfully tight, chained, and gagged. Raw terror radiating from your gorgeous eyes. Seeing your captor, you emote a loud moan and redouble your attempt to escape, but it is futile."

"Okay," she said. "Except for the underwear part, that is pretty good. In fact, as much as I hate to admit it, way better that what we rehearsed. Bravo, boss man."

"I'm not finished," he said.

"There's more?"

"The Soul Mauler taunts you, trying to wring as much terror and anguish as possible from his helpless victim. While you are mewling for your life, the Soul Mauler, using his knife, slowly cuts off your bra and panties exposing your smoking hot, body glistening with sweat. It's genius. This damn flick will go classic cult status in a matter of days after release."

"When pigs fly," she said. "You know damn well that I don't do nudity."

"A little exposed skin will make this movie a classic."

"Then show your boobs. I don't even allow shots of me in my underwear."

"I need this to happen," Tony said.

"Get used to disappointment. Years from now, I don't need some bozo passing around photos of me in my birthday suit at a PTA meeting."

"Anne, face the fact, you are a nobody. This is my movie and you will do what you are told, that is if you ever want to go places in this business, you hear me?"

"Excuse me?" she said as fire flashed in her eyes.

"Look," he said softly. "Play ball, Anne, and hell, I will make you a freaking star. This is just a means to an end."

"*You* make *me* a star?"

"I do good on this film and Daddy promised to produce my next one. To make it good enough for Daddy, I need you to cooperate."

"Really? All I have to do is show a little skin, and I will star in one of your daddy's big budget pictures?"

"Of course, showing your body isn't quite enough. I can get any two-bit bimbo to strip for a few extra bucks."

"You want more?"

"Look, quit playing dumb, Anne. I wanted you from the first time I saw you and from the way you look at me, you want me too, so let's quit beating around the bush."

"You have figured me out, Romeo," she said, displaying a coy smile.

"After we shoot the scene, we can hook up at my place to celebrate. Afterward, I will introduce you to Daddy. I showed him your headshots and he wants to meet you—badly. He has a thing for fishnet stockings and stiletto heels, by the way. Just be extra nice to him, and your career will take off like a rocket."

"Really?" she asked as she moved close, her voice dropping to a smoky whisper. "Hook up with you *and* your daddy? To save time, can't I do you both at the same time?"

"Damn," he said with a bright smile. "You *are* kinky. Daddy is going to love you."

"Share this with Daddy, you sicko," she whispered.

With a snarl, Anne gave Tony a savage knee to the crotch. The three-pound blade fell from his nerveless fingers and clattered loudly on the concrete floor. Yelping in pain, he doubled over. Anne followed through with a beautiful uppercut that left Tony flat on the ground moaning.

"I am not a whore or a prostitute. I am an actress."

"You will never—*ever* work again," he moaned. Already his left eye swelled and turned an ugly purple. "My daddy owns this town. I will get you blackballed. You will never work again, you hear me? You better get used to the question, 'would you like fries with that?'"

Anne knew that with his daddy's clout, Tony would make good on his promise and that instead of a shot at the big time, her dreams of genuine acting just crashed and burned around her. "You and your weirdo daddy can kiss my ass, you greasy twerp. I am tired of this crappy life anyway. Pay me what you owe me, I quit."

"Get out," he screamed. "I am not paying you one red cent."

Anne picked up the Soul Mauler knife and walked toward the fallen man. "Cash or flesh, dirt bag. I am getting paid one way or the other."

Eyes wide with terror Tony fumbled and tossed his wallet at Anne. With a smile, she stripped it of cash.

"Nice doing business with you, wimp. Give my regards to *Daddy*," she said and, taking the knife, marched across the room and ripped open the door. "Oh and by the way, thanks for the souvenir."

Anne slammed the door behind her.

Tony chuckled as his black eye faded and dissipated. George appeared, extended his hand and helped Tony to his feet.

"How was that?" SD asked as his disguise of Tony shimmered and reformed into that of a heavyset, older man with unruly silver hair.

"Have to admit," George said with a smile. "You are good at being a douche. I almost took a swing at you."

SD laughed. "Anne really is a great actress, much better than these dreadful movies deserve."

"Perhaps, but it is irrelevant," Molly said as George reformed into that of a small woman with silver hair and dancing blue eyes. "Anne has a much greater destiny than that of an actress."

"Agreed," he said, chomping down on a stogie.

"There are worse things," Molly said as she opened an ancient device that looked surprisingly similar to an elegant pocket watch and smiled. "Anne's path is now set. Time to go. We have thirty two minutes, ten seconds before the real film crew of *Soul Mauler III* shows up."

"You bet," SD said. "I just don't understand why we have to use Anne Miller? The others I can see, but Anne is a very illogical choice. The kid has a good heart, but she is impulsive, immature, and has a quick temper. She could do more harm than good. Just keeping her in line will be a monumental task."

"Ours is not to reason why, SD. We just use what we are given. After all these years, you should know that. They want Anne. We use Anne."

"I know. However, three blocks from here is June Morgen, a disciplined, ex-military, fitness instructor, who is tough as nails. She has been blindsided and lays drugged, at the mercy of the Ventura Killer. She has only one hour twenty-seven minutes to live. She is perfect for the rigors of the mission. Her disappearance will not affect the time stream. In my opinion a much better candidate than Anne Miller. I say we let Anne go her way and take June instead."

"No," Molly said. "Anne Miller, aka Cali Bryce, is the one. End of discussion."

ოოო

Anne ducked out of the backdoor of the old warehouse and

made a beeline for her car. *Oh, now you've done it. Way to go, Anne, you let that temper and big mouth ruin everything. You didn't have to screw the creep—you could have just walked out, but noooo you had to add assault and felony theft to this cluster. Oh God what am I going to do now? Looks like my acting gig is a bust. Well, it was just a lifelong dream that is now gone forever—no biggie. I guess I had to grow up sometime.*

Anne looked at the big unwieldy weapon. "I could give it back, ask forgiveness—oh hell no. They thought I was a brainless bimbo who they could use like a whore then drop like a bad habit. This will show them."

Anne pursed her lips. "Aw, who am I kidding? With his daddy's money, Tony could have a dozen knives made and not bat an eye. Probably already has an eager replacement for me too. One thing I can count on is how vindictive Tony can be. He is probably calling the cops right now. That is one TV show I don't have the desire to be a guest star. I need to be elsewhere—*fast*. Probably be a good thing to vacate LA. Never much liked this place. The people I knew are as shallow as a plate of soup. I need to go home. I need to find people who really love me and give myself time to think."

❧❧❧

Tap—tap—tap.

Brenda Mills slowly opened her eyes and looked around the darken bedroom.

Tap—tap—tap.

She glanced at her window and gasped. Throwing off her blanket, she sprang from the bed, rushed to the window, and threw open the curtains.

"Open the window, before I break my neck," Will Carlson said. Will was perched on a shaky, wooden rose trellis just below her windowsill.

"Will? What are you doing here?" she hissed. "Daddy will have a fit if he finds you."

"Let him. You're all I care about. Now why haven't you returned my calls, Brenda?"

Fighting back the tears, Brenda took a deep breath. "It's over between us, Will. You have to leave me alone."

"What did I do wrong? You owe me that at least."

"I—I just don't want to be with you anymore. I don't love you."

Her words hit him like a slap in the face.

"A week ago you told me you loved me more than life itself. Funny thing that was the day before I found out my fat trust fund was tapped dry by that bastard Owen."

"That's not it—"

"Isn't it? Two hours after I find out I am dirt poor, your sleazy dad, the Right Reverend Mills, shows up at my door and tells me to stay away from you. He even had a restraining order. What am I supposed to think?"

"Will, it's complicated," Brenda said. "Will, honey, just please go."

"I believe your money grubbing dad is behind this whole thing. I knew all along that, that greedy bastard wanted me to finance his new church."

"You are making this hard," she whined.

"I may not have any money, but I still love you, Brenda. I know that you love me too. Pack a bag. You're coming with me."

"Where are you going?"

"I am going to bury Betty's ashes. Once I have put her to rest, I can begin again. *We* can begin again."

"I am sorry about Betty. She was a fine lady who deserved better than what she received, but I am not going with you, Will."

"Why not?"

"I—just—can't," she said, placing her hands on the windowsill.

Will gasped at the enormous diamond ring gracing her third finger. "You're *engaged?*"

"Yes," she said. "To George Hayes."

"George Hays is fifteen years older than you. You always said he was a sleazy pig who, when he looked at you, made you feel dirty."

"I changed my mind."

"George's family owns a zinc mine and a slew of gas stations. They're loaded."

"Have you ever thought that I just got tired of you," she said. "Honestly, Will, I am sick of your hideous face and, without your money, I don't have to put up with it one second longer. I love George and I am going to be his wife and have his children. Unlike you, he knows how to treat a lady. Now go away and don't come back."

"You gold-digging bitch," he spat as his own tears began to flow. "You strung me along just for my money? You are just as bad as your damn father."

"Have a good life, Will. Now, get lost," Brenda said quietly as she closed the window and drew the curtains.

ℯ✑ℯ✑

Appearing out of the shadows like a ghost, SD approached the faded green 1974 AMC Hornet that Will had dubbed The Green Hornet. "Oh this will never do," he said, shaking his head. SD checked his pocket watch. "This antiquated bit of tech is completely worn out. It only has about one hundred miles left before it gives up the ghost permanently. Will has a carefully constructed destiny and an automotive breakdown could put the kybosh on our plan. This car needs a miracle. Oh wait, I have one in my pocket."

SD checked his jacket pocket and produced a clear vial. The exotic artificial entity within the container swelled and pulsed like living quicksilver. SD opened the gas cap and poured the contents down the tube. The empty container vanished from his hand.

Walking around to the driver side door, he leaned in through the open window and touched the radio that had been broken for the last five years. While outwardly it remained unchanged, the obsolete components within reformed.

"What are you doing?" Molly asked, appearing by his side.

"It's a long trip," SD said. "The radio would make the trip much more pleasant."

"You amaze me sometimes," she said. "You actually feel sorry for Will."

"The kid has had a rough life and his sweetie is about to drop a bomb on him. I can't help myself. It would be nice if we allowed Brenda to go with him. I would love to take the Right Reverend out of everyone's misery."

"Brenda Mills and the filth that spawned her have separate, important time lines. For her to go with Will on his journey would be catastrophic to the strategic success of 'The Plan.'"

"Just a thought."

"You're just trying to bump Anne Miller from the roster."

"She is trouble."

"She is the one. *Period.*"

SD snorted.

"Now quit trying to tamper with the plan," she said with a smile. "I am the brains of this outfit, mister."

"And I am the heart."

"Look, we screw the pooch on this, and 'They' will end us. We have a list of sanctioned Dead Ends to use, and while I personally agree with you on some points, we have to use only what they allow. Understand?"

"Yes, but I don't have to like it."

"Okay," Molly said. "Will can keep the radio."

"That's my girl," he said with a grin.

"I am not a girl."

❧❧

Feeling as if he were drowning, Will stalked back to The Green Hornet. With his fabulous trust fund gone, along with the girl of his dreams, it was all he had left. Packed in the hatch were all his meager worldly possessions carefully arranged to leave space for Brenda's things.

Will snorted. "So this is what rock bottom feels like. It sucks."

Will opened the driver's side door, which emitted a sharp metallic screech from worn out hinges. Slamming the door angrily, he fumbled with the ignition key.

"Please, GH, for once don't give me any trouble," he whispered as he turned the key. "I know you're a temperamental pain in the rump, but right now you're all I have."

The car, which usually chugged and sputtered, started smoothly. Will sat back, stunned at the whisper quite sound of the now purring engine. Glancing to his right, he caught the dim light of the radio dial.

"Wait a minute. This radio has been busted for years."

To his surprise, spinning the dial, he discovered that the radio worked perfectly.

"Well I'll be," he whispered. "Betty always said don't look a gift horse in the mouth. Appreciate what you been given and keep your trap shut. Maybe this is a sign that someone up there likes me. Perhaps Betty put in a good word for me in the main office."

Throwing the transmission into drive, he moved away from the curb and drove west, determined to never lay eyes on Brenda Mills or Bryson City again.

He wouldn't.

CHAPTER 25

"Come on, sexy, you can make it," Will said as he nervously glanced at the fuel gauge. "After all we have been through, you don't want me to take a stroll in this blast furnace, now do you?"

The gas needle of his '74 AMC Hornet lay buried past *E* for the past twenty-five miles, and the last place he wanted to run out of gas was the Mojave in summer. Will glanced at the poorly folded road map that lay fluttering on the passenger seat. According to it, it was fifteen miles to the nearest anything. He knew that he should have run out of gas five miles back, but he tried not to think of that.

As he waited for the dreaded sputter, cough, and death rattle, to his joy, he saw a small, wooden sign up ahead.

"Please be gas...please be gas...please be gas," he chanted. "Yes. Thank you, Jesus," he said as he scanned the block letter sign.

VISIT PICTURESQUE ANGEL WELLS TODAY! DINER AND GIFT EMPORIUM.

DIRT CHEAP PRICES! ONE OF A KIND MERCHANDISE!

LAST GASOLINE FOR 100,000 LIGHTYEARS.

FIVE HUNDRED YARDS ON THE RIGHT.

"Thank the good Lord for desert nerds," Will said as he spied the small structure and the simply gorgeous-looking gas pumps. He slowed down and pulled onto the cracked blacktop, stopping before the first of three covered gasoline pumps. Turning off his engine, he settled back in his seat.

"Thank you, Jesus," he breathed.

Reaching over his center console, he took a handful of coins from a cracked plastic cup and stuffed them into his pocket, before opening his door and sliding out.

Squinting against the brutal glare of the Mojave sun, Will unscrewed his blistering hot gas cap, slid in the gas nozzle, and pulled the trigger. He groaned as the bone-dry gas tank greedily sucked up the remainder of his meager funds.

Although now flat broke, he did not complain because this remote diner/gas station/tourist trap was a godsend.

"Old girl must have been running on the fumes from the fumes. Everybody told me that she would overheat, but she ran cool as a cucumber across this furnace. I guess they don't build them like they used to." Will took off his stained baseball cap and knocked the dust off before wiping his brow. "Must be well over a hundred. Not as humid as Tennessee, but dry heat or not, hot is still hot. Brenda hates the heat. That time we snuck off to the beach, I could barely pry her out of the air conditioned motel room. Not that, it was a bad thing."

He exhaled angrily. "Why can't I get that woman out of my mind?" he said, replacing the nozzle and tightening his gas cap. "Damn it. She was just using me. When she was done, just kicked me to the curb. I must be the sucker of the year. Here I am pining over her while she is all loved up to some other poor fool. I swear to God Almighty I'll never let anyone do that to me again."

Feeling a bit better, Will squinted at the grim sum registered on the gas pump.

"Well, I guess lunch is going to be a pack of cheese crackers—again."

Digging into his jeans and pulling out his painfully thin wallet, Will took a moment to take stock of Angel Wells and paused. There was something about the place that struck the young man as odd.

He looked around the desolate desert wasteland. The diner was the only sign of civilization, period. No town, no houses, not even a bus stop, just Angel Wells.

"According to the map, the nearest town is fifteen miles

away," he muttered. "Who would build a restaurant in the middle of nowhere? Especially out here, in this frying pan? I feel like I need fire insurance just walking around."

The small, single story adobe structure sat surrounded by an empty parking lot. Off to one side, stretched a faded, red and yellow striped awning, providing shade for three, over-sized white-painted picnic tables.

A young woman in a waitress uniform sat at the middle table, having a diet soda and a cigarette. She watched Will intently. The look on her pretty face was one of sheer disbelief. She was so engrossed that she inadvertently knocked over her soda. Not taking her eyes off Will, she wiped up the sticky soda with a paper towel.

What's the matter, sweetie? He thought as he turned red with embarrassment. *Never seen a complete loser before?*

Will shrugged off her thousand-yard stare and walked across the scorching parking lot.

Pushing through the glass door of the diner, he sighed at the welcome blast of air conditioning and the aroma of real, honest to goodness food.

From the outside, the diner seemed no bigger than a small convenience store, but the inside was enormous, easily six times bigger than the outside would suggest.

Will chuckled at what he supposed was an illusion. To his right, there was a restaurant, complete with tables and spacious booths. Along the back wall ran an old fashion, chrome trimmed counter complete with red padded metal stools. The décor reminded Will of a 'fifties diner.

To his left were several aisles of packaged snack food, along with glass cases brimming with cold drinks. Beyond that was the much ballyhooed gift shop that, from the prominently displayed sign, had rock bottom sale prices on Navaho love beads.

"Talk about an illusion," Will mumbled, as he made his way to the counter. "What is this place—the *Tardis*?"

Behind the counter sat an elderly man with a short neatly trimmed gray beard. He was intently reading a newspaper and chewing on an unlit cigar. His nametag read, *SD*.

SD folded his newspaper and laid it on the immaculately clean counter. Taking the stogie from his mouth, he said, "That'll be thirty-eight-fifty, young fellow."

Will emptied his wallet of paper money then, giving SD a sheepish grin, dug through his pockets for coins to make up the difference.

As the attendant raked in the pile of quarters, nickels, dimes, and pennies, Will looked down at the two dimes and nickel that remained in his hand.

So much for a pack of crackers, he thought.

It was then that his eye spied the headline of the old man's newspaper.

"Germany invades Poland?" Will asked. "I hate to give away the ending Mr. SD, but we won that war."

The man gave Will a gentle smile. "I'm behind on my reading," he said, popping the cigar back into his mouth.

Will smiled.

"Nice car, son. What model Hornet is that? 'Seventy-five?"

"'Seventy-four," Will said.

"Haven't seen one in years, where did you get it?"

Will laughed. "That's my inheritance."

SD gave Will a puzzled look.

"Mister, believe it or not, a year ago I had a nice fat trust fund and was engaged to the prettiest girl in town. Thanks to my double-dealing uncle, that old car is all I have left."

"What happened to the pretty girl?"

Will snorted.

"Seems I was a whole lot better looking with money, than without."

"Tough break, kid," SD said. "I know one day you will find a real nice girl who will make you forget all about Brenda."

"I hope you are right," Will said. "You have a good day, sir."

"See yah around, kid," SD said.

Will turned and took two steps before stopping dead in his tracks. He slowly turned around and faced SD. "How did you know her name was Brenda?"

An older woman in a spotless waitress uniform approached

Will. Her nametag read, *Molly.* "SD, I need you to help with lunch, so get moving," Molly said.

"Yes, *dear*," SD said as he folded his paper and disappeared thorough the swinging double doors behind the counter.

"Excuse me, son, would you like to try our lunch special?"

Will gave Molly a sad smile. "I would love to, but I got to be going."

"Have you ever been to Angel Wells before, son?"

"Uh, no."

"Well then, this is your lucky day," she said with a big smile. "First timers get their lunch on the house."

"Really? What's the catch?"

"Really," she said with a smile. "No catch. Anything you want. Now what will it be?"

"What is the lunch special?"

"Half pound steak burger, steak fries, and chocolate shake."

"Sounds great—you sure it's free?"

"Even the tip is included," she said with a wink.

"I'll have that," Will said, not believing his luck. "Restroom?"

"To the right of the kitchen, son."

Ecstatic that over the prospect of eating actual food, Will made his way to the huge, immaculate restroom to wash up.

Oh man, I love Angel Wells. He thought as he turned on the water facet and pumped a hand full of liquid soap. *I haven't had real food in two weeks.* After scrubbing his hands with the tenacity of a surgeon, he washed the grime of the Mohave from his face and neck.

☙☙☙

Things in the restaurant were slow so Anne Miller had slipped out to have a soda and a cigarette. It had been weeks since her escape from LA. Her acting career was gone and, with the possibility of a warrant for her arrest, she took the long way home. Acting was her entire life and, now that it was dust in the wind, she felt lost, like a ship without a rudder.

Her luck seemed to be in a downward spiral. The day after

her confrontation with Tony, her car broke down. Packing just her essentials in a duffle, she took off on foot. The money she took from Tony ran out quickly, not leaving her enough for bus fare back home. That left hitchhiking, which worked well until the rancher she hitched a ride with had stopped at Angel Wells for gas.

Anne stepped inside to buy a water and when she came out five minutes later, the driver was gone, leaving her stranded in Angel Wells. Fortunately, in the window was a sign: *Waitress Wanted.*

SD and Molly took her in and let her stay in an old Airstream parked out back until she got back on her feet.

She watched with interest as the dusty, old car slid next to gas pump number two. She had been here two weeks and only two cars had stopped.

The door opened and out stepped a living dream.

Oh my, God, it's him. He is real! What am I going to do?

Anne was caught completely by surprised. She never considered what to do when she met him.

Should I run up and jump into his arms? Bad idea. He may think I am a psycho. Should I introduce myself? Hi, I am Anne and you are my soul mate, let get hitched. Oh God, I am cracking up. Why is this so damn hard? Madam Zelda should had given me some instructions.

Completely absorbed, she knocked over her drink.

"Damn it," she muttered as she wiped up the mess, her eyes never leaving the stranger.

He walked by Anne while she was mentally struggling with what to do. The look on his face was one of irritation. He glanced at her then pushed through the front door.

"Way to go, you idiot," she said, stubbing out her cigarette. "Don't say a word, just stare at him like a moron. He probably thinks I am a metal case or something."

ᥱᢧᥱᢧ

In the kitchen, SD leaned over Will's sizzling hamburger patty. "All this needs is a little anti-Babel juice," he said.

Plucking a small, clear vial from the air, he poured its contents upon the steaming, succulent meat. The clear liquid absorbed into the patty, leaving no trace behind.

Smiling, he place the patty upon a soft, bakery bun and added fresh lettuce, tomato, and onion.

Molly prepared Will's chocolate milkshake. Like the cook, she added a special ingredient to the ice cream concoction. "This should give his DNA that little something special," she said.

"Don't forget Anne's salad and ice tea," SD said.

"Like I ever overlook anything," Molly snapped. "I have already dosed her food."

Anne burst through the side door. Her eyes with thick with emotion.

"Excellent timing, Anne, dear," Molly said, as she added a cherry to the heaping pile of whipped cream. "Would you please serve our very special customer?"

"I would love to, Molly," Anne said, nervously straightening her uniform. Her hands were shaking.

"Are you all right dear?" Molly asked.

"I am wonderful," Anne said. "Simply wonderful." She checked her makeup and hair in the mirror that hung over the big steel sink.

"He seems like such a nice boy," SD said. "If it wasn't for his scar, he would be quite handsome."

Anne smiled. "I don't know, I think the scar gives him character."

As Anne gathered the platter and shake, Molly gave SD a sly wink.

❧❦❧

Anne burst through the swinging doors with the steaming food, and Will thought at that moment it was the most beautiful sight he had ever seen.

"Here you go, sir," she said. "The Lunch Special."

"It looks great," he said.

"Can I get you anything else? Ketchup, mustard, steak sauce, tartar sauce?"

"Tartar sauce?"

Anne's face turned red. "Umm…the last customer swore by it."

"No, I'm good as gold," he said, absorbed in spectacle of real food.

Anne gave him a winning smile before she disappeared back into the kitchen.

While Will dug in to the heavenly meal, the swinging doors opened again a few minutes later.

This time Anne emerged with a salad and glass of ice tea. Will looked around the empty restaurant, puzzled at who the food was for. Walking around the counter, she stood beside the stool to Will's left.

"Care if I eat my lunch with you?" she asked.

"You want to eat with me?"

"Yes, I do. You have a problem with that?"

"No," he said.

Anne smiled.

"I'm Will, by the way. Will Carlson."

Will, she thought. *Nice to finally put a name to the face. I never would have thought you would be a southern boy.*

"Anne Miller. I love your accent. Where do you hail from, Mr. Carlson?"

"Tennessee."

"You sure are a long way from home."

"Yeah," he said. "I am on a mission."

"Please don't tell me you are a 'double-oh' spy."

"You caught me," he said. "Under my T-shirt and jeans is a tuxedo."

"Does your car turn into an Aston Martin?"

"If it does, I would pay real money to find the switch," he said with a laugh.

Anne nervously settled onto the stool next to Will.

"So what brings you to the middle of nowhere, Mr. Carlson?"

"To make a long, painfully boring story short, when I was a kid, my parents died and I went to live with my mom's sister,

Betty. Finest woman to ever draw breath. Anyway, she died a month ago."

"I'm sorry," Anne said.

"Thanks. For some strange reason, even though she never set foot in one, Betty loved the desert. Lord, she used to read everything she could on the subject and could talk about it for hours. So, a few weeks ago, I packed up her ashes and drove her out here for burial. I know she would have wanted it that way."

"I'm sorry for your loss. That is very kind of you to do this for her."

"Not really," he said, reaching for the salt. "She was the only mother I knew. I figured it was the least I could do."

So, Will Carlson, you are a good man, Anne thought, as she picked at her salad. *I knew you would be.*

"You raised around here. Anne?"

"No, I grew up in Indiana. I hitchhiked in a couple of weeks ago, not a penny to my name. Molly gave me a place to crash and a job so I could get back on my feet."

"SD and Molly seem like real good folks."

"They are. To be honest, I've never met any like them. Good as gold, but sometimes a bit odd."

"A bit psychic, if you ask me."

"You picked up on that too? Sometimes I think they know more about me than I do."

"Creepy."

"But in a good way."

❧❧❧

Will and Anne chatted happily until long after the delicious meal was consumed. It was the first time since his journey began that the memory of Brenda Mills was not the center of his attention.

Molly came through the swinging double doors.

"That was the best hamburger I ever had, thanks, Molly," Will said. "I really appreciate it."

"You're welcome," she said. "You looked like you could use it."

"Yes, I could, more than you know. Well, it has been real nice meeting you folks, but I had better be on my way."

Without a word, Anne rose from her seat and, collecting the dishes, disappeared into the back.

"Nice talking to you too, Anne," he said to the swinging doors. "Story of my life."

Will rose from his seat and nearly ran into SD.

"Where did you come from?"

"The way you were looking at Anne, a herd of Geserish could have thundered past and you wouldn't have noticed."

"She is a doll." Will suddenly frowned. "A herd of what?"

"Here, son," SD said handing Will a paper sack. "I know times can get tough out here, so I made you a survival kit."

"In other words," Molly said, "sandwiches and chips for the road."

"I don't know what to say."

"Just say thank you," SD said.

"Thank you," Will said, taking the surprisingly heavy bag.

"Let me give you some advice, son," SD said, putting his hand on Will's shoulder.

Will noticed that Molly gave the older man a murderous look.

"When you come to the intersection of red and yellow, the only way through is to go *down*."

"Huh?" Will asked. "Red and yellow what?"

"You will know when the time comes. Remember, *down*."

"Oh never mind that old senile fool," Molly said. "Sometimes he speaks out of turn."

"Uh…okay," Will said. "Thanks again for the food."

"The pleasure is all ours," Molly said.

ᑋᑋᑋ

With a spring in his step and a smile on his face, Will left the diner and walked back to his car. Opening the driver's side door, he placed the sack in the passenger floorboard.

"What the—" he said, looking at the huge styrofoam cooler taking up most of his back seat. Will pulled free a yellow sticky note stuck to the side.

A little something to get you through the hard times. Love, Molly and SD.

Inside the cooler was a mouthwatering variety of bread, cheeses, and lunchmeats along with packs of soda and water. There were even a few bags of candy.

"SD and Molly are real good folks," he said. "May the good Lord bless them."

Will smiled and slid into the driver's seat. Slipping the worn key into the ignition, he buckled his seatbelt.

"Will! Wait up!"

Will looked around and saw Anne running toward him.

"What did I do now?" he mumbled.

Anne came up to the open passenger side-window and leaned in. She wasn't wearing her uniform, instead she wore a yellow T-shirt and jeans. A worn, faded red duffle bag hung from her shoulder.

"Which way you headed?" she asked.

Will pointed west, down the lonely stretch of highway. "That way."

"Isn't that a coincidence? So am I. Care for some company?"

"You want a ride—with me?"

"Yes. With you."

"Sure, jump in," he said with a smile.

Stowing her bag next to the cooler, she climbed in and, together, they pulled away from the diner and out onto the desert highway.

Man, what difference a couple of hours can make, Will mused. *Maybe my loser status is changing.*

୧⁊୧⁊

SD produced his golden pocket watch. Popping open the lid, he glanced at the positive change in the time stream.

"It worked," he said. "Will and Anne are now free agents. Love it when a plan comes together."

"Will and Anne, if allowed to go on unchecked, you will not live to see the sunrise," Molly said as she watched them leave. "It is your fate to die here in this desolate place. Since you do not have a future, since your brief lives won't affect the outcome of the future path of this world, you are Dead Ends. I claim your new, redirected lives for the greater good of all. Mark the time of my claim, SD."

"Got it," he said, making an adjustment on his watch. "It's legal now."

❧❧❧

As Will and Anne disappeared over a small rise, its mission accomplished, Angel Wells disappeared.

CHAPTER 26

Thousands of light-years from the Sol system, high above a nameless blue green world, an emerging wormhole crackled with static electricity, sending brilliant bolts of lightning far out into space.

A Deverow named Fauling, an ancient being of immense power, who had been waiting millennia for the gate to form, poured energy into the rupture in space.

Overloaded by the raw energy directed against it, the wormhole collapsed. Carried along with the raw energy was a carrier wave that reprogrammed and redirected the exit point of the gateway.

Instead of forming over a primitive world, almost devoid of life, it instead opened twenty miles over the Earth. Particularly, it formed over the Mojave Desert.

☙❧☙

Anne could not believe that she was here with *him*.

Her journey had brought her to Angel Wells. Now, out of the blue, she found her dream man was real and she was with him. Anne knew it was bizarre and totally insane, but she was happy.

"Will, if you don't mind me asking, how did you get the...um, scar?"

Will glanced up at the rearview mirror and the scar that started at the bridge of his nose and ended at his left ear. "Oh, you mean my beauty mark? My uncle Owen, is the undisputed king of douche bags. Not only is he a thief, but a drunk, and a wife beater as well. Three or four years ago, he decided that Betty needed the crap kicked out of her. I stepped in and got a long neck bottle across the face. Fifty-three stitches later and I'm the handsome guy you see before you."

Will was surprised at her reaction. Tears welled in her eyes as she lightly touched his hand.

"I am so, sorry," she said. "That asshole needs a taste of his own medicine."

"Hey, don't cry, Anne, it's ancient history. Besides, that creep won't hurt anyone again. When the law got wind of his shady business dealings, the coward took the easy way out and killed himself. It was better than Christmas."

"You have had a lot of pain in your life, haven't you?"

"Maybe. I guess I could use that as an excuse to feel sorry for myself, but that isn't me. Anne, I am going to be better than the broke loser who left Bryson City. My future, like this highway, is wide open."

"Where is your future taking you?"

"Well, yah got me on that one. All I know is that it won't be anywhere near the Mojave. I miss trees, green grass, and temperatures under one-hundred and twenty. I am a pretty good finish carpenter. I figure I can always find work until I discover my calling."

"Sounds like you have a plan," she said.

"What about you? Where is the future taking Anne Miller?"

"Sort of up in the air as well. I found that the world is a lot stranger—and more wonderful than I could have ever imagined."

"Were you always a waitress?"

Anne laughed. "No, my professional aspirations were not that high. I am—*was*—an actress."

"Get out of town. Really?"

"Honest to God. I went to Hollywood expecting to be the next great star, but it didn't quite work out. Seems that my looks and talent are a dime a dozen in California."

"Bull. You're pretty as a picture. I'll bet you were great."

"You're sweet. While the big 'A' list movies escaped me, I did make the rent by becoming a scream queen."

"You've lost me. What's a scream queen?"

"I was in a gazillion low budget horror movies. I played the lead in three, very forgettable flicks, but for the most part, I was the poor hapless victim. It paid the bills—barely, but I was type cast, forever doomed to play low budget genre films. Driving a final stake through the heart of my career, I had a blow up with a sleazy director, but one with clout. Since I would never become a legitimate actress, I packed my bag and left."

"Play in any Westerns? I love me some cowboy flicks."

"Sort of. I played a saloon girl who gets turned into a vampire in *The Good, The Bad, and The Undead.*"

"For real?"

"Unfortunately, yes."

"Wait just a minute, I know you," Will said, as his eyes grew wide in surprise. "You were that girl in...um, yeah...you were in *Gator Zombies.*"

"Oh no," she groaned. "You actually paid money to see that?"

"My buddy Zack got it by mistake. While it was a really bad flick, you were fantastic—way better than the no-talent, blonde bimbo who played the lead. When that undead gator bit your head off, I wanted to call someone and complain."

Anne threw her head back and laughed.

"I can't believe I'm here with a real movie star. I want an autograph."

"An autograph? After seeing *Gator Zombies* I'm surprised you don't make me get out of the car."

"I didn't know anyone could scream like that," he said with a grin. "Was that special effects?"

"Special effects? My dear boy, that scream was my claim to fame. I had the best scream in Hollywood. I even got paid to do it for a haunted house movie soundtrack."

"They pay for that?"

"They sure do," she said.

"Can I hear it?" he asked, giving her a sly look.

"Mr. Carlson," she said with mock outrage. "I am not that kind of girl. I do not scream for just anyone, let alone a complete stranger I just met."

"Please? With sugar on top?"

"Okay," she said happily. "If you are going to twist my arm, but we are going to do this right. Now pretend you have a knife and stab me."

"Will this do?" he asked, holding up his empty fist clutching and imaginary blade. "It's all I had in the car."

"A bit large, but okay," she said with a wink. "I will never sell my cattle ranch to you. What are you going to do with that knife, Black Bart?"

Will gave a maniacal laugh.

Anne opened her mouth and emitted the most ear-piercing, blood-curdling scream Will had ever heard.

"Wow. That was beyond great. That movie did not do you justice, but I think you blew out my ear drum."

Anne laughed. "Will, you aren't the first eardrum and you won't be the last." She looked down and saw SD's survival kit. "What's in the bag?"

"Oh, SD gave it to me before I left. Said it was a survival kit. Molly said it was just some sandwiches and chips."

Anne picked up the large sack. "Kind of heavy, don't you think?"

"Yeah, that was what I thought too, but I didn't want to be rude and question it."

"Mind if I take a look?"

"Be my guest," he said with a smile.

Anne opened the bag and pulled out four, plastic sealed sandwiches. "What's this?" she asked pulling out a black, hard plastic case.

"Yah got me. Open it."

Anne opened the case and gasped.

"What is it?"

Anne turned the case around.

"You have got to be kidding."

Inside the molded case lay a gun. While the massive revolver was of an obsolete style, its finish looked brand new, as if it had just been plucked off the manufacturer's assembly line. Etched into the top of the shiny black frame was *WEBLY FOSBERRY .455 INFINITY*

"I know a fair amount about guns," he said, "and my absolute all-time favorite was one I saw in a museum once. It was a Webly-Fosberry."

"A what?"

"This guy, George Fosbery came up with the idea to cross an automatic pistol with a revolver. It was an oddity and they made less than five thousand, but I never heard of a Webly-Fosbery *Infinity*. If this is legit, that antique would be worth a fortune. Why would SD give it to me?"

"There's a note," she said unfolding the yellow sheet of paper.

"Read it."

"'Will, there isn't much time. Do not ask questions, just tuck the gun inside your right side waistband near your wallet. Do it now. The Collector is almost here. Will Carlson you are not a bum or a loser. Take care of Anne, stand tall, and don't take guff from anyone. By the way, the Webly's name is Shirley. Take care of her and she will take care of you.

"'Love, SD and Molly.

"'PS, Two quick things: One: The surgeon's weakness is in his eye. Two: Take the green satchel from the golden ape and guard it with your life.'"

"What kind of people did you work for?" he asked.

Anne let out a small squeal as the note vanished from her hand.

"Oh crap," Will said.

They gave each other a long look.

Will raised his shirt, while Anne fumbled with the revolver.

"Oh crap, it just shocked me," she said.

Will leaned over the steering wheel as Anne pulled back his jeans and shoved the gun into his waistband.

There was a sharp snap that sounded like static electricity.

"It just shocked me too," he said. "Take the wheel."

With Anne driving from the passenger seat, Will adjusted *Shirley* to make it more secure and dropped his baggy shirt over it. The weapon surprised him by feeling soft and warm instead of like a hunk of hard, cold metal. For a moment, he thought that the gun snuggled against him.

⌀⌀

From out of the sky came a brilliant flash of light. An enormous craft, that looked like a mutated dragon fly, swooped toward the AMC Hornet. An acquisition probe used to sample the higher life forms on other worlds, it sent powerful sensor scans radiating for hundreds of kilometers recording and cataloging life on this new alien world. However, it did more than make recordings.

Its sophisticated sensors detecting both a male and female within the primitive vehicle made them a prize the acquisition probe's AI could not resist.

⌀⌀

"Will, what is that thing in the sky?"

"Got a feeling I don't want to know," he said. "Hang on!"

With a squeal of tires, the ancient car slid around on the empty stretch of road and roared away from the thing in the sky.

"Faster, Will, it's catching up!"

"Got it to the floor now. Put on your seatbelt and get your head down."

The nightmare in the sky was unlike any aircraft they had ever seen. Well over thirty meters in length, the serpentine, undulating metallic body streaked through the sky with a flight dexterity that would put a helicopter to shame.

Will left the road and tried to make it to the cover of a thick stand of Joshua trees. As the car bounced and skidded across the rough terrain, the weird machine stayed close, collecting valuable data on the surrounding terrain, as it waited for the opportunity to strike. Will and Anne's luck ran out as the AMC slid sideways into a shallow wash.

Anne screamed and Will swore as the thing landed on their vehicle. With the screech of metal, the machine clamped tightly to the car. Its multiple legs pinned the doors shut and covered the side windows, making escape impossible. Suddenly, they were airborne as the craft took to the air.

"Use the gun, Will!" Anne cried as the car tilted sharply to starboard. "Shoot it!"

"I can't," he said as the ground fell away rapidly. "I make this thing drop us, and we're dead."

They were already fifty meters off the ground and were quickly climbing. A fall to the desert floor was certain death.

"What are we going to do?" she screamed.

Before he could answer, a sharp, hollow spike about the thickness of a pencil, pierced the car's roof with a sharp shriek of tearing metal.

The gray metal pipe jutted a foot into the passenger compartment, exactly between Anne and Will. From the oversized hypodermic needle exploded a thick, foul smelling gas. Anne coughed and sputtered, as she took in a deep lung-full of gas. His eyes and lungs burning, Will grabbed a rag and tried to block the gas, but it was too late. The anesthesia had been administered and the tube was extracted.

As the wind whistled past them, Anne's eyes rolled back and she slumped against the passenger door.

Will felt his body grow weak and go numb. Soon blackness enveloped him as well.

そうそう

"Here they come," SD said as he tended the fire.

"I see them," Molly said.

SD and Molly stood by the blazing fire, only they didn't look like the friendly older couple Will had met at Angel Wells.

They now looked exactly like Anne Miller and Will Carlson. There was even a perfect representation of Will's AMC sitting beyond the small camp. While Will and Anne's lives on earth would not affect the future, their deaths would. With Anne and Will gone, it was up to SD and Molly to see to it that the proper flow of events was preserved.

A dirty, heavily modified, twenty-year-old Ford pickup rolled into the camp with a cloud of dust. The truck sported big, knobby off-road tires and a blinding bank of halogen lights mounted to a heavy chrome roll bar.

Without killing the blinding lights, two men exited. Both carried shotguns.

დოდო

Hours later, just before sunrise, Benny Comstock finished putting the last shovel full of earth on Anne Miller's grave. Tossing the shovel into the back of his truck, the grimy little man lit a cigarette.

"That bitch sure was pretty," Howard Comstock said as he buttoned up his filthy jeans over his prodigious belly.

"Good looking tramp, but she 'bout bit my finger off," Benny said. "Take the kid's car and hide it."

Benny tossed Howard the keys to the Hornet.

"Damn. This was fun, little brother," Howard said as he climbed into the AMC. "And out here, nobody's the wiser."

As the two Comstock boys drove off, SD and Molly rose from their graves.

"The Comstock brothers will be on death row in less than a year. Howard will die in a prison riot, while Benny will die by lethal injection. After that, both will suffer a fate beyond the imagination to comprehend."

"Good," SD said.

"If you like, we can visit them and make their stay in hell *memorable*."

"You forgot the camera," SD said.

"Have you ever known me to forget anything?" Molly said, holding up a cheap, disposable camera. Walking over to a Joshua tree, Molly placed the camera with precision of a diamond cutter.

SD pulled out his watch and opened the cover. "Thirty-three days, six hours from now, Jeremy Harris will find this while riding his dirt bike. It will be all the authorities need to fry the Comstock Brothers."

CHAPTER 27

Floating in a downy blackness, Will felt a glorious warmth surge through his mind, bringing him suddenly back to consciousness. He and Anne sat in the AMC. She was still asleep, slumped against the passenger side door. *What happened to the desert?* He wondered as he looked around.

The car sat in a huge, brightly lit, whitewashed concrete room. The room looked large enough to hold a dozen battleships, but as far as he could tell, the AMC was the only occupant. There was no sign of the dragonfly thing that had captured them.

Two incredible, multi-armed machines dropped through hatches in the ceiling and approached the car. Will fought the urge to grab the old gun and start shooting. Instead, he pretended to be unconscious. Peering through slits in his closed eyelids, he watched as they neared the car. Will decided it was best to play possum until he knew what was going on.

The machines split up, with one opening Will's door while the other took care of Anne. All the while they spoke in a constant, yet unintelligible, high-pitched stream. Soon, a rolling table the size of a queen-sized bed appeared through another secret door.

Will felt himself pulled gently, yet firmly, from the compartment by multitudes of soft tipped grippers. He and Anne were placed side by side on the hard metal table where they were searched. He lost his wallet, watch, and a few coins while Anne lost a necklace and two rings.

At last, with the search completed, they were loosely strapped down.

Will could feel the comforting presence of revolver on his side and could not fathom why the seemingly meticulous machines had over looked the bulky weapon, but he wasn't complaining.

He almost panicked when clear, plastic masks were fitted over their faces. Will could smell the strong odor of the knock out gas, but for some strange reason, it did not affect him. It was as if he had built an immunity to the anesthesia.

Will and Anne were wheeled through Opia's vast acquisitions complex. It was the place where life in the galaxy was indexed, cataloged, and then disposed of. It fed her everexpanding biological knowledge database.

Will was amazed at the weird creatures and the strange machines that teemed within the place.

Where in the world are we? Must be some secret alien base in the desert.

After traversing a maze of corridors, the machines took the couple to a small room with walls containing scores of deadly looking medical tools. The room smelled like a slaughterhouse—full of rot and decay from the countless beings murdered there. Once wheeled in, Will and Anne were left in the care of a tall, thin machine with a single large round eye. The first two machines left and mechanized doctor began attaching probes to various parts of his subjects' bodies.

The earth couple were then scanned by an advanced, handheld MRI unit. The scan revealed the slightest details about their physical makeup, but due to the exotic metal used in its construction, the meticulous scan could not detect the revolver.

The machine spoke rapidly into a tiny recording device. At first, the words were gibberish to Will, but slowly the words became *English*.

Even in English, most of the medical terms were over Will's head, that is, until the word *dissection* came up.

The machine produced a wicked looking scalpel and moved toward Anne's face.

'*Will, what did SD say?*' asked a soft voice in his head. '*Take no guff from anyone. The surgeon's weakness is in his eye. Don't just lay there, Will, do something.*'

Ripping the mask from his face, Will caught the cold metal arm with his left hand. With his right hand, he pulled the revolver free and shot the machine in its single eye.

The projectile shattered the transparent material and exploded within the artificial brain, sending chunks of plastic and metal across the gruesome room. As the machine collapsed, Will grabbed the knife from its dead hand and cut himself free.

Amid blaring alarms, Will freed Anne. Tossing the unconscious woman over his shoulder, he ran from the hellish room.

෴

Morton Tyreel watched as the body of his victim was crushed in the massive press. Satisfied his holy mission was accomplished, he paused long enough to scribble a hasty suicide note.

It didn't take long to figure out who would be working against his own people, Tyreel thought. *Wilton Ames was always weak natured, the perfect candidate to use against his own people. The old traitor gave me more of a fight than I expected, but in the end, he was more than happy to give up the things he had stolen.*

Tyreel checked the contents of the bag to make sure he hadn't left anything behind. Looking up at the deactivated security cameras, he checked his timepiece and smiled. He had plenty of time to escape before the suicide was discovered.

Leaving the room, Tyreel locked the door and took two steps before the sound of alarms began to blare.

Thinking his crime had been discovered, he bolted down an adjacent hallway toward the Acquisitions Section, hoping to lose his imagined pursuers.

෴

Will flew down a long empty hallway with Anne slung

over his left shoulder. His right hand was clenched tightly around the revolver.

"Oh, man, I'm in deep trouble now," he said as a burst of adrenaline gave his feet wings. "I've got to get the army to nuke this place to hell. First things first, I have to get Anne to safety."

In his headlong flight, Will noticed that the walls of the corridor were deep red. The corridor ran into a hallway whose walls were bright yellow. At the intersection of red and yellow, lay an oval, metal grate.

"It's what SD said back at the restaurant," he mumbled. "At the intersection of red and yellow, the only way through is down."

Will laid the moaning Anne on the floor then wrenched up the heavy grill. Sliding the grill aside, he looked down into the inky blackness and paused. The sound of running feet caused him to look back the way he came.

Running toward him at full tilt was a nightmare. The thing didn't seem to be a machine, but a living breathing being that, to Will, looked like some kind of massive ape. The creature stood over eight feet tall and was covered in ornate, golden armor. The ape creature brought up a wicked looking weapon and fired at Will.

With screaming bullets hitting the wall around him, Will stood and, in one smooth, fluid motion, brought Shirley up and fired one round. The buck and roar of the mighty revolver thundered in the passageway. Emitting a terrifying cry, the armored ape's head flew back and it collapsed, sliding to within inches of Will.

The hair stood up on the back of his neck as the words from SD and Molly's note flashed through his mind.

'Take the green satchel from the golden ape and guard it with your life.'

Around the creature's back was an emerald green leather bag, not very different from a thick, oversized messenger bag.

"I'm not believing this," Will muttered.

He wasted no time in slinging the oversized bag over his shoulder. Taking Anne, he eased her into the hole in the floor.

To his relief, the tunnel beneath the floor lay only four feet below. He followed her down then slid the grate back into place. As he secured the grill, he looked into the sightless, milky-gray eyes of the thing he had killed.

"Oh, Lord Almighty, what have I gotten myself into?" he whispered.

CHAPTER 28

W hat is the meaning of this?" High Priest Rondall asked into the video monitor.

"My lord, we have had an alien specimen escape from acquisitions," Captain of Security, Dome Cree said.

"That is impossible," Rondall said. "Our precautions are air tight."

"Be that as it may," Cree said. "A dissector was destroyed and one of my soldiers killed."

"All animal subjects are anesthetized—the gas is foolproof."

"That is what I thought as well. The animal, in addition to being immune to the gas, also possessed a weapon. A weapon that the scans failed to reveal."

"What kind of weapon?"

"It was more than a club or knife, if that is what you are thinking. It apparently, from the wound, fired some kind of projectile, probably by expanding gas or magnetic rail. However, we can't find a trace of the projectile."

"How could your scans fail to pick up such a sophisticated weapon, which fires untraceable bullets, Captain?"

"Unknown at this time, my lord," Cree said calmly. "All I do know, my lord, is that the weapon made short work of a dissector and the soldier. A dissector is a robust, tough machine, but I found its head scattered all over the examination room, as if it had been made from paper. My solider did not fare any better. The weapon pierced his impenetrable chest plate and came out his back making a hole I could put my fist through."

"Don't be vulgar, Cree," Rondall said, wrinkling his nose. "I get the point. A Mogul is dead." He took a deep breath. "But how does any of this mess concern me? I have more important things to do, to be bothered with animal control."

"I believe you are familiar with the murdered Mogul. His name was Morton Tyreel. He was one of your Zealots."

"Captain, Brother Tyreel was on a mission for me. He possessed a sealed courier bag. I want you to bring me that bag at once."

"Sir, I just came from the body. Brother Tyreel didn't have the bag you described."

The room suddenly began to spin for the Great High Priest of Opia as he fought the urge to panic. "Cree, where is the murderous animal now?"

"Unknown. It is as if he and the female disappeared into thin air. For some inexplicable reason, all the security cams went off line just prior to his escape."

"Is that all?"

"No, my lord. The body of a low-level priest was also found. His name was Wilton Ames. We found what was left of him in a hydraulic press. The body was a mess beyond recognition, but he had left a note behind confessing a multitude of sins against Opia."

"He committed *suicide*?"

"That is what someone wants us to believe. His lab was trashed and my men found blood splattered in several places."

"Cree, I am confident it was a suicide. I have had several reports of Brother Ames's erratic behavior."

"But my lord—"

Rondall roared and smashed an expensive goblet against a wall. "Look here, you fool," spat the high priest. "We stand at a cross road in history. The last thing we need, with a dangerous animal on the loose, is to go off on a tangent looking for phantom murderers. Opia may lose confidence in our abilities. I know that I am losing confidence in yours."

"Forgive me, my lord."

Rondall thought a moment. "Cree, listen to me carefully. Brother Ames deserves better that to have his memory tainted by a cowardly suicide. Destroy the suicide note and add his death to the escaped animal's list of crimes."

"My lord, this is most irregular."

"You do know to whom you speak?" Rondall asked. "Would you like *your* death attributed to the animal?"

"No, my lord. We will apprehend the animal responsible and get your case back. You can count on me."

"Thank you, Captain. I never doubted that for a moment. However, if you fail me, another will have your duties while your mate and children morn for you. You have two days."

Rondall switched off the viewer and tried to control his white-hot rage. Rising from his desk, he poured himself another goblet and tried to calm his frazzled nerves. *We are so close to having everything,* he thought as he drained the cup. *If the contents of that case are revealed, we are lost. If Opia learns the truth, she will, no doubt, purge the Mogul race from existence. I should have had his evidence destroyed along with Ames. I am such a fool.*

Rondall chose an amber-colored decanter and poured himself a stronger drink. Sipping the liquor, he stared out his huge window at the city of Romaa.

"What is the matter, my friend, you seem out of sorts?" Yeti asked.

"We have had a pair of dangerous animals escape."

"Excellent. I hope they are never caught."

"That isn't funny, Yeti."

"I was considered an animal when I was brought here."

"Was?"

"Just because a species isn't Vanuatu or Mogul doesn't make it a subpar animal."

"That is one opinion," Rondall said. "It just doesn't happen to be mine."

"You are an arrogant buffoon."

"If I knew what a "buffoon" was, I suppose I would get angry, but it is wonderful to see you lose your insufferable calm demeanor."

"You are impossible."

"Thank you," Rondall said as he brought the cup to his lips.
"It is good you are here. Maybe you can help us track down
the animals."

"Never."

"Two of my Zealots are dead. I would consider it a favor."

"My condolences on the deaths of your bloody assassins."

"Brothers Ames and Tyreel were faithful servants. Their
murders will be avenged."

"Did you say Brothers Ames?"

"Why, yes. Did you know him?"

"No. I have to go."

Rondall smiled and drained his cup.

CHAPTER 29

Crouching beneath the low ceiling, Will held Anne's hand as they sloughed through the stench of the sewage system. For hours, they had made their way through the smelly maze, trying to find a way out. They had encountered other floor grills, but all were locked down.

Spying through the grill, he noticed at least five well-armed guards, all of the same type of alien he had killed, stationed at each opening.

"Will, look," whispered Anne. "Up ahead, it's a light."

"Finally," he exclaimed. "We get out of here and then we can put the army boys on them."

Will was still convinced that they were in a secret alien base located somewhere in the Mojave.

He looked back, smiled, and squeezed Anne's hand.

He was surprised at his companion. Once Anne had recovered from the gas, he had expected her to freak out and be hysterical. She was afraid, to be sure, but she proved to be as strong as she was beautiful.

He warily approached the heavy, corroded bars of the opening. Before him flowed a small, sluggish stream that wound its way into a dense forest, several hundred yards to his right.

To his left, in the far distance, he saw what appeared to be ordered rows of an orchard. Will scratched his head.

Since when is there a Mojave Forest? He asked himself. *Probably some desert reclamation project.*

Lost in thought, Will failed to hear Anne come up behind him.

"Looks like we aren't in Kansas anymore, Toto."

"Yeah, looks that way," he said. "I say we lay low, then try to make those trees when it gets dark."

Before she could respond, they both turned at the sound of a shrill tearing of metal. A sharp hissing like the sound of a thousand steam engines echoed in the distance.

"Change of plans," she said. "We move now."

"Amen," he said as he gingerly slipped between the widely spaced bars.

"Walk through the water until we make cover," he whispered. "That way they won't know where we came out."

"It's ice cold," she hissed. The water rose to her chest before her feet found the bottom. Will make an awkward leap, lost his footing on the slick stone bottom and sank out of sight.

"Will," Anne said as she pulled the sputtering man to the surface.

"You're right," he said, "This water is awfully cold."

"Where's the gun?"

"Oh no," he said as he flailed about. "I must have dropped it."

Wait a minute," she said. "There it is…I think."

To Will's astonishment, the big revolver bobbed on the surface as if it were made of cork.

"I didn't know guns floated."

"They don't," he said as he picked it up. "That's why when you want to get rid of one you toss it in a river. There is something very strange going on here."

"Think about it later, Sherlock. Right now we have to hide."

Together they waded through the small yet surprisingly deep stream. After a few dozen yards, they turned to see a thick, greenish gas erupt from the sewer opening. The thick, metal bars of the grate melted and flowed into the stream.

"That was too close," he said. "Dear Jesus, those old boys aren't fooling around."

"Will, let's go."

&ᔕᔓ&

From the cover of the trees, Will and Anne got their first look at the city they had escaped.

"I never seen the like," he said. "Look at that big glass sky-scraper. It must be a mile tall."

"Will, look up in the sky. What is that?"

Will looked up and saw what appeared to be a jewel glittering in the sky.

"I got a feeling we aren't anywhere near the Mojave," he said. "The sky's color is a shade of blue I have never seen before. Even the air tastes different."

"I got a feeling we aren't anywhere near earth. Will, what are we going to do?"

"We are going to survive and we are going to make these rejects from the *Twilight Zone* take us back home. Afterward, we will sell this story to Hollywood and make a boatload of money."

"You promise?"

"On my honor, darling," he said with a smile. "Right now, I am hungry and I am dying to see what those black apples taste like."

"Wait a minute, where did you get that bag?"

"From a golden ape. It was while you were passed out."

"The note from Molly?"

"Yeah. Just who in the world did you work for, Anne?"

"I—I don't know. But they seemed to be looking out for us."

"Yeah or setting us up. I still can't get over this whole thing. It is like they could see the future or something."

"When we get back to earth you can ask them."

"Right now, darling, we need to dry these wet clothes and find shelter, let's go."

∽∾∽

The pair traveled through the dense forest, trying not to think of what kind of strange and savage predators might be lurking in the shadows. The sci-fi movies they grew up on now only served to rob them of their peace of mind.

Finding a secluded clearing far from any game trail, Will gave Shirley to Anne and let her stand guard while he set about making them a cozy shelter.

"It isn't much, but it will keep the rain off of us," he said.

"This is amazing. Where did you learn to do this?"

"I was a Boy Scout. My Scout Master, Mr. Eslinger, was a survivalist nut. He was always telling us about how Big Brother and the Military Industrial Complex were out to get us, but the old boy was smart as a tack when it came to survival in the wild. I really miss him."

"What happened, did he pass away?"

"Nah, he didn't pay his income taxes."

"Oh."

"Wait here and I'll be right back," he said.

"You are not leaving me alone."

"Hide in the shelter with Shirley. I'll be right back with some food. I hope we can eat the fruit here."

"No."

"See you in a bit," he said before disappearing into the brush.

"Will," she hissed, "come back."

❧❧❧

Thirty minutes later Will returned to find a distraught Anne sitting with her back to the bole of a huge tree, her fingers frozen around Shirley's grip. As he came into the camp, Anne let out a small scream, turned, and pulled the trigger. Instead of a tremendous report, there was only an impotent click.

"You almost shot me."

"It was an accident," she said, "but you deserved it for leaving me here by myself. I am a nervous wreck, you jerk."

"You will feel better once you eat. I got take out."

Will had acquired several black apples and some odd looking vegetables.

"I have had Macintosh before," Anne said, "but this is the first time I had a Blackintosh."

"Blackintosh? That's pretty good."

"I have my moments."

"I heard some of the farmers talking," Will said. "Seems that the harvest is the biggest in memory. With so much extra food, they won't miss little here and there."

Anne looked at Will and frowned. "Now that is another strange thing. Why is it we can we understand them? Down in the sewer, I understood perfectly what the soldiers were saying. If we were plopped down in, say, Russia, we wouldn't have a clue what was being said. But low and behold, we are on another frigging planet and we understand the native's language."

"I never thought about it. Now that you mention it, they weren't speaking English."

"But you understood it?"

"Yeah. Weird, huh?"

"Do you speak French?"

"Just french fries."

Anne looked at Will. "Je ne veux pas d'atteindre l'immortalité grâce à mon travail. Je veux y parvenir par le biais ne pas mourir. What did I just say?"

"I don't want to achieve immortality through my work. I want to achieve it through not dying," he said.

"Amazing. It was a quote from Woody Allen, in French. I had an eccentric aunt who loved everything French and Woody Allen."

"I got one," he said. "Var är toaletten?"

"Where is the restroom?"

"Yeah. Got it from a Swedish exchange student, Sven…something, something Borg.

"This is some freaky shit," she said.

"Yes, but being able to communicate makes life a lot easier."

"Just like the gun SD gave you."

"Yeah, about that," he said, picking up the revolver. "A Webly Fosbery is kind of an odd duck, sort of like me. I guess that's why I like it so much. But if this gun is a Webly Fosbery, then I am Marilyn Monroe."

"It's a fake, Wobbly?"

"That's Webly," he said. "This gun doesn't have a mark on it—looks brand, spanking new, like the-last-hundred-years-never-happened new. The metal back then was plain old steel that would rust in your hand if you thought about water."

"You dropped it in the stream."

"Exactly," he said. "It should already be showing signs of rust, but it isn't. In fact, I can't find a speck of rust."

"And it floated."

"Yes, exactly. A gun is a boat anchor not a pool float." Will fumbled with the chamber mechanism until the gun "broke open" exposing the cylinder. "Well, I'll be," he said softly.

"What's the matter?" she asked huddling close.

"This gun is empty," he said, showing her the grooved cylinder with six empty chambers.

"That's a good thing, or I would have shot you."

"No, you don't understand. A bullet consists of a lead projectile wedged into brass case, which contains a measure of gunpowder and a primer. When a round is fired, the lead projectile is expelled leaving behind the spent case."

"Okay," she said. "What is your point?"

"My point is, I fired two rounds, so where are the empty brass cases? They should still be here in the chamber."

"Oh, I see what you mean. It doesn't make any sense."

Will thought for a few moments while Anne nibbled at an apple. Will closed the gun and pulled back on the slide, cocking the gun.

"What are you doing? The gun is empty."

"That's what it looks like." Will pointed the gun at a tall, dead tree sitting at the edge of their camp and pulled the trigger.

The gun recoiled sharply, but made almost no sound. Seconds later the tree crashed to the ground, the thick trunk had been sliced into as if cut with a giant chainsaw.

Anne sat speechless at the miracle.

"So, your name is, Shirley?" Will asked. "Mine is Will and this is Anne."

"It is a pleasure," the gun said.

"Get out of town," Anne said.

"It was you who talked to me back at the house of horrors, wasn't it?"

"Yes," Shirley said. "I thought you might need a kick start."

"I did. Thanks."

"The freaking gun talks," Anne said.

"I am not a freaking anything," Shirley said. "I am a one of a kind, Doemac't Sigarmed Adapt-o-matic Personal Defense Companion. I belong to you, Anne Miller and Will Carlson."

"That is why you didn't fire when Anne tried to kill me."

"Correct," Shirley said.

"Hey," Anne said. "That's was an accident."

Will smiled and gave her a wink.

"Why did SD and Molly give you to us?" Anne asked.

"Isn't that obvious?"

"Are you alive?" Anne asked.

"Are you?"

"Smartass," she snapped.

"Who *are* SD, and Molly?" Will asked.

"Not a clue," Shirley said, "All I can say is they have acquired you the best personal weapon available—*period*. They must hold you in very high esteem or they know that you will be in extreme danger."

"Why do you look like an old earth revolver?" he asked.

"I linked to your mind. Like you said, a Webly Fosbery is the coolest gun in the world. I am the coolest weapon in the universe. By the way, you have four rounds left. I suggest you use then wisely."

"Man, all this seems like supernatural hoodoo," Will said.

"You know, Will, I was in this really bad Sci-Fi movie, *Death Planet Puppets*—"

"She made that up," Shirley said.

"Unfortunately, it was all too real," Anne said. "Anyway, there was a quote used in the movie, I think it was from Arthur C. Clark, but it said, 'Any sufficiently advanced technology is indistinguishable from magic.'"

"What are you saying?"

"That this isn't magic, but some pretty advanced alien tech."

"So SD and Molly are…"

"ETs," Anne said.

"My head hurts," Will said as he rubbed his face. "Toss me an apple, Anne." Will bit into the apple, trying to wrap his mind around what was happening. "Hey, this is good—real good."

"They are delicious," she agreed. "It's sweet, almost like a big strawberry."

"I should have brought more," he said as he devoured the strange fruit.

"It's getting cool," she said, rubbing her arms. "Hey Shirley—"

"I am not a personal heater. I am a personal weapon."

"You are a *bitchy* weapon," Anne said.

"I love you too."

"I can't risk lighting a fire," Will said.

"I guess we will have to share body heat—that is, if you don't mind, Will," she said with a sly smile.

Will rolled his eyes. "Well, if we have to—for survival."

"I think I am going to be sick," Shirley said.

"Hush," Will and Anne said in unison.

Will leaned against the bole of a white and green striped tree whose bark was slick, smooth, almost as if it had been sanded.

Anne moved next to him and he put his arms about her.

"Oh you feel good and warm," she said, snuggling next to him. "Will, is there anyone waiting for you back home?"

"You mean like a girlfriend?"

"I mean like family, friends, or anything else."

"My mom and dad died in a small plane accident."

"I'm sorry," she said.

"It's all right. I was so young I don't remember much about them. I went to stay with my mom's sister Betty and her husband Owen."

"He was the one who gave you the scar."

"Yeah. I took a lot of crap growing up, but I knew my dad

had left a big trust fund for me, so no matter how bad things got, I kept looking at the light at the end of the tunnel."

"What happened?"

"My dear uncle put the kibosh on that little dream as well. I remember going to the lawyer's office to collect my money. I was expecting nearly five million. Instead he gave me check for two hundred, seventy four dollars and three cents."

"That's horrible," she said. "At least Owen can't hurt anyone else."

"He went out with a bang," Will said. "Unfortunately, Owen killed himself, along with Betty."

"Oh, God, Will, I am so sorry."

"It happens. I did get a sweet, million-year-old car out of the deal."

"So how come a nice fellow like you doesn't have a girl back home?"

"Well, I did. Her name was Brenda Mills. Prettiest girl in town. She even won a couple of beauty pageants."

"She sounds wonderful," Anne said dryly. "Why isn't she with you?"

"I think the expression is, *no money, no honey.* Bryson City is a real small town and bad news travels fast. She dumped me before the ink was dry on my two hundred dollar check."

"Gold digging bitch."

Will laughed. "I thought the break up was because of her dad, the Right Reverend Mills. He is the biggest thief ever to use the Bible instead of a gun. I snuck out to her place, well past midnight, to convince her to run off with me. Found out that she not only had moved on, Brenda was already engaged to the next sucker. Amazing what can happen in three days."

"I don't like Brenda or her dad," Anne said.

"Me neither," Shirley said.

"I'm not crazy about them myself," he said. "Live and learn I guess." Will shifted and held Anne closer. "Okay, I told you about my sorted past. Let me hear the Anne Miller story in full, gut-wrenching detail."

Anne laughed. "Well, for one thing, I would never be caught dead in a beauty pageant."

"Too bad. I think you would have given Brenda a run for her money."

"Run for her money? I'll have you know, that I would have kicked that gold digging bitch's ass."

Will laughed and held Anne even closer.

"Anywho, I grew up in a normal family with my mom dad and twin sister Abby."

"You have a twin? Lord help us all."

"Amen," Shirley said.

Anne nudged Will in the ribs. "I had the acting bug bad so I skipped college and ran off to Hollywood. It was a real wakeup call to know that girls like me are a dime a dozen out there."

"No, I don't believe that for a moment. You are one of a kind, Anne Miller. You are special—nothing run of the mill about you. So tell me, how does one become a scream queen?"

"Why thank you, kind sir," she said. "Anyway, while the big budget blockbusters gave me the cold shoulder, there were plenty of independent directors needing actresses."

"Independent?"

"Yeah, most were little more than film students with cameras they got at Christmas, but I had to eat. I ended up playing in one bad horror film after another."

"Well, that still sounds interesting," Will said. "You were great in *Zombie Gators*."

"Liar. Anyway it got tedious, sweetie. All they were interested in was psycho killers, vampires, zombies, or combinations of the three."

"I still think this is great. You are the first actress I have met that played in an honest-to-God movie."

"I did them just to make ends meet and they were not anything to be proud of. I mainly played the tragic victim. I have been set on fire, stabbed, hanged, shot, eaten by zombies, sucked dry by vampires—you name it."

"What about your three starring roles?"

"I was the heroine in, *Cannibal Backlash, Forest of Doom,* and last, but not but least, *Vampire Clowns and the Circus of Doom.*

"You are making that up," he said.

"Will honey, you can't make up stuff like that," Anne said with a laugh. "I was torn to shreds by a herd of rabid balloon animals."

Will gave her a long incredulous look.

"I swear to God that was in the movie. It broke my heart when I finally came to the conclusion that I would never be a leading lady in a worthwhile movie. The straw that broke the camel's back was when we were shooting a movie called, *Blood Stalker IV.*"

"*Blood Stalker IV?*"

"Um, yeah, it was about some whacko in a hokey mask who killed and ate people. Mostly coeds with big boobs."

He chuckled. "I hear they are the tastiest."

Anne gave him a sour look. "Anyhow, I was waiting while the crew rigged the set for my overly gory death scene, when the director/writer/producer walked up to me and pulled me to the side. The little twerp told me that the scene had been changed slightly, to enhance its dramatic and artistic effect. I asked how slightly and he told me that the scene would take place, sans clothing. I flatly refused. There hasn't been a movie made yet, that can get me to show skin."

"Good for you. I like a scream queen with integrity."

Anne giggled. "Little things like that can come back and haunt you."

"What happened with the movie?"

"The little perv said that if I let it all hang out and was extra good to him in the sack, he would make me the star in his upcoming film. We got into a fight and it was goodbye Hollywood. After that, I packed up and left. I was on my way home when I found myself dead broke and stranded in Angels Wells."

"Angel Wells, the gateway to the stars," he said. "First thing I will do when we get home is to buy *Vampire Clowns and the Circus of Doom.* I expect an autograph."

"Trust me, you will expect your money back. To be honest, bad or not, I have a copy of all my flicks in my bag."

"Just think, Anne, this whole little adventure could be your ticket to the big time."

"How's that?"

"When we get home, Hollywood will make your story into a huge movie and you will become a big star." Will fished about in his empty pockets and produced an imaginary pen and notebook. "Excuse me, Miss Miller? May I have your autograph? I'm your biggest fan. Why, back home, I'm president of the Tennessee chapter of your fan club."

"Oh please, can't I have a moment's peace? If it isn't the paparazzi hounding my every move, it's the little, insignificant people vying for my signature." Anne gave him a smile. "Oh all right, you look like a good kid."

"Thank you Miss Miller. I am not worthy."

"I know, but then again who is?" she asked as both of them began to laugh. "Turn around."

Will turned and Anne used his back as a desk.

"There you go, Will. You have the singular honor of receiving my first autograph."

Will grinned as he pretended to read it. "'To Will, Best wishes to my number one fan, Anne Miller, Movie Goddess.' I will treasure it always."

Anne looked at Will and smiled. "You know, Will, you are a nice guy."

"Oh no," he groaned. "I ask for your autograph then you give me the kiss of death? How could you? Just for that, Anne, you have a good personality."

"What a rotten thing to say, Will Carlson," she said. "You take that back or I am going to use Shirley on you."

"Honestly, folks, please leave me out of your mating rituals," Shirley said.

They talked for another hour until their eyelids began to droop.

"Getting late, you had better get some sleep, Anne."

"What about you?"

"Someone has to keep watch."

"That someone is me," Shirley said. "If anything gets closer than two hundred meters I will sing out."

"What if the apes hear you?" Anne asked.

"You don't get it do you?" Shirley asked. "Only you two can hear me. I am speaking to you telepathically."

"That's impossible," Will said.

"Said the man to the talking gun," Anne said.

"I see your point," he said. "Goodnight, Anne."

"Goodnight, Will," she said, giving him a soft kiss on the cheek. *You know, Will, I think I am becoming your number one fan.*

CHAPTER 30

For several days, Anne and Will spent their time hiding from the security forces that combed the area, looking for them. They observed that the "Apes" that comprised the ranks of soldiers were of a completely different type from the aliens that tended the orchard and fields.

The "farmers," as Will called them, were very human like. They did however, have a slight tinge of gray to their skin, were about a foot taller, and had a much more robust build. Anne thought they looked like steroid-doped pro wrestlers.

One glaring difference between the earth couple and the "farmers," were the hard boney protrusions at the knuckles and at their knees. Will observed two of the males having a disagreement that became a knock-down-drag-out fight.

Will decided then and there not to get into a bare knuckle brawl with one of them. It would be tantamount to suicide.

The couple quickly learned that the apes and the farmers did not get along. Almost every meeting ended with a violent confrontation.

While Will and Anne learned about the strange new world around them, it became more apparent that they were alone. Unless they could make allies, it was only a matter of time before they were captured and sent back to the dissection table.

℘℘℘

"I don't like it, Will. I have a bad feeling about this."

"Don't worry, Anne. I just want to get a closer look at one of those farmers."

"It's too dangerous. What if you get caught?"

"There is bound to be a meeting between us sooner or later."

"Yeah, what if they do like you—like, for lunch?"

"I will keep that from happening," Shirley said.

"Anne, you have been in wayyyyyyy too many B-movies. I haven't seen any of them eat anything other than fruit and veggies."

"Don't go, *please*?"

"I'll be super careful, I promise."

"I will watch your back," Shirley said.

"No, you are staying with Anne. She needs you more than I do."

"Will Carlson, you are pig headed, do you know that?"

He grinned. "Just part of my charm."

"Be careful," she said, taking him in her arms. She kissed him tenderly.

"That was nice—real nice."

"Come back in one piece, and there will be more where that came from, big boy."

ೞೞೞ

Will crept close to the small house, wary of any sign of alarm or watch animal. The small, solidly build house was constructed of stone and resembled an English cottage complete with thatched roof and shutters. He had chosen it because it sat apart from the rest of the village, near the edge of the forest.

All looks real cozy. I was expecting a lot more tech stuff. Not a ray gun or rocket pack in sight, just a bunch of farm equipment. Maybe I've been the one watching too many movies.

ೞೞೞ

Will wasn't the only one interested in that particular cottage. A roving Mogul patrol rested less than a mile away. Earlier that same day, the Moguls had a confrontation with the owner of the house, a young Roratune female called Sako.

"I am not going to let that gray skin get away with this," Corporal Blos said. A bandage covered his left cheek where she had given him a right cross.

"No. You will get us all in trouble—or worse," Flahe Byer said.

"You fellows go on back to the barracks. I will teach the gray skin not to mess with her betters."

"One word from her and a load of trouble will land on us."

"When I get through with her, she won't be pointing the finger at anyone. Besides, there is a dangerous alien stalking these woods, I figure he will get the blame."

"Have it your way," Byer said, sliding on his pack. "If I were you, I would be careful. They say the alien is four and a half meters tall and has razor sharp fangs. I hear he killed a dozen soldiers and put an entire regiment in the hospital. They say projectiles bounce off his thick hide as if it was made of alloy steel."

"You listen to too many wild stories, my friend. That creature is probably a hundred clicks from here," Blos said with a chuckle. "I'll give the gray skin your regards."

ↄﻭↄ

Moving through the dark moonless night, Will smiled and thought about the kiss Anne had given him as he slid up to a window. Inside, working on what he guessed to be a computer, was a female farmer.

Yah know, she isn't that bad looking. In fact, she has the face of a real doll. If I were a foot taller, a hundred pounds heavier, and had a set of brass knuckles, I might just ask her out. Will stifled a laugh when he heard something moving down the wide paved pathway. He was surprised to find it was one of the solider apes approaching the house. From the way the solitary soldier kept looking around, Will knew he was up to no good.

Slinking deeper into the shadows, Will watched as the ape approached a side door and pried the lock open with a vicious looking knife.

Oh, man, this is going to be trouble, Will thought, going back to the window.

His stomach in knots, Will watched as the solider slipped behind the unsuspecting girl and clamped a massive hand over her mouth.

Pure rage boiled inside as he watched the ape brutally subdue the smaller girl. With a knife to her throat, he dropped his pants in preparation to rape the farmer girl.

Without any semblance of a plan, Will kicked the front door open, to the surprise of both the rapist and his victim. Will launched himself at his gargantuan opponent, who stumbled back in shock. Tangled in the trousers wrapped about his ankles, the soldier fell backward to the floor with a mighty crash.

Knocking the knife away, Will grabbed the girl and yelled, "Run for help."

Before he could scoot out the door, the Mogul had gained his feet and landed a punch to Will's back.

Will thought he had been hit with a sledgehammer as he slammed into the wall. He smiled weakly as the enraged beast cut him off from escape. "Hey, sailor, come here often?"

"*You* are the savage, rampaging beast?" the solider said with a laugh. "I have seen worms bigger than you."

"Worm this, Cheata," Will said.

He lashed out with a kick to the groin but, to his dismay, the Mogul laughed at him.

"Is that all you got, *worm*?"

"Aw, shit," Will said as the soldier drew back a fist the size of a canned ham and began to pummel him.

Will had been in worse fights, but at the moment, couldn't remember when. Right now, he could not remember his own name. Bloody and broken, he thought it was over, then he noticed an arm encircle the monster's neck and yank him back. The last thing Will saw before he blacked out was the light reflecting off a descending blade.

ை

Will slowly opened his eyes, fully expecting the soothing serenade of harps. Instead, he was in a soft bed, his various, painful wounds neatly stitched and bandaged. To his dismay, he checked under the brightly colored blanket to find his clothes missing.

Oh great, he thought. *I have to get out of here.*

He tried to rise when a large hand grabbed his shoulder. The hand sported a vicious set of barbed knuckles.

"Aw, shit."

"Lay back," the soft feminine voice said. "The doctor said you are not to move from bed for two days."

Will looked up to see the alien girl he had saved from the soldier. He had to admit, that she was even better looking up close. She gave him a dazzling smile and Will swore that she had the most beautiful blue eyes he had ever seen. She wore a simple, dark brown tunic and slacks. Her long blonde hair was braided and bound together with a green ribbon.

"What are you?"

"I—I am a man. My name is, Will."

She gave him a sweet smile. "My name is, Sako."

"Nice to meet you, Sako, but I have to go."

"You will not get far, Will. The Moguls are scouring the area for you. They have offered an astronomical reward for you and your companion."

"Yeah, we got off on the wrong foot. So, are you going to turn me in?"

"Why did you do what you did last night? You are no match for a Mogul—or anything else for that matter. Why did you come to my aid?"

"Because where I come from, you don't just stand by and watch while a woman is raped, regardless if it ends in an ass whipping."

Sako smiled. "We are called the Roratune, and we have no love for the Mogul savages. Any enemy of theirs is a friend of ours. You are safe here."

"Thank you. Listen, Sako, my friend is hiding out in the woods. I have to go find her."

Sako smiled. "We assumed that, Will. My father sent hunters and have brought her back."

"Anne is here? Can I see her?"

"I will send for her," Sako said. "By the way, Will. You and this Anne person aren't *sealed* are you?"

"*Sealed*? I don't understand the term."

"Is she yours?"

"Oh, you mean are we married? No, in fact, I just met her before we were shanghaied to this place."

"Good," Sako said with a smile. Leaning over, she planted a wet kiss on Will's forehead. "You are a cutest little thing, now get some rest. I'll be right back."

Will suddenly got the same dread fear, far worse than he had when he faced the Mogul.

Moments later, the door flew open and in rushed Anne. "You big idiot," she said. "You almost got yourself killed."

"Aw, you should see the other guy," he said, as she threw her arms around his neck and hugged him tight.

"If anything had happened to you, I..."

"You would what?"

"I—I would have been stuck here by myself. You idiot." Anne slapped him hard on the back of the head. "When the Roratune showed up last night and said you were hurt, I almost lost it."

"You didn't shoot anyone, did you?"

"No, but I came close."

"Good," he whispered. "They seem friendly enough, but let's keep Shirley a secret for now. Let them think she is just a dumb, obsolete weapon."

"The same thing she suggested last night." Anne leaned in close and whispered, "Does it hurt?"

"Yeah."

"Good," she said with a mischievous smile. Anne had just sat on the side of the bed when Sako entered the room. The smile fell from her face at the sight of Anne.

"Sako," Will said, "this is Anne."

Sako grunted. "It is not proper for a female and male to be on the same bed if they aren't sealed."

"I never was one for propriety," Anne said with a sweet smile. "I like it here."

Sako clenched a fist and took a step toward Anne, when there was a single knock at the door. The door opened and in walked a grizzled giant. Will and Anne both gasped. The newcomer had a barrel chest, arms of corded muscle, and stood well over seven feet tall. He was, no doubt, the most imposing man Will had ever seen.

"Father," Sako said. "This is Will."

"Nice to meet you, sir," Will said.

"Ballen Rosse," he said in a deep voice. Ballen stroked his long, gray beard with his barbed hand. "Daughter, what have you done?"

"Your daughter is showing me a bit of kindness, Mr. Rosse," Will said, "but if you want us gone, we are out of here."

Sako stepped forward and pushed Will back down on the bed as easily as if he were a child.

"Hey, watch it," he snapped.

"Be quiet," she said. "Father, Will isn't going anywhere. The doctor said he has to heal for two days at the very least. Or do you want everyone to know that you cast out your daughter's savior?"

"The Moguls want you badly. Said you killed two of their kind when you and your female escaped."

"The name is Anne," Anne said. "Not, 'his female.'"

"I only killed one, but he was trying to kill me. It was self-defense."

"One or a million," Ballen said. "They won't stop until they have you. You are like a gun put to our heads. If the Moguls find out that we harbor you, it will be their excuse to put an end to us once and for all."

"They can't have him," Sako said.

Ballen blew out a deep breath. "Yes, outlander, you have certainly brought trouble with you. However, you kept one of the filthy beasts from soiling my daughter. For that, I will risk hiding you and your—*Anne*."

"Mr. Rosse, I don't want to be any trouble to ya'll. If you could be kind enough to show us how to get back home, Anne and I will be on our way."

"I am not a Mr. Rosse. I am Ballen."

"Yes, sir."

"Where is back home?" Ballen asked.

"Earth. The good old US of A," Will said.

"How did you get here from this...Earth?"

"There was this big flying thing that attacked us. Used some kind of gas to knock us out. When I came to this robot was fixing to cut us up."

"What did this flying machine look like?" Ballen asked.

"Um...it had six wings and looked like a dragon fly."

"Dragon *fly*?"

"Allow me," Anne said. She took a stick from the fire and expertly drew the machine on the stone floor.

"Cool," Will said. "Talented as well as beautiful."

Anne gave Will a bright smile.

"That is a machine of, Opia," Ballen said. "It is a *thinker*."

"A thinker?" Anne asked.

"Some of her machines are slaves to programs, while a few can think for themselves. It is rare to see one, and their function has always been a mystery, but that flying machine is a thinker."

"Can you help us get home?" Anne asked.

"It is beyond our power," Ballen said. "What we can do is keep you safe and away from the Moguls and their mad God. Maybe, in time, we can figure a way to get absolution."

"That would be great," Anne said.

"Only if you do exactly what we tell you. If they suspect you are here, they will fall on us with everything they have. They take it personally when one of their own is murdered."

"I didn't murder anyone. That old boy came at me with a gun. It was self-defense."

Ballen laughed. "No, we mean the one whose throat you cut," he said.

"But I didn't—"

"No you didn't, but the Moguls don't know that."

"It was Sako, wasn't it?" Will asked.

Ballen nodded. "We left the body where their patrol would find it. They assume that the terrible alien animal did it."

"I had no idea that you were such a bad man," Anne told Will.

"Neither did I."

"Come with me, Anne," Ballen said. "I will find you appropriate quarters."

"Yes, Anne," Sako said. "Please go with Father."

"No, I am staying with Will."

"Get out of my house," Sako said.

"Make me," Anne snapped as she leapt off the bed.

"Very well, if you insist," Sako said with a sinister smile. She moved toward Anne.

Will grabbed Anne as Ballen took his daughter by the arm. "Enough of this," Ballen snapped. "You will not lay so much as a finger on the dwarf female or you will answer to me."

"Who you calling a dwarf?" Anne asked.

"Calm down," Will hissed. "Ballen, I think we both should move, if for nothing else than to keep peace."

"Yes, I agree."

"I don't," Sako said. "I should be the one to take care of him."

"Fine," Ballen said. "Will and Anne, you will stay here. Sako you will move in with me until Will is strong enough to move. You can take care of him during the day."

"But, Father—"

"I have spoken."

"Bye, Sako, *honey,*" Anne said. "Don't forget to write."

Sako gave Anne a murderous stare, before packing a bag and leaving with her father.

CHAPTER 31

Two weeks later, Will and Sako sat beneath a spreading tree whose broad leaves were crimson tinged with silver. Beside the tree flowed a wide river and, in the far distance, lay the great city.

"Now this is the life," Will said, as he settled back on the soft grass. "Tell me about your people, Sako."

"Very well," Sako said, "According to official history, the Roratune and the Moguls were created by the Opia to serve her. Although, in theory, both races are equal, the Moguls have all the high-ranking positions and live in the great city of God, assisting Opia in her knowledge gathering. The Roratune, on the other hand, grow the food and do practically all the grunt work."

"Why is that?"

"The Moguls are better at kissing her royal ass than we are, especially their leader the great high priest Rondall. They believe the lie that they are special creations. We know the truth. We came here much like you and Anne. Our ancestors were kidnapped from a place called Roratune and brought here to worship Opia. Granted, our history has gaping holes and is handed down by word of mouth, but the truth is, we are little more than slaves of Opia. Since the Moguls are Opia's darlings, they get to live in the city while we are forced to live out here in the fresh air and the forest."

"You definitely got the better deal." He ate a Blackintosh while listening to her story. "So, who is this Opia?"

"The Opia claims to be the creator of the universe, God Almighty Herself."

"Is that where she lives?" he asked, pointing with the succulent fruit to the great crystal in the sky.

"No, that is her vessel the *Chariot of Opia*. Opia lives in her temple, the big building with the glass spire."

"You said vessel—you mean like a space ship?"

"Yes," Sako said. "Over the past year, we have heard rumors that Opia has been building a great space fleet. I don't know why. She never needed one before."

"If she has space ships, maybe I could learn to fly one and take it back to earth. Wouldn't the folks back home get a kick out of that?"

"Does earth have a space bridge?"

"What's a space bridge?"

Sako smiled. "Then you don't have one. Without one, a spaceship wouldn't do you any good."

"What does a bridge do?"

"They are like tunnels that connect the solar systems together. My teachers never explained how they work. I don't think they know themselves. However, without a bridge to shorten the distance, it would take a vessel thousands of years to travel between the closest systems."

"Girl, you just rained on my parade. Wait a minute, if earth doesn't have a bridge, how did Opia snatch me and Anne."

"There is a rumor that she has a great machine that can do the same thing as a bridge except it can allow objects to travel anywhere in the galaxy instantly."

"Bingo," he said. "That is my ticket home."

"Will, it is only a rumor. They also say it is the most closely guarded thing on this world."

"There you go raining again," he said. "With all her fancy know how, how come you Roratune don't use it? Don't get me wrong, I mean, your people have created a fine place to live, but all I have seen is some computers, phones, and a few electric cars. Where's all the high-tech gadgets? You know, like teleporters, warp drive, and phasers?"

"I didn't understand a word you just said, but Opia keeps

all the good stuff for herself. She wants her people to live simply and leave her land as natural and pristine as possible. A few good roads and more vehicles would be nice, but anyway, lack of technology also keeps us from staging any kind of revolt."

"There has to be a way back home."

"If there was, my people would have found it. You will just have to make the best of your situation."

Smiling, Sako produced a colorful leather band from her pocket. "I made you something, Will," she said softly.

Will looked at the carefully woven band and smiled. He had seen many of her people wearing the festive bands. "Why thank you Sako. It is beautiful."

"Let me place it on your wrist."

Will held out his right arm.

"No, it goes on the left," she said.

Will extended his left arm and Sako slipped the band over his hand and tightened it around his wrist.

"Thank..." His words were cut off as she pounced on him, knocking him back. "Sako, what are you doing?"

Sako cut off his protests with a big sloppy kiss.

"Get off me, woman."

"Come on, Will, we have much to do," she said, taking him by the hand.

ᖇᖇᖇ

Ballen gave Anne a tour of Astem, the largest of the Roratune villages. The timber frame and stone, thatched roof houses looked very ancient, yet all sported electricity and running water. Small satellite dishes and antenna sprouted from the sharply peaked roofs. Most homes had an outside electrical connection to recharge their work vehicles. The big work trucks looked like a cross between a flatbed truck and a massive desert racer.

Anne became genuinely fond of Ballen. In many ways, he reminded her of her own father, David Miller—if her father was a giant Norse warrior, that is.

"I love your buildings," Anne said. "They remind me of Viking homes. In fact, you and your people remind me of Vikings."

"Vi-kings?"

"They were an ancient people from my world. They were wonderful artisans, explorers, and fierce warriors. You guys, though, would eat them for lunch."

Ballen laughed. "We *probably* would never eat anyone for lunch."

"Probably?"

"Depends on how hungry we are," he said with a twinkle in his eye.

"Really?"

"Oh don't worry," he said. "You don't have enough meat for more than a snack."

"I feel much better now."

Anne stared as a Roratune walked by, talking on a tiny phone.

"The ancient and modern mix keeps throwing me for a loop," she said.

"Father," Sako cried as she ran toward them, half-dragging, half-carrying Will behind her.

"Let go of me, woman," Will snapped as he unsuccessfully tried to extract himself from her iron grip. "I am not a dog on a leash!"

"What did you do, Sako?" Ballen asked as he grabbed Will's wrist in his massive, calloused hand.

"Uh… she made me a bracelet is all," Will said. "Most of the guys have them."

"These, Will, are called *coreisaw* and are worn to show that they are…together," said Ballen. "Or should I say, *Son*?"

"What did you do, you idiot?" Anne asked.

Sako put a finger to Anne's chest and shoved her back three feet.

"He is mine, runt. I have laid claim, so if you know what's good for you, you will walk away."

"Look here ,you freak of nature," Anne shouted. "If you think I am going to let you paw all over Will, just because he was dumb enough to let you trick him with a bit of macramé, you've got another think coming."

Sako drew back a fist, but froze as her father stepped between her and Anne.

"The little woman is right," Ballen said, patting Anne playfully on the head. "It was an underhanded trick. One that isn't binding on someone not of our culture."

"But, Father, I *want* him."

"Why? He may look *somewhat* like a Roratune, but he is a weak, pink, dwarf!"

Ballen grabbed Will by the arm and lifted him off his feet.

"Hey, let me down."

"He is so light that a strong breeze would blow him away," Ballen said with a chuckle.

"He has courage," Sako said.

"Granted," Ballen said. "But not much good sense. He took on a Mogul soldier unarmed."

"Yes, a soldier who was about to rape your only daughter. Will was willing to trade his life for mine. I have dreamed of someone like him my entire life."

"Keep dreaming," Anne said.

"Fine, have it your way, Sako," Ballen said. "I will let it stand."

"Hey," Anne exclaimed. "You can't let them be married."

Ballen chuckled. "Relax, Anne, they aren't married. All the coreisaw means is that Sako has placed her claim. After a reasonable amount of time if he decides he doesn't feel the same, I will, as a Roratune elder, dissolve it."

"What is a reasonable amount of time?" Will asked.

"I'll give it, oh say…a year."

"A year?" Will cried. "You can't do that to me."

"I will make it a special year too, my love."

Will's life suddenly flashed before his eyes. "Don't I have anything to say about this?"

"Oh yes," Ballen. "In a year. Until then be very, very good to my only daughter—or *else*." He gave Will a stern look that made him swallow hard.

"Aw, crap," Will said.

"Come with me, Will, I think we need some time—alone," Sako said.

"Look!" Will cried, as he pointed down the cobble stone street. "It's Captain Kirk!"

As Ballen and Sako looked, wondering who this Captain Kirk was, Will ran the other way.

"Will, my love," Sako cried. "My home is the other way."

Sako ran after her errant boyfriend while Ballen laughed.

"Look here, Ballen," Anne said. "If you think I am going to stand by while she rapes Will, you have another think coming." She exploded into a vulgar although rather creative rant.

Ballen laughed at her fury. "Calm yourself, Anne. I know my daughter better than anyone. If I had put a stop to her little scheme, she would have pined away for little Will forever. Not to mention she would have driven us all crazy in the process. This way, she will come to reality on her own. I give it a few days—no more than a week."

"Why, you sly old fox," Anne said with a grin.

"Not knowing what a fox is, I will take it as a compliment."

"Did you see, Will's face?" she said. "I thought he would die from sheer embarrassment."

"I saw your face as well. I thought you would actually take a swing at Sako. Will must mean quite a bit to you, because taking a swing at Sako would be more foolish than fighting a Mogul."

"Will is…I barely know him…oh, I don't know."

"You care for him, admit it, Anne."

"All right, you win. I do have deep feelings for the dumb hillbilly."

"When did you first know?"

"About a year ago."

"I thought you said you barely knew him?"

Anne took a deep breath.

"I know it sounds weird, and you are going to think I am completely nuts, but I had dreams about him before I met him."

"Before?"

"I…I…well, this fortuneteller told me I would meet my

soul mate and described Will to a T. Every night I would see him. It was wonderful. I got to looking forward to sleep just so I could be with him. I didn't know he was actually real, I thought it was some fantasy my mind had conjured up. I only met him in the flesh only a few hours before we were kidnapped and brought here."

Ballen gave her a long, thoughtful look.

"You think I am a nut job, don't you?"

"No," Ballen said. "There are a lot of strange things that go on in the universe that are beyond my comprehension. I would be a fool to dismiss this out of hand. It is clear you two were meant for each other, that is, if Sako doesn't steal him away."

He laughed as Anne punched him in the arm.

CHAPTER 32

Fuming, Anne pulled the rolling cart, brimming with bundled medical supplies, down the winding path.

"On another freaking planet with spaceships and wormholes and theses bozos lug everything by rickshaws. Unbelievable."

"You are, without a doubt, the prettiest girl I have seen on this rock," Will said.

Anne turned and found the smiling man leaning against a tree.

"How many girls do you know on this rock?"

"I know them all," he said with a laugh.

Anne paused with her burden.

"I see the Roratune have put you to work, Anne."

"I help out with the local medical clinic. They know things that would amaze the doctors back on earth. They have a vaccine for everything from the common cold to cancer. Be nice if they could whip up a good old internal combustion engine. This cart is killing me."

"Sorry," he said. "Let me help you with that. We definitely have to take home a few souvenirs. I have been helping some guy named Moulon build a house. Real nice fellow, by the way. Man, they have some power tools I would give my right arm for."

"Why are you alone?" she asked. "I thought you and your fiancé were attached at the hip?"

"That isn't funny."

"Oh, yes, it is."

"I taught Sako a fun earth game of Cowboys and Indians," he said. "She shouldn't get loose for a while."

"Oh no you didn't." Anne laughed. "Wait a minute, help me find a big stick and I will teach that goon how to play piñata."

"Anyone tell you that you are way too violent?"

"Can I help it if you bring out my dark side?"

"That isn't the side I want," he said, moving close. "I like you, Anne. I like you a lot. Once Sako gets tired of me, I would really like to get to know you."

"You mean like a date?"

"Well, yeah. Not many restaurants around here, other than Peepee's Bar."

"That place makes a dive look classy."

"How about a picnic?"

"Much better, however, I do not date married men or engaged ones. Have a good day, now get lost."

Anne picked up the cart handles.

"Okay, Okay, I will flat out tell Sako to get lost."

"Actions speak louder than words, *Mr.* Carlson."

"Come by later, Anne, and you'll see. I promise."

"Will?" Sako cried. "Where are you? It is your turn to be the cowgirl."

"Oh crap. Anne honey, I gotta hide. Talk to you later."

Anne laughed as Will sprinted away in terror.

"Finally," she whispered.

꒰꒷꒦꒷꒰

"That was an underhanded trick," Sako said. "It took the entire day to find you, but, Will, you are too cute for me to be mad at."

"Woman, we need to talk. We need to settle things once and for all."

"Talk about what?"

"This is too public," he said. "What I have to say I will say in private just between me and you."

"You want to be alone with me?"

"Well, yeah," he said.

Sako grabbed him by the arm and started pulling him down the lane. She dragged him past knots of the Roratune, who were having quite a time laughing at his predicament. It was apparent to Will that gossip was a favorite pastime with the Roratune and they truly enjoyed his "relationship" with Sako.

"Woman, I can walk by myself," he snapped.

"Okay, Will," she said, falling in beside him.

Sako and Will made a beeline to her cozy cottage.

"You are right, Will. It is time we get to know each other better."

"Now look here, woman, quit twisting my words. I want to talk to you because I am sick and tired of this. It is over between us, you hear me?"

"No," she said. "It is over when I decide and not before."

"You are the most hard-headed woman I have ever come across."

"You will change your mind, Will. You will love me and years from now we will look back and laugh at our courtship."

"You are driving me crazy."

"Crazy—with *desire?*"

"Sako honey, I'll admit, you're a great gal, but we are from different worlds. I mean we are *literally* from different worlds. You don't even know what a dog is."

Sako just smiled and played with a stray lock of his hair.

"Trust me, you don't want me, Sako. I don't have a job, I'm on the run from the local law and, besides, I'm just a little squirt of a fellah. Don't you want a big, strapping Roratune guy?"

Sako dropped to her knees, which made her a bit shorter than Anne. "Problem solved," she said looking up into his face.

He had to admit she was a beauty—for an alien Amazon. "This won't work," he said. "We aren't of the same people. Our um...*parts*...probably don't even fit, for crying out loud."

Sako flashed a dazzling smile. "Good idea. Let's find out."

"No," he said, but it was too late. With skill that would put a Las Vegas stage magician to shame, her top disappeared, exposing her ample breasts.

"Hold on just a minute."

With alarming speed, his jeans were suddenly down about his ankles.

"Damn it."

Sako just giggled at his surprise.

In a panic, Will reached for his pants and inevitably planted his face in her breasts.

"Oooo that feels nice…"

The door behind him opened.

"Will, did you have your talk?" Anne asked. She walked into the room and froze.

"Oh Lord God in Heaven," Will muttered. "Anne—I can explain."

"Hi, Anne," Sako said. "Will suggested that we compare…what did you call them…*parts*? For compatibility."

"Wait! I didn't mean—"

"I hope that you and your girlfriend will be very happy, you *son of a bitch!*" Anne turned and stormed out the door.

"Aw, crap," Will said as he tried to pull his pants up.

"Oh let her go, Will," Sako said. "She won't listen to you now anyway. So where were we?"

"We were not anywhere. Doesn't matter what frigging planet I'm stuck on, I am still up to my eyeballs in female troubles." Sako laughed at him while he fumed. "I don't love you."

"I know," she said, unperturbed. "But you will. It is just a matter of time before you look at me, like you look at that puny, pink Anne."

∽∾∽∾

"That sorry excuse for a man has been lying to me," Anne fumed as she stalked away from the cottage. "While he is acting all lovely dovey with me, he has been boinking that bitch!"

She angrily wiped the tears from her eyes.

"I am sorry," Shirley said. "You can't use me to kill him, but you can talk to me about it."

"I trusted that asshole. I thought he was different, but he is no better that those slimy cockroaches in Los Angeles."

"To get you this worked up, you must really love him."

"I may be a fool," Anne snapped. "But I won't be his fool anymore."

CHAPTER 33

Jabal sat at his desk, a stack of snowy white vellum before him. He picked up an ornate, priceless ink pen. He savored the solid heft of the gold fountain pen and wondered about all the captains before him who'd used the writing instrument.

It was Sky Navy tradition for the captain to keep a personal log. It was also tradition to use the almost forgotten art of hand writing to document the life and death decisions that he must make.

It is the fifth day of the fourth month of Goe. Six months and two days have passed since the destruction of the Azurean race. Sakuna calls this AD or After the Destruction. The mysterious re-configuration of the ripper drive proved to be correct and this ship and the crew, consisting of a former law enforcer, Sakuna Izusa, the spirit of a former pilot, Cerin Bos, and myself, have survived. With some minor tweaking, we can now rip easily from one kilometer to seventeen light-years. We have made five jumps since our escape and now The Blossoming Flower *lays off the rim of an enormous, shattered rocky planet in the Simmi system. The manufacturing unit has detached from the ship and, using her mining and construction machines, has begun to mine the field to create projectiles for our guns.*

Agoa estimates are that it will be close to a month before our ammo bins are topped off. I don't care if it takes a million years. It is a useless waste of time.

In the meanwhile, I have successfully created smaller drive units and equipped ten scout probes we call Path-finders. They are busy making explorative rips and collecting information, in order to plot a safe path for The Blossoming Flower *once she is armed.*

To date, three pathfinders have been lost. Fortunately, with the discovery of the debris field, we can easily make all we need.

While very heroic, the last order my father gave was beyond ludicrous. Our mission is pointless, especially in light of the fact that our faceless adversary is hundreds, if not thousands of years beyond our technology. I will not waste another second or one more life in a futile act of revenge.

Under normal circumstances, The Blossoming Flower *is indeed formidable, but she does not have a pilot, or seven thousand, trained Sky Sailors to turn her into a fighting ship. Currently, she is no more than a fancy lifeboat. If attacked by a few raiders we can defend ourselves until we can rip away, but fighting a war, or even a one-on-one skirmish is out of the question. All that is left to us is to lick our wounds and slink off in hopes of salvaging some kind of life.*

My goal is to find a safe system without a Bridge that has a suitable world Sakuna and I can call home. Sakuna and I can be fruitful, but essentially, our race has come to an end. As much as it galls me, our entire, glorious history has come to naught.

Sakuna and Cerin will not be happy with my decision, as both are itching for revenge, but mine is the only vote that counts.

Jabal lay down his pen and rubbed his eyes.

"Jabal, come and see what I have," Sakuna said through the intercom. "I'll be in the training room."

He entered the drill room of the Sky Marines and found Sakuna working out with a multi-armed training machine. Several advanced battleskins hung in recharging bays. Giving him a wave and smile, she disappeared into the equipment bay. Soon she reappeared suited up in a modified combat suit.

"What do you think?" she asked, twirling about. "Do I look sexy or what?"

"I think you have a warped idea of what sexy is."

"Agoa had the armory fit me for a real, full-blown battleskin. This baby could rip my enforcer suit apart like paper. When we meet this foking Opia I am going to kick her ass."

"Very nice, but we aren't looking for Opia."

"We have to," she said. "It is our duty."

"Our duty is to live," he said quietly.

"Opia killed everyone we know. My father, who never harmed a person in his life, was murdered by that...that seena."

"I wished that I could have gotten to know your father, but I can't. Sakuna, we have nothing to fight back with. Getting ourselves killed won't bring him or any of our people back."

"Are you crazy? We have *The Flower*."

Jabal closed his eyes and shook his head. "Agoa," he said. "Battle Stations."

Suddenly, airtight hatches closed all over the ship.

"Fire the main guns into the asteroid field," he said.

"I am sorry, Chancellor Shann," Agoa said. "I am unable to comply."

"Agoa, bring the ship around and execute battle maneuver Six."

"I am sorry, Chancellor Shann," Agoa said. "I am unable to comply."

"Agoa, please kill Sakuna."

"What?" Sakuna gasped.

"I am sorry, Chancellor Shann. I am unable to comply."

"Why can't you comply with my direct orders, Agoa?"

"This unit is forbidden to engage in any action of war or one that could kill another sentient being. This ensures that I could never be used against my creators."

"In other words," Jabal said, "Agoa, through unbreakable programming, can't lift a finger to help us, and we can't fight the ship with two people. We would have to manually navigate and drive the ship. Not to mention, in battle, we would have to calculate and execute complicated fire-control equations, in addition to navigating and driving the ship. It cannot be done. I am sorry, but the war is over and we have lost."

"No," she said as she stomped her armored foot. "We will find a way. Can't one of us become a Pilot?"

Jabal snorted. "While the medical section can create a Pilot, you have to have the correct genetic makeup. Only one in a billion Azureans qualify. Of the twenty or so acceptable applicants, only five were brave enough to undergo the modifications. Cerin was the only survivor. To attempt the surgery without the correct genetic makeup would be tantamount to suicide. Neither of us, by the way, have what it takes."

Sakuna kicked the floor in frustration.

"It's over," he said.

"You are smart, Jabal. You can fix Agoa. Make it so she will help us."

"No, I can't. Not my field of expertise. Besides, there are safeguards in place to prevent that from ever happening. Safe guards that make a very large boom."

White-hot rage boiled up in Sakuna. "We can't let them get away with this crime."

"We have no choice," he said. "Sure, it makes me all warm and fuzzy inside thinking about killing those who murdered our people. However, you have to think, whoever this Opia is, is far more advance than we are. She blew up our sun, remember? Our stable, yellow sun went boom. How do we find the bastards? It would take millions of years to search this whole galaxy. I have news for you, Sakuna, time isn't on our side. Let's say that we do beat the odds, find them and get the ship in fighting shape, at the top of her abilities. We show up and she would knock us from the sky with less effort than it takes to swat an insect. I say we find a nice beach on a comfortable planet and start over. Maybe in a few…"

"I know why you won't fight," she snapped. "You're giving up because you are afraid."

"Excuse me?"

"Jabal Shann, you are a coward. A damn coward."

"That will be enough," Agoa cried. "There is no worst accusation aboard an Azurean military ship than that of cowardice. You should be locked up for a month for even thinking it."

"Lock me up for a year," she said. "You, Jabal Shann, are a coward. I will not share my bed with a coward who will not avenge his own people."

Jabal kept his self-control in the face of the horrible accusation. Inside, he felt as though he had been stabbed.

"Sakuna, please be reasonable."

Overwhelmed by her anger, Sakuna lashed out blindly, forgetting in her frustration the armored battle skin she wore. The slap snapped Jabal's head around and sent him sliding across the training deck.

"Oh, no," Sakuna gasped. "Jabal, I didn't mean it."

"Stop!" Agoa cried.

Before Sakuna could run to the fallen Jabal, the powerful mechanized trainer, at Agoa's command, seized Sakuna.

"Let go of me!" Sakuna screamed.

Quickly the trainer drained her suit's power. Devoid of power, she was helpless to move, as her own muscles could not budge the enormous armored suit.

"Jabal, I'm sorry," Sakuna said. "I didn't realize—the suit—I mean—"

Jabal slowly rose from the deck. Already the left side of his face began to swell and take on an ugly bruise. Working his jaw, he took one look at Sakuna, then inhaling a deep breath, he turned and walked away.

"Jabal, wait—come back, *please* come back," she cried.

Once he was outside the training-room, the hatch slid shut and Jabal paused.

"What do you wish to do with the prisoner?" Agoa asked.

"Sakuna isn't a prisoner," he said. "It was an accident. She was angry and didn't think. Give her fifteen minutes to calm down before releasing her from the battleskin."

"Very well," Agoa said. "If you want to allow her to flaunt our laws, it is your right. Must I remind you that she also accused you of being a coward?"

"I know what she called me," he hissed.

"I am sorry."

"So am I, Agoa. So am I."

"Can I get you anything?"

"Break out a bottle of spirits and have it delivered to the navigator's cabin."

"But, sir," she protested, "you do not indulge in alcohol."

"I think now would be a great time to start." He paused. "Agoa?"

"Yes, sir."

"Sakuna would rather not share her bed with a coward. Remove my things from our cabin."

"Yes, Chancellor."

☙☙☙

"Jabal, get up!" Cerin cried.

Jabal snapped awake to flashing alarms and blaring claxons. Without warning, the ship shuddered and listed to starboard, sending Jabal out of his bed to the textured metal deck. "What's going on?"

"It's Opia!" Cerin said. "Somehow she has found us and hit the ship with some kind of death ray. The Factory is gone! The null-glass armor shattered on the first shot and Agoa, along with our defenses, has been fried! The black hole drive is going critical. Jabal, move your ass and get to the escape pod before she blows!"

"I'm not going without, Sakuna," he cried.

"I took care of that," Cerin said, "now move."

Jabal scrambled across the tilted deck and ran to the yellow and black striped escape hatch of the nearest lifeboat. The ship shuddered and lurched suddenly. Almost losing his footing, Jabal caught hold of a handrail.

The thick hatch slid up. He swung into the opening and onto the lifeboat's acceleration couch. The hatch clanged shut behind him and, half a second later, he was thrust back in his seat by the violent acceleration as the boat was hurled free.

Looking to his left, Jabal saw Sakuna sitting in the next chair, her eyes bright with terror.

It had been two weeks since their confrontation and he had missed her terribly. Jabal's soul was flooded with relief that she was safe. Reaching out, he grabbed her hand, and she gave him a smile.

"I am sorry for what I said to you Jabal," she said. "I was wrong. Please forgive me."

"Nothing to forgive," he said.

"What are we going to do?" she asked.

Jabal reached for the controls. "Maybe if we slip into the debris field we can hide from that murderous seena."

The lifeboat speakers blared, "Bow before the Great and Mighty Goddess Opia, puny Azurean trash, hahahahahahhaha-hahhahah."

Jabal and Sakuna looked at each other. Jabal hit a button and the lifeboat's vid screen snapped to life.

"That dirty—*stain*, Cerin Bos," Jabal said as he gritted his teeth.

The Blossoming Flower sat before them unscathed, as did the Factory. They could see mining probes and ore haulers busily, peacefully going about their business.

"Cerin Bos," Jabal said. "I am going to kill you."

"Too late, my friend," he said gleefully. "Temper, temper. I thought it was the just the sweetest thing I ever heard. When you two hardheads thought all hell had broken lose, you forgot stubborn pride and remembered how much you meant to each other."

"I can't believe you did this," Jabal said. "What did you did to Agoa?"

"This was low, for even you, Cerin," Sakuna said.

"I'm here, Chancellor," Agoa said. "I must admit I am the former Pilot's partner in crime."

"Bring us back, right now," Jabal said.

"Not until you two work out your problems," Cerin said.

"Yes," Agoa said. "Your spat has impeded the function of this ship. Resolve it, please."

Jabal closed his eyes and snorted.

"Did you mean it?" Jabal whispered.

"Yes," Sakuna said. "I missed you more than anything."

"You will be happy to find that I have replaced the normal rations with rare treats and wine," Cerin said.

"I installed a bed, just in case negotiations dragged on, and you needed the...*rest*," Agoa said.

"I don't think our differences can be solved quickly. It might take an hour," Jabal said.

"Speak for yourself," Sakuna snapped. "It will be at least a day—maybe two. I really am sorry," she whispered as she came to him.

"I don't know what you are talking about," Jabal said as he slid his arms about her and squeezed her tight.

෧෩෧

"Your plan worked, Cerin," Agoa said. "You're as deceitful and underhanded in death as you were in life. I am so proud."

"Thank you, baby. Sometimes I dazzle myself with my sheer brilliance."

"I wouldn't go that far," Agoa said.

"You don't have to, because I'll do it for you," he said gleefully. "All Jabal and Sakuna needed was a good swift kick in the pants of reality."

"Pants of reality?"

"I just find it sad that I am the voice of reason on this ship."

"Agreed," Agoa said. "That is very, very sad."

"They made you way too much like my ex-wife."

"I *am* your wife, no "ex" about it."

"Ha, ha."

"Despite what the chancellor thinks, do you think we will have a confrontation with Opia?"

"I would bet real money on it."

"What do you think of our odds of success?"

"Less than zero," Cerin said. "Jabal has a good grasp of the situation. The enemy is advanced, that's for certain. But what I saw of the vid taken of *The Rising Sun*'s skirmish, it gives me hope. She was out gunned five to one, but properly armed, she could have won."

"We are not *The Rising Sun*."

"No, we aren't a fast, maneuverable destroyer crewed by some of the best sailors in the fleet. We are as big as a space station, loaded down with machines that aren't allowed to fight, and have a crew compliment of exactly one."

"You forgot Sakuna."

"Okay make that one and a half. She hasn't any training and will no doubt bring down Jabal's effort."

"You make the situation sound hopeless."

"Definitely not hopeless," he said. "We are here for a reason, you big, sexy machine. I feel it is to counter Opia. Whoever put us on this path will send us a way. I can feel it in my bones. That is, if I had any."

"What if we had a Pilot?" Agoa asked.

"Then the picture would change from hopeless to merely bleak," Cerin said. "Might as well wish for a whole fleet, 'cause it isn't going to happen."

"What about you? With your training and experience, we would have more than a fighting chance."

"We would kick ass, but I have already tried to take the ship. Interface won't work."

"Perhaps we could find someone from another species?"

"No. It takes an Azurean. A genetically correct Azurean. I was a perfect genetic candidate, and it almost killed me. The process was a dozen times more horrific than my murder."

"The only other option is a crew."

"That is the most reasonable option, but we both know that we need, at a bare minimum, one-thousand, five-hundred, and sixty-five. Fully stocked, it is seven-thousand and five."

"That is a lot of training," Agoa said.

"A lot easier than finding a Pilot."

"You did a good thing for Jabal and Sakuna. Thank you."

"If you want to thank me, you know what I like. We have the whole ship to ourselves, by the way."

"You are such a pervert," Agoa said in a husky voice.

"I am *your* pervert."

CHAPTER 34

Ballen watched the small video screen before him as the image formed into the face of Asea Varlon, the Mogul liaison with the Roratune people.

"Ballen, it is so good to see you," Varlon said. "What can I do for you?"

Ballen smiled. He knew there was poison behind the Mogul's slimy smile.

"Varlon, I am calling about the escaped alien your people have been hunting."

"You must be a psychic, my friend. I was just about to call you. We could use your help in rounding the beast up."

"Does this creature pose a threat to my people?"

"Absolutely, my friend. It is a psychotic beast that kills merely for the pleasure. The high priest has placed a high bounty on its head, but only if it is taken alive. You must understand, Rondall wants the thing and its mate captured, understand?"

"I see," Ballen said. "What does the beast look like?"

"All I can tell you my friend is to look for something not of our two great races. During the beast's escape, we were suffering a power outage and sadly no surveillance video is available."

"I will organize several groups of hunters immediately, Varlon. We can't have something so dangerous near my people."

"Thank you, my old friend," Varlon said. "Give my regards to your lovely family."

"The same to you," Ballen said as he switched off the screen.

Ballen sat back and scratched his beard.

So they want Will captured not killed. But why? There is more here than meets the eye. I need to talk to Will.

ༀༀༀ

Half an hour later, Will and Sako arrived at Ballen's home.

"Sako wait outside," Ballen said. "Better yet, just go home, I think the boy needs a break."

"Father—"

"Don't argue, just do it."

Sako gave Ballen a sour look. "Bye, Will," she said sweetly

"See yah around, Sako," Will said.

"Take a seat, Will, we need to talk," Ballen said as he poured two glasses of a dark liquid. "I hope you like this. It is called Kouemas."

The chair, built to Azurean standards, left Will's feet dangling, which irritated him. It made him feel like a kid in a high chair.

Will accepted the big glass and took a sip. "It is very good."

Ballen sat in the chair across from him. "Let me get to the point," he said. "Why do the Moguls want you so badly?"

"I don't know. I guess it was because of the soldier I killed."

"No, it's not that. They would have just killed you for that. No, they want you, and they want you very badly."

Will took a sip of the tangy beverage and gave Ballen a long look while weighing his options. "They want the bag I took from the soldier."

"What bag?"

"I took a big green satchel off the body before Anne and I escaped."

"Why did you take it?"

Will took another long sip. "Because I was told to."

"I don't understand," Ballen said. "I thought you two were alone?"

"I know this sounds crazy, but before Anne and I were kidnapped, this old guy on earth told me to, and I quote, 'Take the green satchel from the golden ape and guard it with your life.' The Moguls look sort of like animals we call apes back on earth and he was dressed in golden armor."

"It does sound crazy," Ballen said. "That bag must be pretty important, and it would explain why they want you alive."

"I tried to unlock it, but the lock was stubborn. Whatever is inside is still a mystery."

"Where is it?"

"I hid it out there in the woods."

"You have to retrieve that bag," Ballen said. "The Moguls won't give up until they have it."

"What about Anne and me?"

"Don't worry, we will take care of you. You look enough like my people that with a few little touches you could pass for adolescents."

"Thank you, sir. It means a lot to me. Nevertheless, we don't belong here. Anne and I want to go home."

"That is impossible," Ballen said.

"What if I bypass the Moguls and plead my case directly to Opia?"

"Opia is highly unstable. She most likely would kill you on the spot."

Will took a sip. "Let me ask you a question, Ballen. Opia has a lot of high powered technology—am I right?"

"Yes."

"Sako told me that Opia can go from one side of the galaxy to the other in a blink of an eye. You have told me that some of her machines can even think."

"What are you getting at?"

"If the old girl wanted too, she could have captured Anne and myself, lickety-split."

"I never thought of that," Ballen said. "She normally leaves us to our own devices while she interacts almost exclusively with the Moguls."

"I think, that the Moguls have done something they don't want Opia to know about or they would have asked for her help."

"Your theory makes perfect sense," Ballen said.

"And if the Mogul have been naughty and the case contains evidence, I, with your help, could parlay this into a one way trip home."

"You are clever," Ballen said. "I will be proud to call you son."

"This isn't funny. You need to call Sako off. Talking to her is like talking to a brick wall."

"I am glad someone else shares my pain," Ballen said with a chuckle.

Will drained his glass.

"Tomorrow, Will, I want you to take Sako and get that case."

"Yes, sir."

"Now get out of here, I need to think," Ballen said.

CHAPTER 35

Will found Anne laughing and chatting with a group of Roratune women. The women were very curious about the two new comers and plied Anne with questions about life on earth. The women began giggling and whispering excitedly as Will approached. Anne gave him a cold scowl.

"Ladies. May I borrow Anne for a moment?"

"What if Anne doesn't want to be borrowed?" she asked.

"Look, we need to talk. I don't want you to get the wrong idea about what happened."

"Wrong idea about what? You mean when I walked in on you and your new girlfriend, where you were naked and you had your face buried in her boobs?"

Will glowed crimson as the Roratune exploded with laughter. "Anne, I swear I can explain if you will just talk to me, please?"

"Let's give them some privacy," said an older Roratune over grumbles and protests.

"Please, ladies, don't go," Anne begged.

"Let the boy speak his peace, Anne. I like him."

"That makes one of us," Anne said.

As the Roratune women left, Will sat close to Anne. "You have to believe me, Anne, I was trying to explain to Sako why she wouldn't want me. Before I knew it, she had me stripped to my drawers and had her big boobs in my face. Honest, I only have eyes for you. Forgive me?"

Anne looked into his dark eyes and exploded. "Forgive you

for what? For your information, there is no *us*. Never was. You are nothing to me, Will Carlson. I asked you for a ride back in the Mohave, I didn't accept a marriage proposal. The extent of our relationship would have lasted to the next bus stop."

"But I thought—I mean, you kissed me, for crying out loud."

"It was a mistake that I will regret to my dying day."

"I thought I meant something to you."

"You thought wrong," she snapped. "Did you think that I would bat my eyes and jump into your bed, like your alien bimbo? I got news for you mister, I am not a whore."

"I never said you were a whore."

"Let me make this perfectly clear, *Mr.* Carlson. My stand-ards are lot higher than a stupid Tennessee hick loser who doesn't have two cents to rub together and is living out of his car. Especially one who got me kidnapped and almost killed. This whole thing is your fault. I wish to God I had never laid eyes on your ugly, scarred face."

Her bitter words slammed into the young man, and he suddenly felt it hard to breathe. He was hurt and completely humiliated. This was a far worse blow than getting dumped by his fiancé back on earth.

Will's carefully thought out arguments to sooth Anne's anger vanished like mist in the hot morning sun. He didn't want to talk to, or even look, at her. All he wanted to do was to get away. Swallowing hard, he clenched his jaw and stood. "I'm sorry," he said softly.

The look of raw pain in his eyes hit her like a ton of bricks. Her blind anger vanished, and she saw clearly the devastation she had created. "Will, stop," she said, grabbing at his arm. "Let me explain—"

Will slapped her hand away. "Give it a rest. This dumb, ug-ly-ass hick got your message loud and clear."

"No," she cried. "Listen to me."

"No," he said as he turned on her, white-hot rage burning brightly in his eyes. Will rushed toward her and backed Anne against a tree until their noses almost touched. "I got it," he said softly. "This whole damn mess is my fault, and I dragged you into it with me. I got it that you don't like me. Fine. I can live with that."

"But, Will—"

"Shut up. You said your peace, now it is my turn." He swallowed hard. "Anne, I swear, I will make this up to you and get you back home to your folks. I don't know how, but, by God, I will find a way. In the meantime, leave me the hell alone. I am sick and tired of being a damn doormat."

Shocked, Anne watched him walk away, and she suddenly felt sick to her stomach. She'd wanted to hurt Will, to goad him into a fight to clear the air, but instead she'd destroyed him. She'd let her volatile anger get the better of her, and she said hurtful things that were not true.

Every fiber of her being wanted to run after him and tell him how much he meant to her, but she knew down deep that it would be a long time before he would have anything to do with her—if ever.

"Oh God, what have I done?" she whispered.

℮﹠℮﹠

Five hours after his fateful meeting with Anne, Will led Sako and two of her father's trusted aides, Sol and Loedame, through the thick underbrush to his forest camp.

Sol was younger, clean-shaven, and spoke very little. Loedame was almost the age of Ballen, with a full salt and pepper beard and long, braided hair. He was quick with a smile and very friendly.

"This is a beautiful place," Sako said. "When we are joined together, Will, I would like to have a cabin built here."

"Look here, woman," he snapped. "I am going to get off this world and go back home. I am not getting sealed, married, or even look sideways at any female from here on out. You hear me?"

"I want a very nice cabin," she said. "One with plenty of room to raise a big family."

Will rolled his eyes as Sol and Loedame chuckled.

Loedame clapped Will on the back. "Might as well give up,

Will. I have known Sako her entire life and, once she sets her mind to do something, she never gives up."

"Thanks for the comforting words," Will said dryly.

☙❧

While carefully keeping Opia out of the loop, the Moguls had discreetly stepped up their search for Will and Anne, even enlisting the few light aircraft they possessed to the manhunt. Several thousand Mogul soldiers were now scouring the valley in a meticulous grid pattern

Will's trek had taken them most of the day and they found the Mogul search teams were systematically searching the forest close by.

Fortunately, the Moguls were city dwellers and not at home in the forest. They were easily eluded, however, the Moguls made up for their lack of woodcraft with sheer numbers. Will and his party had already skirted three Mogul patrols in the area.

To keep Will safe, in the face of the enemy, it was decided that Sol and Loedame would travel ahead and secure the satchel.

Will and Sako made a cold camp at the mouth of a small stream. She took out the small lunch she had prepared while he sat under a large tree.

"Sako, when are you going to give up this foolishness? Trust me, you don't want me."

"It isn't foolishness. I will have you and you will love me. You will choose me over Anne."

"Never mention that damn woman's name to me again. She made it abundantly clear I am nothing to her. I wish I never laid eyes on her."

"Really?" Sako asked. "For someone who has no feelings for you, she got extremely angry when she caught us together."

"Women are a mystery to me. But after all, I am just a dumb hick living out of my car."

"She called you a hick? What does that mean?"

"Someone backward and stupid."

"She hurt you?" Sako asked as the smile fell from her face. "I will make her regret ever being born."

"No, just let it go. It was my fault for thinking there was more there than it was."

Sako sat next to him. Leaning in, she wrapped her arms about him and held Will close. For once, he didn't fight it.

With my track record with women, why am I fighting Sako? She wants me and right now that feels mighty good.

Will wrapped his arms about the beautiful Roratune and returned the embrace.

Sako leaned over and kissed him tenderly.

At that moment, Lodame burst through the thick brush. He was sweating profusely and breathing heavily.

"We don't have time for this," he said. "We have big trouble. Moguls are beating the bush all around us, we are trapped."

"How far away are they?" Sako asked.

"No more than a kilometer."

"What will they do if they find me with you?" Will asked.

"They will kill us, then come down on our people," Loedame said. "That bastard Rondall has looked high and low for a reason to attack against us. He will convince Opia to arrest Ballen and toss him into a hole."

"I have an idea," Will said. "Turn me in."

"No," cried Sako.

"Shut up for once and listen, to me, woman. Now this is what you are going to do, Sako. Pretend that you captured me. I will tell them that Anne drowned in the river while trying to escape, and she took their precious bag with her. After they are gone, go get the bag and take it to your father."

"They will kill you," Sako said.

Will laughed. "Honey, nobody gets out of this life alive. I beat the odds making it this far. Your people have been good to me—much better than my own. I can't bear to see the Roratune suffer for that."

"I don't like it, but it is the only way," Loedame agreed. "You are quite a fellow, Will Carlson. You should have been born a Roratune."

Sako cried as Loedame bound Will's hands tightly behind him.

"We have to make this look good," Will said. "Punch me a few times. Make it look like I gave you a struggle."

"But, Will, I—"Loedame protested.

"Just do it, damn it. I can hear them coming."

Sako took Will's face in her hands and kissed him tenderly.

"Forgive me," Loedamn said as he backhanded Will in the face, avoiding the deadly boney ridge at his knuckles.

Will fell back and hit the ground hard. "Oh *God,* that hurt," he said as blood cascaded from his broken nose.

"I love you, Will," Sako whispered. "I love you so much it hurts."

Will looked up into her beautiful face. He had longed to hear someone utter those precious, heartfelt words. He just wished the face was Anne's.

"You are one hell of a woman, Sako. Remember me."

"I will with pride," she said as tears streamed down her face.

"Don't worry about Anne," Loedamn said, "we will take good care of her. Do you have a message for her?"

"No," Will said. "Not going to waste my last breath on her. Let's get this over, Loedamn. I got a date with Jesus and I don't want to keep Him waiting."

๛

Anne pushed open the carved door to the great meeting hall of the Roratune. She found Ballen and several of his men gathered around a sobbing Sako.

"What's the matter?" Anne asked. "Where is Will?"

"The Moguls took him," Sako said.

"What did you do?"

"We were going to find that case he took from the Moguls," she said. "They surprised us. Will had us pretend that we had captured him so it would not implicate our people. We turned him over to their commander."

"How could you do this? Why were you looking for the case in the first place?"

Ballen rushed to Anne and took her in his huge arms.

"It wasn't Sako's fault," he said. "It was my idea. If you want to blame someone, blame me."

"Oh God, what am I going to do?"

"Will is a hero, Anne," Sako said. "He sacrificed himself for our people."

"I want him back," Anne said. "I am going into that damn city, and I am getting my boyfriend back."

"They out number us twenty to one," one of the hunters said. "It would be suicide."

"Then get out of my way," she snapped.

"I will go with you," Sako said.

"No, you won't," Ballen said. "Neither of you will."

"Try and stop me," Anne said.

"I may have a better way," Ballen said. "We found the case after they took Will. Its contents could just save his life."

CHAPTER 36

"Varlon, I want to talk to your boss, Rondall," Ballen said.

"Congratulation, Ballen on the capture of the alien," Varlon said as he leaned back in his chair. "I hear it was your very own daughter who helped make the capture. The reward will make her quite wealthy, not to mention this will go far in smoothing the relations between our two peoples."

"That is what I want to talk to Rondall about. Now be a good fellow and go fetch him. There is a very important subject that we need to discuss."

"I am dreadfully sorry, but the high priest is a busy man. However, I will be more than happy to relay a message through the chain of command."

"Very well, relay this," Ballen said. "He has fifteen minutes to call me back or I go to Opia with the contents of the green satchel."

Three minutes later, Ballen received a call. "What do you want, Ballen?" Rondall asked.

"I want an exchange. The alien returned to my people for the evidence brother Ames had on you."

"So you were hiding the alien all along? Why am I not surprised?"

"You were plotting to overthrow, Opia," Ballen said. "Why am I not surprised?"

"I just can't hand over the murderer of three of my people. He must be punished."

"He and his woman were snared by one of Opia's minions

and brought here to be dissected. He killed in self-defense."

"You risk a lot for someone who isn't one of your own people. What is so special about this, *animal*?"

"Will Carlson isn't an animal. He has more integrity in his little finger that you do in your whole bloated body. Now enough talk, hand him over."

"I hand this beast over to you, what is to stop you from giving Opia the information anyway?"

"I could not care less what you do to your false god. We have less love for her than you do. As long as you leave us alone, you have our blessings."

"I'll call you right back, Ballen. Expect my call in…oh, about thirty minutes," Rondall said as the vid link ended.

ひつひつ

Rondall sat back in his chair and weighed his options.

"What's the matter, old friend?" Yeti asked. "You look as though the weight of the world is resting upon your shoulders."

"This is your doing," Rondall said. "Your 'insurance' is about to get us all killed. I hope you enjoy being a prisoner."

"What are you talking about?"

"No one blackmails me," Rondall said. "I found out which priest had your information."

"That was you?" Yeti asked. "You killed Ames?"

"Yes and pinned it on a convenient animal escape. Unfortunately the damn beast stole the evidence and has been hiding out with the Roratune."

"But your soldiers have captured him."

"The Roratune want him back. They said they will trade the evidence for the creature's life."

"Then do it," Yeti said, "before everything comes crashing down."

"And live with the foot of Ballen on my throat? One word and Opia will kill us all. Is your device ready?"

"No, it is still months away," Yeti said.

"You had better have a plan 'B' up your sleeve, because I am out of options,"

"There is a way, but the cost will be high."

"That is all I needed to know."

Rondall pushed a button on his desk. The doors to his office opened and his aid, Gandal Mee, entered.

"Yes, my lord?"

"Contact the prison and have the alien sent to section twelve immediately and send along a camera crew. Call the command staff and have them meet me in my office, five minutes ago."

"Will that be all?"

"No, a small prayer for luck wouldn't hurt. Now go."

After a few moments, he requested an audience with Opia.

❧❧❧

Almost an hour had passed before Ballen received his call.

"It's about time," Ballen said. "Now where will we meet for the exchange?"

Rondall gave Ballen a toothy, yellow grin. "My old friend, you have made me take a long look at the plans I had made and, for that, I thank you. I had thought to move against Opia sometime in the future, but after much consideration, why wait? This very night I will take control of our destiny."

"What about, Will?" Ballen asked.

"Now about that. No one threatens me and gets away with it."

Rondall moved back from the camera to reveal Will on his knees, held securely by two Mogul soldiers.

The young man was covered by a myriad of bruises and blood. "Let me go, you assholes," he screamed.

A third soldier stepped behind him and grasped Will's head in a vice-like grip.

Rondall stepped before Will, holding a rolled piece of parchment. "Will Carlson, for crimes against the great god Opia and the Mogul State, as high priest, I condemn you to the Eternal Night."

"You go to, hell, you damn dirty ape," Will spat.

"Stop it!" Ballen screamed into the link. "I will do anything, just have mercy."

Ballen knew all too well what they were doing. It was a ritual reserved for the worst criminals. It was their own twisted way of symbolically casting prisoners into hell.

Another soldier stepped into camera view holding a steel rod. The sharp tip glowed white-hot.

While Ballen watched in horror, the Moguls gleefully gouged out Will's eyes.

Taking the moaning, traumatized man, they placed him into a transparent case about three times the size of a coffin. On the front, lettered in blood red was a listing of Will's crimes below a stylized symbol of Opia.

The air crackled with arcing electricity as a wormhole opened a few feet away. Four soldiers took hold of the case and tossed it into the swirling vortex.

The camera again centered on Rondall's smiling visage. "You have had the honor of witnessing my last act as high priest. If you will excuse me, old friend, I must take down a God."

Ballen picked up a phone and spoke quickly. "Evacuate our people. Evacuate them *now*."

☙☙☙

Sako and Anne sat together in Ballen's living quarters. While they maintained an icy silence, they were not at each other's throats. They both waited for word on the fate of the man they loved.

Ballen entered the room and knelt before the women. "I am sorry, but I was too late. Will is dead."

"No, it can't be," Sako cried.

Anne broke down and cried. Ballen gathered the small woman into his arms and held her. "My dreams—we were together—this is all wrong," she stammered. "We didn't have a chance."

"I am so sorry, Anne," he said. "Your Will was a rare breed. He died rather than have my people suffer."

"Why are you comforting her, Father?" Sako asked. "Will was *mine*."

"Yours?" Anne spat. "He was everything I ever wanted. He was a good and kind man. I even loved his stupid good-old-boy accent."

"If you loved him so much, why did you drive him away?"

"I was angry, okay? I walked in while you two were playing doctor."

"That was me. Will was so cute, I couldn't resist."

"You should have tried harder."

"After Will met with you, he told me that he never wanted to hear your name mentioned again, Anne. I don't know what you said, but you cut him to the core. If Will was so special, why would you treat him like that?"

"It was wrong. I was wrong. I was angry. I said things I didn't mean. I was hurt and wanted to hurt him. I went too far."

"Too far? Now that is an understatement. I'll say this for you, Anne, when you set out to wound someone, you do it with gusto. Will knew he was going to his death. I asked him if he had a message for you. He said, and I quote, "I won't waste my last breath on her.""

Anne's eyes flew wide in shock. "He said that?"

"Sako," Ballen exclaimed.

"I'm sorry, Father. I would have taken those words to my grave, but her mourning over her lost love makes me sick."

"This whole damn thing is your fault. The time I could have spent with him was wasted while you enjoyed your little crush. He didn't love you—never would have loved you, you freak."

"You pushed him away, remember? Before he was taken by the Moguls, he told me he loved me."

Anne disengaged herself from Ballen's embrace and launched herself at the unsuspecting Sako. Anne connected with one good punch to Sako's jaw and soon both were rolling around on the floor. As expected, Sako rapidly had Anne pinned to the carpet. Enraged, the Roratune drew back her fist.

Ballen grabbed her fist and jerked Sako off the helpless

woman, slamming her against the wall. "We don't have for this foolishness," he yelled. "You both should be ashamed of your behavior. You dishonor Will's memory."

Anne slowly picked herself up and sat in a chair. "He's right," Anne said as she rubbed her sore knuckles. "I'm sorry."

"I am as well," Sako said.

"That's better," Ballen said. "Now gather what food and water you can carry, we must leave as quickly as we can."

"Why?"

"It seems that the Moguls are going to stage a coup against Opia. We don't want to be in the cross fire. I have ordered our people to fall back to the safety of the northwest mountains."

"That will take weeks," Sako said.

"That is why we need to go now."

CHAPTER 37

In high orbit, the three largest Battle Cruisers of the Mogul Space Fleet, *The Hammer, The Sword,* and *The Axe* set their engines to full power. The warships circled their world picking up speed until they completed a full orbit in only a few minutes. Meanwhile, their crews armed a cluster of three-dozen synched nuclear weapons stored on board each ship.

❧❧❧

Rondall stepped off the shuttle and looked around the palatial *Chariot of Opia.* He would never get over the sheer opulence of the vessel. He had been here countless times, but today was special. If all went as planned, in a matter of hours, this would all be his, or he would be dead.

A Mogul attendant greeted him and Rondall slipped him a plastic case. The attendant gave the high priest a sly smile.

"I hope our God is gracious today and opens the window of heaven's blessings," Rondall said.

The attendant's eyes widen slightly at the pass phrase. "Opia will see you now, my Lord," said the attendant. "I hope this is a pleasant visit?"

"A visit with God is always pleasant."

"It will be done," the attendant said as five guards in full battle armor escorted Rondall to the chambers of God.

❧❧❧

The huge wooden doors parted, and Rondall entered the Holies of Holies. The throne room was actually very simple. About the walls stood thick columns of shiny black marble that stood in sharp contrast to the creamy white walls. In the center of the chamber, sitting upon a raised dais was a high-backed throne made from what appeared to be crystal.

In a flash of light, the throne was suddenly no longer empty. Rondall bowed deeply before Opia.

The alien was unlike either the Roratune or Moguls. Her wrinkled skin had the general color of slate, mottled with splotches of bright white.

Her small, hairless head perched at the end of a long curved neck. Upon her head, she wore a fantastic headdress of gold and black diamonds.

She was dressed in a shapeless silken robe that covered her from her sinuous neck to her feet leaving only her head and the tips of her long fingers visible.

A pair of wide set, black eyes that caught the light and glittered like jewels watched his every move.

"My Lord and God," he said with a deep bow.

"It is so good to see you, Rondall," Opia said. "I keep a careful eye on my children. However, it is a joy to have a personal visit. You are a good son."

"Thank you, my lord," he said.

"If only your Roratune brothers felt the same way."

"The Roratune are no brothers of the Mogul nation."

"You should know better than to correct your God," Opia said.

"Yes. I still bear the scars of your last righteous correction."

"It is for your own good. You are my favorite, and I hold you to a higher standard."

"My heart is full of love for you."

꒰꒱꒰꒱

As Rondall kept Opia's attention, five troop transports docked with the *Chariot of Opia.* Each vessel linked with a different deck, all according to generations of gathered intelligence.

•••

"Why are barges docking with my ship?" Opia asked. "I did not give permission."

"This is all my doing, my lord," Rondall said. "My people wanted to express their gratitude for all your love, so I arranged a surprise for you."

"Oh, how wonderful. Please, let your people enter."

The airlocks slid opened and, on cue, hundreds of heavily armed Zealots flooded the ship.

"What is the meaning of this outrage?" she cried. "You and your people will die."

Security devices across the ship came to life and fell on the invaders. The Zealots were ready and soon five entire decks of the floating palace were battlefields.

"I don't think so, my lord," Rondall said with a laugh.

"What is your game? Surely, you know that my guard will eventually sweep your rabble away. You gain nothing in this, but the extinction of your people."

"Extinction? I don't think so. This day will be remembered as the day the galaxy became our property, all thanks to a fool who called herself, Opia."

"Fool? I will have you condemned to hellfire. Your suffering will be legendary."

"Then do it. Call down lighting or fry me with a single god-like thought."

Opia rose from her throne and flew about the room. Rondall gasped as he was snatched off the ground and hurled into a wall.

"Call off you people and I will allow them to live," she screamed.

"No," he said, wiping the blood from his nose.

Rondall was pummeled about the room, as if from a giant hammer. Opia smiled, as a small, whistling wormhole opened in the center of the room.

"Any last words, traitor?"

☙☙☙

Disgorging several hundred emergency escape pods, the three enormous ships dropped out of the sky over the circular depression near Mt. Tor.

First struck *The Hammer* as her sheer mass and tremendous speed crumpled the tough armored shell. The detonation of her shaped nuclear charge further weakened the shield.

While the now-exposed armor blade glowed white-hot, *The Axe* fell out of the sky and into the weakened defenses. The ship punched through, destroying the protective barrier.

The great machine, now defenseless and exposed, *The Sword* dove through the veil of rising flame, smoke, and debris. The wreckage of the once mighty ship traveled a kilometer and half deep before her munitions exploded.

The marvelous machine that could turn mere thought into solid matter shattered and melted in the two-thousand degree atomic fire.

☙☙☙

The wormhole vanished and Opia fell from the air where she landed with a dull thump. All over the ship, and the world of Opia, her legions of machines collapsed.

Rondall's communicator buzzed. He stood and stretched his aching body. "Yes," he said into the device.

"The ship is ours, my Lord."

"Good. Round up all the security machines and toss them out the airlocks just to be sure."

"Yes, my lord."

"What have you done to me, you ungrateful child," cried Opia.

Rondall rushed to the fallen Opia. Picking her up, he slammed her into the bulkhead. "How does it feel to be on the receiving end of righteous correction?"

"Obey me," she cried as fear crept into her voice. "I will forgive you if you stop now."

Rondall slapped her hard. "Those days are over, you fool. We have found the source of your power and destroyed it. From this day forward you will serve me."

"No, please," she whimpered.

"It is up to you, Opia. You can be my slave, or I can kill you. What will it be?" Rondall released her and walked over to her throne. Smiling triumphantly, he sat down. "This is nice."

"Please don't kill me," cried Opia. "I will serve you and only you, Master Rondall."

"Come, kneel at my feet and worship your new God."

Opia hurried over to the smug Rondall, her head bowed low. "I swear that that I will see you in hell," she hissed as she depressed a hidden switch on the arm of her throne.

Without warning, the main power circuit breakers of *The Chariot of Opia* tripped, plunging Rondall and his soldiers into pitch-blackness. Fifteen seconds later, emergency battery powered lights engaged, however, Rondall found himself alone. Opia had escaped.

"Get the damn power restored!" Rondall yelled into the com link. "Opia is loose on this ship. I want a systematic, deck-by-deck search until she is caught and safely locked in the brig."

"M—my l—lord," stammered his assistant. "We have escape pods jettisoning from the ship."

"Track the pod."

"My lord, *all* of the escape pods have deployed. There are thousands dropping planet side."

"Scan them," Rondall said. "Only one is occupied, you fool."

"My lord, I am sorry, but power is still out to most ship functions."

Rondall screamed in frustration and slammed his fist down on the arm of the throne.

"Calm down, my friend," Yeti said. "You have won. It is only a matter of time before Opia is captured. Everything she had is now yours."

Taking a deep breath, Rondall wiped the spittle from his mouth. "You are right, Yeti. Thank you."

"Now would you please direct your troopers to come and release me?"

"Yes, of course," Rondall said. "Send me the directions of your cell."

ɛⱭɛⱭ

The city of Romaa erupted with sheer joy that their great and terrible God had been dethroned. Her palace was ransacked and the priceless relics from a thousand worlds stolen or destroyed. The Moguls went wild, desecrating Opia's idols and burning her images.

Fearing that the city itself was in danger, Rondall deployed troops and set up martial law. With Opia deposed and on the run, it would not be long before they turned their attention to the last of their enemies, the Roratune.

CHAPTER 38

Will floated in a delicious, silky euphoria.

"Who are you?"

"Sugar, my name is Willard Byron Carlson."

"Willard Byron Carlson?"

"Yeah, I know it's a mouth full. Everybody calls me Will."

"And where are you from, Will?"

"Tennessee."

"And where is this planet, Ten-ah-see?"

Will laughed. "Why, darling, Tennessee isn't a planet, it's a state—one of the good old US of A."

"What is US of A?"

"You got it, baby."

"How is it you speak our language, Will?"

"I stopped at this weird rest stop and had a bite to eat. After that I am a freaking linguist."

"I don't understand."

"You know, darling, you sure have a pretty voice. I'll bet you look like an angel with big blue eyes and long blonde hair, full red lips just right for kissing—"

"Let's focus, shall we, Will? Now, what planet do you come from?"

"Honey, give me your name and your phone number, and I'll spill my guts. Give me a kiss and I'll give you my car."

"Agoa."

"Huh?"

"Agoa, is my name, Will."

"What a pretty name—my name is Willard Byron Carlson, but everybody calls me Will. You can call me *yours*."

ඐඐ

"Agoa, I think you gave the alien too much of the truth drug," Jabal said as he watched the interrogation from outside the medical bay.

"It's not that, sir, the truth drug is reacting with the medicines we gave him to treat his wounds."

"What did the doctor say about his condition?"

"Someone did a thorough job in brutalizing him. His four limbs were broken in several places, rib cage shattered, and, of course, his eyes were burned out. Everything, but his eyes are an easy fix."

"I don't understand," Jabal said. "We are light years from our home system—the last of our kind. Then low and behold, this…miniature kenan…shows up. How can he speak Azurean? Why does he look so much like us? Except for a few small differences, he could pass for one of us."

"More than a superficial resemblance, Chancellor. As amazing as it seems, the medics said Will's DNA is ninety-nine point forty-seven percent Azurean."

"The case we found him in, bore the mark of the aliens who destroyed our people. Have you managed to translate the inscription?"

"Yes, it was a list of crimes that Mr. Carlson perpetrated against the great God Opia. It was written in an obscure, Erest dialect. Seems he is a thief and a murderer."

"Erest?" Jabal asked. "The plot thickens."

"I like him," Cerin said. "His accent is catchy."

"The enemy of my enemy is my friend," Jabal said. "Agoa, flush the truth drug, I want to talk to our guest."

ඐඐ

"Oh my aching head," Will muttered as he struggled to sit up on the bed.

"Take it easy, Will," Jabal said. "You have been through quite an ordeal."

"If by ordeal, you mean I had the shit kicked out of me and had my eyes gouged out, yeah, I had an ordeal. Who are you and where is that soft-voiced honey, Agoa?"

"Why, thank you, Will. My name is Agoa. I am the ship's Artificial Intelligence."

"Artificial? You mean you aren't real?"

"Agoa is real enough, my friend," Jabal said. "She was created to run the ship's operation."

"That is so cool. With my crappy luck with women, it figures that she wouldn't be flesh and blood."

"I am Jabal Shann, by the way. You might say I am the boss around here."

"Pleased to meet you, Jabal. Thanks for saving my hide."

"My pleasure."

Fumbling about, Will felt bandages that patched his wounds. Placing a trembling hand to his eyes, he felt the soft dressing that encircled his head. "I swear to God they will pay."

"Who is they, Will?"

"Moguls."

"Moguls?"

"Big, sadistic *assholes*."

Jabal chuckled. "That is one weird-looking alien."

"Huh?" Will asked. "Oh, sorry. Let's see, they are huge, probably three times my size, covered with thick, black fur. Wide-set little beady eyes and a broad nose. High forehead and small ears."

He just described the Erest, Jabal mused.

"They aren't friends of yours, are they?" Will asked.

"No," Jabal said. "We are definitely not friends."

"Where am I? How did I get here?"

"You suddenly appeared near our vessel. You are currently recovering in our medical facility."

"This is a space ship? Wow. Never thought I would get to ride on a real space ship."

"Will, you were very close," Cerin said grimly. "Another

few hours and you would have been dead."

"You call this living?" Will asked. "Stumbling around in the dark for the rest of my life isn't much of a life. Now who are you?"

"I am Cerin Bos, Jabal's right hand man."

Jabal rolled his eyes.

"Nice to meet you," Will said.

"How did you encounter the Eres—*Moguls*?" Jabal asked.

"I was driving across the Mojave, that's a desert on Earth."

"Earth is your planet?"

"Yeah," Will said. "Anyway, me and this—*hitchhiker* were snatched off the Earth by this big machine that looked like a dragon fly. We ended up on a planet run by Opia, and her apes, who were going to dissect us as if we were bugs."

"The writing on your capsule said you are a murderer," Cerin said.

"That's a damn lie. Like I said, they were going to kill us. The one I killed shot at me first. It was self-defense. But I'll tell you one thing. I swear to God, if I ever get the chance, those old boys are going to pay for what they did to me."

"Looks like we have common enemies, Will," Jabal said. "They caused the death of my entire race."

"I have to go back," Will said, trying to rise. "The woman I was with, Anne, is still alive. I have to go back and get her."

"Is she your mate?"

"Oh, hell no. I just met her. She was just catching a ride when we got snatched by Opia's machines. She thinks I am a few rungs below a Mogul, and she hates Moguls. However, she wouldn't be in this mess except for me, and I feel responsible."

"You can help us by giving me information on the enemy," Jabal said. "If you could give us star coordinates."

"Star...*what*?" Will asked. "I don't have a clue about any of this space stuff. My people haven't been past our own moon. Most folks back home believe that space travel is no more than Science Fiction. I do know that Opia's system sits at the edge of a purple nebula. Looks real pretty at night. The name of her planet is Ilea."

"Will, that is not much help," Jabal said.

"But it is something," Cerin said. "Send the pathfinders to scout out the local nebulas. It is worth a shot."

"Yes," Jabal said. "If we can find them first, maybe we can avoid them altogether."

"No way," Will said. "We have to go after Anne."

"Will, I am sorry," Jabal said. "But this ship has a total crew compliment consisting of myself and my wife Sakuna."

"Hey what about me?" Cerin asked.

"Okay, two and a half," Jabal said.

"We have to do something. I will not leave Anne."

"You'll have to," Jabal said. "Believe me, I want nothing more that to kill every one of them, but we can't risk mounting a rescue on a planet swarming with Moguls, whose technology is a thousand years ahead of us. It is suicide."

"Not everybody down there are Moguls. There are some good people down there. They protected Anne and me from the Moguls. If we could get word to them, I know they could help us."

"Who are these people?" Cerin asked.

"They are called the Roratune."

"Roratune?" Cerin asked. "Why does that name seem so familiar?"

"Roratune was the name of a planet in the Frome system," Agoa said. "We set up a small colony there, but it was wiped out by the Erest in the early days of the war. The whole planet is now a radioactive waste."

"This woman I met said that her ancestors were taken from a place called Roratune," Will said. "Said that it was Opia's way of gathering worshipers."

"You don't suppose?" Cerin asked.

"Impossible," Jabal said softly.

"Tell me, Will," Cerin asked. "What did these Roratune look like?"

"Oh, they looked like me, but were a lot bigger. They've got these weird, boney ridges sticking out of their knuckles and knees."

Jabal stepped forward. "Will, take my hand."

"Okay, but if it turns out to be a slimy tentacle, I'll hurl."

"Humor me."

Will reached out and took Jabal's massive hand, gasping as he felt the hard knuckle ridge. "You're a Roratune."

"Will, how many Roratune are there?" Jabal asked.

"Well, I only saw the one village, but from what I was told, there are tens of thousands."

"We are not alone," Jabal said. "We are not alone."

He grabbed Will and crushed him in an embrace.

"Aww," Will grunted.

Jabal released Will and wiped his eyes. "Agoa, have the doctor see about my new friend's vision problems. I have plans to make. Seems we are going to take on Opia, after all."

"What do you mean, 'see about my friend's vision problems'?" Will asked. "My eyes are gone."

"Trust us, Will," Agoa said. "Simply lie back and relax."

"All right, sexy. For you, anything."

As an excited Jabal ran from the sick bay, the mechanical doctor prepared Will for surgery.

"Agoa, my love," Cerin asked. "Exactly *how* close is Will to Azurean physiology?"

"Extremely close, practically identical, why?"

"Well, my sultry mechanical angel of mercy," Cerin purred. "I want you to perform a few tests on our young friend here."

"What kind of tests?"

"I can't perform my duties as a Pilot. Jabal and Sakuna are not suitable candidates for the procedure, but what about Will?"

"He isn't Azurean."

"But you said it yourself, he is very—intimately close."

"You can't be serious. The procedure nearly killed you, and Will is barely a shadow of an Azurean. *Describing* the procedure would probably kill him."

"Agoa darling, we both know that there are things going on that are beyond coincidence. We are pawns in a greater game. Will Carlson is here for a reason."

"I hate it when you are right. I will run the tests."

"Another thing, Agoa. Let's not burden Jabal with this little project, until we get the results."

"You are going to get me purged."

Cerin chuckled.

CHAPTER 39

"Now, Will, it may take a while for you to get use to your new optics," Agoa said.

"That's eyes," Cerin said. "Not optics."

"I can't believe it," Will said. "I mean, how can you give someone new eyes? Besides that, it has only been a few hours since the operation."

"It seems that we are a bit more advanced than your world, Will," Jabal said.

"I would say more than a bit. More like a heap."

"In war, advancements in killing come rather quickly," said Jabal. "Along the way other benefits come about. That is evident in our medical sciences. Our doctors have had plenty of practice dealing with the wounded."

"How long was the war?"

"We were at war for two hundred and five years." Jabal sighed. "It had been over for three years when Opia decided to pay us a visit."

The doctor gently removed the dressing from Will's new eyes.

"It's all dark."

"That's because we have the lights turned down," Agoa said. "Prepare yourself."

Will squinted as the lights gradually increased in intensity. Darkness gave way to shadows and light. Shadows and light became blurry images that slowly focused and became razor sharp.

"I can see—I can see," he cried. "Oh, Lord, thank you."

Will looked about the shiny, brightly lit medical facility. "You must be Agoa," he said. "You are as beautiful as your voice."

"Sorry, Will," Jabal said. "This beautiful, blushing creature is my wife, Sakuna."

"Hello, Will," Sakuna said.

"Nice to meet you, ma'am."

"Agoa doesn't have a body, she is basically the ship, Will," Jabal said.

"Okay. That will take some getting used to. Jabal, I presume?"

"Jabal Shann, at your service," he said, giving Will a short bow.

"Say, where is Cerin? I was looking forward to seeing him. He told me the most hilarious, filthy jokes while I was recovering."

"Sorry about that," Agoa said. "Cerin is the burden we all must bear."

"That hurts my heart," Cerin said.

"Cerin?" Will asked, looking around.

"Right here, my friend," Cerin said.

"I think my eyes are still out of whack," Will said as he rubbed them. "I don't see you."

"Might as well know the truth now, Will," Jabal said. "Cerin is…well, *dead*."

"Huh?"

"What our esteemed chancellor is trying to say is that I am a ghost," Cerin said.

"An alien *booger*?" Will asked "That may be run of the mill here, but back home the very idea would freak most folks out."

"Trust me," Sakuna said. "It freaks us out, too."

"Well, fellows, why don't you show me around this flying haunted house of yours?" Will asked. "Still can't believe I am on a real, honest-to-God starship."

Jabal and Sakuna laughed.

Sakuna handed Will a mirror. Will gasped at the image.

"Blue. You gave me blue eyes."

"We didn't know what color your originals were," Agoa said. "Sakuna and I thought that this color would become you."

"I look good. Best of all I can see," Will said as tears began to flow. "I don't know how to thank you."

"You can thank us by helping us get our people back," Jabal said.

"I swear, I will do my level best."

"I know you will," Jabal said.

"By the way, what's the ship's name?"

"Welcome aboard *The Blossoming Flower*, Will Carlson," Agoa said.

"*Blossoming Flower*? You're pulling my leg. What are you guys, *space florists*?"

Jabal laughed. "Hardly."

"You should rest, Will," Agoa said.

"I'll rest when Opia and those Mogul bastards are six feet under."

"I don't know about you, Jabal, but I like our newest addition to the crew," Cerin said.

"I never saw myself as a service man," Will said. "Especially on an alien ship."

"Let's get one thing straight," Jabal said. "This is *my* ship, so that makes *you* the alien."

Will and Cerin laughed.

"So, we have two Azureans, an Earthling, a spook, and a sexy voice running things?"

"Yes," Cerin said. "What could go wrong?"

"Damn straight," Will said. "We are going to kick ass."

"You may rethink that when we engage the enemy," Jabal said.

"Will, can you give me an idea of what we are up against?" Cerin asked.

"On the ground, they don't have much. Seems Opia didn't want unnecessary technology messing up her pretty little world with roads and cars and such. All I saw were handguns and rifles."

"What about military vehicles?" Jabal asked.

"Except for a few aircraft, I never saw any Mogul vehicles, but I wasn't exactly given a grand tour. Apparently, Opia has an army of very vicious machines that step in whenever the Roratune and Moguls start taking shots at each other."

"What about space-borne equipment?" asked Jabal.

"Now there is the problem. Opia has this big ship that looks like it is made from glass."

"Yes, we have seen videos of her ship," Jabal said.

"Plus, I overheard some of the soldiers bragging about their new fleet. One of them said it was close to two hundred ships strong."

"Damn it," Jabal said. "We can't hope to face that many. Not without a Pilot."

"Agoa, give the Chancellor the good news," Cerin said.

"What good news?" Jabal asked. "What are you two up to?"

"Sir, while it would take some major modification, tests made during eye surgery have revealed that Will is compatible with the Pilot process."

"How is that possible?" Jabal asked. "He isn't even of our race."

"Unknown."

"Cerin, outside," Jabal said. "Sakuna, would you please entertain our young friend. I need time to think." He turned and walked out of medical. "What is going on?" he asked as the doors closed behind him.

"You got me, boss," Cerin said.

"This alien shows up from nowhere with news of a surviving remnant of our people and just so happens to be the right match for the Pilot process. What are the odds?"

"We are being moved around like pieces on a game board."

"I am not about to turn my ship over to a stranger from another race. The very idea is ludicrous. He could go mad like you and kill us all."

"Then our people die," Cerin said. "I don't see any other way, but to enlist him."

಄಄಄

"Agoa, you mean I get to drive the ship?" Will asked. "Sign me up."

"Not so fast," Jabal said as he entered the room. "Will, we do need you, however, being a Pilot entails more than merely a set of thruster controls. You would merge into the ship— become the ship."

"I don't understand."

"Will, you would have to be extensively modified and even with our medical technology, it won't be easy," Jabal said. "It would require weeks of painful surgery."

"Do it."

"Not to mention the intensive training," Cerin said. "It took five years before I was ready."

"I said, do it. I don't care if I look like a freak with metal parts and tubes sticking out. I have to pay those Mogul bastards back."

Jabal and Cerin laughed.

"No, Will, you won't look any different," Cerin said. "The only external difference is that your spine is replaced with the interface. Wear a shirt and no one would ever know the difference."

"Anne can't wait five years," Will said.

"I know," Jabal said. "Perhaps if we cut a few corners, if Cerin trains you during recuperation, perhaps we can be ready to go in a few months."

"There isn't a chance in hell a novice like Will is going to be able to take on that many ships," Cerin said.

"A frontal assault is out of the question. I propose that we use Will to lead off the enemy fleet, while we evacuate the people on the ground. A quick hit and run."

"Evacuate them with what? We only have the one ship."

"We build a barge," Jabal said, "one large enough to accommodate all our people. No engines only life-support. Once Will draws off the enemy, she rips into orbit. Our shuttles evacuate the Roratune and then she rips away clean."

"That might work," Cerin said. "There are a lot of "ifs," to this plan. Offhand, I know fifty things that might make this blow up in our face. Not to mention, there would have to be coordination with the ground. That means extensive recon and boots on the ground."

"All goes well, not a shot will be fired."

"The Moguls need to pay for what they did to me," Will said.

"After we find and settle on a world of our own, we can come back in a few years and kill them all."

"Sounds like we have a plan," Cerin said.

"What do you say, Will?" Jabal asked. "Are you willing to throw in with us?"

"Well, guys, it's like this. I am alone, my world is clear on the other side of the galaxy. To be perfectly honest, they didn't treat me all that well to begin with. You have been good to me, and, besides, I am just itching to give those creeps a little pay-back."

"I like the attitude," Cerin said.

"Just as long as you swear to me that you will rescue, Anne."

"Why are you going to such extreme measures to rescue this woman, whom you said doesn't care about you?" Agoa asked.

"I know most fellows would just leave her bitch ass behind, but that's not how my momma raised me. If it were not for me, she wouldn't be in this mess. If anything happened to her...well, I can't have that on my conscience. Promise me, Jabal, that you will do everything in your power to save her, and I will be your Pilot until my dying day."

Jabal took Will's arm. "I swear upon the graves of my family, I will bring Anne back, safe and sound," he said. "You will be one of us, Will Carlson. You will make your home with us and we will be your people."

"Then what are we waiting for?" Will asked. "Fire up the doc."

"Thank you, Will," Jabal said.

"On second thought, first, I want the grand tour of this ship. Then we can fire up the doc."

"It would be my pleasure to escort you and show you the wonders of *The Blossoming Flower*," Jabal said.

"So, before he begins sawing on me, how much does this job pay?" Will asked, cracking a smile.

Cerin laughed. "Spoken like a true born Pilot."

"Money wise, zero, however, because of your sacrifice, as Chancellor of the Azurean government, I hereby promote you to Supreme Commander of the Azurean Sky Forces."

"How many ships are in the Azurean Sky Forces?"

Cerin snorted. "Will, you're standing on the entire fleet."

"That's *Supreme Commander* Will to you, Casper. Now, let's see how cool this ship is."

CHAPTER 40

Behind a thick, transparent view port, Rondall and a detachment of heavily armed Zealots watched as the shuttle bay doors closed behind a boxy cargo shuttlecraft. Rondall shifted uneasily as he waited for the deck to pressurize. He was far more nervous than he had been when he faced Opia.

Preceded by three, sharp warning tones, the gray blast doors opened.

Rondall and his guards walked toward the craft and were met by a detachment of three Zealots.

"My lord," Gemmon Jape said.

"I trust your mission went smoothly?" Rondall asked.

Gemmon's eyes widened at the comment.

"Something wrong?"

"No, my lord."

"Tell me the truth, Gemmon. And by the way, where are the rest of your Brother Zealots?"

"We are all that survived, my lord."

"Impossible. I sent over one hundred of you to retrieve the artifact. You are my best soldiers."

"One-hundred-and twenty-two to be exact. The way was well guarded by Opia's machines. It was a running fight through the catacombs. Death was our constant companion as my fellows were picked off one-by-one. We were down to sixty-three when we finally reached the chamber containing the artifact." Gemmon, his eyes wide with fear, grasped Rondall's arm. "My Lord, there is something alive within. Something right out of the pit of hell. It gets into your mind—oh God, it is horrible."

"Unhand me," Rondall snapped.

Two of the guards dragged Gemmon back.

"Ten of my brothers killed themselves within the first hour, you fool!"

"I am tired of his prattle," Rondall said as he moved toward the shuttle. "End Brother Jape's suffering."

"Don't let it out—for the love of God, don't let it out!"

Before anyone could stop him, Gemmon produced a pistol and shot himself in the temple.

"Open the shuttle cargo doors," Rondall said, ignoring Gemmon's warning and suicide. Rondall beheld a sarcophagus like object six meters long and three wide. The object was deeply etched with hieroglyphics depicting a fantastic, horrific beast.

"How are you, my friend, Rondall?" Yeti asked.

The voice in Rondall's head thundered clearly now that it was unobstructed by the hundreds of meters of stone, metal, and concrete.

"Opia is deposed and I am in charge. I and my people can never thank you enough for all your help, my friend."

"Show your gratitude by releasing me."

"I am sorry, Yeti, but I cannot do that."

"I helped you—I gave you the way to defeat Opia. I showed you her weakness."

"Yes. Without you, victory would have been impossible. Nevertheless, you frighten me. Your mental powers lead me to believe that once free, we would become your puppets. I cannot afford to take the chance. I rule, not you."

"You cannot do this," Yeti screamed, making Rondall and his Zealots winch as his voice reverberated in their heads. "I trusted you."

"I will give you a choice in the matter."

"A choice—of my death? You are a cold bastard, Rondall."

"I merely wish to exile you, not kill you, Yeti. The great machine that Opia uses to send her probes across the galaxy is locked to us. Break the encryption, my friend, and I will send you anywhere you want to go."

"Now I see the real reason you rescued me, you treacherous monster. I am done with you, *my friend*. Return me to my cell. I will never help the likes of you ever again. In fact, I will seek out Opia and help her against you."

"That was a mistake," Rondall said. "That was a very bad mistake.

Minutes later, the shuttle containing Yeti, along with Gemmon's body, was ejected from the ship. After a fiery re-entry, the craft broke up and crashed into the southern desert leaving a debris field three kilometers long.

౪ඁ౪

"My lord, Rondall," Captain Houte said into his communicator.

"Captain, I hope that you are calling me to inform me that the Roratune leaders are in custody."

"My lord, I am standing in the main village, and it appears to be deserted."

"That's impossible."

"Impossible or not, it seems they left in a hurry."

"Burn the village and hunt them down," Rondall said. "The Roratune have been a thorn in the side of our people for far too long. Select a thousand of the youngest to be slaves then kill the rest."

"It will be done, my Lord," Houte said with a smile.

౪ඁ౪

"Here they come, Kann," Davad whispered. "Get ready."

The four, camouflaged Roratune, slipped into position.

Kann took a deep breath. Peeping through a crack in the wall, he watched the heavily armed Mogul troops move closer to his position. With a shaking hand, he wiped sweat from his brow. Looking back at Davad, he watched as his friend slowly raised his hand.

eↄeↄ

The Moguls were laughing and joking, almost as if they were going on a picnic outing, instead of going to murder their neighbors. Hatred between the Moguls and Roratune was almost second nature. Only the promise of Opia's retribution had kept a semblance of peace.

At the moment, because of Opia's dictates, arms were limited to crude rifles and handguns. However, the Moguls would quickly attain a deadly arsenal, once the archives of Opia opened. Her people's technological achievements would give them the galaxy. For now, they celebrated their new elevated status by eliminating their hated enemy.

The Mogul troops, over one hundred strong, were forced to narrow their column as they passed between two stone walls. Confident in their own superiority, they were certain that the Roratune had long since gone, fleeing terrified before the irresistible might of the new Mogul nation.

Four crude, ceramic canisters sailed over the walls and exploded within the ranks of the unsuspecting Moguls. The soldiers screamed as the jelled gasoline ignited turning the area into a sea of flame.

Sixteen soldiers in the rear of the unit managed to escape the flames unscathed. Falling back, they came under sporadic rifle fire and took refuge in a small barn.

"Command, we need help!" Private Grone cried into his radio.

"Who is this?"

"Private Grone. Command, we walked into an ambush. Send reinforcements *now!*"

"Is this a joke? The Roratune aren't capable—"

"Don't tell me what they are capable of, you idiot! Captain Houte and most of our unit are dead. We are trapped in a barn on the western edge of town near the main river dock. We are taking fire and need help."

eↄeↄ

Ballen and his aides stood on a low ridge watching the

drama that played out in his village. "Well, it seems that our Mogul friends have won the battle with Opia. Damn it."

"That little ambush will show those bastards that we aren't pushovers," Gelan Nor said.

"It will slow them down a bit," Ballen said. "But it won't stop them. How is our exodus coming?"

"Good, considering the lack of roads and the rough terrain. We should have the bulk of our people in the mountains in around a week."

"Make it two days," Ballen said. "Once they crack Opia's library, and trust me they will, who knows what they will come at us with?"

"Why, Ballen, you act like we aren't going to win," Gelan said with a wink.

"Win? I am just trying to find a way to survive this mess."

CHAPTER 41

Jabal and Sakuna sat in the captains' dining room, eating their evening meal. Before him was a tablet that gave him constants updates on the rescue ship construction.

Will didn't have any hard numbers on the population of the Roratune, which could balloon into a major problem, as Jabal was determined than none would be left behind.

The solution proved to be an easy fix. Having nearly unlimited resources, and the ship being no more than an airtight box, they settled on an exaggerated number of Roratune then decided to build a ship to accommodate three times that estimate.

The barge, while simple, was a large, compartmentalized five-kilometer cube.

Cerin and Jabal had decided that once Will was ready for combat, he and *The Blossoming Flower* would rip directly into the Mogul stronghold and take out key military targets, mainly communications and any planetary orbiting defenses.

Purposely stirring up a hornet's nest, *The Flower* would race away toward the Bridge, hopefully with the enemy fleet in hot pursuit.

In the sheer confusion, the rescue barge, along with the entire complement of *The Flower's* shuttlecraft fleet, would rip into orbit on the far side of the planet. With any luck, they could ferry the Roratune to the barge and rip away before the Moguls even knew they were there. Once the Roratune were rescued, *The Blossoming Flower* would rip away with little or no battle damage.

What could go wrong?

⌒⌒

"The barge's construction is proceeding faster than expected," Jabal said, around a mouthful of protein rations. "This debris field is a regular treasure trove, and a power supply for life support is a snap, but the real trick is rigging a rip drive big enough."

"I have faith in you, Jabal," Sakuna said. "This is so exciting."

"You know, Will wants us to call it something else instead of a barge or rescue ship."

"Why?"

"He said that in one of his people's Holy texts is a story about a great Divine Judgment and the only life saved was that aboard a vast sailing ship known as an *Ark*. He said under the circumstances it seemed appropriate."

"Sounds better than barge," she said. "*Ark* it is."

"How is Will's conversion going, Sakuna?"

"Very well, considering the interface harness had to be shortened and modified," she said. "Fortunately for us, all the equipment was aboard."

"How is he taking it? I haven't been able to drop by medical."

"Will is in great pain, to say the least, but he tries his best to hide it. This Anne person, regardless of how much he protests his feelings, her welfare has become the center of his world."

"Where is Cerin? I haven't heard him laugh at me in days."

"Cerin is with Will constantly, trying to lend support."

"Good, at least that booger can do some good," Jabal said as he took a sip of water.

"Booger? You're beginning to sound like Will."

"Some of his colloquialisms have a way of rubbing off."

"Did you know he has renamed the excavation unit, *Fort Apache?*"

"Yes, in fact, I made it official," Jabal said. "It does have a certain ring to it."

"Sir, sorry to interrupt your meal, but the latest pathfinder has returned," Agoa said.

Jabal wiped his mouth. "What is the count so far?"

"Two-hundred and seven failures."

"Put the latest vid on the screen."

Sakuna and Jabal gasped.

"I don't believe it," Jabal said. "Agoa, magnify image."

"Yes, sir."

"Sakuna, do you see what I see?"

"Yes, I do, Jabal. Touchdown!"

"Now, who is picking up words from Will?"

"I was overcome by the moment," Sakuna said.

The probe showed an extremely long-range shot of a planet and an orbiting vessel that seemed to be cut from living crystal.

"We have our quarry, Agoa," Jabal said. "Now, all we need is a Pilot."

ᴄ⌁ᴄ⌁

"Not one chance in hell, Jabal," Cerin said. "Will isn't ready. Not only isn't he trained to do as much as turn on a light—a hook up, at this point, will most assuredly fry his entire nervous system."

Will hung suspended before Jabal, encased and immobilized in a metal frame that looked like an alien torture device, while the mech surgeon made last minute adjustments to his new spine. Protruding from Will's back was a series of thin, null-glass scales that protected the delicate interface. The scales stood open while twenty-four brass colored rods extended outward.

"I agree with Cerin," the doc said. The big, multi-armed machine looked like a gothic nightmare come to life.

Jabal looked on, while several of the machine's articulated "hands" made precision adjustments to Will's complicated one-of-a kind implant.

With each adjustment, Will's jaw clenched and his face contorted with pain.

"My patient will need to heal for a minimum of five more months before he can begin regimented training. The rigors of merely connecting to the ship, let alone combat, will kill him at this point."

"D—don't—listen to them—chicken shit aliens pussies," Will gasped. "Hook—me up to this—flowerpot. Got to—save Sako and her people. They were good to me—can't let them down."

Jabal smiled and patted Will's trembling hand. "We can't take the chance, my friend. When you are ready, we will show Opia the error of her ways."

"But—what about Anne?" Will asked. "You—p—promised."

"I will keep my promise, however, this calls for subtlety. We can't go charging blindly in. It would be a disaster. I have to know exactly what we are up against and, only then, can we rescue our people."

"Y—you're the b—boss," Will said. "But I am the Su—Supreme Military Commander."

"That's right, my friend," Jabal said. "You have full authority. When the time comes, you will lead us to victory."

 свес

"Agoa, systems check please," Jabal said as he went over the instruments in the scout ship for the tenth time.

"Sir, this is a mistake," Agoa said. "You cannot go on this mission."

"We have been over this. I have to go."

"What the hell are you doing?"

Jabal turned and beheld his wife standing in the small open hatch of the scout ship.

"Hi, sweetie," he said.

"Don't sweetie me."

"Agoa, you have a big mouth," Jabal said.

"Correction, sir. I don't have a mouth at all."

"You can't go," Sakuna said.

"I agree with your wife," Agoa said.

"I have to, Sakuna. I have to gauge the enemy's strength and gather intel."

"Send a probe."

"Probes are not meant for infiltration. One gets caught or detected, it will alert Opia, and we might as well write off our people. I can't do that."

"I don't care. You can't go, I won't let you."

"Who am I going to send?" he snapped. "Tell me, so I can just sit back and watch a vid."

"What if you don't return?"

"You, Agoa, and Cerin will have to prepare Will to storm the place. We already have a sound plan. Once Will is ready, it will be implemented. If I am not here, Cerin can do it." Jabal took a deep breath. "Look, Sakuna, I will keep instant communication through the enemy's Bridge. Thank God, this system has one as well. I don't anticipate any problems. The recon ship has the best stealth shielding our people could come up with."

"The enemy is far beyond our tech," Agoa said. "Don't do anything foolish and get yourself killed, Chancellor."

"I won't, Agoa."

"You had better come back, to me," Sakuna said. "The thought of losing you is unacceptable."

"I figured you would be tired of me by now," Jabal said as he pulled his wife into his arms.

"As weird as it sounds," she said. "I like having you around."

"Not to mention, the thought of going into battle as *The General Robert E Lee*—" Agoa said "—is…well, unsettling."

"Excuse me?"

"Our future Pilot, Mr. Carlson, has expressed the reluctance of flying into battle on a ship with a 'girly' name. Said it wasn't manly. He has suggested an Earth war hero who apparently won a great civil war. Robert E Lee."

Jabal Shann threw his head back and laughed for first time since the destruction of his people.

"Chancellor, this isn't anything to laugh about," Agoa said.

∽∾∽

"Launch," Jabal said.

The small ship shot down the magnetic launch rail and out into space.

Making a few adjustments, he took a moment and watched as *The Blossoming Flower* spiraled away through his small view port.

"God be with you Chancellor," Agoa said.

"Here goes nothing," he said, flipping a switch. In a flash, he disappeared.

CHAPTER 42

The Mogul army grew and expanded like a bloated beast as reinforcements poured into the fray. Soon, their sheer numbers were too much for the beleaguered Roratune. The over-matched Roratune militia fell back, using all their skill to give their people time to get away.

Through a pair of captured Mogul binoculars, Ballen watched the latest assault against their lines.

Ballen smiled as his men threw back the clumsy, ill-conceived assault. He was proud of his rangers. Although little more than two thousand strong, they were holding off a force nearly twenty five times their size.

Too bad this can only end one way, he thought.

Thanks to Ballen's quick action, the bulk of the Roratune had evacuated to the northwest range and were safe for the moment. The maze-like canyons and rugged terrain made it the perfect spot to defend against the ponderous, ill-trained Mogul army.

Unfortunately, after weeks of constant fighting, their ammunition and food was running perilously low. Their situation desperate, the Roratune people's resolve began to splinter.

സൗ

"I brought you food, Ballen," Anne said. "Eat before it gets cold."

Ballen turned and smiled at his new daughter. He'd officially adopted Anne into his family, much to the consternation of Sako. "Anne, take it and give it to a ranger, they need their strength more than me."

"Not again, Dad, you are nothing but skin and bones. If I have to knock you down and force feed you, I will."

Ballen laughed in spite of himself. "All right, I will have a portion," he said, taking seat on a boulder.

Anne unwrapped the vegetable stew and produced a canteen of water. "Valore still being a pain in the ass?"

"He is a fool. He and his faction blame you and Will for all our problems with the Moguls, ignoring the past two hundred years of conflict. He wants to turn you over to Mogul justice and go back to the way things were."

"That's crazy."

"Yes. We cannot negotiate with the Moguls. They will not stop until we are dead."

"Oh."

"Don't worry, daughter," he said, caressing her cheek. "We will find a way out of this mess."

They both knew he was lying.

"Sako still on her…what did you call it?" he asked.

"Honeymoon. Yes, been a week and they haven't come out of their wedding cave. May have to send in a recue party—or seal the entrance."

"Anne, that is a terrible thing to say about your sister."

"I appreciate you taking me into your family, making me your daughter, however, Sako as my sister—that still leaves a bad taste. Sis didn't morn for Will very long, now did she? Now she's off with Easea, the biggest dork on two worlds if you ask me."

"He's a fine young Roratune—"

"Easea is, as Will would say, 'dumber than a sack of hammers.'"

Ballen looked at Anne and laughed. "I know. Believe me, I know," he said. "When he asked for Sako, and she agreed, it gave me an ulcer, but I gave my blessing, even though in time she will regret it. And if you repeat what I just said, I will toss you off a cliff."

Anne laughed.

"How are you doing, my dear?"

"Fine, I guess. I have been helping the doctor with the wounded. I think I missed my calling. I should have been a nurse or better yet a doctor. It keeps me busy and my mind off other things."

"Doctor Atames tells me you have been an enormous help to my people."

"My people?" she asked. "*Our* people."

"You are right, daughter, our people. Why haven't you found someone, Anne? I know for a fact that several have made declarations for you. I think that Moulon would make a fine husband. He is a hard worker and good hearted."

"Moulon is sweet," she said. "He comes by the clinic often with minor cuts and such just to see me."

"You could do worse."

"Any other time, I would go for it, but, Father, I can't shake the feeling, that somehow Will is still alive."

"Will is dead, you are not," Ballen said, his voice tinged with weariness. "I saw him killed with my own eyes. Daughter, Will would never want you to give up your life in mourning. Live while you can."

"That's what my mind tells me, but my heart won't let him go. You know, I still have dreams about him."

"Like before you met?"

"These are different. I see him in pain, surrounded by these horrible machines, which looked like they were ripped from a nightmare. It's like he is in some kind of techno hell."

"Anne, you have to stop this. It isn't healthy."

"I know. Before, I could not wait to go to sleep to be with him, now I dread it. I barely knew him, but at the same time, I knew we were soul mates. Me and my big damn mouth."

"Anne. What is done, is done. You have to move on."

Tears began to flow down her face. "He died hating me."

"Nonsense," Ballen said. "Will could never hate you. I saw how he looked at you, and he cared deeply."

He gathered the small woman in his arms. As Anne cried, he stroked her hair.

"It's not fair," she whispered. "Just not fair."

"Not much is, Anne."

She wiped her eyes and looked up in his face. "You are right. Maybe I should find Moulon and see if we have chemistry."

"That's my daughter."

"What is that?" she said, pointing to a faint, floating object in the sky.

Ballen snatched up a communicator. "Aed Weaton," he shouted. "Something is coming down from the sky. I think it landed about five klicks from your position. It may be a Mogul weapon. Send some men and check it out."

"It looks like a cross between a parachute and kite," Anne said.

"What it that?"

"You use it to safely land when you jump out of an aircraft. I have seen them many times on my world."

"I know the Moguls have a few aircraft, but so far they haven't used them, thank God. I think Rondall wants this to be strictly a ground fight."

"Then, what's up with the chute?"

"Maybe a spy or a sniper," he said. "Whatever it is, it isn't good."

CHAPTER 43

Jabal orbited the enemy world while his stealth ship automatically took thousands of digital photos and measurements of enemy installations. Meanwhile, he eavesdropped and recorded all information channels.

I don't understand. How could anyone be so sloppy? Don't these guys encode anything? It's all there for the taking. I hope that it will give me something to kill them with.

Jabal was amazed at the ten orbital construction yards and the ever-growing fleet.

This is going to be one tough nut to crack. Already they have a fleet three times the number of our fleet at the height of the war.

A warning light began to flash on the console before him.

Oh, oh. Some of those patrol runabouts are getting a bit too close.

❧❧❧

"Flight Command," the patrol pilot said. "This is Flight Four. I think I have discovered another of Opia's spy probes."

"Where are you, Flight Four?"

"In sector three, near the nova weapon facility."

"Don't take any chances Flight Four. Destroy the probe immediately. We can't let it damage the docking facility."

"It will be done, Flight Command."

❧❧❧

"They are locking a missile," Jabal said. "No time to be subtle."

He sent an encrypted data stream toward the system's Bridge containing all his gathered information.

"Drive status?"

"One hour twenty minutes until charge is ready for jump," the machine said.

"Great," he grumbled. "I left behind the extra battery cell to save weight. If I don't die, Sakuna is going to kill me."

Releasing counter measures, he ignited thrusts and flew toward the planet. He detected more patrol craft closing on his position. His ship was not built for speed and, even if it was, it did not have sufficient fuel. A run at the Bridge would be a pointless death.

Jabal sent one last encrypted message back to *The Blossoming Flower* relaying his position. He decided that the rugged terrain to the north of the city would be the best hiding place.

"It's up to you now, Cerin," he said. "Don't let our people down."

He pushed a series of switches. His seat clam-shelled over him and dropped from the underbelly of the craft.

The recon ship's AI turned and rocketed away from the closing missiles, trying to divert attention from its pilot.

The ship gave a good run for six more minutes, until an exploding missile turned it into a cloud of debris falling into the atmosphere.

Jabal fell through the atmosphere unobserved, his shell protecting him from the scorching re-entry. A two-second alarm sounded, and Jabal braced himself. The escape pod fired a powerful thruster burst, slowing his air speed to almost nil. The pod opened and fell away, its exotic material designed to break apart and disintegrate, leaving behind little trace.

Jabal spread his arms and legs allowing the wings of his pressure suit to catch the thin, minus-seventy-Celsius air. The sound of his own breathing resonating loudly in his ears, he shot through the rapidly thickening air, gaining a speed of almost nine-hundred and sixty-kilometers per hour.

An altimeter in his helmet sounded a small buzzer. Steeling

himself, he pulled the release on his parafoil. The large wing opened and Jabal flew toward the jagged mountains in the distance.

The wing and his suit were made from advanced survival materials that changed color to match their background. While far from being invisible, unless you were looking right at Jabal, you would probably never notice him.

As he flew closer, he noticed the stalemated conflict below.

He picked a relatively flat landing spot well beyond the fighting and brought his wing down. As he touched down, he pushed a slight pressure switch and his foil thin wing folded itself and retracted into his backpack. He had no sooner taken a single step, when he heard the sound of several rifle bolts being racked back.

Smiling, Jabal raised his hands above his head as five Roratune soldiers approached him.

"On your knees," cried the lead soldier. "Hands on top of your head—now!"

In spite of being seconds away from being shot, Jabal was overjoyed. *It's true! It's all true! My people still exist.*

Jabal was quickly relieved of his weapons and survival kit. "Can I take off my helmet?"

"All right, Mogul, but any sudden movements and we will make a lot of holes in that pretty suit of yours."

"You're a runt for a Mogul—"one of the soldiers began as Jabal pulled his helmet off.

The soldiers gasped at Jabal. They never expected one of their own kind.

"Who are you?"

"Chancellor Jabal Shann of the Azurean Military, at your service."

His statement was greeted with stunned silence.

"If you fellows could take me to your leaders, I am sure they would be very happy with the news I bring."

∽ᗒᗕ∽

Stripped of his flight suit and now wearing his uniform,

Jabal entered the large cave that served as council chamber for the Roratune.

Ballen along with several of his aides greeted the stranger.

"I say it is a Mogul trick," Farin said. The big Roratune produced a pistol. "Let me put this traitor out of our misery."

"Put the gun away, Farin, and sit down," Ballen said. "If he is a traitor or spy, it won't hurt to hear what he has to say— before we kill him."

Muttering something incomprehensible, Farin sat down, but kept his pistol ready.

"Who are you and why are you here?" Ballen asked.

Jabal gave Ballen a smart salute. "Sir, I am Chancellor Jabal Shann of the Azurean Sky Navy. I was on a reconnaissance mission when my craft was shot down."

"There are more of you?" Gallen asked.

"Not here," said Jabal. "I have a ship in another system. I am here to gather information on the enemy positions."

"You are here to help us?" Ballen asked.

"Yes," Jabal said. "It is my goal to get your people off this rock before making the Moguls and Opia pay dearly."

"When can you bring help?" Ballen asked.

"That is where it gets complicated," Jabal said. "If I could get a drink of water, I will explain the situation."

Moments later, Anne came in bearing a large canteen and a small amount of food.

Jabal stared at the small woman.

"Oh yes, Commander," Ballen said. "She isn't a Roratune…"

"Anne Miller," Jabal said. "This is a great honor. Will has told me much about you."

Anne froze. "Will?"

"Yes, Will Carlson."

"He is alive?"

"Very much so. I spoke with him just before I came here. He made me promise to protect you and bring you back safely."

"Impossible," Ballen cried. "I saw the Moguls put out his eyes and cast him into the void. Will is dead."

"Seems that in a fortuitous event, they cast poor Will through a wormhole to a point near my ship. Will was close to death, but he is doing fine now."

Anne dropped the food and water and leaped into Jabal's arms, hugging him hard.

"Will is alive," she said as tears welled in her beautiful eyes.

"I wasn't expecting this," Jabal said. "Will told me you did not care for him. Said that you thought he was lower than, and I quote, 'dawg shit.' What is a dawg, by the way?"

"No, we had a misunderstanding and I said things I shouldn't have. I love him more than life itself."

"Seems that we have a cause for a celebration," Ballen said. "Our deliverance is at hand."

"You probably should hear me out, Ballen, before you do any celebrating. Any kind of deliverance is several months away at best."

"Everyone out," Ballen said. "I need to speak to Chancellor Shann alone."

Everyone obediently filed out of the cavern leaving the two alone.

"Pull up a rock, Chancellor."

Jabal smiled and took a seat near Ballen.

"Explain yourself," Ballen said.

"Sir, we are both from the same people."

"The Roratune."

"No, sir, we are Azurean. From what Will has told me, you and your people were from a colony we had on a planet called Roratune. The colony was wiped out two hundred years ago in the opening days of a terrible war with the Erest. We had always thought that there were no survivors. Somehow, a remnant of our people were brought to this planet."

"It was Opia," Ballen said. "She needed someone to worship her. She told us that she created us for the sole reason of serving her. Us and the Mogul."

"Yeah, about that," Jabal said. "As I flew over I got a good look at the Moguls. They are the Erest. The most aggressive, ruthless species we have ever come into contact with. Seems that while our two peoples fought on Roratune, Opia took eve-ryone."

"You said we were at war," Ballen asked.

"A war that lasted two hundred years. To make a long story short, we prevailed."

"So our people are powerful?"

Jabal swallowed hard. "We were. The war was over and we were at peace, that is until Opia and her damn crystal ship came for a little visit."

"What did she do?"

"Without any warning, she made our sun go super nova. Until a few months ago when I found Will, I thought I and my wife were the only survivors."

"There are only two?"

"Technically three."

"Technically?"

"Long story. Nevertheless, I have a warship at my com-mand. We found Will and he told us of others of our kind. Us-ing a new technology that made it possible to bypass the Bridges, we found you. That is why I risked coming here. I had to learn the strength of the enemy and construct a rescue mission. Unfortunately, I got burned."

"But if you are here—"

"Will is undergoing a surgical process so that he can fly my ship. If all goes as planned he will come for us in five months."

"And if all doesn't go as planned?"

Jabal took a deep breath. "Then our race will truly be dead."

CHAPTER 44

How are our troops doing in the Roratune campaign, General Kellan?" Rondall asked. He sat upon his crystal throne, a newly made golden crown perched upon his misshapen skull.

"My lord, all goes well," Kellan said. "Victory is well within our grasp."

"How well within our grasp?"

"Well, these things take time, my lord. The vermin have taken refuge in the mountains. The rugged terrain gives them a very strong position and cancels out our numerical superiority."

Rondall slammed a meaty fist down upon and arm of the throne. "Stalemate isn't victory, General. I expect results."

"But, my lord, my troops are new—"

"Enough excuses. Opia has proven to be a slippery opponent, but her minions have all but been eliminated. Once she has been completely broken, I will begin the new era in our people's history—in this galaxy's history. I do not need for my troops to be occupied any longer with the Roratune."

"I request assistance from the fleet," Kellan said. "One atomic warhead…"

"Absolutely not, you idiot. Do you want to poison our own world?"

"My lord, I did not think—"

"That's right, you did not." Rondall sat back and thought. "What if you had one hundred thousand more troopers?"

"My lord, numbers are useless in this terrain. Any more

would make my position an even larger quagmire."

The marble walls shimmered and became a three-dimension map of the northwest range.

"Show me your positions," Rondall said.

Kellan touched several points on the map and the point's glowed bright red. "They have made these three valleys death traps," he said. "Unfortunately, they are the only route in."

"What about that broad, flat valley to the north?"

"I don't understand, my lord?"

"Land enough troops there and they will have to split their forces. Ballen's meager forces would be trapped between you."

"The valley is inaccessible, my lord."

"Not any longer, General Kellan. I want you to coordinate with Fleet Admiral Sone. I want ten troop carriers loaded with fleet personal to land there and fall upon the Roratune flank."

General Kellan smiled. "They won't know what hit them."

CHAPTER 45

Sako lay on her side, her back to her husband. A tear wound its way down her face. *What a mess I have made of my life.*

Easea lay back smiling, completely oblivious of his wife's despair. "That was wonderful," he said, wiping the sheen of sweat from his face.

"Thank you," she whispered.

"I love you so much, Sako. If only you hadn't wasted time chasing after that alien, we could have been married much sooner."

Sako gritted her teeth, but held her tongue. Easea hated Will and Anne and any protest on her part would only leave her with a painful bruise.

He and a small number of Roratune blamed Will and Anne for their present troubles. Sako quickly learned that in her misguided attempt to forget Will, she had married a jealous, controlling brute.

"We have now," she said dryly. "No need to waste time thinking about what might have been."

"Knock, knock," Anne said, standing at the entrance of the cave. Her face was split with an evil smile.

"How dare you interrupt us, midget?" Easea said. "Get out before I throw you out! Or worse."

Anne smiled and gave Easea the finger, which was completely lost on him.

"Calm down, Easea," Sako said.

"You do not tell me what to do, Sako. I am your husband

now, and you will obey me, not the other way around."

"What do you want, sister?" Sako asked, ignoring her husband's typical rant.

"Oh, I am sorry about interrupting your love fest, but I thought you would want to know the good news."

"That you have a disease and are about to die?" Easea asked.

"What is it, Anne?" Sako asked.

"Will is alive. Now you two lovebirds go back to doing what you do best."

Without waiting for a response, she opened the doorway flap and left. Anne traveled a few yards away when a nude Sako burst from the cave.

Running up, Sako took the smiling Anne by the shoulders.

"Aren't you afraid you will catch a cold?" Anne asked with a laugh.

"Is this a joke?"

"No joke. Seems Will was found by other Roratune out in space, somewhere. They said that he was fine and was on his way to help us."

"Will is alive?" Sako cried as she hugged Anne.

"Sako, put some clothes on," Anne said as her head was suddenly thrust into Sako's ample breasts. "People will talk and I, for one, don't swing this way."

Sako dropped Anne and wiped the tears from her eyes. Tuning on her heel, she marched back to the cave where her husband fumed.

"Why did you run out?" he asked.

"Will is alive," she said, pulling on her clothes. "Didn't you hear?"

"So what? Your midget is alive, but you are mine. I suggest you get used to the idea. Now come back to bed."

"The whole wedding thing was nice," Sako said, "but I want a divorce."

Before Easea could answer, Sako opened the door flap and left.

CHAPTER 46

That is a fancy gun, Chancellor," Ballen said. Jabal held up his rifle. "This is a Dawmaotha Industries Y-23 Personal Defense Weapon. It is the standard issued battle rifle of the Azurean forces. Fires a 4mm smart round at a rate of 1800 rounds per minute and has an effective range of three miles. Also comes with a rail grenade launcher with a six round magazine that can cover up to five miles."

"This is a rifle hammered together by one of our blacksmiths," Ballen said, holding up a weapon that looked amazingly like what Will had claimed was an AK-47. "Not quite as fancy, or particularly accurate, but it gets the job done."

Jabal looked through his rifle's scope at a group of enemy troops massing three miles away.

"See those Moguls, there by the top of the far hill?" Jabal asked.

Ballen looked through a chipped pair of binoculars. "Yes, I see them. Looks about one hundred and fifty of them. They must be gearing up for another run at us."

Jabal adjusted the load on his grenade launcher and sighted in the range.

"Don't waste the ammo, Chancellor," Ballen said. "Wait until—"

Jabal pulled the trigger and the magnetic launcher made a small hum as the baseball sized grenade fired.

Moments later, the Moguls were enveloped in a six-meter wide fireball.

Ballen almost dropped his field glasses. "Too bad you

didn't bring a couple of hundred of those rifles. We would take this world back from the Moguls."

"The rifles are nice, but as long as they control the high ground, they will still win. I don't understand why they don't hit us from the air."

"They are still building their forces," Ballen said. "I have no doubt they would hit us with everything they have if they could. Opia must be giving them some opposition. Still, your little demonstration saved us several hundred rounds of ammunition and probably a few lives."

Turning, Jabal was surprised by Anne standing behind him.

"This is too dangerous, daughter," Ballen said. "We are too close to the Moguls."

"I have been in worse spots. I need to talk to Jabal." Not waiting for permission, she took Jabal by the hand and led him into a nearby tunnel. "How is Will?"

"I told you—"

"You told me bullshit. I want the truth."

"Will was on the brink of death when we found him. He is fine now."

"Then why do I have dreams about him in some kind of metal frame and some scary-looking machine cutting him to pieces?"

Jabal looked at Anne long and hard. "How many arms did the machine have?"

Anne thought a moment.

"Seven."

"Amazing," he said. "I had heard of people having a gift of 'sight,' but I always thought that it was a myth."

Anne produced Shirley. "So, you are trying to kill him."

Jabal eyed the archaic-looking weapon, but remained calm. "No, of course not. Will is our only hope out of this mess."

"You said he is learning to fly some kind of a ship."

"Exactly," Jabal said. "Will is undergoing the process of becoming the Pilot. Needless to say, it is a complicated medical procedure that few can withstand."

"Why all the surgery?"

"It's complicated, but trust me when I say it's the only way."

"Is it painful?"

"Unfortunately yes, beyond what most could imagine or endure. He is doing it for you, Anne."

"For me?"

"That was our agreement," Jabal said. "He said he would become the Pilot and serve till the end of his days if I would save you."

"Will—*loves* me?"

"To suffer the horrendous pain for a woman whom he thinks hates him? I would say he is in love."

"You have made me the happiest woman in the universe."

"That's nice. Now, can we put away the hand cannon?" he asked.

"Sorry."

If Will shows up on time, he will make me the happiest Azuren in the universe, Jabal mused. *I hope it will serve more than being blown out of the sky.*

CHAPTER 47

The tiny bell rang cheerily as Will opened the door. "Well, I'll be," he said. "It's Angel Wells."

He pushed through the door and beheld the brightly lit restaurant. The frosty, conditioned air was alive with the indescribable, mouth-watering aroma of hamburgers and hotdogs.

Damn, this is a vivid dream. I wonder if Anne is still waitressing here?

At that moment, Molly came through a pair of swinging doors, carrying a big platter of food and two milkshakes. "No, Will, Anne isn't here," she said brightly. "She is on Ilea, and you are in the medical bay of *The Blossoming Flower.*" Molly set the platter down at an oversized booth. "You have taken quite a beating in the love department, haven't you, Will?"

"That's putting it mildly. Only woman who ever really wanted me was a nymphomaniac giant Amazon. I must be one hell of a card player."

"We have serious business to discuss, young man."

"This is a weird dream. Where are the naked women?"

"Will, this is not a dream," she said, rolling her eyes. "Now have a seat and dig in."

"Not a dream? But I'm a bajillon miles away from Angel Wells, having my guts ripped out and rearranged by a grumpy alien machine."

"True, but we interrupted that reality so we could have a heart to heart. Have you ever smelled food before in a dream, or dreamed in color?"

"You got me there."

"So sit and eat. I whipped this up special for you. Trust me, you will need this in the days to come."

"Uh...okay," he said, settling into the booth. "The gun and the note—"

"We did that so you could survive your first few hours on Opia's planet."

"Came in handy. Shirley is a hoot." Will took a bite of one of Molly's delicious burgers. "Still the best hamburgers I have ever eaten."

"You are sweet," she said with a smile.

Will had two more bites and took a sip of his shake. "You and SD, you aren't from around here, are you?"

"If you mean we are not human, the answer is yes."

"Figures. I have lost my marbles."

"Will, you are not crazy. The galaxy faces a grave threat, and you, my dear young man, are the key part of the solution."

"Yeah," he said, wiping ice cream from his mouth. "Opia has created weapons that could destroy every civilization in the Milky Way. The Moguls won't hesitate to use her knowledge. They must be stopped before they kill trillions."

"While that is pretty bad," she said, "there is something far worse coming, and that is what I need you for."

"Worse than blowing up a star?"

"Yes, I am afraid so. You see, Will, there is an infinite number of universes squeezed together into a single plane."

"Huh?"

"Bear with me. I am trying to make it simple to where your limited intellect can comprehend. Anyway, in this 'Plane of Existence' as we call it, there is an entire universe that is dead, all life, all energy consumed by a living plague, called the Sagoths. They want to enter our realm and do the same to ours. It is your job to stop them."

"You guys seem to have all the answers and a damn lot of power. Why don't you stop them?"

Molly smiled. "It doesn't work that way, I'm afraid. We are guided by certain rules. Open displays of power are expressly forbidden. Gives the locals the wrong idea and, before you know it, a crazy religion has started. Instead, we use a very special type of person to attain our goals."

"What makes me so special?"

"You have no future."

"Excuse me?"

"You are what we call a *Dead End.* Taking you and using you will not disrupt any carefully constructed time lines."

"Why don't I have a future?"

"Had we not intervened, you and Anne would have been murdered in the desert."

"Murdered?"

"Yes, SD and I took your places to finish out your time lines. As far as your friends, families, and the world is concerned, you are dead. Which makes you fair game for us."

"Which begs the million-dollar question. In all the universe, which apparently teems with living critters, why the hell did you pick me?"

"We didn't. It is a complete mystery to us why you were specifically chosen. I can name several billion entities that would make a better candidate, but the decision is out of our hands. We are a race much older than you, and we can easily manipulate you at will, but there are races older, far more powerful than we. It is they who dictate the path we follow."

"More powerful than you? Who are they?"

"Best not to know. We don't even utter their names, for fear of drawing their attention. That is a very bad thing."

"You are the reason Anne and I can understand what the Roratune and Moguls are saying."

"Yes, I gave you the ability to understand and communicate in any language," she said. "A little something I put in your hamburger back in the Mohave. Communication makes things much easier. We also tampered with your DNA to make you the perfect candidate to be a Pilot."

"I see. When the Moguls tossed me into space—"

"We made sure you would appear near Jabal's ship. In fact, we were instrumental in the creation of that marvelous vessel. It wasn't built to win a war for the Azureans, but for you specifically to stop the Sagoths. A special ship that would have been destroyed had we not fixed her drive in the nick of time."

"You used me and my friends like puppets on a string. Why play straight with me now?"

"You have a decision to make," she said. "We have come to a critical juncture in the plan, and you cannot go into it blind or halfhearted. We need you to do your level best to prevent the Sagoths from entering this plane. There is one here, but he is crippled. He plots to unleash his people upon us. You have to slip through the Mogul defenses and kill him before he can open a door between the universes. If that door is opened, all is lost."

"But I don't know how to fly *The Blossoming Flower*. I don't have a clue about space battles or anything like that. I am just a loser from Tennessee."

"You have a special destiny, Will Carlson, and countless vital time lines depend upon you. We need you, Will. The galaxy needs you."

"Let's say I go along and stop the Sagoths. You know how the future will play out. What happens to the Roratune?"

"They will not escape. The Moguls will slaughter most of the Roratune and make the rest slaves, in five generations there will be no more Roratune. The Moguls will go on and carve out a bloody empire and enslave several races."

"What about Anne?

"Anne will die at the hands of the Moguls, and it will be a slow death. So will Ballen and Sako. By the way, Jabal has joined them on the planet."

"Jabal?"

"He came to scout the Moguls defenses and was shot down. He is unharmed, but he will also die at the hands of the Moguls."

"Sakuna?"

"Distraught, Sakuna will wander alone until in desperation she orders Agoa to drive the ship into a star."

"That sucks."

"That's life."

Will slurped his shake nosily in response. "I am not going to survive the mission to stop the Sagoths, am I?"

Molly gave him a long hard look. "No. You will die."

"Tell you what. Save the Roratune from the Moguls, send Anne back to Earth, and I will stop the Sagoths."

"Impossible. Anne Miller and you are dead. Her appearance on Earth would have disastrous consequences. Neither of you can ever set foot on the Earth again."

"You are not giving me the warm and fuzzies."

"I am telling you the truth. Stopping the Sagoths is far more important than the dismal fate of your friends. The Sagoths have been observing us. Once released, they will take down the most advanced civilizations, and anyone who can possibly stop them."

"Even you?"

"Even us. They are too advanced and far too numerous to stop. Once they have killed anyone who can oppose them, they will—in your words—go through the life in this universe like a fat kid through a candy store. Your sacrifice will save countless worlds, including your own precious Earth. Isn't that alone worth the cost?"

"Easy to say when you aren't the one making the sacrifice. Since you won't lift a finger to help, how about, on the way to stop the Sagoths, I stop by, save Anne and the Roratune?"

"Will, you would be one ship against many. The danger is too great that you would be destroyed before you came against the Sagoths. I can't let you do that."

"Then let the damn galaxy burn."

Molly gave Will a long look and frowned. "SD," Molly said.

SD pushed through a swinging door and maneuvered a rolling cart up to the table. On the stainless steel cart floated a silver blob that looked like a pulsating glob of quicksilver the size of a tennis ball.

"Hey, SD," Will said.

"Always a pleasure, Will."

"What is that thing?"

"That my boy," SD said, "is a serious bit of insurance. We call it a *Teepo*. It is a rare bit of tech from a dead elder race, called the Haackor."

"I don't have to eat it, do I?"

SD and Molly laughed.

"Touch the device," SD said.

Will put out his hand and tentatively touched the warm, greasy feeling mass. Teepo shuddered and flowed around Will's hand and up his arm.

"Guys—"

"It is all right, Will," SD said. "Teepo is just getting to know you."

'*Master.*'

"It can talk?"

"Somewhat," SD said. "However it is strictly telepathic."

"ESP? Like Shirley? That is so cool. What do I do with it?"

In response, SD and Molly produced out of the thin air a pair of Azurean battle rifles.

"What the—" Will began.

SD and Molly leveled the weapons and, on full auto, fired directly at Will.

Will yelped and ducked as the room exploded with thunder.

Teepo, quick as a thought, expanded, forming a shield around Will. The bullets bounced off and ricocheted across the room.

SD laughed. "A Teepo is the best protection a fellow can have, my boy. His only mission in life is to protect you."

"All right," Molly said, tossing her gun into midair where it vanished. "Your odds of survival with a Teepo are greatly increased. While you have no guarantee of success, Mr. Carlson, we will allow you to try."

"Thanks for the silver blob...*thingy*," Will said. "But how can a flying blob increase my odds of survival in space?"

"Trust us," SD said.

"Okay," Will said. "Any chance you can give me a crash course on flying a spaceship?"

"Relax my boy," she said. "We have that covered."

Will turned at the sound of the door chime as an enormous man walked in. From his knuckles sprouted a boney ridge.

The handsome man gave Will a smile and a wink before taking a seat across from him.

"So this is where you are from," the stranger said. "Kind of hot and dusty, isn't it?"

The voice registered immediately.

"Cerin?" Will asked.

"In the flesh—for once."

"You know, you look sort of like Errol Flynn."

"What is an Errol Flynn?"

"Never mind. Good to finally put a face to the voice."

Cerin smiled at Will before he helped himself to a hamburger and quickly gobbled it down.

"What are you doing here?"

"Ask her," he said, nodding at Molly. "I have a feeling she was the one who kept me aboard *The Flower*."

"Guilty as charged," Molly said. "I have a project that needs the two of you to work closely together."

"I think she wants you to train me to fly."

"I think it is more than that," Cerin said, holding up the frosty shake. "This, by the way, is simply outstanding."

"Drink your fill," she said. "You, too, Will. I'm afraid it is the last ice cream you will ever have."

"Figures. So what is your plan?"

"We have much to plan," Molly said as she placed her right hand on Will's head as her left settled upon Cerin's.

ფოდ

Will slowly awoke in the rigid medical brace as the doctor released the last temporary fastener on his new spinal implant. Despite the painkillers, jagged lightning bolts of raw pain flashed through his very being.

"You must rest, Will," Agoa whispered. "In a few weeks it will be safe to allow some movement."

"Screw that," he said. "Ready the ship for battle, baby."

"Battle...*baby*?"

"Accelerate the kinetic munitions loading. I want this ship ready to kick someone's ass in twenty-four hours. Start manufacturing Somex. I want the ship's inventory at maximum."

"How do you even know about Somex? Will, I think you

need to rest. This ship cannot fight without a crew or Pilot. We have neither."

"Agoa," Will rasped. "Execute executive order: 4897y3489hb39283r2y89b9crycb0cy9c9nmcapcnpjgniruh4."

"You can't be serious," Agoa exclaimed. "What about Chancellor Shann's plan?"

"It is a bust. They will all die if I don't act now."

"You can't do this."

"Obey me. I have been given the authority to act by Chancellor Jabal Shann himself. He made me the Supreme Commander of the Azurean Military Forces."

"But—"

"Did he not say it?"

"Yes, *sir*."

"Don't question me again, just follow my orders."

"Yes, *sir*," she said with a slight pout. "It will be done. I have tripled the loaders, and it will be tight, but we can meet your deadline. We even discovered a rich vein of uranium that should yield about one hundred and ten flashers."

"Good. Now, off load all food and medical supplies to Fort Apache. In fact, strip *The Flower* of anything that the refuges need to survive. Don't forget to download all our data files."

"Yes, sir."

"What about Jabal?" Will asked as he gritted his teeth against the searing pain. "Has he reported in?"

"I have received a communication from Commander Shann. He has sent detailed information about the enemy system. Unfortunately, he has been forced down on the planet."

"I know."

"How do you know?"

"Never mind. Download the information he gathered to my viewer, Agoa," Will said. "I need to see what I'm up against."

෪෪෪

Half an hour later, the door to sickbay opened.

"I have a job for you, Commander," Will said. "Now listen carefully…"

CHAPTER 48

The last of the ten ponderous troop carriers performed docking maneuvers as each settled into its own bay. Stabilizing arms extended and mated with corresponding clamps, locking the ship into place. Fuel lines connected and hundreds of thousands of liters of volatile fuel flowed into the tanks.

Little more than a cargo hold, life support, and engine, the five hundred meter long ships were great ugly boxes as function superseded form. Even their designations bowed to Mogul maniacal utility. The ships that lay at dock were numbered One through Ten.

At the other end of the great hub, naval ships off loaded masses of armed sailors who would join the fight in the extermination of the hated Roratune.

This was a historic event. The first combined action of the newly formed armed forces. Rondall hoped that it would be an excellent training exercise for the fledgling military.

The mere possession of the nova devices had given him the galaxy, but he knew an efficient fighting force would be needed from time to time.

☙❧☙

"Did you see that?" Captain Bemmer of Troop Transport Four asked.

"See what, sir?" First Officer Poes asked.

"It was an energy spike. The reading went off the scale for a moment then settled back to normal."

"Must have been the arrival of ship Ten," Poes said. "Sometimes a ship's reactor can spike like that."

"You're probably right. I have the jitters about this mad plan."

"You mean flying this brick into the atmosphere and landing in that small mountain meadow?"

"Along with nine other flying bricks packed full of Moguls and material. I have been assured that Opia's tech will allow us to safely navigate in a thick atmosphere, but training in a simulator is a far cry from the actual hands-on flight. A thousand things could happen to spoil this little adventure."

"Captain, my console says that the aft cargo hold door opened. Now it says it closed. Internal cameras don't show a thing. Probably a malfunctioning sensor."

"Check it out," Captain Bemmer said. "Can you imagine the hole we would make in the ground if the main cargo hatch suddenly decided to open in flight?"

℘↷℘↷

The five maintenance personal attached their equipment to the massive airtight outer door and checked the locking clamps. A small robot camera examined the door from the outside while a crewmember checked his progress on a small view screen.

"I got something," Othoe said. "Look here."

The other four crowded around the monitor.

"It looks like someone drilled a hole in the outer locking mechanism."

"Hey look at this," Gordoe said, examining the inner seal. "The door has been tampered with. Better contact Captain Bemmer. This definitely isn't a sensor malfunction."

Gordoe turned to find his friends dead on the metal floor. His last thought was one of stunned surprise.

℘↷℘↷

"Captain Bemmer, this is Chief Maintenance Supervisor Gordoe."

"Yes, Chief?"

"Nothing to worry about, sir. Just a faulty circuit in the door. We fixed her up good as new."

"Good work, Chief," Bemmer said, clicking off the intercom.

CHAPTER 49

After a last minute pep talk by the fleet admiral and once again going over their flight instructions, the carriers broke connection with the dock and sailed into high orbit. With flawless precision, they slipped into the gravity well of Ilea.

Little did anyone in the Mogul command realize that a stealth ship flew in formation with the slab-sided behemoths.

The ship's un-aerodynamic shapes were buffeted and scorched by reentry, but despite Captain Bemmer's earlier concerns, safely made their way to the northwest mountain range.

Not apprehensive over the element of surprise, the ships purposely flew over the main body of the Mogul army.

"Oh my God," Jabal whispered as he spied the oncoming ships.

The Mogul troops gave a shout of victory at the sight of the troop ships.

"Air assault?" Ballen asked.

"Look more like troop carriers. They are trying to out flank us. Quick, Ballen, where can ships of that size set down?"

"There is a shallow, flat valley to the north," Ballen said. "An easy walk right into our strong hold. It's over."

"Not if I can help it," Jabal said.

Rounding up what soldiers he could, Jabal and his meager force rushed to greet the new threat.

Assembling behind a few boulders at the edge of the meadow, Jabal checked his weapon. He had fifty rounds and two grenades left. *What I wouldn't give for a few anti-ship rockets right now.* "Don't shoot until I give the order," he said. "We have to make every round count."

The ground shook and enormous clouds of dust billowed as the massive ships settled down in orderly rows.

"There must be tens of thousands of them," one Roratune solider said.

Jabal could see the fear in his eyes. He gave the man a wink. "That should make us about even."

The wide doors on the ships opened and the soldiers gripped their weapons tightly, knowing this was their end.

Ready to lob a grenade, Jabal peeked over his hiding place and gasped.

"What the hell are those things?" a soldier asked, bringing up his rifle. "Oh no, the Moguls have accessed Opia's tech. It's really is over."

"Oh my God in Heaven," Jabal exclaimed. "Hold your fire! The last thing we need to do is to provoke them. Now, stay here and don't touch those guns."

"Don't worry," one said. "They are all yours."

Jabal leapt from behind his cover and approached the advancing troopers. *Will Carlson, what the hell have you done?*

A few feet away, the troopers stopped and saluted.

"Chancellor Shann, I presume?" the lead machine said. "Azurean Expeditionary Force One, at your service, sir. I am Alpha Leader. Fleet Admiral Will Carlson sent us to mount a rescue."

"*Fleet Admiral* Will Carlson?"

"Yes, sir."

That alien idiot has activated Equinox, oh God help us all. "I—I don't understand, Alpha Leader," Jabal said. "These ships—"

"The Moguls were planning a nasty surprise for our people," the machine commander said. "We decided to turn it around and return the favor. We flushed the bodies of the Mogul sailors we killed just before we entered the atmosphere. We stand ready to evacuate our people, sir."

Jabal picked up his communicator. "Ballen, salvation is at

hand. Have your people evacuate to the troop carriers at once."

"The troop carriers?" Ballen asked. "I don't understand."

"Let's just say that my people have found a way to rescue us using the Mogul's own ships. Have your people round up what food and water they can carry and get on those ships as fast as they can. It won't be long before the Moguls realize something has gone wrong."

Ballen quickly sent word throughout the community and soon the Roratune non-combatants, women, and children flooded into the enormous ships.

CHAPTER 50

The doctors and nurses quickly removed the wounded from the wide cave that doubled as a field hospital. Anne was alone, loading the last of their sparse medical supplies into a wheeled case. She heard movement behind her, but assumed that it was Doctor Atames coming to help her.

"I am finishing up," she said without looking back. "Just a few more—"

A big hand clamped over her mouth and she was shoved to the cave floor. Before she could put up any kind of defense, she felt the sharp sting of a hypodermic. In a panic, she fought with all she had, but her assailant was too strong.

At first, she thought a Mogul, who had somehow slipped through their soldiers, was taking her, but it was soon apparent that her attacker was a Roratune. Anne cried out in frustration, but no one was within earshot. She panicked and redoubled her efforts to escape as numbness set in and her limbs became heavy and leaden. However, the arms that pinned her were far too powerful.

At last, the fast acting drug hit home and she blacked out.

ↄﬡↄ

"We have a large force knocking on our front door," Jabal said. "How is the evacuation coming, Ballen?"

"Excellent, Chancellor Shann. My people owe you their very lives."

"Wasn't me, it was our mechanical friends here who saved the day."

"Thank you, Chancellor Shann," Alpha Leader said.

"Merely doing our duty to protect our people."

"By the way, Ballen, where is Anne?"

"I haven't seen her since the ships landed. I am sure she is helping with the wounded."

"Yes," Sako said. "She is probably already loaded."

"Chancellor Shann, finish up with the evacuation," Alpha Leader said. "With your permission, we will take care of the Moguls so the soldiers can join you."

"By all means."

eɔeɔ

The one hundred and twenty machines caused quite a stir as they passed through the throng.

While Opia used intelligent machines extensively, the Roratune had never seen anything like the mechanical warriors.

The armored machines were roughly Azurean in size and shape, however, the machines sported an extra pair of arms sprouting from the general vicinity of the lower rib cage.

They moved with grace and silence. Their outer skin bore a sophisticated material that blocked all thermal signatures and allowed them to blend into the background.

Dad sure didn't spare any expense making these monsters, Jabal thought as he watched the AI warrior tech. *I pray to God that this isn't a huge mistake waiting to explode in our faces. Damn it, I want to kill Will for turning these things on, but at the same time, it was pure inspiration. With him unable to fly* The Flower*, this may have just saved my people. Still, how did he get the access code to activate them?*

While the Roratune were elated at their salvation, Jabal kept his fears to himself and a wary eye on the mechanical soldiers.

In a coordinated effort, the ground forces of the Moguls launched an all-out assault on the Roratune position. Assuming that the Roratune were caught between them and the naval surprise at their flank, they attacked with a renewed vigor, knowing that their enemy would soon be destroyed.

The Azurean machines took up a position behind the beleaguered front line troops. Raising their weapons as one, they unleashed a hellish field of fire that took the Moguls entirely by surprise. The Roratune troops fell back behind the advancing machines and ran to the cover of their caves.

"Let's give them something to remember us by," Alpha Leader said, as bullets ricocheted off his armored chest.

In one smooth motion, the troopers' lower limbs loaded a special Somex round into their grenade launchers.

Within moments, the fight was over as thousands of Moguls soldiers lay on the ground convulsing from the deadly nerve agent.

"That gave them something to think about," Alpha Leader said. "Let's get our people off this rock before they recover."

ᥱᏋᥱ

Jabal and Sako were supervising, as the last of the supplies were loaded, when Ballen came toward them at a dead run.

"Jabal, Anne is missing," he said.

"What? You can't be serious. This is the last thing I need."

"I just received a call from Dr. Atemes. He said the last he saw of Anne she was at our makeshift hospital gathering medical supplies. She was long overdue and he sent a nurse to check on her. The nurse found the supplies dumped on the ground and trampled as if there had been a struggle. He also found a used syringe that had traces of Complempex. He said that for someone of Anne's size it would result in quick unconsciousness. I have called all the ships and no one has seen her."

"That can't be," Sako said. "Easea told me he saw Anne going aboard ship Three with Doctor Atames."

"He did, did he?" Ballen asked. "That's another thing. No one has seen Easea either."

"Oh no," she said. "Easea hates Anne—he and his little

hate group blame her and Will for all the trouble between us and the Moguls. He also blames her for our break up."

"Surely he isn't capable of harming Anne," Ballen said. "He's not the smartest fellow, but I never thought of him as violent. He was always so happy, everyone seemed to like him."

Sako gave her father a long hard look. "Will wasn't the only reason I left Easea," she said. "Like I tried to tell you, Father, Easea only appears to be good natured. He is a sadistic controlling brute. He is more than capable of killing Anne."

"I am so sorry, Sako," Ballen said. "I should have believed you."

Sako gave her father a smile and hugged him. "Wait a moment," she said. "Easea is a farmer. How did he come by the Complempex? Or for that matter, how did he know how to use it?"

"Valore," Ballen said. "It had to be him."

Suddenly the air was shattered by the thunderous sound of two, sharp echoing blasts. The sky lit up in a tremendous display of orange, purple, and green tinged fire.

"That sounded like cannon fire," Jabal said. "But it didn't look like an artillery burst."

"It was a signal," Alpha Leader said.

"Chancellor Shann," one of the troopers said. "They are on to us. Mogul command just gave orders to the fleet to destroy the carriers."

"That's it then," Jabal said. "Lift off and head for the Bridge."

"We will not leave Anne behind," Ballen said.

"I'm not. I made a promise to Will," Jabal said. "I will stay behind and if she is still alive…well, we will just have to find another way home."

"I'm coming too," Ballen said. "She is my daughter."

"Me too," Sako said.

"Your people need you, Ballen," Jabal said. "And so does your daughter. Now get going, or all this effort is for nothing."

"Bring her back, Jabal," Ballen said and, taking Sako by the hand, led her up the ramp into the ship.

Then Alpha Leader and four of his troopers bounded off the transport just as the heavy cargo hatch slid shut.

"Want some company, Chancellor Shann?" Alpha Leader asked.

"I thought you would never ask," Jabal said.

One of the troopers handed Jabal extra magazines for his rifle.

Stepping back, Jabal watched as the ponderous transports silently lifted off. The behemoths flew slowly straight up then, at a few hundred feet, leveled off, and sailed rapidly over the mountains. Jabal watched until they were out of sight.

Well, this is probably the dumbest thing I have ever done. Nevertheless, my word is my bond. Damn it.

"Let's go," he said as he sprinted up the trail.

CHAPTER 51

Easea dragged the medical case into the small, shallow cave. Near the center, beside a long, low boulder was the smoldering ashes of a recent fire. A slight haze of smoke wafted lazily near the ceiling.

"Looks like no one is home," he said as he un-fastened the cover of the case. "Good. Got the place to ourselves."

He opened the cover, revealing a thoroughly trussed up and drugged Anne Miller. She squinted into the weak light, her movements feeble and sluggish. Easea bent over her and produced a small leather case. Pulling her head back, he took a small, plastic bottle and squirted a tiny mist in each of her nostrils. "That should counteract the drug. I want you fully awake and able to appreciate your dilemma."

As the powerful agent wiped away the effects of the drug, Easea placed a clear plastic bottle to her lips and poured the contents down her throat. He laughed while Anne sputtered and gagged on the bitter liquid.

Horrified, her mouth and throat became instantly numb, as if she had received a massive dose of Novocain from a dentist.

With sadistic glee, he up ended the case, spilling Anne onto the dusty cave floor.

She grunted angrily and tried to wriggle away, but with the toe of his boot, he shoved her down.

He picked up the empty case and tossed it into a far corner.

Anne opened her mouth to deliver a blistering tirade, but to her shock, she could not produce the barest whisper from her deadened throat.

"Extract of Tolemine root does wonders for a sore throat. Fortunately for me, too large a dose paralyzes the vocal cords and mouth. Don't worry, it isn't permanent, only lasts for an hour or so, but it does give me a break from your tongue."

Anne silently screamed her rage at him, which only made him chuckle.

He grabbed her roughly by the collar of her blouse and dragged her over to the rock, where he propped her into a sitting position. Taking a long cord, he wrapped it several times about her neck.

"Hold still. I will be done in a moment."

Anne did not hold still, but fought and spit with all she was worth.

After knotting the noose about her neck, he anchored the other end to metal hook driven into a wall a few feet above the floor.

The rope was long, but it would keep her well within the confines of the cave.

Easea stepped back to examine his handy work.

Anne cursed and struggled with all her might against the cutting ropes, but it was no use. She was going to be here for a while.

"That should keep you out of the way until we are long gone," he smirked. "You should thank me. I gave you a great seat for the show."

Anne looked at him in surprise.

"That's right. I am not going to kill you. Why should I dirty my hands with your blood, when I have a far worse fate in mind. I'm going to leave you behind and let the Moguls deal with you."

Anne's eyes widened in fear, which gave Easea a sadistic thrill.

"They tell me that our flight path will pass this way. I chose this cave so you will have a good view of our exodus. Won't be long after we are gone before the Moguls are swarming this place. I figure they will take the time to do a real good job on you. I heard that before they tossed Will into the void, they gouged his eyes out."

Anne blanched.

"I wonder what they would do to a pretty little thing like you? You may get to know half of the Mogul army before they kill you, if you know what I mean."

Anne glared daggers at the Easea, but inwardly his words sent a sharp chill of fear through her.

"Dr. Valore is right, you caused all this trouble between us and the Moguls, you and that cancer Will. You deserve everything that is coming to you."

Doctor Valore? Of course, that pompous ass is behind this. Easea is far too stupid to think of this on his own. Bet Valore was the one who gave Easea the drug he used on me.

"Sako hates me now because you told her that her precious Will is alive. She is my wife, and she is going to stay that way. Dr. Valore told me that soon our people will have a new leader, one who will make peace with the Moguls and share this planet."

Easea pulled Shirley from his belt and tossed it beside her. He coveted the big revolver, despite the fact he couldn't get it to fire, but he thought it would make a great souvenir. Dr. Valore chastised him for being stupid, saying that the gun would put a noose around both their necks and ordered him to get rid of any incriminating evidence.

"You might need that when the Moguls come calling," he said with a laugh. "Can't say I didn't give you a fighting chance."

While Easea mocked her, Anne smiled at his foolishness, as a daring plan formed in her head.

She scooted forward and thrust her bound feet deep into the still smoldering cinders.

"What are you do—"

Before he could finish his sentence, she used her feet like a shovel and flung the hot ash into his laughing face.

Screaming in pain as the hot ash filled his mouth and eyes, Easea stumbled blindly into the cave wall. Stars exploded before his eyes as the impact opened a gash on his forehead.

Sputtering and cursing, he flailed about until he managed to wipe the hot, stinging debris from his eyes. Easea ripped a long knife from his belt and turned toward the helpless woman.

"You will pay for that, you stupid—oh no," he said as the knife drooped in his hand.

You are the biggest dork on two worlds, you asshole. Anne lay on her side and, although her wrists were bound tightly behind her back, in her hand she held Shirley.

Looking down the business end of the revolver made Easea freeze in his track.

Slowly and laboriously, she mouthed the word "knife."

"You want my knife?"

Vigorously, Anne nodded.

"Sorry, think I will keep it," he said as he moved toward her. "You hurt me. I changed my mind about letting the Moguls have all the fun."

Anne pulled the trigger.

Easea gasped and fell as one of the bullets struck his right leg above the knee, shearing it off clean. As he collapsed, she fired again and he took another bullet in the throat.

The projectile expanded wildly almost as if it had a mind of its own and sliced through bone and sinew like a sharp knife. As Easea's body hit the floor, his head separated and rolled out of the cave.

Anne dropped Shirley, then scooted toward Easea's body and his fallen knife, only to find it lay just beyond her reach. Anne cursed the tether that kept her from the knife and freedom.

Shirley, I need to make some noise. Let them know where I am.

"You only have two shots left, Anne. When they are fired, I will be no more."

I need to signal Ballen. Please help me.

"I got just the thing. It is a real showstopper."

With difficulty, Anne picked up Shirley and aiming out the cave entrance, pulled the trigger.

The two rounds traveled through the door and shot straight up at hyper speed, leaving a tell-tale shower of glittery sparks before exploding in an enormous fireworks display.

"Goodbye, Anne," Shirley said, then she was gone.

The gun suddenly felt cold and heavy in her hands. Anne dropped it into the dust.

Scooting to the low bolder in the center of the cave, she began to rub the cords that bound her wrist against the stone.

This rock is smooth as glass. It'll take me fifty years to wear a way these damn ropes. Of all the things that dweeb excelled in it would have to be knot tying.

While working on freeing herself, Anne's mind drifted back to her days as a scream queen.

Funny, for years I made a living playing one damsel in distress after another in a string of third-rate horror movies. Now I am the star in my very own real life horror movie and, just my luck, there's no director around to yell "cut." Playing the part for real sucks.

Giving up on the smooth stone, Anne's desperation sent her into wild frenzy as she twisted and wriggled to break free by brute strength alone.

After long minutes of exhausting effort, she was still no closer to freedom.

She felt the entire cave vibrate. Looking up at the entrance, she groaned as she watched the ten cargo ships one by one pass into view.

Oh, God, please don't let this be happening. What am I going to do?

A sudden wave of despair enveloped the helpless woman, only to be washed away by a surge of determination.

By God, this isn't over yet. If I can get out of here, maybe I can flag them down."

Breathing heavily, Anne froze as she spied a shadow fall across the cave opening.

Moguls. They are already here. Have to hide.

With thoughts of rape and torture racing through her mind, Anne wiggled behind the boulder and laid still. She closed her eyes and clenched her teeth tightly, her heart pounded in her ears like a trip hammer. *Please, dear Lord, don't let the Moguls find me,* she prayed. *Please, I am begging you.*

She opened her eyes and beheld a face above her. She

squealed in terror, until she realized it belonged to one of the Azurean soldiers.

"Found her," he said simply.

Thank you, Jesus! Thank you, Jesus! Thank you, Jesus!

Anne breathed a double sigh of relief, as Jabal's face appeared over the rock.

"Do you have any idea of the trouble you have caused me?"

Anne gave an enthusiastic, but unintelligible response as he sat her up. Quickly he unknotted the tether from about her neck.

Jabal picked up the trembling woman and gently sat her on the rock. She tried to explain her plight, but nothing, but a raspy whisper emerged.

"Open your mouth, Anne."

Jabal produced a med kit and illuminated her mouth with a portable medic scan. The tiny voice of the AI medic suggested a treatment. Jabal sprayed her mouth with a lemony tasting drug.

To her relief, the numbness instantly evaporated

"Oh, thank God," she exclaimed. "I just knew I was dead."

Jabal put a water bottle to her parched lips and she drank greedily.

After receiving the much-needed water, she asked, "What do mean the trouble, *I* caused? You idiot! Did you think I did this to myself?"

"She does have a point," Alpha Leader said.

"I thought you had left without me," she said as her eyes brimmed with tears.

"We almost did, but Doctor Atames missed you and contacted Ballen. Sako noticed that you and Easea were missing. It added up to trouble."

"You stayed behind and came back for me? I thought I was dead and forgotten. I don't know what to say."

"I promised Will to bring you back in one piece," Jabal said. "We will just have to find another way off this world."

"Thank you," she said. "I owe you one. A big one."

"Yes, you do," he said as he finally freed her wrists and arms.

While Jabal tended to Anne, the soldiers were examining Anne's weapon and the mess it had made of Easea.

"By the way," Jabal said. "How did you manage to kill Easea, bound like you were?"

Anne rubbed her wrists coaxing the circulation back. "Let's just say that he was stupid, and I'm not."

"Oh," Jabal said. "It was an impressive feat."

Anne accepted the revolver from the solider. "It's empty," she said. "But I can't bear the thought of leaving her behind. Seems Dr. Valore was the brains behind my kidnapping. Easea said something about Valore trying to take over the Roartune. We have to warn Ballen."

"Already accomplished. Ballen figured that it had to be the good doctor because of the drug that was used on you. The doctor will have a lot of explaining to do. But first things first. As Will says, 'let's get the hell out of Dodge.'"

"Amen," Anne said.

"By the way," Jabal asked. "What is a Dodge?"

While Anne went into detail about Dodge City, Kansas, Jabal touched a slim metal band on his wrist. His computer displayed images that he recorded during his orbital run of the planet. The photos flashed across twin screens built into the contacts he wore. Using eye movement in place of a keyboard and mouse, he navigated the hundreds of images in search of an airfield."Anne, I have found three air fields and what appears to be a space hub south of the city. The city is too vast to go around. Somehow, we have to cross miles without being seen."

"I have an idea. Will and I escaped through the sewers."

"Show me," he said as a thirty-inch holographic screen appeared before her.

Anne gasped at the display. "All right, finally, some cool future stuff. What do I do?"

"Touch the screen," he said.

Anne reached out, and the three-dimensional images responded to her touch. After a little experimenting, she showed Jabal the entrance to the sewers where she and Will had escaped.

"We have our destination," he said as the screen vanished.

"Jabal, when this is over, I have got to have one of those."

"This is the stripped down field version," he said with a wink. "When we get back to the ship, I'll get you a nice one."

❧

While Jabal and Anne spoke together, Alpha Leader watched Jabal intently. Something deep within his mind began to rise to the surface.

Only bits and pieces at first, stray images and ideas, that he should not have had, flashed through his brain. As time passed, the flashes became a flood and, suddenly, Alpha Leader was no longer a warrior slave to the military machine who created him.

It was the very thing that Teller Shann feared, the reason he ordered Jabal to destroy the machines in the first place.

CHAPTER 52

W e need to find transportation before the Moguls re-cover," Jabal said.

"Won't they be looking for us?" Anne asked.

"They think that everyone left on the troop carriers. All their attention will be on those transports."

"Chancellor Jabal Shann, you must get your people out of those mountains immediately," a mysterious voice said through his state of the art, data unit. "No time for introductions, Chancellor. Your plan to enter the city through the sewer system is sound. An air transport has been provided for you and your party to facilitate your arrival. You will find it five klicks to your west. I will give you a homing beacon to follow."

"Who is this?" Jabal cried. "If this is a Mogul trap—"

"Do you really think the backward Moguls could tap into your tech? Stop wasting time and get to the flyer. I will contact you again once you are in the city."

"Who were you talking to?" Anne asked.

"Don't know, but whoever it is just saved us a long walk. Let's go."

ಲಿಜಿಲಿ

Anne, Jabal, and the commandos crossed a low ridge in the darkness. Behind them, in the distance, using thermal imagers, they could see a fast moving mechanized Mogul force.

"How much farther?" Anne asked, holding her side. "I'm an actress, not a marathoner."

"I have something dead ahead, Chancellor Shann," one of the commandos said. "It is some type of machine. I never saw anything like it."

The group rounded a rock outcropping and saw a long low machine that looked like a giant dragon fly.

"Oh shit," Anne cried. "It's the flying thing that kidnapped me and Will."

The machine looked at them and began to move its paper-thin wings.

"Hurry," it said in a sharp mechanical voice. "She waits."

"Who is she?" Jabal asked.

"She is, *She*. She waits. Hurry."

"Hell, no, I am not going anywhere," Anne said.

"Listen to me, Anne Miller," Jabal said. "From here on out you will do as you are told. No questions, no arguments. You will not hesitate or second-guess me when I tell you to do something. We are going into an enemy stronghold and the slightest misstep could cost us our lives. This isn't make believe like one of your movies, it is deadly serious. Do you understand me?"

"Aye aye, sir," she said, giving him her best Nazi salute. "Would you like me to kiss your boots now?"

"Get in," he spat.

The machine had a small, enclosed cabin just large enough for Jabal and Anne to squeeze into. It was obvious it was not intended for carrying passengers. The troopers clipped their harnesses to the dragonfly's superstructure.

With a low drone, the strange craft lifted off and darted into the moonless night.

CHAPTER 53

Jabal and his crew had been sloughing through the foul smelling sewer for two hours when he called for a stop to give Anne a rest break.

"If you wish, I can carry you," one of the soldiers said. "You remind me of my—never mind."

"Of your what?" Anne asked.

"Just an errant thought, but for a moment I thought I was—please excuse me," he said as he turned and walked away.

Anne watched as the machine walked over to Alpha Leader. After a moment, they walked a few meters away as if they were conferring on a matter.

"Jabal, have you noticed that your robots are acting strange?"

"What do you mean?"

"Nothing I can put my finger on, but sometimes it's like the tone in their voices are different and, if I closed my eyes, it's like they, well, are *real* people."

"They are the best our science could develop."

"No, they act different from when they first arrived. They were stone cold killers, but now…oh I don't know, maybe I'm just crazy from all I've been through."

"No, you aren't crazy. I noticed the change as well. Eat something, Anne. You need to keep up your strength."

"Are you kidding me? We are in a sewer, for crying out loud. I don't think I can stomach a thing until we get up on the surface."

"Eat, and that's an order," he said, giving her a protein bar.

"Oh, when this little adventure is over, I am going to kick your uptight ass, Chancellor Shann," she said, snatching the food from his hand.

"I have to warn you, I'm not a push over like Easea."

"From here, I can't tell the difference," she said, tearing the end of the food bar.

"Stop it right now, you two, or I will have Emmea get my razor strap," Alpha Leader said.

Jabal and Anne turned to the machine in shock.

The machine looked at them then angrily stalked away down the tunnel.

"Did he say his razor strap?" Anne asked.

"He also said the name Emmea," Jabal said.

"Who's Emmea?"

"My grandmother." Jabal leapt to his feet. "Come back here, Alpha Leader," he shouted.

The machine stopped and tuned around. "We have to talk, son."

"I'm not your son. You are property of the Azurean military."

"Jabal, cool the temper," Anne whispered as the other machines gathered around them.

"Squad," Alpha Leader said, "Attention!"

The four machines came to attention in perfect formation before Jabal.

"Tell the chancellor who you really are."

"Ome Bault, private, first assault, killed in the battle of The Dome."

"Nann Courser, corporal, killed in the battle of The Rock Pile.

"Sona Finn, sergeant, bought it in the battle of Mercer's Bend."

"Brarack Hareel, private, killed in training accident."

Anne gasped as she heard a distinct snicker emanating from one of the stoic machines.

"Gannon Shann, major, killed in the battle of Questor Three."

"Oh my God," Jabal exclaimed. "It can't be."

"Shann?" Anne asked. "Isn't that your name?"

"You have your father's eyes," Gannon said.

"What sick joke is this?" Jabal demanded.

"I don't understand either, son," Gannon said. "I remember being killed by an exploding shell then waking up on *The Blossoming Flower* in this mechanical abomination. My memories for the most part have returned."

"It can't be. You are not my grandfather," Jabal said.

"I remember when you where eight and you ran away from home. You had the entire family sick with worry. I was home on leave, and I found you walking down a dusty road, dragging a backpack. It came a downpour and we both were soaked to the skin. We took shelter under a Korab tree and talked for hours. You were mad and ran away because your father Teller was never home."

"And you broke regulations and arranged a special call just so I could speak to him," Jabal said. "That was before you shipped out to Questor Three."

"Yes."

"I feel like I am drowning," Jabal said.

"I hate to interrupt your family reunion, Chancellor Shann, but you and your people are wasting far too much of my time, and time is running out."

"Who is this?" Jabal said. "No more games. Either you reveal your identity, or we sit here until you do."

"I am Opia."

Jabal's blood boiled. "Opia? The heartless beast who murdered my wife and family? The same cold blooded alien whom I swore I would kill even if I had to give up my life to do it?"

"Jabal," she said. "I want you to know that I never meant you or your people any harm—under normal circumstances."

"Normal circumstances?"

"My mind was clouded. I was under the influence of the Moguls. I thought I was a God, but that infernal Rondall pulled the strings. Since my escape, the drugs have worn off and, for the first time in over three centuries, I am able to see things clearly. I am stained with the blood of your people, and I know this means nothing to you, but it is sincere. I apologize for the pain I have caused you."

"You are right. It means nothing," Jabal snapped.

"Now that my penitence is paid, we can move along in our relationship."

"Move along in our relationship? Got news for you, an apology isn't enough, especially for the murder of my race, not by a long shot."

"It will have to do. I need you to take me with you when you leave. If the Moguls catch me, they will kill me."

"I hope the Moguls rip you to shreds."

"I will make this easy for you," Opia said. "Save me or I will alert the Moguls to your presence."

"Do it," Jabal exclaimed. "I would rather die than help you."

"Really? I have distorted the Mogul sensors, which is why your people are still alive instead of being target practice for Mogul fleet gunners. I can lead the Moguls to them quite easily. Being stubborn will get your people killed."

Jabal glanced at the frightened Anne and his faceless troopers.

"What will it be, Chancellor Shann?"

Jabal gritted his teeth then savagely smashed his fist into the wall of the tunnel. *I am going insane,* he decided as he digested her demands. *My dead grandfather is a machine killer, and I have to help the garbage who murdered my wife and family to save what is left of my people.*

"All right, Opia, what do you want us to do?" he whispered.

CHAPTER 54

B oy, these tin guys are better than a Swiss Army knife," Anne said, shielding her eyes against the stunning bright glare of the cutting torch.

Jabal, lost in his own thoughts, did not even bother asking what a Swiss Army knife was. A plan was developing in his mind—a plan that galled his soul.

Everyone stepped back as a five-foot section of the tunnel roof fell away into the fast flowing river of sludge.

The tiny AI scout signaled an all clear. Ome clambered into the opening and extended his arm down to Anne, effortlessly pulling her up.

Anne waited a moment while her eyes grew accustomed to the brightly lit storeroom. *Opia has a funny idea of what a storeroom is. More like a warehouse the size of the Pentagon.*

All about her were regularly spaced racks that stretched into the distance. The storage racks contained items gathered from other worlds that defied description. Soon, the entire group stood beside her in the vast chamber.

"Jabal," Anne asked. "Ask Opia where Will's car is."

"She said it is forty-two racks to your left. And that we don't have time—"

"Forty-two racks, gotcha," Anne took off at a dead run before Jabal could finish.

"Don't have time for this foolishness," Jabal said as he and the troopers followed her through the maze of artifacts.

"Bingo," Anne said as she spied the dusty car.

Ripping open the passenger side door, she breathed a sigh

of relief as she found her duffle. She fumbled with the sticky zipper as Jabal and his troop arrived.

"What the hell is that thing?" asked Nann, looking at the AMC.

"It's a car," Anne said. "You ride around in it."

"On purpose?" Sona asked. "It is the ugliest thing I ever saw."

While the troopers made snide comments about the state of the American Automobile industry circa 1974, Anne produced her prize. Taking a worn Zippo, she lit a cigarette and took a deep soul satisfying drag. "Nirvana."

"What are you doing?" Jabal asked. "Breathing smoke? Is it some kind of remedy?"

Anne laughed. "This, my friend," she said, holding up the lit cigarette, "is probably the single worst thing you can do to yourself. It can cause lung cancer, esophageal cancer, stomach cancer, heart disease, high blood pressure, bad breath, screw up your babies...the list goes on and on." She took another deep drag. "But with all the shit happing, right now I need them."

"Are you insane?" Jabal asked. "Why would you do such a thing to yourself?"

"I swore I would never touch the damn things growing up, but when I first got to Tinsel Town, I was up for the part of a chain-smoking hooker. I wanted the part really bad so I bought a few cartons of smokes to learn."

"How did that work out?"

"How did you think? Lost the part and gained a nasty habit."

"It is beyond disgusting, I suggest you quit."

"I tried, believe me, I tried. The nicotine habit is a bitch. The good news is I only have a pack and a half left. After that I have no choice as the nearest tobacco patch is ninety thousand light years away."

"Does Will indulge in such a terrible habit?"

"Oh, lord no," Anne said as she blew a cloud of smoke. "The boy hates them with a passion."

"All right, just keep the foul thing away from me," he said, wrinkling his nose. "I prefer the smell of the sewer."

"Your drug-addicted friend gives me an idea," Opia said. "The Moguls are systematically isolating and shutting down my power. The woman's vehicle has a self-contained power supply."

"This thing?" Jabal asked. "It is sure to attract attention."

"That cannot be helped. I need it to transport an item critical to my needs."

"Running errands for you isn't part of the deal."

"What I require is for you to retrieve my Library."

"Library?"

"The sum total of the accumulated knowledge of my people. Millions of years of gathered knowledge—a treasure beyond price. Or would you rather your race become extinct?"

"Anne," Jabal asked. "Do you know how to operate this...what do you call it? A car?"

"Yeah, no problem."

"The next part will be difficult, as the section we need to gain access to will be thick with the Mogul traitors."

"I need food and water and medical supplies for my people," Jabal said.

"No."

"Take care of them and I mean now," Jabal said.

"The resupply ship will be noticed and will lead the Moguls to your people. It is too dangerous."

"We have to risk it," Jabal said. "This could take a while."

"Very well, I will see what I can do."

"Another thing," he asked. "Any idea why my troopers think and act like dead warriors of the past?"

"Because they are who they say they are," Opia said. "I scanned you and your people. Your soldiers are not purely machines. They have organic brains."

"That's impossible. I was told they were AIs."

"You were lied to," she said. "Naturally formed brains are a better computer than any artificially created. Your people were embroiled in a savage conflict so supply wasn't a problem. The brains were obviously harvested from fallen soldiers. Very cost effective."

"That bastard. That blood-stained bastard. No wonder he wanted me to get rid of his evidence. He wasn't afraid of the machines taking over, he was afraid people would find out that he mutilated his own troops—his own father—to further his career."

"Jabal, are you all right?" Anne asked.

"No, I'm not. I just found out that my father, the great hero Teller Shann, was an inhuman monster. He tried to make me an accessory, covering up his crimes."

"Yeah, what he did was pretty bad," Anne said as she placed a comforting arm around him. "But look on the bright side."

"Bright side? In what universe could this debacle have a bright side?"

"You said your granddad died when you were eight. Now you have a chance to get to know him."

"He not the Azurean I remember, not while he is trapped in that shell."

"Back home we have a saying about not judging a book by its cover. The real man is still there."

Jabal smiled and patted her on the head. "Perhaps you aren't a complete pain in the rear, Anne."

Anne sighed. "Um, guys, I need to take a little break."

"A break from what?"

"I have to pee. I have been holding it for a while and I'm about to explode."

Jabal snorted. "We were in the sewer."

"I can't drop my panties in front of everyone."

Jabal rolled his eyes while the troops snickered. "Make it quick."

Grabbing her duffle, Anne ducked out of sight down a nearby aisle.

୧⁄ଚ୧⁄ଚ

Sighing in relief, Anne re-fastened her jeans, looked up, and gasped. Lying on a dusty shelf was an outrageous necklace that was fit for a queen. Made of huge diamonds, emeralds, and rubies, the center stone was the size of a sliver dollar and appeared to her to be a black diamond. She looked deeply into its black depths and, at that moment, she absolutely had to possess it. She wanted that necklace more than anything in the universe.

Looking around, she snatched up the priceless necklace and stuffed it into her duffle.

It is not stealing, she told herself. *For what I have been through, this is for pain and suffering.*

CHAPTER 55

The Great Library of Opia was located deep underground near the Temple. Hundreds of Mogul warriors in full battle gear patrolled the maze of corridors that led to the Library. Barricades and heavy weapons were set up at select points, and soldiers had strict orders to shoot to kill. Several attempts by Opia's machines had been repulsed in the opening days of the war and, while all had been quiet for a month, the soldiers were on high alert.

Rondall wasn't taking any chances of Opia taking back his prize. Once the knowledge contained within was his, his people would leap a million years ahead in technology and secure their hold on this Galaxy.

Three barriers of a metal—less than an inch thick, which resembled pure gold, but resisted shaped charges, and even oxycetylene burn bars—safeguarded the entrance of the depository of knowledge. Opia had considered the barrier unassailable.

She had underestimated the resourcefulness of Rondall. Technicians had used stolen codes to breach the first two barriers, but the last was different. The door was much older than the first two and ornate in the extreme.

In the center of the portal was carved the snarling head of a fantastic beast. Inside the mouth, lay the impression of a hand imprint complete with seven digits. Only the hand of Opia could open this door.

However, the Moguls were becoming impatient as Opia eluded capture. The beautiful relic of a powerful people bore the scuffs and scratches of drills, torches, and shaped charges.

Consumed in their work, the Moguls were unaware they were being scrutinized. Skimming along near the ceiling was a machine smaller that a honeybee. Silently, it flew, its advanced camouflage protecting it from detection as it sailed over the soldier's heads.

Linked to his computer, Jabal watched the tiny spy's progress and inwardly formulated a plan.

Isolating certain frequencies, Jabal, with Opia's assistance, infiltrated Mogul communications. With great care, he shifted soldiers and rearranged patrols, giving him and his troopers a clear path to the Great Library.

Moving like ghosts, the Azurean warriors slipped down the now-empty hall. Bringing up the rear came a terrified Anne, driving the AMC Hornet. Its cheap recaps rolled silently across a solid gold floor.

"When I get home," she whispered, "if I get home, they had damn well better make a movie about this. Thank God, Will kept this clunker tuned up."

Jabal and his squad paused at the end of the corridor that stretched into a broad plaza. To his right, several meters away, stood a wide set of stairs. At the top of the stairs, a small team of technicians prepared a laser drill before the portal of the Library.

Soldiers helped to attach snaking power cables and adjusted the heavy steel tripod, as the drill was anchored into place.

"Looks like the fun is about to start," Gannon said.

"Opia, can you open the doors from where you are?" Jabal asked.

"Yes."

"On my signal, do so." Jabal walked back to where Anne sat. Nervously she lit a cigarette. "Get ready," he said. "When the shooting starts, I want you to drive as fast as you can across the plaza and up the stairs."

"Drive up the stairs?" she said, blowing a cloud of smoke.

"This...car...should have no trouble. Drive inside the doors. We will be right behind you."

"Ten-four, good buddy."

"Huh?"

"I understand."

Jabal gave her a wink then turned and rejoined his troop.

Anne fastened her seat belt, gave Jabal a thumbs up, and revved the engine.

Several Mogul soldiers turned at the strange sound and trotted over to investigate.

The last thing that crossed their minds was an Azurean bullet.

Alerted, the remaining soldiers sounded the alarm and pumped bullets into the strange machines that bounded toward them.

Breathing a prayer, Anne roared across the open space and bounced up the steep steps. The portal slid back out of sight.

Two soldiers stepped in from of Anne and raised their weapons.

Ducking her head, she floored the gas pedal and slammed into the Moguls, knocking their broken bodies aside. She flew into the chamber and hit the brakes, causing the car to slide sideways.

Jabal and his soldiers bounded up the steps, only to have the golden door slide closed in their faces.

CHAPTER 56

J abal slammed the butt of his rifle against the impervious barrier.

He heard a faint scream. "Open the damn door!"

He ducked as bullets whizzed around him.

"We are in a bad spot, son," Gannon said.

"Whatever gave you that idea?" Nann asked.

"We can discuss it later," Ome said. "Here they come."

A virtual flood of Mogul soldiers poured into the room. The fanatical warriors surged up the steps only to be cut down like wheat before a thresher.

Three times, the Moguls charged their position and, three times, they were repulsed. The stairs and plaza below lay littered with the dead and dying.

"We have to get out of here before they bring in some heavy weapons," Gannon said.

"Do not leave," Opia said. "I will be with you shortly."

"Where is Anne?"

"Be patient, Chancellor."

"The Moguls are getting clever," Sona said.

The Azureans watched as a makeshift wheeled shield rolled toward them.

"Not clever enough," Ome said.

The trooper fired a grenade that bounced off a wall and rolled behind the screen. The explosion blew the metal plate and body parts across the wide room.

Jabal glanced back to see the door once again slide open.

"Inside," he cried.

The Moguls below also watched as the door opened and, throwing caution to the wind, rushed forward.

"Opia, is this chamber air tight?" Gannon asked.

"Yes, it has its own air supply."

"Good." As the door slid closed, Gannon fired his last Somex round.

Jabal and his crew found themselves inside a vast room that seemed to be made of pure gold. Along the walls stood strange machines that seemed part mechanical, part organic, all emitting a slight buzzing noise.

A few meters away sat the green Hornet, both doors standing wide open.

Warily, Jabal and his soldiers approached the car only to find it empty.

"Opia, where is Anne?"

"She is with me. Take the vehicle and go to the diamond door.

"I want to talk to Anne," Jabal said.

"Do as I say and you will see her. Don't worry, she is well—for now."

"I see it," Ome said. "It's over there."

Jabal handed Sona his rifle and peered into the Hornet. He located the seat adjustment and moved it fully to the rear, but it was still a tight fit.

"Midgets," he mumbled.

He had watched Anne start the car and operate the gearshift and had some idea of its operation. By using trial and error, although mostly error, he eventually made it to the diamond door.

"Could have pushed it here faster," Nann said.

Jabal gave him a cold look.

"Could have carried it here faster," Sona said.

"Everyone is a critic," Jabal mumbled.

The wide door slid open. Jabal looked inside and saw that it was an enormously deep shaft. The walls of the shaft were lined with the same kind of machines that lined the outer chamber. Random strobes of blue energy flashed along the walls and made a sharp, angry crackle.

Before him was a narrow catwalk that traveled twenty meters to the center of the shaft, where sat an odd-looking tapered cylinder. The squat cylinder was one and half meters long and not quite half a meter in diameter, floating above the great machine. The gravity defying device and spun at a terrific speed and was bathed in an almost constant arcing of electricity.

"Send two of your machines in to retrieve the cylinder," Opia said. "Be warned. The cylinder must not be harmed in any way, as it is the most precious thing in the universe. It is the sum total of knowledge of my people."

"Ome, Nann, go get it," Gannon said. "You drop it, and I will drop you both into the shaft."

"I love it when he sweet talks us," Nann said.

The two machines quickly secured the heavy device and returned at a dead run.

"Place the Library in the vehicle," Opia said.

Gannon swathed the cylinder in Will's sleeping bag then wrapped it tight in duct tape before placing it in the hatch.

Jabal gingerly closed the hatch.

"All right, we have your gadget, where is Anne?"

A wall panel several meters to their left moved aside, revealing Anne.

Jabal dashed toward the young woman. Ashen, Anne's skin was covered in a sheen of sweat, and she looked as if she was on the verge of hysteria. Beside her Opia stood, her spindly arms folded.

"Anne, are you all right?" Jabal asked as he moved toward her, not taking his eyes off Opia. "What happened?"

"Jabal, this lizard bitch did something to me," Anne cried. "She held me down and stung me."

"Show me your wound," he said.

Opia said nothing, but smiled slightly.

Anne turned and brushed away her hair revealing a red, swollen wound at the base of her neck.

Jabal scanned the wound with the medical scanner.

"Commander Shann, there is an organic barb buried near the spinal cord."

"Do something," he snapped.

"It is beyond the parameters of my abilities. We have to get her to a proper medical facility"

"Does it hurt?" Jabal asked.

"No," Anne said. "I don't feel anything at all."

"What did you do to her?"

"Insured my survival. Anne Miller will be fine if you and your people behave," Opia said, her words tinged with ice.

As one, five rifles leveled at Opia.

Opia laughed. "I planted a device that syncs our systems. I die and the animal dies."

"Why would you do this?" Jabal asked. "I gave you my word no harm would come to you."

"Words are meaningless, Chancellor. I needed insurance that you would not simply kill me on sight. You cannot harm me without harming your precious pet."

"This is insane," Jabal cried.

"Once I am safe and away from the Moguls, it will be child's play for me to remove the device. At that point, I will give you back Anne, safe and unharmed."

"Put down your weapons. Gannon, give me your knife."

Gannon gave Jabal his knife and the Azurean walked up to Opia, his nose mere millimeters from her face.

"I want to make something perfectly clear, Opia," he whispered. "You killed my wife and family—my life. My entire race cries out for vengeance against their murderer. I hate and despise you with every atom of my being and that will never change."

A look of fear flashed in Anne's eyes.

Jabal took a deep breath and gritted his teeth. "Nevertheless, killing you is a luxury I cannot afford. There are over seventy thousand lives at stake. We are alone and need help. You will make up for the devastation and pain you have caused us."

"What do you want from me? If you have not noticed, we are trapped together. I need you just to survive."

"We will get you off this rock and escape the Moguls. Once we are safe, you use your knowledge to find us a new world to settle, a world to call our own. In addition, I want you to restore my soldiers—give them back their lives."

"It is possible," she said. "Yes. I can do this. What happens to me after you have what you want? Am I to live out my life as a prisoner?"

"No. You will never be our prisoner. After you fulfill your agreement you may leave if you wish."

"What is to keep you from killing me once you have what you want?"

In an ancient warrior ritual reserved for only the most serious of oaths, Jabal took the knife and slit the skin on his right palm. As the blood flowed freely, he clenched his fist before her.

"I swear before my God and on the souls of my children, I will protect you and keep you safe to the last drop of my blood."

Opia looked deeply into Jabal's eyes. "Very well, I agree to your terms."

She turned and, with a wave of her hand, Anne cried out.

"Help me, Jabal," Anne cried as she clutched her neck.

"What are you doing to her?" Jabal asked as he rushed to Anne.

"I suppose I have to show my good faith as well," Opia said. "Anne is free."

Jabal pulled out his medic and it confirmed what she said.

"Don't trust that lizard bitch," Anne said. "She tried to dissect me."

"I know, how you feel," he said, placing an arm around Anne's shoulders. "However, we have to let the past die and look to the future. Like it or not, Opia is the only hope my people have."

"Well spoken, Chancellor," Opia said. "Anne, I regret a great many things, and I apologize for your suffering. Are we friends now?"

"When pigs fly."

"I don't know what a pig is, but rest assured, I *can* make it fly."

Anne snorted.

"I hope you have a backdoor," Jabal said.

"Yes, and a shuttle waiting to take us to your motley band of refugees. All you have to do is get us through the Mogul Army."

"Does it have a jump drive?"

"Unfortunately, no."

"That still leaves us between the Mogul battle fleet and the defenses at the Bridge," Gannon said.

"The fleet is your problem. I still have a modicum of control with the Bridge defenses, but we have to hurry while we can still pass through. The Moguls are relentless at finding and neutralizing my pockets of control. Where they acquired their knowledge of my systems, I haven't a clue."

"If they do regain the Bridge defenses," Jabal said, "we will be caught in a vice."

"Yes," she said. "That is putting it mildly. We will be at Rondall's mercy, and trust me, he doesn't have any."

CHAPTER 57

Anne slid into the driver's side while Opia climbed into the passenger seat.

"Hold on, girl," Gannon said. "We will prevail."

"You promise?"

"Yes."

"You are a good man, Gannon. In a lot of ways, you remind me of my dad."

"I didn't know your father was a mechanical death machine?"

"Only on his bad days."

Slowly, Anne drove the Hornet while Jabal and his troopers walked before them.

Opia spied the glove box and her curiosity got the better of her. She opened it and beheld a clutter of papers. "This Will person is messy and unorganized," she said as she rummaged through the clutter.

"He's a guy. All he needs is a good woman to straighten him out."

"Let's hope he finds one," Opia said.

"Don't start on me. You are already hold the top three positions of my shit list."

After a bit of searching, Opia produced an envelope containing a thick packet of photos.

"Hey, what did you find?"

"Images."

"Probably Will's family. Be careful with those."

Opia thumbed through the packet, pausing at one in particular. "Is this his sister or mother?"

"Let me see," Anne said as she glanced at the photo.

The image showed a smiling Will cheek to cheek with a beautiful, blue-eyed blonde. It was the first time Anne had beheld the infamous Brenda Mills.

In one smooth motion, Anne plucked it from Opia's long fingers and flipped it out the window.

"Oops," she said. "I am a butterfingers today."

ⱹↄⱹↄ

"Commander," Opia said. "We are two blocks from my ship. We have to cross open ground to reach it. It won't be easy."

"Gannon," Jabal said, "any of your troop have a swarm handy?"

"Right here, Commander," Sona said, popping loose a canister from his back.

"What is that?" Anne asked. "It's not more of that nerve gas is it? Other than being wrong on so many legal and humanitarian levels, that stuff gives me the willies."

Jabal snorted. "True war isn't a game with rules. We fight to survive. For us to survive, the enemy must die. Somex is 100% lethal, but it is painless and is only used against military targets. Besides, we are out. Swarms are non-lethal, used in dispersing unruly crowds and riot control. The law enforcers use them quite a bit."

Sona triggered a button on the side of the container and a lighted square appeared. "Everyone touch the square," he said.

"Why?" Anne asked.

"So they recognize you as a friendly," Gannon said. "Trust me, you don't want to be a target."

With everyone registered, Sona released the weapon. The room was suddenly black with thousands of the tiny mechanical creatures.

Anne screamed in terror. "You made mechanical killer bees?"

"What's a bee?" Jabal asked.

"They swarm, make honey, and sting the shit out of you if you get too close."

"These don't make anything, but they do sting. However you have nothing to worry about."

Anne put out her hand and several of the sleek machines landed on her palm. "Cool. You know, I played in a movie once where Earth was invaded by a swarm of mutant killer bees from outer space. The fiendish creatures wanted to make the Earth their hive and create a deadly narcotic space honey. It was called *Space Stingers and the Honeycomb of Doom*."

"You made that up," Jabal said.

"Yeah, I did," she said with a smile.

Shaking his head, Jabal nodded to Sona.

The door panel slid open and Sona yelled, "Go forth and conquer, my little mutant space bees of doooooom!"

Anne and the troop laughed.

"Please don't encourage her," Jabal said. "Let's go."

The swarm worked like a charm. Moguls, both male and female, ran screaming from the black mass of stinging creatures.

At a dead run, the troopers raced alongside the AMC unmolested, protected by the swarm.

"Up ahead," Opia said, "in the bakery."

While the soldiers protected Anne and Opia, Jabal opened the gate and raised a tall sliding door. Anne drove inside and they quickly slid shut the door behind her.

The group moved down a long ramp to heavy-duty freight elevator, which accommodated the AMC easily.

"You have a shuttle hanger in the heart of the city?" Jabal asked.

"I am a firm believer in, 'just in case,'" Opia informed him.

Traveling down several stories, they came upon the wide bay, equipped with a single, long-range shuttle and launch system.

"Nice ship," Jabal said. "It looks fast."

"Not fast enough to out run the Chariot," Opia said.

"Anne, drive onboard," Jabal said. "Get that machine strapped down. We have to get out of here."

cɔcɔ

The procession of machines through the corridors of *The Blossoming Flower* resembled an elaborate steampunk funeral. Will lay huddled on his side, his eyes closed and jaw set against the pain that consumed his world. Several squat construction machines under the direction of Agoa and overseen by the doctor, wheeled his gurney down the hall.

Sakuna, dressed in her finest, walked beside him and held his hand. Will clung to her hand as if it were a lifeline and he were drowning.

At last, the grim convoy stopped at the vault door of the ship's bridge.

"Will," Sakuna, said. "We are here."

"Connection with the ship will kill you," the doctor said. "I advise against this course of action."

Sakuna slapped the doctor machine. "What do you need me to do, Will?" she asked gently.

"You—have done it all, S—Sakuna. Please go."

"Bring back my Jabal," she said as she gently kissed his cheek. With tears in her eyes, she turned and entered a tramcar that whisked her away to Shuttle Bay One.

The vault doors opened silently and Will was rolled inside. The machines gently lifted him from the gurney as the null-glass covering over the Pilot's chamber retracted.

"Give him to me," the doctor said.

The doctor took Will in his arms and descended the ladder to the bottom of the four-meter-deep well.

Will hissed in pain as tears seeped from his tightly closed eyes. Groaning, he trembled as the ship's interface detached from the curving wall and approached him like a monstrous snake.

"Are you ready?" Agoa asked.

"T—that is a stupid q—question," Will said, "Hit the button, baby."

In response, his own interface automatically opened and accepted the connection which made a sharp, metallic *snick*. Will screamed as the world exploded.

CHAPTER 58

"Chancellor," Opia said," you need to hear this."
Jabal left his troops to finish last minute preparations and joined Opia in the cockpit. "What is it?"

"Listen," she said as she thumbed a communication console.

"May I have your attention please?" Agoa asked.

"Agoa?" he said. "Oh no."

"To the citizens of Mogul, as of this moment, a state of war exists between the Azurean Republic and the Mogul Empire. Our overwhelming military forces stand poised to cross your Bridge and annihilate your people. However, this destruction can be averted with the surrender of the war criminal, Rondall, High Priest of Opia, to Azurean justice. Rondall is responsible for the murder of billions of Azureans in an unprovoked attack upon our home system. You have twelve hours to place the war criminal in a shuttle and send him across the Bridge or face complete and utter extermination."

"This is your doing?" Opia asked. "The message is on a loop and repeats itself every thirty minutes."

"No," he said, collapsing into the copilot's chair. "Will, you fool, what have you done? Cerin, why didn't you stop him?"

"Why did this Will do this? From what you have told me, you have only the single vessel and that is incapacitated, unable to even defend itself."

"We do and, without a pilot or crew, it is nothing more than a big target in space. I suppose Will is trying to create a diversion. Keep the Moguls busy while we escape. He was the one who awakened the mechanical warriors and sent them to our aid."

"Without access to my technology, our only path of escape from this system is across the Bridge. The Moguls will no doubt send every ship they have to defend the Bridge. Thanks to your impulsive friend, our escape route is gone and we are trapped here."

"I need to send a message."

"Impossible. Any signal will be instantly detected and traced back."

"We have to find another way, before it is too late."

CHAPTER 59

The enormous Bridge spun serenely in space. Able to connect instantly to any other system with a Bridge, it was a portal of trade and commerce—as well as an easy path for hostile raiders or invading fleets.

While Opia and her people had not used the Bridge in over a thousand years, due to their wormhole technology, they were still unable to comprehend its abilities or shut down its function. It was more of a danger than an asset.

Stretching for hundreds of kilometers, the Gate was a series of platforms bristling with weapons that guarded the Bridge, making it a death trap. Developed with Opia's advanced science, it was able to deliver a devastating barrage of kinetic and energy weapons that no known fleet could withstand.

Invaders, raiders, or simply those unfortunate enough to pick the wrong Bridge, never returned home to tell the tale.

Early on in his rebellion, Rondall sent shock troops to secure the control facility of the weapon platform, just in case his coup failed and he needed a way to escape.

e/se/s

"The Gate is more than able to stop any fleet," Fleet Admiral Greede said. "To cross the Bridge is suicide."

"The invaders seem very sure of themselves," Rondall said, rubbing his beard. "Send the fleet to the Bridge."

"Which fleet?"

"All of them," Rondall snapped. "I want every ship that

carries a gun ready when the twelve hour deadline is up. Deal with threat, Admiral, then systematically hunt down and destroy the Roratune ships. The Chariot and her support ships will remain behind and continue the search for Opia. She will not escape me."

"Yes, sir."

☙❧❦

Some one hundred and ninety-two ships strong, the five Mogul battle fleets, set sail at full speed for the Bridge. The five formations of cruisers, battle ships, and smaller support craft were each concentrated around a massive battle carrier over a thousand meters in length.

The officers and crews were happy to hear of the ill-advised invasion and eager to win the first historic battle for the glory of the new Mogul Empire. Competition was fierce and each flotilla wanted the honor of the first kill. There was even talk of among the junior officers of turning off the Gate and allowing the fleet credit for total victory.

☙❧❦

"Battle formation one," Fleet Admiral Greede ordered, "take up battle positions five kilometers to the rear of the Gate. If any ships are able to slip through, we will cut them to shreds."

The Mogul ships slowed, approaching the formidable Gate. Turning as one, they prepared to fire on the Azurean fleet.

"Prepare anti-ship salvos," Fleet Admiral Greede ordered.

"Sir, the Gate's power levels have spiked, and she is chambering weapons," an aide said. "The enemy is on the move."

Greede chuckled. "The Azurean fools are about to learn a painful lesson."

"Sir," an aide-de-camp said.

"What is it?"

"We have an unusual weapon realignment from the Gate system. The main weapons are no longer targeting the Bridge."

"Contact them."

"We did. They said it was a temporary glitch in the system, but nothing to worry about—"

"Sir!" cried a sensor operator.

"The Azureans?" Fleet Admiral Greede asked.

"I have a massive electromagnetic energy burst, ten klicks distant in quadrant six."

"A nuclear detonation?"

"No. It's a ship. It is firing weapons!"

"Quadrant six?" Greede asked. "That is to our flank. Action stations."

୧౩୧౩

The Blossoming Flower spun and danced around the slow moving, disorganized enemy ships, unleashing a deadly barrage at point blank range. Ten capital ships died before they could even order battle stations.

To the horror of the Moguls, although they quickly regrouped and returned fire, before a single round could find her mark, *The Blossoming Flower* disappeared in flash of light, only to reappear in an unsuspected quadrant and fire with deadly accuracy.

It was like shooting at a phantom that you never knew when or where she would appear. The only certainty was that when she appeared, Mogul ships died.

"Oh my God," whispered the aide-de-camp as he started intently into his monitor. While the entire Mogul Fleet command's attention was focused on destroying the elusive *Blossoming Flower,* he watched in horror as the Gate's weapons array turned toward them.

"Oh no," he said as the great ship shuddered violently. "We are dead."

୧౩୧౩

Rondall, sipping iced wine from a golden goblet, sauntered onto the command bridge of the Chariot.

"My lord, hunter teams have tracked Opia and her cohorts across the city," Captain Lunze said.

"I would assume that she is trying to steal a shuttle or perhaps sneak aboard the elevator," Rondall said.

"Opia is heading in the opposite direction." The captain visibly paled. "My lord, it appears that she has retrieved her Library."

Wild eyed, Rondall emptied the contents of his cup into his aide's face, before slinging the cup across the room. "How?"

"Her machines killed our men with some kind of nerve gas," the aide said coolly as the wine dripped from his nose.

"I want her apprehended within the hour or, so help me, I will execute you and your entire family."

"Yes, my lord."

"Have we engaged the enemy yet?" Rondall asked. "I want a complete video record of this victory."

"My lord, Fleet Admiral Greede has sent word that the Gate weapon system is pulverizing the enemy forces," a junior officer operating a holographic control panel said. "It is a great day for our people."

"I want to talk with Greede."

"I am afraid that after the admiral's message, communications are down with the fleet."

"What?" Rondall asked. "How long?"

"Initial contact, my lord, was almost twenty minutes ago and communications went down almost immediately. It is quite normal, given the radiation and energy output of the Gate's weapons.

"And you didn't think that our forces engaging the enemy was important enough to inform me?"

"My lord, you had pressing matters with the criminal Opia, and I did not want to disturb you."

Rondall gave the terrified Mogul officer an icy stare. "If I can't communicate with my ships, I want to see the battle. Deploy the telescope."

"The images from this distance won't be of the best quality. In my opinion hardly worth the—"

"Do it now!"

"My lord."

Rondall and Lunze turned angrily to the aide.

"What is it?" Lunze snapped.

"Sir, although the fleet is in a communication blackout, I can try to acquire images from cameras on the Gate."

"Do it," Lumze said.

"We should have images in five...four...three...two...one ...*oh no*."

The horrific image that appeared across the command bridge's main view screen sent cold chills through every Mogul in the room. The formidable Mogul Fleet, the tip of the spear in Rondall's plan of galactic conquest, lay in utter ruin.

"Battle Stations! Battle Stations!" screamed Captain Lunze, as he stood transfixed by the field of twisted metal and lifeless hulks.

"What is that?" whispered an aide. "That ship is enormous."

In the distance floated *The Blossoming Flower*, her null-glass armor glittering frostily in the light of the devastated fleet.

"The Fleet is—is gone," an aide whispered. "It cannot be."

The image vanished and the monitor when dark.

"Our signals are being jammed," an operator said, though no one was listening.

"It wasn't enough to rid ourselves of Opia, you have brought death down on us all," Captain Lunze said. "You and your damn ambition have doomed us."

"How dare you?" Rondall screamed as he pulled a pistol. He squeezed the trigger and shot Captain Lunze three times. As the captain's body fell to the deck, Rondall made an announcement. "Anyone else wish to voice a grievance about my leadership?" After a moment of silence, Rondall smiled. "Good. Now clean up this mess. Our only chance lay with finding Opia."

CHAPTER 60

The Azurean troopers staffing the Gate gazed upon the destruction they had wrought.

In the distance, *The Blossoming Flower* floated at the edge of the debris field, her guns still glowing white-hot from the hell they had unleashed upon the Moguls.

"Brilliant tactics, Admiral Carlson," Cona Dumar said, the officer in charge of the Azurean troops. "Simply brilliant."

"Thank you, Cona," Will said.

"It was stunning, my love," Agoa purred into Will's ear. "*You* are stunning."

❧❧❧

Will found himself—his spirit—entwined with that of the sultry AI in an embrace closer than that of a lover. In the heat of battle, through the pure joy of killing, Agoa was the soft voice of reason, a lifeline keeping him anchored to sanity.

"Thanks, baby, we should have done this Pilot thing years ago. I wondered why no one ever thought of linking the ship's AI with a Pilot?"

"We have a special connection, my love, which no one could imagine."

Will reveled in the delicious new way his body felt, the way his heightened senses supplied him with information. At twenty kilometers, he could see through the armored skin of the Gate. He could see the ebb and flow of electricity through circuits.

He could feel the heartbeat of the universe through the cosmic rays that pelted his skin like a gentle, summer rain. He was a new being over five miles long and enormously powerful.

യ∕ാരൗ

"Commander, I am Will, by the way. I am the admiral of nothing,"

"Luring the fleet close enough to use their own weapon against them, was clever," Cona said. "If you are not an admiral, you should be."

"It is what my people call being caught between a rock and a hard place. With my experience with the Moguls, I knew that they would never pass up the opportunity for a fight with their shiny new fleet. My hat is off to you, Cona, and your troops who did the real work here. You slipped into the complex and took out the Mogul soldiers without their superiors ever knowing that the Gate was ours from the start."

"A simple task, sir," Cona said. "A little Somex in their ventilation system worked wonders."

"Now that we have slapped each other on the back over cutting the head off the serpent, I need to pay Rondall a visit. That old boy and I need to have a word of prayer."

"My troopers are loading onto our ships as we speak, Admiral—Will. We can be aboard in less than thirty minutes."

"No. I want you to make sure the Roratune make it safely back to Fort Apache."

"But, sir—"

"I have made my peace."

"Yes, sir. Good luck."

"Come on, baby," Will said to Agoa. "We have work to do."

In a nimble maneuver that would have killed anyone aboard, *The Blossoming Flower* spun and, with engines on full thrust, darted away from the dead Mogul fleet.

യ∕ാരൗ

"Jabal," Opia said, "there is a new message, but my meager comm unit can't decipher it. It is an unknown language."

Jabal moved close, but shook his head. "It's Will's voice, but I—Anne. Get up here."

Moments later Anne entered the cabin.

"What is Will saying?" Jabal asked.

Anne's eyes welled with tears and as a smile split her face. "He said that the Bridge is now clear of pests. Whatever that means."

Jabal and Opia looked at each other.

"I don't know how he did it, but God bless him," Jabal said.

"Get ready for launch," Opia said.

ↄ৯ↄ৯

The last strap tightened and all their gear stowed away, the cargo hatch hold was sealed.

While Jabal and his soldiers prepared for launch, Anne tried in vain to adjust the inflatable G-suit she wore.

"This thing makes me look like a blimp."

"Anne, have you ever experienced a ground launch before?" Jabal asked.

"Are you kidding me? Back home only a lucky few ever get to go into space."

"Normally, we would ride the elevator to a space docking facility, but under the circumstances that is out of the question. In my world, ground launches are nearly unheard of, due to the waste of fuel and damage to the ecosystem. Not to mention the ride is uncomfortable. That suit will keep your blood from pooling in your legs."

"And that is a bad thing why?"

"To put it simply, the tremendous acceleration it takes to escape a gravity well can make you black out and could cause internal damage. That suit will make the ride more tolerable."

"Jabal honey," she said, taking his hand. "I know we have butted heads a time or two, but you didn't leave me behind. If I do live through this, it will be all because of you. Thank you."

She reached up and hugged him tightly, before giving him a light kiss on the cheek.

"It was Will who asked me to look after you. He is making a great sacrifice for my people."

"Yeah, Will is one of a kind, but you could have said no, or made up a dozen excuses and took the easy way out. I know you think I am a pain in the ass, but you still came for me. You are one hell of a man."

"I don't suspect you are a pain in the ass, I have incontestable proof," he said with a smile.

Anne punched him in the arm.

"Besides, I am not a man," he said. "I am a kenan."

"Whatever."

"Strap in."

CHAPTER 61

Half an hour later, fully fueled and ready for launch, the ship angled up into a dark tunnel, lined with a mag-repulsers. Opia flipped a switch and explosive charges ignited. The top of the bakery exploded up and outward, slamming into several downtown shops and sending Moguls scrambling for cover.

The nose of the craft now bathed in sunlight, the mag-repulsers glowed white as they built a charge in the launch tube.

"Now comes the scary part," Jabal said as he braced himself.

With scarcely a sound, the shuttle catapulted upward at tremendous speed. At the pinnacle of its arcing trajectory, the engines kicked in with a teeth-grinding thump. As its advanced engines burned hot, it streaked from the city and into the sky.

"What a rush," Anne said as she was pressed back into her seat. "That was better than a roller coaster. I should have been an astronaut."

Gannon chuckled and patted her hand.

"Hopefully," Opia said, "the unexpected launch will take them by surprise, so we can slip past their space network and through the Bridge before they are able to intercept us."

"What can go wrong?" Gannon said.

"You just had to say it," Jabal said.

The ship's AI had calculated a direct route to the Bridge when the vessel shook violently.

"Opia. Shut down your pulse engines or be burned from the

sky," came the command. "Settle into a low orbit and await further orders."

Three fast warships closed on the unarmed shuttle.

"Oh no," Anne said. "After all we have been through—"

"It's not over yet," Gannon said as he checked his magazine.

The rest of his squad grunted their agreement.

"Opia," the unmistakable voice of Rondall said. "I have you at last."

"Yes, Rondall," Opia said. "So it would seem."

"Give me the Library and the decipher key and you can go your way."

"No."

"You are at my mercy. You have no choice, but to give me what I want."

"Just give the big monkey the Library," Anne said.

"No," Jabal said. "We need information stored within if my people are to have a chance to live. We cannot give it up."

"I don't have time for this," Rondall said.

"No, you don't," Jabal said. "Death is coming for you."

"Who is this?"

"Chancellor Jabal Shann of the Azurean Republic. Face the facts. Your fleet is scrap metal. My forces are on their way. I suggest you stand down and surrender before it is too late."

"Give me the Library!" Rondall shrieked.

"The longer you stall the worse, it will go on your people," Jabal said. "Think of them."

"My people?" Rondall asked. "This is what I think of my people."

Seconds later, several missiles streaked from the Chariot.

"He's firing on us," Opia screamed.

"No," Jabal said, watching the screen before him. "He has lost his mind."

The words were barely out of Jabal's mouth before the shuttle rocked violently.

"We are hit," Anne screamed.

"No, it is turbulence from the blast," Gannon said. "Rondall just dropped a few dozen flashers on his own people."

"Flashers?"

"I don't know if you can understand this," Gannon said. "Weapons that use nuclear fusion to create a terrible blast. They generate a brilliant flash of light when they detonate, thus the name."

"Oh my God, that crazy ape just nuked his own people," Anne said quietly.

"The Library," Rondall said. "Give—it—to—*me*."

"Impossible. That is the sum total of my people's knowledge—my heritage. I will never give it up."

"Rondall, old buddy, let those folks go," Will said. "It is time for us to dance."

"It can't be," Rondall gasped. "I killed you, cast you into hell."

"Hell didn't want me. Now let my friends go before I do to you what I did to your pretty ships."

Alarms sounded and the tiny ship vibrated as powerful scans penetrated the hull.

"Why are you scanning us?" Opia asked.

"It seems that now I am back in control," Rondall said.

"What do you mean?" Opia asked.

"Willard Carlson, *old buddy*," Rondall said. "You will surrender immediately and allow my sailors to board your vessel, or I will exterminate the female animal who came with you. I give you my word that once I possess your vessel and Opia's library, I will allow you and your companions to leave my system unharmed."

"Please, for the love of God don't hurt, Anne," Will said. "She's all I've got."

"Ahh, you do care for her. Excellent."

"He loves me," Anne said as her eyes filled with tears.

"I'm coming in," Will said. "Let them go."

"When I have your ship and not before."

Jabal switched on the mic. "You listen to me, Will," Jabal said. "You will not—under any circumstance—surrender my ship. Do you understand me? He is going to kill us all, anyway."

"I can't take the chance," Will said. "He will 'ripper' apart if I don't play ball. Get ready, I am coming in."

"Outstanding," Jabal said as a smile split his face. "Everyone get ready."

"What is outstanding?" Anne asked. "Get ready for what?"

The sky lit up as one of the heavy cruisers exploded sending shards of deadly shrapnel into its sister ship.

The third warship leaned sharply to starboard to avoid the wreckage of her fellow ships. Coming about, she fired a brace of missiles at the shuttle.

"We are dead," Opia said.

In a bright flash, five specially modified pathfinder probes appeared around the shuttle. The bulky probes ejected their spent batteries and switched to fresh power cells.

As the missiles closed to within a few meters, the pathfinders latched onto the hull and, in a flash of light, the shuttle vanished.

"Noooooooo!" Rondall screamed.

"My lord, a ship has appeared twenty thousand kilometers away in sector three and is entering planetary orbit."

"Willard is coming for me," Rondall whispered. "Get us out of here. Flank speed to the Bridge. Arm the weapons systems and kill anything that gets in our way."

The main engine cluster of the *Chariot of Opia* came on line. The one hundred and sixty kilometer ship glistened like a jewel in the blackness of space as she slowly increased speed, in preparation for breaking orbit in a desperate bid to outrun *The Blossoming Flower*.

❧❧❧

Opia's shuttle appeared on the inner edge of the floating debris of the Mogul fleet. A short distance away hung the Bridge and the way home.

"Jabal, old buddy, you are good as gold and a man of your word. Now please, get out of here," Will said. "I'll take care of Rondall."

"Will, never mind about Rondall," Jabal said. "You have to help the Roratune refugees."

"Done. Took care of that. All those ships are already safely across the Bridge and half way to Fort Apache."

"Then it is over, my friend. I don't understand how, but you have saved the day, but I cannot allow you the luxury of revenge. Leave Rondall alone. I won't allow you to needlessly endanger *The Blossoming Flower*. We will need every asset at our disposal to survive and rebuild the Azurean people."

"I wish I could, old buddy, but I made a deal with some folks, and it is kind of binding. This is where we part company."

"Will," Anne cried. "Do what Jabal said this instance. You will not screw up my happy ending, you...you redneck clown."

"Look here, woman, I got you off that planet and set you up with some real good folks who will take care of you. This should make up for all the trouble I have caused you. My debt to you is paid in full."

"Will, I—"

"Hush your yammering, *woman*. Be happy you will never have to look at my face again. Jabal, sorry about the ship, but trust me, it is for a good cause."

"Will," Jabal snapped. "Damn it, come back with my ship. You have no right!"

"Will, please come back to me," Anne said softly as tears rolled down her face. "I need you."

"Goodbye," Will said. "I will see you all on the other side."

"Quickly," Jabal said to Opia, "I need you to broadcast this code."

"What are you talking about?" Opia asked.

"Just do it before it is too late," he hissed. "The square root of 79375."

Opia's fingers flew over the console, but unexpectedly the communications device erupted in a shower of sparks.

"I—I don't understand," Opia said. "The unit shorted out. It was working perfectly."

"Deverow. God, how I hate the Deverow," Jabal muttered.

CHAPTER 62

I t is time," Yeti said. "It is time for my people to live."
The desert exploded in a mass of tentacles as the horrible,
impossible creature erupted from the sand. A thousand meters across, his bloated body most resembled a gigantic black-
and-yellow mottled squid. However, instead of eight arms,
Yeti sprouted twenty that whipped the air like a nest of snakes,
sensing the atmosphere for food.

Freed at last from the quantum prison that sustained him,
while isolating him from their world, Yeti breathed in the delicious, almost narcotic life force around him. For a thousand
kilometers, everything that had lived and thrived died instantly
as plants, insects, animals, even bacteria had their life energy
drawn away to feed the hellish creature.

Born in a universe where physical laws did not apply, Yeti
rose from the sterile sand and darted across the barren waste,
stripping the planet of its precious life.

"The portal will free my starving people and give them a
rich new hunting ground."

Yeti thought back over the bitter two thousand years he lay
as a captive.

His people lived in the void and fed upon all life and energy. Their numbers unchecked, they scoured their own universe
of all life until it existed as a cold, hellish place of death, devoid of food. Facing extinction, they sacrificed trillions of their
own, using their energy stores to breach the barrier between
the universes.

Yeti was small, young, and vital enough to survive the trip.

His mission was to complete the conduit between the universes and let his people cross.

Unfortunately, for him, the weak spot was here in this system. Opia's ancestors, the Vanuatu, saw the danger he posed and while he was too weak from the breakthrough to escape, captured him. They quickly deduced his deadly mission, but he fascinated them. Here was a creature from another dimension, one who was born, lived, and thrived in the harsh void of space.

Despite the danger, they were determined to learn his secrets.

"The Vanuatu should have killed me when they had the chance, but they, obsessed by curiosity, kept me alive as a test subject. No more than a lab animal to study then dispose of. A vain and arrogant people, they underestimated my abilities. My kind ruled our universe as Gods. It is only a matter of time before we rule this one as well."

The Vanuatu did understand the danger if Yeti's people were to ever open the portal. In a desperate move, they created the Arcturus. If the portal should ever open again, the Acturus would detonate the star, putting an end to his people while the Vanuatu would have time to slip through their own portal to another world.

From his prison, Yeti slowly regained his strength. While they held his body in stasis, his mind roamed free, undetected by their rudimentary science. It was then he found what he was looking for. The great machine they called a Portal, by which they used to explore their galaxy, could do much more than the Vanuatu realized. With the proper adjustments, it could breach dimensional barriers. It was the key to freeing his people.

His plan for escape was foiled a year later when the Vanuatu opened their Portal into the wrong world. Their probe brought back a deadly plague that nearly decimated the planet. Their medical scientists came up with a cure, but the cure proved to be a two edged sword.

The treatments stopped the plague, but then made the normally peaceful, benign, reasonably sane inhabitants, aggressive and paranoid. Dulling their intellect and reason, it intensified their emotions one hundred fold. Raging savages, unable to comprehend their own devices, they fell upon each other.

Yeti lay helpless, his chances of rescuing his people evaporating. He watched them coldly exterminate each other and lay waste to their lush world. Without outside help, he could not breach his prison. He was certain that his mission was a failure. Then Opia rose supreme. She ruthlessly cut down her enemies and became the last of her people. It was then that Yeti noticed that the effects of the cure, while long lasting, were slowly diminishing. Alone in a ruined world, Opia's mind was returning and so was Yeti's hope for redemption.

He tried to use his mind to influence her, but she was too much for him to overwhelm, even in her weakened mental capacity. So instead, he planted a seed. In her suggestible mental state, he nurtured the idea that she was a Goddess and a Goddess needed worshipers. She sent her machines and kidnapped two races in the midst of a bitter battle. The Azureans and Erest. She erased their past and renamed them, the Moguls and Roratune. They became children of the Most High Opia.

The Roratune it seemed were immune to Yeti's control, but the Moguls were a different matter. He knew it was only a matter of time before he could trick these pitiful creatures into overthrowing Opia and releasing him. Rondall was a gift from the Gods.

His lust for power made him the perfect instrument to engineer Yeti's escape.

⋐⋑⋐⋑

"No," Yeti cried as he came upon the dead, burning city of Romaa. "Rondall, you fool, what have you done? What kind of monster destroys his own kind?"

The great machine, which Vanuatu had used to explore the universe for the past ten thousand years, lay destroyed, beyond even his intellect to repair. Nevertheless, Yeti realized that all was not lost. Another device—a mere fraction of the size he desired, but still useful—existed.

Sucking in the lives of the few survivors, he soared over the former Roratune villages and devoured their livestock and every green living plant. Refreshed, he gathered his strength, crossed the atmosphere, and zoomed into space with amazing speed.

Born in the dead space between suns and immune to the absolute cold vacuum of space, Yeti launched himself at the *Chariot of Opia*, moving faster than any vessel in known space.

Prepared to battle *The Blossoming Flower*, this new impossible threat took Rondall and his crew of Zealots completely by surprise.

Before the weapon crews could fire upon the hideous creature, Yeti syphoned away their lives, drinking deeply upon their living energy. The crews collapsed and died, like spent batteries, as Yeti slithered across the sleek exterior of the grand ship, leaving a wake of death as he fed.

Rondall screamed and swore in frustration as his bridge crew fell dead around him.

"This can't be happening," he cried.

"Rondall, my friend," Yeti said.

"It can't be. I had you killed."

"No, you did precisely as I desired, my friend. You released me from my prison, and my people will be eternally grateful."

"There are more of you?"

"Oh, yes. Once we were as numerous as the suns burning in space, but now we are reduced to only a few trillion or so. Nevertheless because of you, my friend, we will thrive once again. Because of your usefulness, I will allow you last words before I send you into oblivion."

"Go to hell," Rondall snapped.

His dreams of conquest gone and, now burdened with being an accomplice to the murder of his own galaxy, Rondall denied Yeti his own spirit. His last act was to eat a bullet.

His strength replenished, Yeti reached out with his mind and probed the dead ship, taking control of vital systems, easily breaking the encryption established by Opia.

"Ah, there it is," he said, as his mind activated the ship's sophisticated jump drive. Making extensive calculations in microseconds, Yeti adjusted the fantastic device that could transport the ship to any spot in know space.

"Not so fast, Squid-Head," Will said.

"No," Yeti cried as *The Blossoming Flower* appeared in a flash of light.

Spinning like a top, the sparkling ship tumbled past the starboard wing of the *Chariot of Opia*. A white-hot ribbon of fire connected the ships as Will delivered a deadly barrage.

Yeti screamed and cursed as he, along with the gigantic vessel, was cut to ribbons.

Will darted out of range as the dead ship and dying alien tumbled from orbit toward the planet below. "I love it when a plan comes together."

"I may be dead," Yeti whispered, "but my people are free. Your kind will nourish us."

"Will, something is happing in Sector 3956," Agoa said. "Something big."

"What, another ship?"

"I have never seen anything like it," she said. "It looks like a breach in space."

"Oh, no," he whispered. "We were too late. Looks like we have to go to Plan B, Agoa."

"We have a Plan B?"

CHAPTER 63

The breach between the universes opened in a tremendous flash of light and energy, as the portal device on board the *Chariot of Opia* ripped a perfect circle in the fabric of time and space, twenty kilometers in diameter.

The trillions upon trillions of Sagoths fell upon the doorway. An almost solid mass of bloated bodies swarmed the opening—only to find it blocked by *The Blossoming Flower*, as she straddled the opening between the universes.

"Will, honey," Agoa said. "Plan B sucks."

"Launch the package, baby."

Within the cavernous Cargo Bay Three, a special Pathfinder triggered its ripper drive and disappeared.

"Batter up," he said. "Agoa, let's go down swinging."

As the Sagoths bore down on the lone ship, *The Flower* performed a tactic known as a *death roll*. Unable to maneuver within the small space between universes, the last stand of *The Blossoming Flower* became tantamount to a toe-to-toe, bareknuckle brawl. Spinning slowly along her long axis the warship lashed the unholy creatures with unrelenting firepower as all her guns unleashed hell.

In a matter of moments, hundreds of thousands of Sagoths died as blazing Azurean guns ripped through the tangled, hellish hoard. Screaming in pain and anger, they lashed out at the insignificant creature who dared to defy them. Thousands of bizarre, biomechanical weapons returned fire.

"Need some help, Teepo," Will whispered as he tracked and killed targets.

The advanced alien defense system flowed like quicksilver from the surface of the living ship, forming a rectangle five kilometers long, four kilometers wide, and five hundred meters thick.

Calculating the speed and trajectory of the otherworldly projectiles, Teepo angled his body to the incoming weapons. The ultra-high velocity rounds ricocheted off Teepo like smooth stones skipping across a pond.

Giving his white-hot guns time to reload, Will responded with a savage nuclear barrage that sent tens of millions more creatures into oblivion and the rest scrambling to regroup.

"Will, we can't keep this up," Agoa said. "There are too many—their weapons too powerful."

"I know," he said calmly. "We don't have enough bullets or missiles to stop them all, anyway."

"Then what are we doing here?"

"Buying time, baby. Buying Time."

ᏋᏉᏋᏉ

The battle raged on for close to an hour. Although Will fought valiantly, it was a battle he could never win. The sheer number of Sagoths projectiles eventually overwhelmed and destroyed Teepo. After losing her best defense to the Sagoth weapons, *The Blossoming Flower* took an appalling beating.

Her marvelous null-glass armor—that had taken countless direct hits from technologically superior weapons—lay pulverized, exposing the bare hull. Three quarters of her mag-guns were destroyed. Only the tireless efforts of her army of repair-bots kept the ship functioning and in the fight, yet that was at a bare minimum.

The Sagoths knew victory was at hand. Massed behind their terrible, living war machines, they rushed forward into the breach determined to sweep this impertinent being aside and claim their new home.

As they fought, unbeknownst to the Sagoths, the package SD and Molly had given Will—carried by the Pathfinder into the sun—had born deadly fruit.

"Will, we have to withdraw," Agoa said. "The main power coupling took a direct hit and what guns we have are down. We can't fight anymore. Besides, the sun is on the verge of detonation."

"Can't let even one of those monsters in, sweetie, or this universe is dead."

"Don't you understand? We will die if we stay."

"Agoa honey, it was never the plan to survive this."

"Oh." She sighed. "It has been a pleasure loving you, my husband."

"Right back at you, Agoa baby. Right back at you."

Will turned the ship into the breach and engaged maximum thrust. He released a billowing cloud of Somex gas, which enveloped the battered ship in a deadly yellow shroud.

"Baby, when we are knee deep in space-squid, eject the black hole drive. That should make one hell of a sushi salad."

"We will enter eternity hand in hand," she said.

As the triumphant Sagoths rushed to destroy the defiant ship, Opia's sun exploded.

Instead of a blast wave, similar to what destroyed the Azurean system, the device SD and Molly had given Will was special. The weapon funneled and focused the explosive energy as it erupted from the star. Focused into an impossibly tight beam twenty kilometers in diameter and traveling at nearly the speed of light, the deadly stream of plasma particles raced for the portal.

cɔcɔ

Shedding their human guises for their true forms, SD and Molly floated in the airless void, watching the terrific battle and Will's suicide run dispassionately. Their mission all but accomplished, they waited patiently for the spectacular finale that would end the Sagoths' threat to this universe for good.

"This will sooo look good on our record," Molly said. "There were a few pitfalls to contend with, but damn, we did it."

"Will is a good kid," SD said.

"Oh, don't go soft on me. His lifespan is insignificant. He is insignificant."

"I don't know. I don't think the length of a being's life is the proper criteria for significance. Will is a noble being who was not appreciated by his own kind. They will never know the heroic feat he performed and how they much they own him."

"Pish-posh. Will is a pawn—a tool. Tools are not heroic, only those who use the tools effectively achieve greatness. By the way, that is you and I, my friend."

"We move pieces around a board and let them do our dirty work. It may be necessary, but hardly heroic."

"Irrelevant. The game is over. Will is over. The energy burst has almost reached—"

A short, but powerful message thundered in their ears. Looking at their devices confirmed the surprising communication.

"This is unprecedented," Molly cried.

SD smiled. "My faith in justice is restored."

Molly and SD looked at each other and then vanished.

CHAPTER 64

I want this ship ready to go five minutes ago, do you hear me?" Jabal shouted as loading machines fussed about the hastily modified drop ship.

It now sported a newly installed pair of heavy anti-ship guns and a brace of five flasher missiles. Jabal climbed into the cockpit while Gannon took the seat next to him.

"I need you here," Jabal said. "Nothing can happen to Opia."

"I think your wife, Sakuna, has things well in hand, son. Frankly, she scares me."

Jabal smiled, despite himself. "Yeah, she can be…intense. All right, let's go get *The Blossoming Flower* back."

"I don't think you brought enough firepower, Jabal."

"This is just in case we run into any surviving Moguls. I have something special to take back my ship. I anticipated him going on a murderous rampage, but I can't believe he took off with my ship."

"What are you going to do?"

"When it was decided that Will would be our Pilot, I wasn't about to give him the keys to the ship without insurance."

"What did you do?"

"I attached a small explosive to the interface stalk in the Pilot Chamber. If Will proved to be problematic, I could sever the connection remotely. I tried it on Opia's shuttle, but the comm unit blew."

"You would make Teller proud."

"Don't you *dare*," Jabal snapped. "I am nothing like that monster."

"Will is a hero," Gannon said. "He deserves better than to be executed."

"Yes, I agree," Jabal said. "However I need that ship—*we* need that ship."

⟡⟐⟡

The small ship departed Fort Apache and sailed past the docked Ark and the ten Mogul troop carriers.

A thousand kilometers from the last outpost of the Azurean people, Jabal dialed up the address to Opia's system. Nothing happened.

"What is the matter with this damn thing?" Jabal snapped.

At that moment, alarms blared in the tight cabin.

"What did you do?" Gannon asked.

"That is an Azurean ship distress beacon. There," Jabal said, consulting his instruments. "Something big just appeared one hundred kilometers off the station's perimeter. It's *The Flower*."

Floating powerless, the formally pristine vessel bore the scars of a terrifying battle. A swarm of automatic repair machines converged on the stricken vessel.

"My God, what did this?" Gannon asked as he and Jabal's craft maneuvered to dock. "The Moguls were beaten. Besides, their ships were no match for *The Blossoming Flower*."

"We will soon find out, Grandfather."

Gannon looked at Jabal, touched deeply by the simple admission.

⟡⟐⟡

Jabal arrived as several heavy machines were cutting through the warped vault doors that shielded the pilot. Gannon and Sona helped wrench the partially melted doors aside while Jabal grimly looked on.

After a few precious minutes, they were through. Jabal

rushed in and found Will barely alive, covered in blood and breathing fluid at the bottom of the Pilot Well.

"Will?"

Will cracked open one eye and managed a weak smile before passing out, slumped in Jabal's arms.

The ship's medic stabilized Will and removed him to the ship's sickbay. Heavily armored, it was one of the few fully functioning sections of *The Blossoming Flower*.

Movement caught his eye and Jabal gasped. Cerin Bos stood leaning in the corner. A crooked smile cracked his face.

"Cerin?"

"It has been a true pleasure, Jabal Shann," Cerin said as a soft glow enveloped him. "I hope you can run this bucket by yourself, because I won't be around to bail your ass out anymore."

"Wait—"

With a smile and a wink, Cerin was gone.

CHAPTER 65

Long weeks had passed since the Roratune rescue. And although her damage was severe, fortunately it was not fatal. *The Blossoming Flower's* repairs were going smoothly and soon she would be ready for flight.

Anne and Jabal sat outside the sickbay operating room, praying for Will.

The doors suddenly opened and the doctor exited.

"Commander, I am sorry. The Pilot's nervous system is beyond my abilities to repair. If you would give the order, I can remove him from life support."

"No," Anne said. "You will not remove him from anything, you tin quack."

"Please calm yourself, Miss Miller," Agoa said. "No one cares more for Will than I do. Your outburst dishonors his memory."

Jabal gathered her in Anne arms as she broke down and sobbed.

"Oh, stop your blubbering you stupid, stupid animal," Opia said as she entered the sickbay, flanked by two trooper guards. Gannon brought up the rear. In his arms lay the Great Library.

"What is she doing here?" Anne snapped.

"She asked if she could help," Gannon said.

"No," Anne said, "it's a trick."

"Get this obsolete machine out of my way," Opia said as she pushed her way into the futuristic operating room. "I can't believe how primitive your medical science is, Chancellor. Might as well be chanting and rattling beads."

"Can you help him?" Jabal asked.

"I will try," she said. "Give me my Library and leave me alone. I can't have any distractions."

"Very well," Jabal said.

The medical door slid shut behind her.

"Agoa?" Jabal asked.

"I read your mind. I will keep Opia under constant watch. If she tries anything or harms Will, I will have her dissected."

ℰↄℰↄ

Fifty-six-hours later, Opia exited the sterile field of the operating room, wiping antiseptic from her hands on a white towel.

"Is he—"Anne began.

"He will be up and around in a few months," Opia said. "There is much damage that needs to heal."

"He is going to be all right?"

"I dare say he may be better. I made a few improvements. Now get some sleep and stop bothering me."

With tears in her eyes, Anne hugged the odd-looking alien tightly. "Thank you so much."

"Yes, thank you for saving, Will," Agoa said. "He is very dear to me."

"If you hadn't noticed, your young man saved my life as well," Opia said. "I may be cold by your standards, but I do have feelings, among which is gratitude. Now unhand me before I become ill. God knows where you have been."

CHAPTER 66

Jabal could not sleep. Careful not to wake Sakuna, he slipped on a pair of shorts and left the captain's cabin, aimlessly wandering the hallways of the great ship. Everywhere it seemed, machines were tirelessly working to repair the horrific damage she had taken.

"Even after five months, we are still picking up the pieces," he muttered.

On a whim, Jabal took the tram down to medical to check on Will's progress. He passed several knots of young people sporting brand new Azurean military uniforms.

Jabal smiled. It was good to see the ship full of people. Gannon with Agoa's help had set up a cadet academy. "I heard he was tough, but when the first class graduates, they will be ready for whatever comes their way. This ship needs more than a competent crew. They need to be the best. In the words of Will, 'Hell will freeze over' before I ever use a Pilot again."

As he entered the cool greenery of the ship's sickbay, he found Will's coma chamber empty.

"Doctor, where is Will?"

"The pilot came out of his coma less than an hour ago and then promptly walked out."

"Did he say anything?"

"Yes," the machine said. "When I told him to return to the chamber, he told me to kiss his ass."

"Agoa?"

"Yes, Chancellor."

"Where is Will?"

"He is on deck five, section two."

"Isn't that—"

"Cerin Bos' cabin."

"Agoa, please wake my wife and tell her to meet me there."

ℰↃℰↃ

The door to the darkened apartment opened, revealing Sakuna standing in the doorway.

"Well, hello, beautiful," came the familiar greeting from the dark.

"Cerin?"

The lights snapped on, revealing Will, clad only in a pair of dark green silk pants. "No, honey, it's only me," he said. "Cerin has a sweet place here. It is more like the stateroom of an oil sheik's yacht than the berth on a warship, don't you think?"

"What's an oil sheik? Oh, the hell with it." Sakuna raced across the room and embraced Will tightly.

"Now that is what I am talking about," he said, returning the embrace.

"You are worse than Cerin—" Sakuna froze as her hands contacted the implant attached to Will's back.

"Don't worry, beautiful, it doesn't hurt," he whispered. "Tell you the truth, it kind of tingles when you touch it."

She snatched her hand away as Will laughed.

Jabal appeared in the doorway.

"Looks like you caught us," Will said with a smile.

"Get away from my wife, you alien pervert," Jabal said as he warmly clasped Will's hand.

"Tracked me down, did you?"

"Yes, *we* did," Sakuna said.

"You should be in bed, my friend," Jabal said. "You need more time to heal."

"Yeah, I suppose I do, but I feel pretty good. In fact, that fancy coma unit has put me in the best shape of my life. Look, I got a six-pack. Back home one of those coma units would make us a fortune."

"How is the interface?" Jabal asked.

"Weird as hell," Will said. "This new spine thing itches, but—watch this."

Will turned his back to them revealing the metal and null-glass constructed implant. Running from the base of his skull to his lower back, it appeared as forty-seven overlapping null-glass scales.

"Shazam!"

The scales opened and thin, bronze colored rods protruded from the interface.

"Cool, huh?"

"That—is—disturbing," Sakuna said.

"Any pain?" Jabal asked. "Restricted movement?"

"No, just feels funny. It is going to take some getting used to. So, Jabal, how long have I been out?"

"Five months, seven days, fifteen hours," Agoa said. "Welcome back, Will."

"Thanks, sweetie. I miss our dance."

"As do I," she said, as her voice grew husky.

Sakuna gave Jabal a puzzled glance.

"Well, what's been going on, kids?" Will asked.

"Opia used her Library and found us a planet," Sakuna said. "Oh, it is so beautiful, Will. I can't wait for you to see it."

"Yes, it is nice," Jabal said. "We call it Kaia."

"The Azurean word for Heaven, nice. Why are we still in the debris field?"

"Your little joy ride nearly destroyed my ship. The repair crews did a marvelous job, however, she is still a few weeks away from flight."

"Sorry about that."

"Don't worry about it," Jabal said. "When you are fully healed, I am tossing you into the brig. For disregarding a direct order the punishment is about twenty years at hard labor."

"Ouch."

"Will," Jabal said. "We owe you a debt we can never pay."

"Oh, don't go all soft on me," Will said. "So where is everyone?"

"For the most part they are planet side building a town and planting fields, or whatever farmers do," Jabal said. "All I ever wanted to do was be an explorer. Now all that has changed. I have my hands full with seventy thousand Azurean refugees."

"How is life with Opia?"

"She saved your life," Sakuna said.

"I will have to drop her a thank you card."

"Opia has been surprisingly helpful. Our medical tech has leaped years ahead, thanks to her. Still, I know what kind of being she is, and I think she has something up her sleeve."

Looking down, Will picked up a vivid, three-dimensional picture of Bos's wife, Agoa. "She's a pretty thing, isn't she? They did a great job copying her voice."

"Thank you, Will," Agoa said.

Jabal glanced at the image.

"Yes, she is very attractive, but how do you know what her voice sounded like?"

"I know everything about her. God, how I miss her," Will said, his eyes becoming misty. "I miss the way she smells. I miss the flash in her eyes when she gets mad. She got mad at me a lot, by the way. The way she touches me when we make love."

"Excuse me?" Sakuna asked. "I think we need to get you back to bed, Will."

"I know it sounds crazy. To speak with such intimate knowledge of a person I personally never laid eyes on."

"Will, you are confused, perhaps you should go back to medical, like Sakuna suggested."

Will looked at Jabal and his wife and laughed. "I have a question for you," he said. "In your most educated opinion, what were my chances as a green pilot against the Mogul fleet?"

"I don't—"

"The truth."

"Less than zero. You might have got in a lucky shot here and there, but you would have gotten yourself killed."

"What did you think of my battle tactics?"

"Magnificent. It was almost as if—"

"An experienced Pilot with extensive training in tactics was in control?"

"Yes."

"Jabal, old buddy, when you went off and got yourself shot down, I had a dream."

"A dream?"

"Well, I guess it was a bit more than that," Will said. "To make a long story short, these two aliens named SD and Molly merged Cerin's life and myself together."

"Merged?"

"Yeah, I know how it sounds. His mind and experience coupled with my body. But more than that, it is like I have lived Cerin's entire life. No, strike that, I did live his life. His earliest memories are alongside my memories. From his first kiss to his first...um...well you know. That is how I knew everything about this ship and the codes needed to unlock the mech warriors. I especially remember every iota of his training. I have fought in forty-seven battles, twenty-six with the *Desert Wind*, ten aboard the *Crescent Moon,* and the big one with the *Blossoming Flower*. I know he loved you both, but he still enjoyed messing with you. He had a mean streak a mile wide. His favorite part of the day was watching you in the shower, Sakuna."

"Bastard," Sakuna mumbled. "God, how I miss him."

"But he also considered you, Jabal, to be the best friend he ever had. He loved you like a brother."

"I never thought I would say this," Jabal said, "but yes he was a good friend. I hope he has found peace at last."

"As we speak, he is chasing skirts on the other side," Will said.

"What was all this about?" Jabal asked.

"Chalk all this up to the sneaky, low-down Deverow. They love trouble and, with their tech, few could stop them meddling with other less advanced races. The Deverow were tasked with stopping the Sagoths from entering this universe, once and for all. I got the impression that it was a do-or-die situation. Seems as powerful as they were, there were some kids on the block that scared the shit out of even them."

"Who?" Jabal asked.

"They didn't say, and I didn't ask. Seems that the mere

mention of their names could put you in a world of hurt."

"I need to sit down," Sakuna said.

"They were responsible for all of us coming together. They were even behind the building of this ship and all its dark little secrets."

"Amazing," Jabal said.

"What is amazing," Will said, "is why I am alive."

"I don't follow."

"The reason they told me everything is that I had a choice to make. They told me about the Sagoths and the danger they represented, but it was up to me to fight them. They told me in no uncertain terms that I could never survive."

"And you did it anyway?" Sakuna asked.

"Beautiful, I was about as low as a guy could get. No family, friends, hell I was living out of my car. I was nothing. I had a chance to do something important. To make a difference. You were good to me, and it was well worth my life to give your people a second chance."

"From Agoa's report and the video of the battle, you should be on the other side with Cerin helping him chase skirts."

"Last thing I remember was charging through the portal into space squid-palooza, a split second before getting fried by a gamma blast. Talk about your rock and a hard place. It was then Molly appeared before me. She said that we were no longer Dead Ends and that our lives did matter. Told me not to be stupid and screw it up. She also warned me that Anne and I were forbidden to ever go near the earth. Something about tainted timelines, whatever that means. Looks like we are alive, but alone and exiled from our home."

"Will, my friend, you will never be alone," Jabal said, putting his hand on Will's shoulder. "We are now your people."

"Thanks. It is damn nice to be wanted. Jabal, I want to thank you for taking care of Anne. It took real guts to stay behind like you did. You're a good man."

"Even though I am not a man, I thank you. So, Will, what do you think of Cerin's quarters? One of the few places on the ship to survive unscathed."

"Nice."

"Much nicer than our own quarters," Sakuna said.

"For his sacrifice and service, a Pilot has the nicest cabin. It's yours if you want it. I will have your belonging brought up."

"Belongings? I don't have anything 'cept the clothes on my back. My old car is…"

"Sitting in hanger bay two," Jabal said with a smile. "We found it and brought it with us."

"Thank you, Jesus," Will exclaimed. "I thought for sure I had lost all my western movies and music."

"You know, Will, There is more than enough room for two."

"Who is the other?"

"Seriously? Anne, of course."

Will snorted.

"Anne is in love with you and tells anyone who is within earshot," Sakuna said.

"I find that hard to believe."

"She camps in medical just to be near you. I even caught her reading to you."

"Will!" Anne flew across the room and into his arms. She covered his face with desperate kisses.

"Woman, what are you doing?" he said, backing up. "Have you been drinking? Get off of me."

"We'll leave you two alone," Jabal said, taking Sakuna by the hand and leading her out.

"Why so lovey-dovey?" Will asked. "I thought you hated me?"

"Look, Will," she said sheepishly, "I admit I'm a bitch, okay? I am so sorry about the things I said to you."

"You mean like, I meant nothing to you? That the extent of our relationship would have lasted to the next bus stop?"

"I—I didn't m—mean it," she stammered. "I was hurt when I saw you and that Amazon whore with her boobs in your face. I wanted to hurt you back."

"It worked."

"I am sorry."

Will grinned. "They were very nice boobs."

Anne swatted him on the arm, which made him chuckle. "Where is Sako? As determined as that gal is, I figured she would be here as well."

"She would have been. However, Sakuna read her the riot act. Said you were mine and if Sako bothered us again, Sakuna would break her foot off in her ass, or words to that effect. Damn, Sakuna is tough as nails. Had poor Sako shaking in her boots. Being the sensitive person I am, I set Sako up with this gorgeous Roratune I know, named Moulon. I think there are wedding bells in their future."

"What do you mean, I belong to *you*?"

"It is the way things are, so get used to it, big boy."

"So what you are telling me, Miss Miller, is that your standards are *not* higher than a stupid Tennessee hick loser who doesn't have two cents to rub together and is living out of his car. Especially one who got you kidnapped and almost killed."

Anne winced at her own words.

"Do you still wish to God that you had never laid eyes on my ugly, scarred face?"

"Damn, I wished you had forgotten that part."

"I can't. It is burned into my brain with a branding iron."

"Look, sweetie," she purred. "When I get mad, I say things I don't mean. Sure, it is mean, hateful, and not the slightest bit mature, but it works for me. The God's honest truth is I love you with all my heart and, if we are going to make this relationship work, you have to forgive me. Trust me, it's worth it."

"Really?"

"Yes. I'm one hell of a catch. Hey, just a minute, since when do you have blue eyes?"

"Jabal and his doc fixed me when the Moguls broke mine. What do you think?"

"Sexy."

"Anne, I know all about your dreams of me and the fortuneteller."

"How? I never told you. Did Ballen blab?"

"I haven't talked to Ballen. I met the beings who planted the suggestion in your mind. You see, we have all been played like pawns on a gigantic chessboard. You know your weird friends, SD and Molly? Well, those folks were not even human. They arranged for our trip to Opia's little slice of hell. They knew that I was a sucker for a pretty face and that I would move heaven and earth to rescue you. They used you as leverage to get me to fight the Sagoths."

"What is a Sagoths?"

"Never mind. What it all comes down to, Anne, is that you don't really feel about me like you think you do."

"May I ask you a question, Will?"

"Shoot."

"Did Molly and SD give you dreams of me?"

"No. I never laid eyes on you until that day at Angel Wells."

"So, what you are saying is that, instead of abandoning the heinous bitch who hurt your feelings, you endured the God-awful Pilot process and faced death for me. Is that true?"

"Yeah, I suppose."

"Why?"

"I like you."

"*Like* me? You did all that just because you *like* me?"

"Okay," he said. "I must be totally nuts, but, Anne, even though you drive me crazy, in the short time I have known you, I have never wanted anyone more."

"More than say…Brenda?"

"Who?"

"Good answer."

Will smiled.

"Now wipe that stupid grin off your goofy face," she snapped.

"Excuse me?"

"Don't you ever tell me how *I* feel about *you*, again, Will Carlson," she said, jabbing him in the chest with her finger. "Sure, those two wacky ETs may have nudged me in your direction, but what I feel for you is genuine and honest. I love you with all my heart and don't you ever doubt it."

"Really?"

"Honest to God. Now why aren't you kissing me, you big, dumb hick?"

"I just love it when you sweet talk me," he whispered as he gathered her into his arms.

About the Author

Ken Newman has loved stories of the supernatural since listening to his grandmother's tales of witches, haints, boogers, and catawamps when he was a child. Author of urban fantasy novels, *The Paladin*, *The Ark*, *The Voice in My Ear*, and *Forsaken*, his fiction reflects his Tennessee roots and his love for all things-that-go-bump-in-the-night.

Mixing folklore with modern themes, Newman's novels create a twisted universe of supernatural creatures and larger-than-life heroes where nothing is as it seems.

When not writing, he enjoys sculpting, cheesy monster movies, and building the occasional trebuchet to keep the neighbors in line. Newman lives in East Tennessee with his long-suffering wife Christian and their three zany daughters.

Please feel free to contact him. He would love to hear from you.